THE RIVER CITY CHRONICLES

J. SCOTT COATSWORTH

Published by
Other Worlds Ink
PO Box 19341, Sacramento, CA 95819

ed180929-amz

 Formatted with Vellum

This book is dedicated first and foremost to my husband Mark, who told me that if I wanted to be a writer, I should just get off my ass and do it. Without him, none of this would have been possible. Love you truly, madly, deeply mio Marco…

I also wanted to dedicate this book to Damon, the first guy I was ever with. Damon was a beautiful human being and the reason I finally came out. He left us far too soon.

CONTENTS

FOREWORD

I've written and published a number of short stories, novellas and full-length novels, but "The River City Chronicles" holds a special place in my little writer heart.

It's my love letter to my current home-town—Sacramento. When my husband Mark and I moved here from the Bay Area, I had no idea how many amazing people we would meet, or how this place would get under my skin.

Sacramento has a few nicknames—The City of Trees, The Big Tomato (thanks to a giant red water tower), and Sactown. But my favorite is the River City. Sacramento sits at the confluence of the Sacramento and American Rivers, and the rivers are an important part of life here, from the severe flooding they once caused to the recreational opportunities and drinking water they give us today.

In 2015, when I decided to attempt a serial story for my blog, I turned to one of my first published novellas, "Between the Lines." It's the story of a gay couple brought together by a little bit of magic. I've always had a soft spot for magical realism, and I decided to bring a little of it to Sacramento.

Sam and Brad, the couple from "Between the Lines," are two of the characters in the rambling ensemble that is River City.

I admit to being influenced by the amazing Armisted Maupin, who famously wrote the first few books of Tales of the City as his paean to San Francisco in the 1970's. Maupin is the master of a story-in-a-chapter. As one of our many gigs, Mark and I teach a local Italian language group. Over the last several years we've been reading the first book in Maupin's series, in Italian.

Many of the places mentioned in this story are real, and I include them here with love. Locals will recognize them, just as they will recognize the image on the cover.

There are also a few invented places. *Ragazzi* is not a real Sacramento restaurant, but I do have a particular site in mind for it.

And regular readers of mine will recognize the Everyday Grind coffee chain, which pops up again and again. The main EG in Sacramento occupies the same space as a certain Berkeley coffee chain in Midtown.

I hope you have as much fun reading this as I did writing it. It truly has been an adventure, and I'm looking forward to jumping back in with these characters again soon to see where they go next.

Welcome to River City.

LIST OF CHARACTERS

Major Characters:

- **Ben Hammond:** 35 – Trans author and barista working on his first novel
- **Brad Weston:** 30 – Runs the LGBT Center, former chief of staff for GOP senator, partner to Sam
- **Carmelina di Rosa:** 55 – Semi-retired, redhead, lost her husband Arthur three months ago
- **Dave Ramos:** 47 – Human resources consultant and Carmelina di Rosa's tenant
- **Diego Bellei:** 47 – The chef at Ragazzi restaurant, married to Matteo Bianco.
- **Marcos Ramirez:** 39 – Web designer and gay playboy who works with the LGBT center
- **Marissa Sutton:** 17 – Bisexual homeless teenager who turns up at Ragazzi for the cooking class
- **Matteo Bianco:** 47 – Co-owner and host at Ragazzi restaurant, married to Diego Bellei.
- **Sam Fuller:** 23 – Suspense novel writer, working on second novel, partner to Brad Weston

~

Minor Repeating Characters:

- **Andrea Smith:** deceased - Carmelina's daughter
- **Arthur di Rosa:** deceased – Carmelina's husband
- **Dana Pearce:** Matteo and Diego's immigration lawyer
- **Daniele Amoroso:** 40 – Italian suitor interested in Carmelina
- **Darryl Smith:** Andrea's adoptive father
- **Ella Jackson-Cucinelli:** 32 – Caucasian woman recently transferred to Sacramento from Chicago
- **Emily Stamp:** P.I. hired by Carmelina
- **Giovanni "Gio" Mazzocco:** Diego's son
- **Jason Clark:** One of Marissa's friends at McClatchy High
- **Jessica Sutton:** Marissa's adoptive mother
- **Loylene Davies:** friend of Carmelina's
- **Luna Mazzocco:** Diego's Ex and Gio's mother
- **Max Cucinelli:** Matteo and Diego's immigration lawyer
- **"Moms" Cucinelli:** Mother to Max and Ella, trans woman
- **Rex Ward:** Owner of the Twink tattoo shop
- **Ricky Martinez:** One of the homeless kids from the LGBT center
- **Tristan Dayton:** Marissa's boyfriend
- **Valentina Bellei:** Diego's sister who lives in Italy

1. RAGAZZI

Matteo stared out the restaurant window into the darkness of Folsom Boulevard. It was getting dark earlier as summer edged into fall. Streetlights flickered on as cars drifted by, looking for parking or making the trip out of Midtown toward home.

The sign on the window read "Ragazzi" (the boys), lettered in a beautiful golden script just two months old. Investing in this little restaurant his uncle had left to them when he'd passed away had been their ticket out of Italy. But now with each passing day, as seats sat empty and tomatoes, pasta, and garlic went uneaten, the worry was gnawing ever deeper into Matteo's gut.

Behind him in the open, modernized kitchen, Diego was busy cooking—his mother's lasagne, some fresh fish from San Francisco, and some of the newer Italian dishes they'd brought with them from Bologna. The smells of boiling sauce and fresh-cooked pasta that emanated from the kitchen were entrancing.

They'd sent the rest of the staff —Max and Justin—home for the evening. The three customers who had shown up so far didn't justify the cost of keeping their waiter and busboy on hand.

Matteo stopped at the couple's table in front of the other window. "*Buona sera*," he said, smiling his brightest Italian smile.

"Hi," the man said, smiling back at him. He was a gentleman in about his mid-fifties, wearing a golf shirt and floppy hat. "Kinda quiet tonight, huh?"

"It always gets busier later," Matteo lied smoothly. "Pleasure to have you here. Can I get you anything else?"

"A little more wine, please?" the woman said, holding out her glass so the charm bracelet on her wrist jangled.

"Of course." He bowed and ducked into the kitchen.

He gave Diego a quick peck on the cheek.

His husband and chef waved him off with a snort. "*Più tardi. Sto preparando la cena.*"

"I can see that. Dinner for a hundred, is it? It's dead out there again tonight."

Diego shot him a dirty look.

Matteo retrieved the bottle of wine from the case and returned to fill up his guests' glasses. "What brings you in tonight?" *Maybe they saw our ad....*

"Just walking by and we were hungry. I miss the old place though.... What was it called, honey?"

Her husband scratched his chin. "Little Italy, I think?"

"That's it! It was the cutest place. Checkered tablecloths, those great Italian bottles with the melted wax… so Italian."

Matteo groaned inside. "So glad you came in" was all he said with another smile.

Four hours later and he'd served a grand total of five customers. At least they'd all been drinkers. Wine was all that was keeping the place open these days.

Diego closed down the kitchen, and they sat together at the big round *famiglia* table in the middle of the place, the blinds on the windows closed, and counted their earnings.

"$203," Matteo announced, tucking the cash and deposit slip into the bank sleeve for deposit. "Another hundred days like that this month and we can pay the rent." He sighed. He'd been sure, when they made their plans to come here, that America would be their land of opportunity.

Some days he longed to return to *Italia*. Sure, the government was corrupt, and the taxes were too high, and the opportunities were rare. But with all her flaws, it was still his home.

He wasn't sure that this place ever would be. The Americans had such strange customs—eating at five in the evening, drinking everything with ice, and going everywhere in their cars instead of on foot.

Diego looked up from his half-finished plate of lasagne. He took a slow sip of his wine and said softly "*Ho un'idea.*"

Matteo looked up. "What kind of idea?" He was doggedly sticking to his plan to become fluent in English by speaking it every chance he got. Diego was less diligent about his practice.

"*Una scuola di cucina. Posso insegnare a questi Americani a cuocere meglio.*"

"A cooking school? Here in the restaurant?" The idea was crazy. They had no experience as teachers. Sure, Diego was a fantastic self-taught chef, but how would they get things started?

They'd already spent a lot of money on advertisements—radio, newspaper, even nailed to posts around town—and had yet to hit upon the magic formula to bring people in the door. Why should this be any different?

"*Ho fatto questo.*" Diego pulled a flier off the chair next to him, handing it to Matteo.

"Learn to Cooking," Matteo read. "Give Classes With An Italian Chef How Easy It Is." He laughed. "OK, the grammar needs a bit of work. But maybe we could do something with this...."

"Not maybe. Can." Diego grinned. "I can."

Matteo looked around at the modern *enoteca* they had created. It had gone from the sadly out of date Little Italy restaurant they had found when they'd first arrived to something sparkling and modern and new.

They had sold their house in Bologna and mortgaged everything they had to make this dream come true. It would be a shame to lose it all and be sent back to Italy with their tails between their legs.

"Okay," he said, taking Diego's hand in his. "I'll tell you what. Send me the file, and I'll clean it up a bit. We'll put these out around the neighborhood and see what happens. When do you want to start?"

Diego grinned. "*Domenica prossima?*"

"A week from Sunday, it is." He grasped the little golden cross his mother had given him before she passed away and said a little prayer to her. "*Ti prego. Mi manca, mamma.*"

Then they put away the dishes and turned out the restaurant lights. Matteo teased Diego with a kiss and then pulled him up the staircase at the back of the restaurant to their apartment.

On the table, the flier sparkled for a moment before becoming dark once more.

2. THE REDHEAD

Carmelina ducked into her bathroom one last time, checking her frizzy red hair. It was all over the place, as usual. There was only so much you could do with yourself once you passed fifty, and it was, after all, the first time she'd left the house for fun since Arthur had passed away.

Not that tonight was going to be *fun*. She was joining the Merry Widows Club—three women who had also lost their significant others. Loylene had invited her, and she hadn't had the heart to say no.

Loylene was a sweetheart, but she was totally caught up in Tupperware and counting calories. Carmelina had never counted calories in her life—she had her gorgeous Italian hips to prove it.

Marjorie was a bit of a bitch. Carmelina had often wondered if the woman's husband had died just to get away from her nagging.

She barely knew Violet, who was, as her name suggested, a wallflower who never spoke above a peep.

She kissed Arthur's photo on the mantel on her way out, the one where he was scowling because they'd been late to dinner for their twentieth anniversary. And true to form, she was late now, due to be at the little restaurant at five p.m.—in just five minutes.

Still, she was sure she had enough time to check her lipstick one last time.

~

It was a quarter to six when she finally arrived at the One Speed, the little pizza place the Club had chosen. Despite the fact that she lived just a couple miles away in River Park, it had taken her almost half an hour to get there due to a road project on H Street. And parking had been horrific. If only she'd left earlier.

"Hi girls," she said, sliding smoothly into the open seat.

The other women had black veils on, something she found a bit morbid. Sure, she had lost Arthur less than three months before, after thirty wonderful years together. But she had given up on wearing black after the first week, and these women had been bereaved for more than a year.

Marjorie gave her a sour look. "You forgot your veil. And you're an *hour* late."

"Forty-five minutes," she shot back, picking up the menu. "And I guess I left mine at the dry cleaners."

Loylene flashed her a perky smile. "Oh, that's all right," she said, opening up her large, woven pastel-peach purse. "I brought an extra, just in case." She handed over a veil that had seen better days—creased and wrinkled and caked with little bits of something.

"Thank you, darlin', but I won't put you out. I'll bring my own next time." She set it aside.

Violet nodded and said something unintelligible.

"What was that?" Carmelina was *starving*. She ached to move past the pleasantries and get her meal ordered.

"She said she's happy you're here." Marjorie's severe tone left no doubt as to how *she* felt about the matter.

"Shall we order?" Carmelina said, trying to move things along. "The minestrone soup looks good. I'll bet all they have to do is ladle that into a bowl…."

"The ritual first." Marjorie's tone brooked no argument.

"The what?" Carmelina asked.

"The ritual," Loylene said, pulling a small green Tupperware container out of her voluminous purse. She popped open the lid, displaying a bunch of small, folded pieces of white paper, and set it in on the table. "Each of us takes one of these, reads it, and then describes what her husband or…" She glanced at Violet. "…spouse liked."

Carmelina rolled her eyes. "Does it take long?" Her stomach rumbled.

"I'll go first," Marjorie said, ignoring her. She took a piece of paper and read aloud. "Clothing." She stared off into space for a long moment. Carmelina was starting to worry about her when her eyes suddenly refocused and she smiled mistily. "Tube socks. Martin loved his tube socks."

"Very good," Loylene said, putting the box in front of Violet, who picked a piece of paper, and read it quietly.

"Burnt toast," she said softly with no further explanation.

Carmelina's stomach rumbled.

"Okay," Loylene said with a frown. She drew her own paper. "Ah, TV Show. Um… that's a hard one. He watched so many. Davis *lived* in front of the television."

"Hoarders?" Carmelina suggested helpfully. She'd been to Loylene's house.

"Ice Road Truckers," Loylene said triumphantly. "Your turn."

Carmelina obediently took a piece of paper, and then stared at it blankly. Printed on the paper was "favorite kink." She looked up. All three women were staring at her expectantly. "The 49ers. Favorite sports team," she lied and shoved the paper back in the box.

Violet's phone buzzed. "Sorry, I've got to take this. It's Sylvie." She took the phone outside.

"Sylvie?" Carmelina asked.

Loylene nodded. "Her wife. Violet's an honorary member. Sylvie's not actually dead, just working."

Carmelina shook her head. This had been a bad idea. "Can we just order? I haven't had a bite to eat since breakfast." She waved at their waiter.

"First we share the objects we brought that belonged to our spouses," Marjorie said, pulling out an old pair of athletic socks with red stripes from her purse.

"Oh hell no." Carmelina pushed away from the table and threw down her menu, ignoring Loylene's shocked expression. "I'm sorry, Loylene, but grieving at home is better than this." She stormed out of the restaurant with just the right amount of righteous indignation, or so she would tell herself later.

As she walked back to her car, something stuck to her shoe.

It was a green sheet of paper. She turned it over. "Italian Cooking School —Come Learn From The Best." It was for a restaurant called "Ragazzi," and the classes started on Sunday. She looked at the address. It was right across the street.

How had she never noticed it before?

She stuffed the flier into her purse and drove home, where gelato awaited her.

3. ON THE STREET

Marissa set her backpack on the toilet tank, where it wouldn't get all nasty from the bathroom floor. Coffee shop bathrooms were better than gas station stalls, but only in degree of *ick*.

She made sure the door was locked firmly behind her and started into her routine. Shucking her T-shirt and jeans, she ran the tap water and gave herself a quick wash with the bar of soap she'd bought at the corner market, pulling it out of one of her precious ziplock bags. She rinsed as well as she could, and then dried off with paper towels from the dispenser.

A little bit of soap went into her hair—she missed her shampoo days, but soap was cheaper.

Her close-cropped brown hair had been unevenly bleached with peroxide. She used a little soap from the dispenser for gel, pulling her hair up into points. At least it smelled good.

She stared into the mirror, trying to recognize her own face. Her snow-white skin was clean now, her brown eyes clear. But she still looked like a stranger to herself. Three months on the street, and she felt like a different person.

Someone pounded on the door. "I know you're in there," a shrill female voice said. "This restroom is for paying customers only!"

"Done in a minute!" she shouted back.

She put her jeans and T-shirt back on and brushed with some of the cheap off-brand toothpaste they'd given her at the Center. It tasted like cinnamon. She checked her teeth—they looked clean enough.

Packing everything back up, she checked herself over once more, deciding she looked okay. Young and disheveled, maybe. But she didn't *seem* homeless.

She closed her backpack and reached for the door. Something was stuck to the sole of her shoe. She reached down to grab the green piece of paper, glancing at it—she almost threw it away, but the word "free" caught her attention.

It was an ad for a cooking class at some restaurant out in East Sac. The first lesson was free, and you got to eat what you cooked.

She folded it up and shoved it into her pocket, slipping from the restroom and out the back door before the manager could catch her.

It was just a few blocks from the coffee shop at 19th and J to the LGBT Center, where the youth support group met every Friday night. It was one of the few times Marissa felt like a "normal" girl these days.

She sat down on the steps of the restored Victorian building, wondering how soon it was going to start getting cold at night. She'd been on the streets since just after school ended, when her parents had thrown her out of their house in Granite Bay after her mother had caught her kissing another girl. Religion ran deep in the Sutton family, and of the many things that were taboo, being a spiky-haired dyke was near the top of the list.

"Hey lez!" Ricky Martinez called from down the block.

"Hey gay boy," she shouted back. "You're early." Ricky usually showed up fifteen minutes late, the poster boy for *gay time*. "Hey, I like the 'hawk."

He sank down next to her on the stairs, dropping his pack, and she ran her hand over his bright pink fauxhawk appreciatively.

"Thanks. Did it myself. Justin seems to like it too." Justin was the guy Ricky was seeing. Ten years older and rich as shit.

"Nice. I'm starving. What time is it?"

Ricky checked his phone. Damn, she missed having a phone.

"Five after seven. He's late. Hey, I like the new art." He pointed at the skull she had tattooed on her arm. It was still a little red.

Some of the other seventeen to twenty-ones were starting to show up now. "Thanks. Rex did it for me at the shop for free."

"You don't have to blow him, do you?"

She giggled. "No. I do work for him, clean up the shop, greet the customers. He pays me under the table."

"Shit. Sorry, I forgot."

She shook her head. "It's all right. How's Justin treating you?"

He pulled out a gold chain from under his shirt. "Not bad."

She whistled. "You know you're his rent boy, right?"

"He never pays me. He *loves* me."

She eyed the necklace, raising an eyebrow.

"He never pays me *in cash*."

Marissa snorted. "I hope they have something besides cupcakes tonight. My stomach churned all night last week after group."

"Oh, about that…" He unzipped his backpack and held out a brown paper sack. "I couldn't finish it…."

She turned away. "I don't want your fucking pity."

"Never. Total respect."

She *was* starving. "You sure?"

"Here, take it. If you don't eat it, it goes in the trash."

Her stomach rumbled. "Give me that," she said, snatching it out of his hands. There was half a Subway sandwich inside and an unopened bag of chips. "You bought this for me," she said accusingly.

He shook his head. "They gave me an extra bag by mistake."

She seriously doubted that but said nothing. Her stomach had roared to life at the sight of the meal. "What, no soda?"

"You're unbe-fucking-lievable." He grinned and pulled out a can of Wild Cherry Pepsi. Ice cold. Popping it open, he handed it to her.

She gulped it down. *Oh my God, it tastes incredible.* Then she wolfed down the sandwich. When she ate, it was usually at the food kitchen, where the cook didn't seem to know what pepper, salt, or seasonings were. And she drank a lot of lukewarm water.

"You know I'm not giving you a hand job for this, right?" she said, glaring at him.

"Eeeew…"

"Just so we're clear." She gave him a quick peck on the forehead. "Thanks."

At that moment, the door to the Center opened noisily, and Brad gestured all of them inside with a smile.

4. THE EVERYDAY GRIND

Marcos Ramirez practically jumped out of his skin. He loved hanging out here at the Everyday Grind, sitting under the shade of the giant oak tree that towered over the wooden patio fronting the MARRS Building. But the noisy traffic along J Street, just feet away, sometimes got the better of him.

Still today was a good day. He had a new paying client—River City Real Estate, a local company that badly needed to update their circa-2005 website. OK, so he kinda hated this sort of work. He missed the good old days when web design had been an art, when you built sites from scratch with a little HTML and some graphic design expertise. These days it was much more rote. Start with Wordpress (or Blogger or Joomla), add a few extensions (or plugins or widgets) and upload a few pictures and boom… instant website.

Plus no one had ever told him that the bulk of his time would go into all the other boring stuff—finding new clients, cold calls, invoicing, tracking and reports. And taxes.

Oh God, how he hated taxes.

But today the sun was shining, the Farmer's Market was in full swing on the street in front of him, and he had an honest-to-goodness paying client to work for.

He took a deep breath and sipped his extra-hot decaf two-pump sugar-free skinny vanilla latte and dove in.

The next two hours flew by. Although the work had grown a bit boring, he knew his stuff. He found a template he liked and got into the guts of it, redesigning it to match the look and feel of his client's logo and style. He added one of his favorite database extensions and configured it to handle the fields he needed to import from the old site. Then he downloaded the data from the existing site and imported it to the new one.

Soon he had a rough first draft to ship back to his contact at River City.

"Can you spare a dollar?" a young girl with blond spiky hair asked from the sidewalk below.

"Just a sec." He rummaged through his wallet and handed her a five.

"Thanks," she said, flashing him a bright smile.

"'Welcome!" He downed the last of his now-cold coffee and stood, stretching and working out the kinks in his neck from being hunched over his laptop.

"Working hard, I see," a guy at the next table said.

He was handsome enough—maybe five years younger than Marcos's thirty-nine. He had fine features, thick blond hair, and blue eyes and wore a sharp dark-gray suit with a black shirt and yellow tie.

"Yeah, programming."

"I always hated that crap." The guy half-stood and held out a hand. "I'm Dennis." His smile was just a little too white.

"Marcos," he replied, taking the man's hand. *Nice firm handshake.* "So what do you do?"

"Me? I'm a salesman. I'm in town for the American Cheese Society convention."

Marcos snorted. "Seriously?"

"Seriously. I represent Swisstown Cheese." He handed over a card.

"Okay, that's just awesome."

"Thanks, I think." He ran a hand through his thick blond hair. "Can I ask you something?"

Marcos closed his laptop. "Sure," he said. "Shoot."

"What is there for a guy to do in Sacramento for the afternoon?"

"Let's see. Well, there's the Sac Brew Bike, if you like pub crawls. Or the Crocker, if you like art. And Sacramento has some great theatre, although most of that's at night."

Dennis was grinning.

"What?"

"I was hoping for something a little more… personal."

Marcos was a good-looking guy. His salt-and-pepper hair had only made him more distinguished, and he wasn't too bad looking for his age. But rarely was someone so forward with him, at least not out on the street.

He kinda liked it.

"Sure…. Your place or mine?"

Marcos lay on the bed, naked and sated, wrapped in the white hotel sheets as the sun slanted through the wide windows, imparting an afternoon glow.

Dennis was gone. He'd had to catch a flight back to Des Moines, or Green Bay, or wherever the hell he was from. He'd told Marcos to enjoy the room. It was paid for until four.

The windows looked out over the Capitol Building and park, far nicer than his own view of the back alley from his condo window.

What the hell am I doing with my life?

The thought came to him unbidden. Sex with handsome strangers had been exciting in his teens and twenties. In his thirties, the thrill had started to wear a bit thin. And with forty just around the corner, maybe it was time to get serious.

There *had been* one guy when Marcos had been twenty-five, living on his own after graduating from Corbis Baptist College up north. Franco had been about his age; smart, Italian, cute as hell, and as artistic as Marcos was logical. He'd been the set designer for a local playhouse called the Gay Twenties, and they'd shared an amazing year together.

Before Frank had found a lump on his neck that had metastasized and spread throughout his body.

After that, it had been easier to be alone.

Marcos took a quick shower, washing off Dennis's smell. He missed long showers—maybe one of these days it would rain again in Sacramento.

He found his underwear hanging over the little blue recycle bin. He grinned. It had been an *active* afternoon. As he pulled them out, a green flier came with them.

"Free First Cooking Class," he read, scratching his chin. It didn't say anything about being a gay thing, but Dennis had presumably put it there, and the restaurant was called "Ragazzi," which he remembered meant men. Or boys.

Maybe it was a *sign*.

He pulled on his jeans and stuffed the paper into his pocket, whistling as he walked out the door.

5. FOUR FOR LUNCH

Diego glanced at the clock. It was almost two, and the lunch rush (which today had been four people) was over. His new students should be arriving soon. If there were any. They'd printed up five hundred green fliers after Matteo had helped him with his English, which was terrible. He *knew* he should learn more, but there was so much other work to be done—sourcing his ingredients, preparing the daily menu, cooking. He hadn't realized what a big job this restaurant was going to be.

He cleaned off the serving counter that separated the kitchen and the dining area. Matteo was setting up the chairs for their guests and had cleared all the tables off to one side. Diego planned to demonstrate the making of a piadina, a traditional flatbread from their home province of Emilia Romagna.

He took out a sack of flour, imported from Italy—the American flour just didn't cook the same. He also brought out a can of lard. He'd learned that Americans preferred to use butter or margarine, but lard just tasted better. A little salt, some honey, and baking powder, and he was ready to go.

Matteo had finished the setup. "*Sei pronto?* Are you ready?"

Diego nodded. "*Se dovessi aver bisogno…*" He made a telephone with his right hand.

"Yes, call me if you need me. *Chiamami!*" And with that he disappeared up the stairs.

Diego looked over his translated notes nervously, not sure he was ready for this. But it had been his idea. There was no backing out now.

Diego's phone buzzed. It was Max. He sent the call to voicemail. He wasn't ready to deal with all that just yet. The last time they'd met… well, Matteo would freak out if he found out.

The front door chimed and someone entered. Diego put on a big smile. "*Benvenuta da Ragazzi!*"

~

Carmelina stood outside the door to the restaurant, her hand on the door handle. It was *only* a cooking class. Really not so big a commitment. Hell, she could always run out the door, like she had from the Merry Widows Club, if it didn't suit her.

Loylene had been right about one thing. It was time to move on. Arthur would have wanted her to get back out and live her life again.

Decided, she pushed open the door. It was a cute place, modern and warm, with brick walls and pottery barn colors.

"*Benvenuta da Ragazzi,*" the man behind the kitchen counter said. He looked to be in his mid-forties, with a warm, infectious smile. He was cute. Gay, but cute.

"*Buongiorno*" she managed at last, racking her brain for her conversational Italian. Her mother had been first-generation American, but her grandmother Maria had been from Sicily and had always spoken Italian at home.

"*Parla italiano?*" the man asked, coming out of the kitchen to shake her hand. "*Piacere, sono Diego.*"

"Oh, hi, Diego. No, *non… non parla italiano.* My grandmother… *mia nonna?*"

He nodded.

"*Mia nonna was Italian.*"

"*Capito.* I not speak much English, but I try." He looked at a notepad on the counter. "Have a seat, please."

She took a seat in the front row. Judging by the low turnout so far, the seating arrangement was wildly optimistic.

The front door chimed, and she turned to see a man coming in—a handsome, younger hispanic guy with salt-and-pepper hair. "Is this the cooking class?" he asked.

She nodded. "Diego and I were just talking." She stood and extended a hand. "I'm Carmelina. That's Diego, our teacher today."

"Marcos." They sat down together, Marcos giving Diego the once-over.

Carmelina laughed. "Forget it. I think he's taken. I googled this place earlier. He runs it with his boyfriend."

Marcos blushed "That obvious, huh?"

"My brother Cliff is gay. So do you live in Sac?"

He nodded. "Off of R Street in Midtown. You?"

"River Park."

Diego cleared his throat. "Let's start."

Carmelina sighed. She had hoped this would be a hands-on class.

Diego looked around the room and at the door. No one else had come in. "*Venite!*" he said, gesturing them up from their seats. "*Siamo solo noi tre.* Just three. We do this together." He opened the sack of flour and pulled out a bowl.

Carmelina glanced at Marcos. "I'll get my hands dirty if you will."

Marcos grinned. "I was hoping you'd ask."

It was the beginning of a beautiful friendship.

Marissa rubbed her eyes, glancing at the clock that hung on the wall of the changing room. "Crap," she said. It was already almost one thirty. She was gonna be late.

She pulled on a T-shirt and one of her two pairs of jeans and stumbled out of the room toward the bathroom.

"That you, 'Riss?"

"You were supposed to wake me at noon." She popped into the front to find Rex with a client, tattooing a rainbow unicorn on his bicep. "Sorry."

"You looked like you needed sleep." Rex glanced at her. He looked a bit scary with his mohawk and all his piercings, but he was a pussycat at heart.

"Can't talk. Gotta clean up and run."

She retreated to the shop bathroom. She washed up as best she could and spiked her peroxide hair. In five minutes she was out the door with a wave to Rex.

She jogged down 16th street to the light rail station and caught one of the Gold Line trains toward East Sac.

She wasn't sure why she was going to all this trouble. It's not like she had any real kind of future ahead of her. But the last two nights, she'd been dreaming of Italian food, and now she was craving it like nobody's business.

She hopped off the train and jogged up the street to the restaurant, just ten minutes late, flinging open the door.

Three people awaited her, all older than her parents.

6. PIADINA

looks of judgment on their faces.

The redheaded woman was frowning. The old guy's eyes narrowed as he looked at her. And the man behind the counter said something unintelligible and pointed at her.

She *knew* when she wasn't wanted.

Marissa turned and ducked out the door, letting it slam behind her. She'd find something else for dinner. Better than being stuck in that stuffy place with a bunch of assholes all staring down at her. If she walked back to Midtown, she could use her Rapid Transit money to get a little something to eat.

She pulled the flier out of her pocket and crumpled it up, throwing it into a trash can.

~

Marcos stared at the girl in the yellow jacket who had just entered the restaurant. He *knew* her.

She glared back at him, all rough edges and teenage attitude under her spiky yellow hair. Then he remembered. She was the homeless girl he'd given five bucks to the day before.

He was about to say something when she sniffed and then ran out.

"That was odd." Carmelina shook her head. "Poor thing looked frightened."

Marcos made up his mind. "I'll be right back." He flashed his companions a smile.

Diego nodded. "*Ti aspetteremo.*"

"I think he means we'll wait," Carmelina translated.

"Thanks." He ran after the girl, stepping out into the warm afternoon sunlight, glancing left and right. Then he saw her bright-yellow jacket about a block away.

He dashed after her.

She threw something in the trash. It was the green flier.

He pulled it out. "Hey, wait," he shouted, jogging after her. "Girl with the yellow jacket."

She spun around, frowning. "What?"

He stopped, a little out of breath. "Just give me a sec." He waited for his breathing to slow. "Sorry, I'm not as young as I used to be."

"What do you want?"

"I know you."

"What?"

"From yesterday. I gave you five dollars, over by the Everyday Grind."

She blinked. "Oh, yeah. Thanks." She turned to walk away.

"Wait!"

She looked at him over her shoulder. "I *said* thank you. What else do you want?"

He held out the crumpled flier. "You were coming to the cooking class, weren't you?"

She looked at the paper, her eyes narrowed. "Maybe."

"Look, I know what it's like to be on the streets. I was there for six months when my parents kicked me out for being gay. I'll bet you were kicked out too."

She stared back at him noncommittally, but she didn't leave.

"I'm Marcos." He held out his hand.

"Marissa."

"Come back inside, Marissa. At worst, you'll get a hot meal, and at best you'll make a new friend or two."

She stared at her feet, fidgeting.

"Besides, you do kinda owe me." He grinned at her. "For the five."

"Asshole," she said, but she pushed her way past him, heading back toward Ragazzi.

Marcos followed, still smiling.

~

Carmelina was dredging up a little of her long-lost Italian to chat with Diego. It was slow going, but they managed to get through the niceties—*How are you? Great weather we're having.*

Inside, she was having doubts about this whole cooking class thing. She had grown fond of spending time on her couch in front of her DVR these past three months, and she'd gotten a little rusty at dealing with real people.

Plus the turnout this afternoon was dismal.

Carmelina was about to excuse herself when the door opened again and the blond girl barged in, followed by Marcos, who winked at her.

"Carmelina, this is Marissa. She's… a friend of mine. Marissa, Carmelina."

Marissa shot Marcos an unreadable look.

"Nice to meet you, Marissa," Carmelina said, wondering where the two of them could have met.

"And this is Diego."

Diego held out a hand. "*Piacere.*"

"It means 'my pleasure'," Carmelina whispered to Marissa.

"Um, my pleasure." She shook his hand nervously.

"Now please, wash hands first," Diego said, holding out a metal bowl filled with warm, soapy water.

They each washed their hands and dried them on white towels Diego supplied.

A gay Italian chef, a gay American web designer, and a feisty young girl who looked like she'd just come in off the streets.

Maybe it will be a worthwhile evening after all.

~

Diego surveyed the little group. It was a motley band and far fewer than he'd hoped for, but even the biggest trees started with a small seed.

"Okay, *siete pronti*? Ready?"

They all nodded.

He picked up his translation and read:

"The Piadina is typical flatbread from Emilia Romagna, in Italy. You are able to stuff it with many thins… things: spicy salami, mozzarella, and *basilico* with olive oil, or even sweets: Nutella and blueberries or fresh raspberries."

He glanced up. His class looked *bored. This is going badly.*

He remembered how his mother had taught him to cook, a sparkle in her eyes as she took his hand and showed him what it *felt* like to make the dish.

He took a deep breath and started over. "*Mia mamma…* she make this for me. Like this."

He took Carmelina's hand and guided her to measure out the flour.

Then he showed Marissa how much lard and milk to add. She smiled when he showed her how to fold it into the flour.

Marcos added the remaining ingredients, and as they worked, the smell of fresh dough filled the restaurant.

"*Sentitelo,*" he said, demonstrating by inhaling deeply.

His class followed his lead.

"Oh, that smells good," Carmelina said. "*Buono.*"

"*Si chiama l'impasto,*" he said, holding up the bowl of dough. "*Impasto.* Repeat."

"*Impasto,*" the three said in unison.

The rest of the afternoon passed quickly, and soon they were all enjoying a typical Italian meal together.

At one point, Diego caught Matteo peeking from the darkness of the stairs. He gave Matteo a thumbs up.

Maybe he'd turn into a decent American after all.

See the piadine recipe at the end of the book.

7. CONNECTIONS MADE

MATTEO CREPT DOWN THE STAIRS FROM THEIR SECOND-FLOOR apartment, peeking out from the darkness at the restaurant below.

Diego was standing behind the counter, sleeves rolled up and strong, muscular arms covered with a dusting of flour. He was engrossed with his students as they ate the products of their afternoon labor. The piadina smelled heavenly, and Matteo's stomach rumbled.

Diego had a level of comfort with strangers that Matteo had always envied. Drop him in any crowd, and in five minutes he was among friends. Matteo supposed it had to do with growing up among a gaggle of sisters. Diego had learned his social game early.

Matteo had grown up as an only child. While he understood social graces, he was always ill at ease among strangers. Learning to be the host of Ragazzi had been a big challenge for him. He sighed.

At last, Diego was shooing his students out the door, securing promises from them to return the following Sunday. Matteo waited until Diego locked the door, then bounded down the stairs. "*Com'è andata?* How did it go?" He spoke in both Italian and English, hoping Diego would pick up more of the American tongue.

Diego gave him a quick peck on the cheek. "*Abbastanza bene*, my love," he said. "*Speravo di avere più persone…*"

Matteo forced a smile. "*Sì, solo tre allievi.* Only three people." He surveyed the chaos in the kitchen. "*Avete fatto un casino*! What a mess!"

"*Non importa. Siediti*!" Diego shoved Matteo playfully into a chair next to the bar. He put down a plate and served up a still-warm *piadina*. "*Mangiala mentre metto a posto.* Is very good."

Matteo picked up the warm flatbread sandwich filled with melted mozzarella and took a bite while Diego cleaned up. It tasted delicious.

Diego seemed truly happy here. He hummed *Come un Pittore* while he worked, glancing up to smile at Matteo every now and again. *Still as handsome as when we met.*

Matteo couldn't bear to tell him how bad things were, financially. Another month, maybe two, and they might have to flee back to Italia. But not yet. He put his plate into the sink, washed his hands, and turned to lean back on the sink.

"*Cosa?*" Diego asked, just finishing his cleaning.

"We have a few minutes before dinner." His eyebrows translated that for him.

"*Ma non posso…*"

Matteo reached out to grab Diego's hand, pulling him in for a kiss. "*Poi ti aiuterò io.* I'll help you after."

Diego's eyes twinkled, and he let himself be led upstairs.

Leaving the restaurant, Marcos found Marissa outside smoking one of those vape pipes. "That'll burn out your insides," he said, frowning.

She glared at him and took another puff. "They're healthy. The guy at the vape shop told me so."

Marcos snorted. "You believe everything you hear?"

She shook her head and grinned. "Only what I want to."

Such a brave face. "Can I give you a ride to wherever you're staying?"

Marissa looked up at the sky. "No, it's still warm out. I'll walk."

"I hope you come back next week. It looked like you really enjoyed class."

She shook her head. "It was all right. But I'll be busy." She took a last pull of the e-cig. "Hey… thanks for making me come in. It was nice."

He nodded. "Hey, if it's about the money—"

"I gotta run." She took off down the street.

Marcos watched her go. She had really come alive in the cooking class, and her walls had dropped for a couple hours. He recognized his younger self in her studied indifference—she didn't want anyone to know how scared and lost she was. Someone had helped him. He had to find a way to help her.

~

The radio talking heads were lambasting President Obama again. Carmelina had hardly listened—she hated Sacramento talk radio. It was all conservative bullshit anymore, and she only turned it on for traffic and weather.

It was another unusually warm, sunny Central Valley day. Her lawn had long gone yellow in the drought, and her neighbor's house had taken a beating when a dying tree had dropped a forty-foot branch on the roof.

Her husband, Arthur, used to take care of their yard and the house. It had only been a few months now since he'd died, and already the little things that needed doing were piling up.

She pulled into the Corti Brothers parking lot. She was determined to go home and make those piadina things herself tonight, before she forgot how. She looked over the recipe—the Italian grocer should have everything she needed, though she planned to find a substitute for the lard. Her ass was big enough already. She swept through the store in record time and got into the checkout line. Then she heard a familiar voice behind her.

"Carmelina Di Rosa!"

She steeled herself and plastered a smile on her face. "Vito Barino," she said, turning to face the man. He was a widower, an accountant, and by all accounts a terrible lay. And he'd been after her since the funeral.

"So happy to see you." They kissed cheeks. "If you're free on Tuesday—"

"I have cycling class."

"Or Wednesday—"

"Dinner with friends."

"Or—"

"Washing my hair. Listen, Vito, it was great to see you." She pushed past him to the just-opened express line. He started to follow, but a handsome, dark-haired man in an Italian suit slipped in between them.

"I'm sorry Mister…"

"Barino."

"Barino. But Ms. Di Rosa and I are seeing each other."

Carmelina almost laughed at how poor Vito's face fell. His shoulders slumped and he nodded and wandered away.

She eyed the newcomer—tall, dark and handsome, all warmth and smooth Italian charm. "Seeing each other, huh?" she asked her suitor with an arch of her eyebrow. "I don't even know your name."

"Daniele. So what do you say?"

Why the hell not? "I might be persuaded."

8. RAVIOLI DAYDREAMS

BEN HAMMOND LEANED BACK IN HIS CHAIR, HIS HALF-EATEN PIZZA growing cold on the plate in front of him, his laptop closed. The patio at Pizzeria Urbano was one of his favorite places for lunch—especially while the days were still warm like this, before the chilly weather (and hopefully drought-busting rains) arrived.

The waiter refilled his water glass, but he barely noticed. His eyes were on the redhead walking across the street. She was drop-dead gorgeous. She wouldn't have been out of place on the catwalks of Paris or Milan, with long legs and a sun dress that made her look ethereal. Like an angel fallen to Earth.

He shook his head—he'd stalled long enough. He was halfway through his writing year—he'd been laid off in the spring from Intel with a generous severance package, and he'd been determined to become a successful writer. He was writing the Great African-American Trans Novel, as he liked to call it. When he could pull his thoughts together enough to actually *write*.

He snorted. All the authors he knew were also great procrastinators, so by that measure, he was a *fantastic* writer.

His novel was *not* autobiographical, but he had, of necessity, pulled from his own experiences to write his main character, Jesse. Jesse was at a bit of a crossroads, caught between his family and his desire to live his life openly as a man. It was a place Ben had found himself five years before, when he was thirty, and that he still remembered with pain. His mother hadn't spoken with him since then, and his father had lost his memories to Alzheimers without ever accepting that his daughter was now his son.

Nevertheless, the world still turned. Ben woke up every morning grateful for his new identity, his new life. He looked at himself in the mirror and saw a *man*—his body at long last an external validation of his inner truth.

But poor Jesse wasn't quite there yet.

The redhead… Maybe it was time for Jesse to take a few steps out of his comfort zone and approach his dream girl. Yeah, that could work.

The rest of the chapter he was working on opened up before him in his head, and he could see the words. "She walked by, like a fallen angel…"

He flipped his laptop open and started to write.

∿

Afternoon was fading into evening when he finished the scene. He was meticulous with his writing—never a word out of place—going over and over and over it until it was a polished perfection. Of course, that slowed him down a bit, but he consoled himself with the thought that he wouldn't have as much to do on his second draft.

He slipped his MacBook into his backpack and stretched his arms up behind his head. Writing was hard work. Just keeping still and ignoring the world around you to immerse yourself in a character, in a moment in time that only existed inside your own head, took patience and effort.

He glanced at the time on his phone. It was almost six. Time to go to his night job, which gave him a little human interaction and some cash to play with, outside his normal expenses.

The Everyday Grind was just a few doors down. He pushed open the door and waved at Alexis and Toby behind the counter.

"Cutting it a bit close, aren't you?" Toby said, glancing at his watch.

"Sorry… got caught up in a character." Everyone here knew he was a writer. Half the time when he wasn't working at home, he was here instead, laptop at hand. He eased past Daniele, who was making a latte, and went into the back to stash his pack and grab his apron. He rinsed his face in the sink, willing his mind back to the present, out of his story. His characters were always with him, especially Jesse, but he had to tune them out to do his job.

He looked at himself in the mirror, surprised. He looked *happy*. Laid off, working a part-time job, and writing like a madman, but happy.

∿

They were a quarter hour from closing when the door swung open.

"Hey, Ben!" Marcos Ramirez grinned.

"Hey Marcos… The usual?" The handsome Mexican-American had a huge crush on him, and Ben obliged him. He always tipped well, after all. "You look good tonight. Hot date?"

Marcos laughed. "Only if you're free."

"Sorry, *guapo*—I have a writing date tonight."

"Suit yourself."

"Let's see, extra-hot, two-pump sugar-free skinny vanilla latte, right?"

Marcos grinned. "You forgot decaf."

"Damn." It was a game they always played. "So what's up tonight?"

"Funny you should ask. I'm looking for a girl."

Ben snickered. "Hell has officially frozen over. $4.20 please."

"Not like that." Marcos handed over a five. "I took a cooking course last weekend—"

"You really are turning over a new leaf, aren't you?" Ben handed over the change.

Marcos ignored him. "I took a cooking class, and there was this homeless teen there. I've seen her here before and thought you might know where she hangs out?"

Ben wasn't sure how to take that. "Um, I'm not homeless."

"I know. But you see folks here all the time. She's about five eight, spiky blonde hair, little bit of an attitude…"

"Name?"

"Marissa."

"Let's see." Ben rubbed his neck. "Yeah, there's a girl like that who comes in here Fridays for a coffee. I think she said she goes to the LGBT Center for the youth group there."

"Ah, perfect. Brad might know her…. He runs the Center."

"Glad to help. Hey, what kind of cooking class?" It might be a good distraction.

"Italian. At this restaurant in East Sac called Ragazzi. Sundays at two."

Ben *loved* Italian.

"Marcos? Your drink's ready," Toby called.

"Thanks, Ben," Marcos said, waving as he walked out the door.

Ben was oblivious, daydreaming about ravioli.

9. SPARKLE

Brad Weston closed his office door and sat down, thinking about Meghan, the transgender kid who'd just left. So many queer kids were still kicked out of their homes for coming out. Increased visibility was a double-edged sword. The Laverne Coxs and Caitlyn Jenners of the world had inspired so many to speak their truth, a truth some parents just weren't ready to hear.

His office was a far cry from his last one at the State Capitol, working for a Republican senator, smaller but cozier. He'd left it a year earlier, after he'd come upon a strange medallion that had allowed him see what people around him really thought, and it hadn't been pretty. This office was warmer and filled with books.

The Sacramento LGBT Community Center was small, located in an old two-story Victorian at 20th and L streets, a block from the heart of gay Sacramento.

Every day, rain or shine, he rode his bike here from his home off R Street. He'd never regretted leaving politics, not even for a moment. Here he could touch actual lives. Someone knocked. "Come in," he said. Devon, the front desk volunteer, popped his head in. "Someone to see you," the young man said. "Says his name is Marcos Ramirez?"

Brad smiled. "He's our webmaster. Send him on in. You can leave the door open." He tidied up his desk. He had a thing about organization.

He wondered what Marcos wanted. He hadn't needed to call the web designer in months. Marcos entered the office, smiling. "Hey, Brad, how are you?"

"Good. Can't complain. Yourself?" They hugged, and Brad gestured for Marcos to sit.

"The last week has had its moments."

"How is… Tony?"

Marcos shrugged. "We broke up two weeks ago."

"Ah." Marcos was a bit of a Casanova, never managing to make it work with one guy for more than a month or two. He wondered who had broken the poor guy's heart. "So what brings you in? Is there a problem with the site?"

Marco shook his head. "Actually, I need a favor."

"Sure. Is everything okay?"

"Yeah, I'm great. Look, I took this cooking class on Sunday. It was just something I kinda fell into, but it was pretty great."

"I never thought of you—"

A train rumbled by outside. One of the reasons the rent was cheap. He waited until the noise subsided.

"—as much of a chef."

"Seriously. Anyhow, I met this girl there—"

Brad laughed. "That must be a first."

"Funny. Anyhow, she was a cute little thing… Maybe seventeen? Spiky blonde hair. Marissa."

Brad stared at Marcos. "You're not asking me to divulge private client information, are you? You know I can't."

Marcos nodded. "I know. But she was kicked out of her parents' house and has had a rough time of it. And something *happened* in the class. It was like she came *alive*. But I'm afraid she's not going to come back."

"I'm sorry, Marcos… I just can't help you."

"I just want to know where I might find her." Marcos touched his arm, and the air sparkled.

Brad blinked to clear his eyes. "Why do you care about this so much?"

Marcos broke contact. "I don't know. There's just something about her. I was thrown out too when I was a kid."

"I didn't know that."

"It was tough. I just thought if I could help her…"

"It would be like helping your younger self."

"Yeah. I guess it's stupid, huh? Sorry for wasting your time." Marcos stood to go.

"Wait." He opened his filing cabinet and pulled out Marissa's file. "These files are private. I can't share the information with you. I just want to be clear."

Marcos looked confused. "Yeah, I got that."

"I think I need a coffee. I'm going to make a run to The Everyday Grind. I'll be gone for about ten minutes."

Marcos smiled. He stood and gave Brad another hug. "I understand."

Brad left the Center, enjoying the beautiful late September day. He ordered his usual decaf latte and returned to his office, feeling better.

When he got back, Marcos was gone and the file was where he'd left it on the desk. More or less.

~

Brad put his Schwinn under the stairs in their small but well-manicured backyard and climbed upstairs, hoping Sam had dinner ready. They cooked at home a lot lately—his salary at the Center didn't pay much, and Sam was still working to get his career off the ground. His first book, *Read between the Lines*, was due out next month. The advance had been decent, but they had to be careful.

He found Sam in the kitchen. "Hey, handsome," he said, putting his arms around the younger man's waist and kissing Sam's neck.

Sam turned to kiss him back. "Making tacos tonight. Mom's recipe."

"Sounds good." Brad went to hang his jacket in the coat closet by the front door. "Marcos came in today."

"The web design guy?"

"Yes, him. He wanted to contact one of the Center kids. Hey, can I help?"

"Sure," Sam said. "Chop those green onions, please. What did you do?"

Brad began chopping. "That's the weird thing. I told him I couldn't help him. Confidentiality and all. Then he touched my arm."

"Oooh, should I be jealous?"

"Of this old thing?" Brad laughed. "No, it wasn't like that. But I felt like I *needed* to help him. So I left the file for him to look at and left for a coffee."

Sam set aside the frying pan and turned to face him. The smell of caramelizing onions filled the air. "Is Marcos a good guy?"

"Yeah." He laughed "Bit of a slut, but a good guy."

Sam chuckled. "Then you did the right thing." He gave Brad a hug, and Brad nodded.

"Now let's get dinner finished. I plan to reward you for your good deeds later."

Brad grinned and resumed chopping with renewed vigor.

10. THE DISH ROOM

CARMELINA POWDERED HER CHEEKS, CHECKING HER FACE IN THE
mirror. She'd gone to the hair and nail salons that morning and to Nordstrom
to pick out a new blouse. It wasn't every day that a handsome Italian man
came calling at one's door, after all. The same man who she'd kept waiting for
thirty minutes in her living room.

She checked the time and felt a sudden wave of sadness—the gold Tiffany
watch had been a gift from Arthur on their twentieth wedding anniversary.
She wiped away a tear from her eye with a tissue and shook her head. She was
not going to be sad tonight. She checked the watch again. It was seven ten
p.m. Not bad. She was only twenty minutes behind schedule.

"I'm so sorry to keep you waiting," she said, sweeping into the room.

Daniele stood and smiled. He looked *gorgeous*. She was certain there must
be something wrong with him.

"Nonsense," he said, looking at her appreciatively. "You're worth the wait.
But we should get going—"

She grabbed her purse. "There's one thing you should know about me if
we're going to date. I'm perpetually late."

He laughed. "And I'm perpetually hungry."

Skinny liar.

He ushered her to the car, a Mercedes convertible with the top up. She
hadn't spent two hundred on her hair to have it blown to bits going to dinner.

"So what do you do?" she asked as she slid into the passenger seat.

"Actually, I'm a florist," he said, picking up a beautiful boutonniere from
behind her seat and pining it deftly to her blouse.

Oh God, he's gay.

He must have noticed the look on her face, because he laughed. "I'm not gay. Believe me, I get that all the time. It's a family business. My grandfather started it." He started the car and pulled out onto the street smoothly.

"Was *he* gay?" she asked, a little embarrassed.

"He was married his whole life. But who knows? The way he looked at the young guys from Sac State when they came in…."

She stared at him, surprised. "Really? That's so sad—"

He was grinning like a hyena.

"You're pulling my leg, aren't you?"

"*Ti prendo in giro*, yes."

"You're a real bastard, you know that?"

"I've been told so before." He was still smiling.

"What's your shop called?"

"Fiori Amorosi," he said. "My last name is Amoroso."

She looked at him with new respect. "I've been in the one on Elvas."

He nodded. "I've seen you there before. I'm usually working in back."

Amoroso. "Your last name means "love?"

He turned onto H Street, heading toward Midtown. She loved this area, with its cute cottages and bungalows. "Lov*ing*, actually. You speak Italian?"

"Just enough to get me in trouble." Case in point—a date with a man named *Mr. Loving*.

It could only go downhill from there.

～

They arrived at Mulvaney's Building & Loan fifteen minutes late, but the host took them in right away. Instead of going out to the courtyard, she led them through the kitchen.

"Where are we going?" Was this some kind of joke?

"Surprise."

They entered a room the size of a large closet, surrounded with shelves filled with dishes of all kinds—white plates and metal wire baskets and silver service and pewter and brightly colored glazed pots, platters shaped like fish, and much more. In the middle of the room was a single table with two place settings and a candle.

"What is this? The pantry?"

"It's the Dish Room," the host said. "*Very* romantic." She gave them a wink and left them alone.

"Do you like it?" Daniele asked, pulling out the chair for her.

She looked around, taking it all in. "I don't know yet. It's different."

He sat across from her, looking crestfallen.

"Oh no, it's very nice! I was just surprised, that's all!"

He smiled tentatively. "I know the chef. It's hard to get on short notice."

It was *different*. Maybe she needed a little more *different* in her life. "It's perfect," she said.

The evening was like a fairy tale. Daniele was handsome, kind, and laughed easily. They talked about their Italian families—a little crazy, but more tightly knit than the scarves her mother used to make for her for Christmas.

He had never married—a red flag—but she forgot about it during the warm glow of the evening.

Now and then during the meal, waiters popped in to retrieve a platter or a set of dishes. She decided she found the whole thing utterly charming.

They were looking into each other's eyes over a decadent chocolate mousse when he asked her an unexpected question. "Have you ever had children?"

She felt the usual tension return to her shoulders. She looked away, not sure if she wanted to answer him, reluctant to let reality creep into what had been a wonderful evening. She hardly knew him, after all. But when she looked into his eyes, she saw no malice. Just curiosity.

"I… I had a daughter. When I was fifteen." There. She'd said it. "I wasn't ready. I was so young, so inexperienced. So I gave her away." She looked down at her hands. Even forty years later, she still felt a twinge of guilt and shame over her decision. Maybe he would be spooked and would run away.

Instead, he put his hands on hers, and she looked up at him. "That must have been very hard for you."

She nodded. "You have no idea."

"Here. *Un po' di cioccolato* makes everything better."

She took the proffered bite and smiled. It was delicious. "You're right." What if she hadn't gone to Corti Brothers?

She liked this guy. She *really* liked him. It had been a long time, but… "You know what else makes things better?" She leaned over and whispered into his ear.

He actually *blushed*. Then he called their waiter over. "Check please."

11. SECRETS

It was a Friday evening, and the traffic down J Street was steady. Marcos double checked the address and looked back up at the sign above the doorway.

"Twink." *It's a tattoo shop. Cute.*

Well, this was the only link he had to Marissa's whereabouts. He might as well follow it through. It was about what he expected inside—an old garage with sealed cement floors and an "urban street sign" design motif.

"Be right with you," the artist, a lanky man with long, greying hair, called from one side of the shop, where he was working on an elaborate Chinese dragon tattoo.

"No problem. I'll just look around."

"Suit yourself."

Examples of the shop's art decorated the walls—the usual skulls and pretty women and (of course) dragons, but also shirtless men, cocks and asses, and rainbow flags. Twink lived up to its name.

He took a seat and thumbed through a tattoo book, amazed at the breadth and variety on offer. He had never gotten one and never planned to, but he was fascinated.

The artist finished up his work. Marcos watched as he gently cleaned his client's skin, then dried it and applied some ointment and a bandage. "You're gonna want to take this off in about four hours and then gently clean the skin with some clear, unscented antibacterial soap and pat it dry."

The client laughed. "It's not my first time at the rodeo."

"I know that, Zack, but I'll tell you anyway. If you're too stupid to listen, that's on you. Give it two-to-four weeks to fully heal."

He left the shop, and the artist turned to Marcos. "Welcome to Twink. I'm Rex. What are you looking for today?"

Marcos shook his hand. "I'm not here for a tattoo."

"Are you sure? I could do a Madonna that would look beautiful on your skin."

"The singer or the mother of Jesus?"

Rex laughed. "Up to you."

"Well, thanks. Let me think about it. I'm here looking for a girl."

Rex sized him up. "I wouldn't have guessed."

"Not for me," Marcos said. The joke was getting *old*. "She's a homeless girl I met on Sunday. Her name is Marissa."

Rex frowned. "What did she do?"

"Oh, so you do know her?"

"Who wants to know?"

Marcos sighed. "I met her at a cooking class on Sunday. She was a little skittish, and I'm afraid she's not coming back. Which would be a real shame."

Rex's expression softened. "Leave me your number," he said at last. "If she wants to talk to you, she can use the shop phone."

"Fair enough." Marcos handed over his card. "Tell her I'd be happy to pay for her class, if she wants to come back."

"Will do. She's a good kid."

"I know." He waved and walked out of the shop into the warm September evening.

Diego pulled the last of the lasagna noodles out of the boiling water, laying them in the pan and topping them with a healthy dollop of bolognese sauce and parmesan cheese. He wrapped the whole thing in aluminum foil and slid it into the kitchen's industrial refrigerator for later.

He washed his hands, humming happily to himself. He was really starting to like it here. As if on cue, his phone beeped. He glanced at it as he dried his hands.

It was from Max. *Devo vederti. Domani.* I need to see you. Tomorrow.

He frowned. He texted back, telling the man not to contact him by text again. He didn't want Matteo to find out. *Domani alle tre da* OneSpeed. It was right across the street. He could sneak away for five minutes between lunch and dinner with some excuse. *Va bene.* Diego had a bad feeling about this, but he couldn't let Matteo find out. It would crush him.

Matteo waited in line at El Dorado Savings. He'd come mid-morning, hoping to avoid the lines, but it seemed like everyone else had the same idea.

He liked the bank because it had an Old West theme, and Matteo had always been partial to American cowboys. He'd attended his first Pride Parade a couple months before, just after they had first arrived, and he'd worn a cowboy hat, plaid shirt, jeans, and shit-kicker boots. He'd never felt so sexy or so American.

He reached the teller window and deposited the restaurant's meager earnings from the day before. Hopefully Diego's cooking class would start bringing in a little cash soon. They could really use it.

"I'd like to speak to someone about a loan," he said to the teller, a blonde woman named Doris, in her fifties or sixties.

She smiled. "Let me get someone for you." She handed him his deposit receipt. "Wait right over there."

He took a seat in a cracked-leather seat at the indicated desk. Soon a man about his age, dressed in a white shirt and bowtie, came to sit behind the desk. "Hi there," he said, shaking Matteo's hand firmly. "I'm Davis. I understand you're asking about a loan?"

"Yes. My husband and I own a restaurant—Ragazzi. We have our accounts here."

"Ah yes, one moment. Let me look up your account." Davis stared at the screen. "Here it is—oh."

"Yes, our income has been a little low this month…"

Davis smiled. "Of course. We all have occasional troubles. What other assets do you have? Retirement accounts? Other property? Cash?"

Matteo shook his head. "No. That's why we need the loan. Things will get better. We just need a little more time…"

"Tell you what. You don't have a lot of assets, but here's a loan application. Fill it out and we'll see what we can do." He stood and shook Matteo's hand again. "Have a nice day."

Not a lot of assets? Why would he ask them for money if he already had it? It sounded like a no.

He couldn't let Diego find out. It would crush him.

12. SATURDAY IN HELL

Diego glanced around, for once grateful that the restaurant was empty on a Saturday afternoon. It was five minutes to three.

Matteo was staring out of the window again, looking worried.

"*È tempo…*" Diego said, anxious to send Matteo out the door so he could get to OneSpeed on time. He held out the leather deposit bag. "*Per la banca?*"

Matteo turned, his expression blank. "What?" He saw the bag and nodded. "Again, in English?"

Diego sighed. "Is time. For the bank."

"*It's* time." Matteo smiled. "*Ma stai migliorando.* You're getting better!" He took the bag. "It's quiet. Looks like a good time to go. Will you be okay?"

"*Sì! Senti, mi prenderesti…*" he saw Matteo's stern expression. "Take me a coffee? Everyday Grind?"

Matteo smiled. "Close enough." He pecked Diego on the cheek and waved as he ran out the door. Diego watched as he walked down the street toward the bank. He'd be gone half an hour, if Diego was lucky.

He checked his phone. It was 3:01.

He grabbed his keys and let himself out of the restaurant, flipping over the "closed" sign and locking the door behind him. It was a clear, crisp day.

He looked both ways and then crossed Folsom Avenue to the other restaurant. It was a nice place, modern like Ragazzi. Diego wondered, not for the first time, if they'd made a mistake opening their place so close to this one. Not that they'd had much choice. It was the space Zio Augusto had left to Matteo when he'd passed away the year before.

Diego opened the door, looking around for Max. OneSpeed wasn't packed —for which he was thankful—but it did have a good ten full tables.

"Good afternoon," the hostess, Shelley, said with a sly smile. She had a bit of a crush on him.

"Hi," he said, pointing at Max. "I see…"

She nodded. "Go right on in." She winked at him, making him distinctly uncomfortable.

"*Grazie*." He was eager to get this over with.

Max spoke fluent Italian. It was one of the reasons they had chosen him as their immigration lawyer.

Diego was regretting that choice. "What do you want?" he hissed, sitting down across from Max.

"Seriously, Diego, that's no way to talk with someone who's trying to help you." He slipped a folder across the table.

"What's this?"

"Just the… information… that we were discussing two weeks ago. It's a copy for your files."

Diego opened it up. It contained a copy of his marriage license. "This means nothing."

"Look at the next page."

The waiter stopped by. "Hi, I'm Alex. Can I get you anything? A little water to start?"

"*Non per me.*"

"We're fine," Max said in English. "Can you come back in ten minutes?"

"Sure." He moved on.

Diego turned the page and felt the blood leave his face. "Where did you find this?"

"It took a little digging. Part of my due diligence." He smiled, a sight that turned Diego's stomach. "It could be bad for you with Immigration if they found out. You haven't told Matteo yet, I take it?

Diego shook his head. He hadn't thought it would ever come out. "What do you want?"

"Not all that much." Max sat back, looking at the menu. "The calzones are really good here, I hear."

"I'm not hungry." Diego ripped the menu out of Max's hands. "What do you want?" he shouted.

"Calm down, my dear boy."

Diego looked around. The other patrons and waiters were looking curiously in his direction. He sank back down, glancing at the time on his phone. It was a quarter after. "Matteo will be back soon. What do you *want*?"

Max licked his lips. "Thirty thousand. Money order, cash, whatever. I'll even help you figure out how to fix this."

There's no way. "Matteo pays all the bills. And we don't have that kind of money."

"I'll give you until Wednesday."

"I just told you. I don't…"

Max held up his hand. "Wednesday." He picked his menu back up. "Now let's see, what do I want? Something expensive…"

Diego stormed out.

Marissa stared at her wrists. It was the first time she'd ever worn handcuffs… all because of her stupid parents.

They were supposed to be at the club on Saturdays. Her dad would play a couple of rounds of golf, and her mom would lounge at the spa with the other model moms.

Marissa had planned to get in and out with some of her things—some clothes, her jewelry, and her teddy bear, Nathan.

Now she was here at the county jail on I Street, being processed. They'd let her take Nathan but nothing else.

The officer gave her a once-over. Her nameplate said Doris. "Name?"

"Marissa Sutton."

"First time?"

Marissa nodded. "It was *my own* house."

Doris snorted. "Girl, they all say that. Social Security number?"

"I'm serious. My psycho parents called the police when they found me in my own room. They weren't even supposed to be home."

"You serious?"

Marissa nodded. "They kicked me out months ago for liking girls."

"That's cold." Doris shook her head. "Still gonna need your social."

Marissa rattled it off.

"Age?"

"Seventeen. Eighteen next month." She leaned forward. "Am I gonna have a record?" Her mother was always going on about how bad it was to *have a record.*

"Can't say. Sounds more like a family dispute than a break-in, so maybe you'll get off easy." She handed over her desk phone. "Got anyone to call?"

Marissa shook her head. She didn't want Rex to find out about this. He might kick her out.

She felt something sharp in her pocket. She pulled it out of her tight jeans. It was a folded-up piece of paper.

It was the number for that guy from the cooking thing. Marcos. She *couldn't* call him though. She hardly knew him.

Then again, all he could say was no.

"Yeah, I've got someone."

13.NATHAN

Brad was rousted from bed by someone pounding on the front door. Who the hell was coming by at ten thirty p.m.?

He grabbed the bat he kept next to the bed.

"Who is it?" Sam asked blearily.

"I don't know. I'll find out."

Sam sat up, and Brad smothered the urge to jump back in bed. Screw their visitor. Sam looked adorable with his sleepy eyes and blond hair sticking up at odd angles.

The pounding sounded again.

"Want me to come with?"

"No, just be ready to call 911." They were downtown, after all. Things *happened* here, sometimes. "I'm coming!" Brad shouted to whoever was knocking. He pulled on his robe and clambered down the stairway to the front door. "Who is it?" he called, bat held at ready.

"Brad, it's Marcos. I need your help."

Marcos… the web designer? He unlocked the door. "How the hell did you get my home address?" he asked, staring at the man. "You *do* know I'm married, right?"

Marcos grinned sheepishly. "I know. You had a fundraising party here last year for the Center, remember?"

"Oh, crap. Yeah." He'd forgotten all about it. "So why are you here?"

"I need your help. Remember that girl, Marissa?"

"Yes. What happened?" He was starting to regret having shared the information with Marcos. If anything had happened to her as a result, he could lose his job.

"She's in trouble. She called me from the County Jail up on I Street."

Brad scratched his chin. "Why did she call you?"

"I don't know. I left my number for her where she hangs out. I guess I was the only one she could think of."

"Maybe so. Many of these kids don't have anyone. Hey, come inside. It's cold out there." He let Marcos in and closed the door.

"Who was it?" Sam was standing at the top of the stairs in only his white briefs.

Marcos looked up and whistled.

"Just our web designer."

Sam blushed. "Um, sorry. I'll leave you guys alone." He vanished into the bedroom.

"Come have a seat." Brad ushered Marcos into their small living room.

"Congratulations, Brad. The hubby's quite a catch."

Brad cleared his throat. "Marissa?"

"Oh, yeah, sorry. She said she was framed. She needs me to come get her out, but I don't think they'll let me, since she's underage. You know people there, right?"

Brad nodded. "What was the officer's name?"

"Um… Donna? Dorothy?"

"Doris?"

"Yes. I think so."

"I'll come with you and see what I can do. What will you do if they release her to you?"

Marcos shook his head. "I don't know yet. Get her home and in a warm bed for tonight. I can figure out the rest tomorrow."

Brad touched Marco's shoulder. "Why are you doing this?"

"Because she's me twenty years ago."

Brad nodded. "Okay, let's go. You brought your car?"

～

It took three hours, but the police finally agreed to release Marissa into Marcos's care, after he paid a bond of a thousand and promised to have her back for her court date in a month.

They brought her out, taking off her handcuffs. She was carrying a teddy bear, of all things. It made his heart ache for her.

"You okay?" he asked.

She shrugged.

He took that for a yes. "Come on. We have to get Brad here back home."

"Mister Weston?" her eyes widened.

Brad grinned. "Marcos here asked for my help to get you sprung."

"Thank you!" She threw her arms around him.

Marcos snorted. Fat lot of thanks he'd gotten. "Let's go. We'll drop him off, and then get you situated."

"You can drop me at Twink," Marissa said as if that ended the matter.

"I'm afraid not."

She turned on him. "Why not? I called you. You helped me. Now I'm good."

Marcos took her gently by the shoulders. "You're *not* good. You are facing breaking and entering charges, and you could end up in jail for six months or a year. The *only* reason you're out here and not in there is because I agreed to look after you. Got it?"

She looked shaken but nodded. "No need to be so harsh."

"Sorry." He pulled her in for a quick hug. She was stiff in his arms. "You have to take this seriously." He released her. "Now let's go. Poor Brad is out past his bedtime."

Half an hour later, they arrived at Marco's condo, a modern loft-style apartment off R Street. He unlocked the front door and let her in and flipped on the light switch.

"Wow, this place is luxe."

"Thanks. I like it. Come on, I'll show you your room." He led her through the living room to the guest room, where his parents stayed when they visited. Which was rare.

Marissa looked around the room. "It's… okay."

He saw wetness in the corner of her eyes. "Let me get some fresh sheets for the bed."

He returned a minute later with the sheets and some towels. "There's a bathroom just off the living room. I have my own, so it will be all yours."

She nodded. "And what do I have to do for you?" She started to pull up her shirt.

"Hey, no. No! None of that."

She stared blankly at him and then sank down on the bed and started to cry.

He sat down next to her. "Listen to me," he said, taking her hand. "You're safe here. I'm gay, and even if I weren't, I'd have zero interest in someone your age."

She sniffed. "So why'd you bring me here?"

"Because I was there once too." He picked up the teddy bear. "What's his name?"

"Nathan."

"Nice name." He handed her the bear. "Now get yourself cleaned up and get some sleep with Nathan. We'll figure things out in the morning. Okay?"

She nodded, and he closed the door behind her softly.

What the hell am I getting myself into?

14. LAZY SUNDAY MORNING

Diego had tossed and turned all night, worried that Matteo would discover his secret. Matteo *might* understand. But their marriage license was invalid too, and if the government found out, he might be forced to leave Matteo and go back home. Or worse, Matteo might be forced to go with him, and their dream of building a new life *negli Stati Uniti* would end.

He hadn't meant to do it. Her name had been Luna, and it suited her. She was a little crazy. His parents had wanted him to marry a nice girl, and when he'd met her in college in Padua, she'd seemed perfect.

She was beautiful, funny, and brassy, and she made him laugh. When she asked, he'd said yes. They chose a civil marriage with witnesses only, considered rebellious at the time. Diego's heart had never been in it, but it seemed like a good way to put aside his desire for men. It had never really worked, and they had split up a couple months later.

Diego had signed all the papers, believing that Luna would too. But when she had returned ten years later when Diego was already with Matteo, she had told him that they were still married.

She'd demanded money to keep silent. He *would* have told Matteo then. But Matteo had been dealing with his father's death, and it hadn't been a good time. So Diego had paid her off instead. Now her ghost haunted him.

He sent an email to his sister Valentina in Italy, asking for her advice. She was the only other person who knew his secret.

If he couldn't find another way by Tuesday, he'd have to tell Matteo.

He shut down the laptop and went to prepare for the day.

~

Sam Fuller leaned back in his chair to peer out the window at the sky. "Looks like another beautiful fall day in Sacramento."

Brad frowned over his copy of the Sacbee. "Is it fall already? I thought that started in October."

"It *starts* on the Autumnal Equinox. That was last week. What did they teach you in school?"

"Mathematics, English, and Finding a Man 101."

"Sucks you ended up with me then, huh?" Sam said, laughing.

Brad grunted. "Pass me the syrup."

Sunday mornings were their together time. They usually got up late, enjoyed an extravagant home-cooked breakfast—stuffed french toast today— and enjoyed one another's company. Then Brad would tend to things around the house or sometimes go in to the Center, while Sam wrote. Today was no different. They finished breakfast, and Sam started carting dishes to the sink. When Brad cooked, Sam cleaned. That was the rule.

Something tickled his memory. "Hey, that friend of yours who was here last night…"

"Marcos?"

Sam nodded. "Didn't you say he goes to some kind of Italian cooking thing on Sunday afternoons?"

"I think he mentioned it." Brad dropped the last of the dishes in the sink, making a sticky mess that extended up well above the counter top. "Sure you don't want my help with all this?"

"You cook; I clean. Fair's fair." Sam started scrubbing. "Do you remember where the class was?"

Brad leaned back against the counter, thinking. "Some place over in East Sac. Rico's… Ragato's…"

"Ragazzi?"

"That's it." Brad grinned. "I'm impressed. You been studying?"

Sam blushed. "Kind of. I'm writing an Italian character, and I thought it would be fun to talk to an actual Italian or two about it."

"That's a great idea! And maybe you'll even learn to cook something besides quesadillas."

"And tacos. I make a mean taco too."

Brad laughed. "Besides *American* Mexican food."

Sam shrugged. "You never know."

"You should go. It would do you good to get out of the house for a bit."

Sam nodded. "Will you be okay without me?

"Go. I'll see you for dinner."

Sam smiled. He really was the luckiest guy in Sacramento.

~

Over in an old apartment building in West Sac, another writer luxuriated in bed under his thick comforter, the crisp white sheets softened by a couple days' use. Ben felt calm, serene, secure. Then he realized he was sleeping on his side again, curled up in a fetal position. He groaned.

He'd once read that women tended to sleep on their sides, and sure enough, when his conscious mind was away, his body reverted to form. *A little betrayal.* He rolled over onto his back and lay there for a few minutes, trying to decide if he felt more masculine that way, then decided that it made no real difference.

He sighed. Sometimes he envied the cisgender people who never had to question the basics.

He glanced over at the clock. It was eleven a.m. on Sunday, his day off. He insisted on having that bit of sanity once a week. He rubbed his eyes. He'd been up on a writing bender the night before, fueled by black coffee and a leftover double-chocolate muffin from the bakery on the corner. He had no idea if he'd written something beautiful or a steaming pile of shit. He could never tell right afterward.

Instead, he'd print each chapter out and send it to his friend Sandy in Delaware by mail. She would read it, and after a week, she'd send it back with her notes on a separate page, using the postage paid envelope he supplied.

The whole thing gave his writing time to "compost" before he worked on it again. His non-writing friends thought he was nuts, but it worked for him, and when a chapter came home, it was like Writer's Christmas.

Sunday. There was something he was supposed to do today. Something Marcos had told him about.

Oh yes. It was the ravioli.

He pushed away the covers and ran to the shower. The class started at two, and he still had a few more pages to write today if he was going to make his self-imposed schedule.

It was going to be a busy day.

15. ENTOURAGE

MARCOS STARED AT THE CLOSED BEDROOM DOOR, TRYING TO DECIDE what to do. It was well past ten, and Marissa still hadn't shown her face. He was sure she was still in there. He'd set the alarm the night before, and unless she was a master criminal, she couldn't have gotten out without him knowing.

Clearly, he wasn't cut out to be a parent. He had *no idea* what to do next. Should he barge in and roust her out of bed? Just knock at the door? Bang some pots and pans together in the kitchen? Or just leave her alone?

Indecisive, he returned to his living room, deciding feigned nonchalance was best for the moment. He picked up a copy of the Bee and pretended to read it while he waited.

About ten minutes to eleven, his patience was finally rewarded. The door cracked open, and he turned to see an eye regarding him through the narrow space. "Where's the bathroom again?" Marissa asked.

"Right over here." He pointed. "Are you hungry?"

She opened the door a little farther. "Sure. I guess I could eat *something*. Can I take a shower first?"

He nodded. "Do you like eggs?"

"Why not?" It sounded just a little surly. *Baby steps.*

"I'll give you some privacy." He stepped into the kitchen and started to make breakfast. It was something he was really good at. He'd fed enough one-night stands over the years to fill the new stadium.

As Marcos cracked the eggs, he heard the shower start. He smiled.

She turned up fifteen minutes later, just in time for the hot breakfast he served. Her eyes widened as she took in the meal, and then her emotions slammed shut again. "It looks fine," she said in a monotone, but she sat down at the counter and began to devour it like someone who had been starved for weeks.

He sat down across from her. "So, you want to tell me what happened yesterday?"

"It was no big deal," she said angrily between bites. "I went home to get some of my shit. And my parents came back from the club early."

"And they called the cops *for that?*" He'd thought *his* parents were bad.

"I know, right?" She waved her arm. "They threw me out when I told them I don't like boys. Now they throw me in jail when I try to pick up my things. I *fucking hate* them."

"I know." It was hard enough being a teenager these days.

Marissa finished her meal and looked up at him, searching his face. "I gotta bounce," she said. "Thanks for breakfast." She started to slip out of the chair, but he caught her arm.

"I told you last night, you can't just take off."

She sneered. "So what is this? Prison?"

"You broke into a house. Sure, it was your own. But if your parents press charges… If the cops catch you on the street and not with me, they'll put you back in jail until your court date."

Her face turned a couple shades whiter, and she looked away.

"Look, it's not so bad here. You have your own room. I can take you to get some things—clothes, make-up, whatever—to replace the stuff you lost. It had to feel good to sleep in a real bed again last night, right?"

He could see the war going on inside her head. He remembered how hard it had been to accept help when he'd been on the street. "This place gets really lonely sometimes. You'd be doing me a favor if you'd stay."

She looked up at him. "Really?"

He nodded. He could see things were tipping in his favor. "One more thing."

"What?" A little of the fear returned to her eyes.

"We're going to that cooking class again today."

She relaxed. "Oh, that stupid thing."

But he thought that she sounded secretly pleased.

~

The restaurant was empty.

Matteo stood by the front door, trying to will some of the passersby to come inside. But foot traffic here was low, and no one came in.

He glanced at his watch. It was a quarter to two. Diego had run upstairs to grab a quick shower before class.

Matteo was so proud of him. Even if it came to nothing, it was wonderful to see Diego step up and do something positive. He was such a good cook; it warmed Matteo's heart that Diego was sharing his talent.

He had a lead on a small business loan. He planned to sneak out while Diego held his class. Maybe he could save this restaurant yet.

Poor Diego had seemed especially worried these last few days. He tried to hide it, but with twenty years together, Matteo knew the signs.

He wasn't sleeping well. He was short with the staff. He avoided eye contact.

Maybe he'd found out how bad things really were for their finances. Maybe it was obvious.

Matteo sighed. If he couldn't find a way to fix things, he'd have to tell Diego the truth. Then they'd figure out some way deal to with it.

Someone entered the restaurant. He looked up from his thoughts to see Carmelina, the redhead from the previous week. "*Salve*," he said.

"*Buon giornata!*"

Close enough. "Hi, I'm Matteo, Diego's husband. He should be down in a minute."

"You speak English. Thank God." She flashed him a warm smile. "What are we making today?"

"An appetizer, I think. One of Diego's mother's recipes."

Before she could reply, the door opened again. A Hispanic man and a young girl entered. He remembered them too. "Welcome to Ragazzi."

One last time, the door swung open, and two more people came in—two men, one blond and blue-eyed, and the other darker skinned with beautiful brown eyes. He'd been afraid there would be fewer people this week, but there were almost twice as many.

"Diego," he called upstairs. "You better come down. Your entourage awaits you."

16. MEMORY OF THE HEART

Diego came down the stairs and stopped, staring at the small crowd waiting for him below. Carmelina, Marcos, and Marissa had all returned—he'd been doubtful the girl would come back.

There were two new people too. A handsome, tall blond in a white T-shirt —a bad choice when cooking pasta sauce—and a cute African-American with writerly glasses. Diego liked him immediately.

"*Ciao, amici!*" he said, holding out his arms.

Carmelina kissed him on both cheeks, and Marcos gave Diego a big hug. "New ones?"

Matteo cracked a smile. "We have some new people?" he translated.

"*Yes. Sono Diego…* I am Diego."

Matteo nodded approvingly.

"Hi, I'm Sam," the blond said, shaking his hand in that forceful American way. "I'm an author. I'm writing a story about Italians, so… here I am."

Diego got most of that.

The other man extended his hand. "I'm Ben. I'm a writer too. But I'm just here because I like Italian food."

"*Benvenuti!*" He searched his memory. "Welcome!"

Matteo gave him a quick peck on the cheek. "I have to run out for a few minutes. Good luck with class."

"I don't need."

"I know." Then he was out the door.

Diego sighed. He was still no closer to an answer to his dilemma, and time was running short. But right now he had a class to teach.

"Come." He led everyone over to the counter and pulled out his ingredients— Parmigiano-Reggiano, some dried bread to make bread crumbs, eggs, a little nutmeg, salt, lemon peel, and some chicken broth. "*Oggi... mi dispiace....* This day, we make passatelli."

Marissa stared at the marble counter top in front of her.

The adults around her were wrapped up in the whole cooking class thing. She was wishing she could be anywhere else. If only she were already eighteen or her parents weren't such pricks.

"Marissa." Marcos was elbowing her.

"What?' she hissed, looking up.

Everyone was staring at her.

"Diego wants you to help him."

"Do I have to?" She rolled her eyes.

"Just give it a try. If you hate it, you don't have to come back here next week."

She sighed dramatically. "All right. What do I have to do?"

"Come." Diego motioned for her to join him behind the counter.

She trudged around it and into the kitchen, hoping her displeasure was coming through clearly.

Diego smiled at her and took her hand gently and, with a questioning look as if to ask her permission, guided her to the grated cheese. They poured it into a large metal bowl together and then added the bread crumbs and the eggs. He mimed for her to mix them together.

She took up the whisk and began to blend the eggs into the cheese and bread crumbs. It *was* kind of fun. She took out her anger on the mixture, beating it into submission, mixing the cheese and crumbs and eggs into a dough.

Diego passed the ingredients to the other classmates, pairing Marcos with the redheaded woman—Carmelina, was it?—and the two newcomers together, and soon everyone was making passatelli.

Diego added a little salt, nutmeg, and lemon peel to each bowl. He sprinkled some durum flour in front of each group and mimed kneading the dough. "We say '*impastare.*'"

Marissa sunk her hands into the pasta dough, and the world around her shimmered and changed.

She was in a strange kitchen, sitting at a wooden table kneading the dough. The room was warm and light, so different from the cold stainless steel kitchen she'd grown up with at home. And yet, she felt like she *belonged.*

Something was cooking on the stove, giving off the most wonderful aroma, like chicken soup, and the backsplash was decorated with tiles depicting the Tuscan countryside. Music Marissa was unfamiliar with, light and airy like the kitchen, drifted in from another room.

Marissa felt something alien that she hadn't experienced in months. *Contentment.*

"Hello?" she called, wondering if she was alone and how she'd gotten there. Something about making pasta…

"Be right in, darlin'," a motherly voice called from the other room.

Marissa sat back to knead the dough, a smile on her face.

~

Carmelina found herself transported to a place she hadn't visited since her childhood—her grandmother's house on T Street that always smelled like fresh-baked biscotti. She was a little girl again, helping her nonna prepare dinner. She looked up, and Grandma Elena tousled her hair. *"Sei una brava ragazza,"* she said, smiling down on her granddaughter.

"Grazie, Nonna," Carmelina said, her little fingers deep in the sticky pasta dough,

"Here, use a little flour."

Nonna Elena sprinkled flour on her hands, and she attacked the dough again, intent on kneading it until it was perfect.

~

Marcos looked around, shocked to be back at the youth shelter, where Joe Salvatore had shown him how to cook in the big industrial kitchen that served the facility. The big barrel-chested man was preparing dinner. As a just-out teen, Marcos had been smitten by him.

~

Sam was at home with his own mother in Tucson, whom he hadn't spent any time with in almost a year. But they slipped back into their relationship with the ease of long practice.

~

Ben sat across from a beautiful dark-haired woman in his own kitchen. She was laughing and joking with him as they prepared a meal together in a small kitchen looking out over a tree-lined street.

~

Diego looked around at his students. They were all deep into their kneading, smiles on their faces, but everyone was so quiet. It was a little strange. He cleared his throat. "Ahem."

Nothing.

He banged a pot. "*Attenzione!*"

Everyone looked up. Carmelina shook her head as if she had been in a daze. She looked around sheepishly. "I was remembering when I used to cook with my grandmother."

"*La cucina fa sempre affiorare i ricordi… boh…* the chicken… the kitchen brings the memory of the heart."

Marissa nodded, a strange, faraway look in her eyes.

"Now we make pasta."

See the passatelli recipe at the end of the book.

17. THE X STREET MAFIA

Carmelina finished the last of her passatelli and licked her lips. "Delicious, Diego. *Come si dice* delicious?" She'd never had it before.

"*Delicioso.*"

"*Deliciossso.*"

He laughed, shaking his head. "No. Like this. "*Del-li-zio-so.*"

"Ah, with a *z* sound. *Grazie. Delizioso.*"

"*Perfetto.*" He started moving the dishes to the sink.

"You have a real ear for the language," Marcos said, handing his empty bowl over to Diego.

"My nonna… my grandmother was Italian. I heard it at home all the time when I was a child." She closed her eyes, seeing her grandmother's kitchen again as vividly as if she were still standing there. Something about the recipe, or this place, was magical. "She's been gone thirty years now."

Marcos nodded. "Mine died a few years back."

"Did you enjoy the class, Marissa?" Carmelina asked.

The girl had been surly at first but had really gotten into it.

"Hmm?" The girl's eyes had been closed as she savored the broth and pasta. "Oh yeah, it was fun."

Marcos sighed. "She had a run-in with her folks," he whispered. "She's staying with me for a few days while we figure things out."

"That's great of you to take her in."

"She reminds me of myself when I was younger. I got thrown out of the house for being gay too. I work at home, so I can keep an eye on her."

"What do you do?"

"I'm a web designer."

"I'm not gay," Marissa piped in.

"You're not?" Marcos asked. He looked surprised. "I just assumed…"

"I'm bi. I like boys too."

Carmelina laughed. She decided she liked the girl. She had a spunk to her that reminded her a little of herself as a child. She'd never had grandchildren. She'd given her daughter away when she was fifteen—far too young to care for a child. But she thought about her every day. She touched the gold cross she always wore around her neck, whispering a little prayer.

"Can I help with the clean-up?" she asked Diego. She never let her own guests do the dishes at home, but she always liked to offer.

"*Cosa*?" Diego looked confused.

"Help." She pointed at herself and mimed washing a dish.

"*Ah, no. Grazie.*" He grinned. "Workers come soon."

She nodded. It was too bad the next class was a week away. Unless…

She cleared her throat. "Hey, I have a great idea.…"

Sam was deep in conversation at the other end of the counter with Ben. It wasn't often that he stumbled upon another local writer like this.

"When I write, I feel like Sacramento is another character in the story," Ben said. "I grew up here—I know this cow town like the back of my hand."

"I've only been here for a year, but I'm really starting to like it. It's kind of like Tucson—a big city with the heart and soul of a small town."

"Exactly! There are so many great things going on here that many newcomers never see. Of course, it's just as bad with the folks who have been here forever. They have this fixed idea of what Sacramento *is* and what it *can* be."

"I've seen that." He took the last bite of his passatelli. They reminded him of his mother's home cooking. "Some of Brad's friends say this town will never amount to anything."

"Things are already changing. Midtown, the 'handle district,' has grown so much in the last ten years." He put the district name in air quotes.

"I know. I've seen it in just the last twelve months. Hey, *that's* where I know you from. You're a barista at the Everyday Grind, aren't you?"

"Guilty. You used to come in all the time with that complicated drink order, right?"

Sam laughed. "Brad's favorite. When I worked for him. Long story."

Someone cleared their throat.

Sam turned to see Carmelina addressing them all. "Hey, I have a great idea. Why don't you all come over to my place Thursday night? I'd love to practice this recipe and the one for the piadine from last week."

Marcos turned to Marissa, who just shrugged. *Teenagers.* "Sure, we're in. "

"I can make it," Ben said. "I'm off Thursday."

Carmelina's gaze turned to him.

"I think so.... Where do you live?"

"River Park."

"And that's…?" He was still figuring out the little Sactown neighborhoods.

"About ten minutes from here."

"Let me ask Brad. But if he's in, I'd love to."

Matteo parked his scooter on X Street. Above him, the swoosh of automobiles and the heavier rumble of semi-trucks thundered past.

The farmer's market held here every Sunday under the freeway was over. It had always seemed strange to Matteo to sell fresh vegetables and fruit below the constant procession of vehicles spewing exhaust from above. Then again, many things Americans did seemed strange to him. But he still wanted to be one.

He stepped into the semi-darkness. As his eyes adjusted, he saw the man he had come to meet. His name was Jordan, and he'd come into Ragazzi one day the week before suggesting he might be able to help out if the restaurant was having any financial difficulties. How he'd known, Matteo had no idea, though the empty dining room on a Friday night might have been a clue.

He was leaning against one of the freeway support columns, smoking a cigarette. It was all starting to feel a little mafia-ish.

"Jordan."

"Matteo. Thanks for coming." They shook hands.

"You had a… proposal for me?"

"Yes." He handed Matteo a manila envelope. "It's all in there."

"Nothing illegal, I hope?"

"Let's just say… nothing *too* illegal. Look it over and call me."

"Will do."

He turned and walked away into the gloom.

18. THE LOTTERY

Marcos gave Carmelina a big hug goodbye. There was something about the brassy Italian American woman that appealed to him. She seemed like the type who never took no for an answer and who didn't deal in bullshit. "See you Thursday night."

They had exchanged cell numbers, and she promised to text him the details.

He looked around for Marissa, afraid she had taken off again while he'd been distracted. He found her talking softly with Diego in the kitchen, and was surprised when she gave the chef a big hug. She seemed to connect with everyone but him.

He sighed. They were stuck with each other for now. She was going to have to learn to deal with him. "You ready to go?"

"I'm *coming*." She pushed her way past him out to the street with her usual charm.

Marcos sighed.

They walked in silence to his Prius on one of the side streets behind the restaurant. He unlocked the doors, and she sank into her seat and crossed her arms, looking straight out of the front windshield.

He got into the car and pulled on his seatbelt. This whole pouting thing needed to stop. "I'm not the enemy, you know," he said aloud.

"What?"

"Look, I get it. You've got the whole 'tough kid' thing down pat. You don't need anything, or anyone."

She turned away.

"When someone you love betrays you, it hurts like a sonofabitch. I don't know your whole story, but I see how strong you are. When your parents threw you out, you got up and kept going. You should be proud of that."

There was no response, except for a heavy sigh.

"When my parents threw me out for being gay, I didn't know where to go. I stayed with a friend for a few days until his parents objected, and then I was out on the streets." He closed his eyes, remembering that bleak time. All alone, eating out of trash cans, sleeping in shelters, doorways or back alleys. "I cried every night for a month, and then I got angry. It was so *unfair*, what they did to me. I swore to never let anyone get close to me again."

She glanced back in his direction. It was something.

He pushed on. "I shut off my heart, so no one would ever hurt me again." And it had worked, better than he would have ever guessed. Here he was closing in on forty, and he was all alone.

She was looking at him now.

"Once you block everyone out, you never get hurt again like that first time. But you end up being all alone."

"I *fucking* hate them."

"Your parents?"

Marissa shook her head. "They're *not* my parents. When they kicked me out, my mother… Jessica… told me she wished they had never adopted me." Her voice shook with emotion.

"Shit… you didn't know?"

The angry look she flashed him gave him the answer.

"Look, I've made a mess of my own life," he said, "but I've learned one thing. You can't change the things people do to you. But you *can* choose how you respond." He'd made a lot of bad choices. He'd pretty much ruined every relationship he'd ever started. But he was convinced that he had made a good one here.

"I guess."

"Your adopted parents dealt you a shitty hand, no question. You can be miserable and sick about it, and close yourself off from the world." He touched her shoulder. "Does that hurt them, or you?"

She was silent for a long time. He let her think. She needed to come to it on her own.

At last she mumbled something.

"What was that?" he asked gently.

"They're my parents. They weren't *supposed* to leave me!" Her voice cracked a little, and his heart nearly broke for her.

"No, they weren't." He released his seat belt and put his arms around her, rocking her gently.

Her arms went around him and she started to cry.

Marcos just held her and patted her back, knowing he was exactly where he was supposed to be in the universe at that moment.

~

Matteo sat at the back of the Everyday Grind, espresso in hand, staring at the manila envelope from Jordan that sat on the table. He had no idea what was inside.

Like a lottery ticket. As long as he didn't check the contents, he could make it into whatever he wanted it to be—something that would save Ragazzi and their lives together in the United States.

So many things here were different from Italy. He loved his new job and the people, but Americans prioritized their families differently than the Italians. They lived their lives in a more transient way, moving from place to place and job to job. It was a kind of freedom, and he loved them for that. But in celebrating it, Americans often lost sight of family, community, and connection.

Still, he loved this place he now called home.

He considered what might be inside the envelope. Maybe Jordan worked for a mafia organization and they wanted to use Ragazzi to launder money.

Maybe he was independently wealthy—one of those angel investors they always talked about on TV. Or maybe he was a billionaire benefactor who had just handed Matteo an envelope of cash, like on one of the reality shows.

He looked around self-consciously in case someone was filming him, but no one was paying the slightest attention to him.

Whatever happened next, he and Diego loved each other. They would come out of this together okay, somehow.

He picked up the envelope and broke the seal, spilling the contents out onto the table.

He stared at the pile in disbelief. It was made up of more than a hundred blue-and-white twenty-percent-off coupons to Bed Bath and Beyond. He snorted. *Some lottery ticket.*

Jordan was nuts.

He laughed because he didn't want to cry.

19. CARAMEL

It wasn't *right*. Sam scrolled back a couple pages, trying to figure out where his story was going off track. He was introducing his new Italian character in his political thriller, *Red as the Night*, and it just felt... off. Something in the story line wasn't working. He knew what this was. He was too close to the writing. He needed a break.

He glanced up at the clock. It was a quarter after one. He leaned back in his chair, stretching out his arms above his head and considered his options. 15L for a quick burger? Coffee and a scone at the Everyday Grind? Or should he make a couple sandwiches and surprise Brad at the Center?

The front door slammed. He looked over his shoulder from his little office in the front of the house. "Brad?"

"Yup, just me. I thought I'd come grab you and take you out to lunch to celebrate. I just won the Hoffsledder grant. Can you take a break?" He popped into the room and gave Sam a peck on the cheek.

"Your timing is totes perfect." He ignored Brad's frown. "I'm stuck on my latest scene, and I could use a break." He closed his laptop. "Is that the one you've been working on for the last few months?" Sam ducked into the hall bath to run a comb through his hair, deciding that he looked presentable enough for public consumption.

"That's the one," Brad called from the hall. "How about the Federalist? I've been dying for a good pizza."

"Sounds good."

Brad came up behind him and slipped his arms around Sam's waist. Sam felt the usual thrill as Brad nuzzled his neck. They'd been together almost a year, and he still felt excited by Brad's touch.

"How hungry are you?" Brad asked with *that* smile.

Sam turned around and kissed him. "I could wait a few more minutes if you had something else in mind...."

~

An hour later, they arrived at the Federalist, a collection of shipping containers welded together into one of Sactown's trendiest back-alley restaurants.

Brad ordered, and then they took a seat at one of the picnic tables in the ultra-casual place. "Tell me about the grant," Sam said. He was always enthusiastic about Brad's work. That was one of the things Brad loved about him.

"It's for $100,000, dedicated to expanding LGBTIQ youth training programs. We beat out twenty other community centers for the money."

"That's amazing! I'm so proud of you."

"We can make it go a long way." Brad realized he was so wrapped up in his own news he hadn't asked Sam about his cooking class. "How about you? You didn't tell me about your adventure yesterday."

"Adventure?"

"The restaurant thing?"

Sam grinned. "It was great. I don't know why we've never been to that place before. It's run by a gay Italian couple."

"Really? What's it called?" Brad liked to support the gay places in town.

"Ragazzi—it means 'guys.' The food we made was great. And the strangest thing happened while we were cooking."

Brad frowned. "Did the owner make a pass at you?"

"No. Jealous much?" Sam laughed. "It was nothing like that. We were kneading dough for this pasta soup, and for a minute, I swear I was back in my mom's kitchen in Tucson."

Brad snorted. "What did they put in those noodles?"

"Don't be an ass. It was a magical moment."

"Maybe your subconscious is trying to tell you something. Like you should call your mother."

"Yeah, you're probably right. Hey, are you free Thursday night?"

Brad checked his calendar. "Looks like it. Why?"

"We've been invited to dinner to make some of that magical pasta."

~

The Grind was especially busy for a Monday afternoon. Ben wiped the counter for the nth time after a customer spilled his vanilla soy cappuccino.

"I'm so sorry," the man said.

"Not a big deal. It happens all the time." Ben gave him a reassuring smile. "Can I make you another?"

"Please. I need something to take the edge off. It's been a helluva day."

He laughed. "I know what you mean. Give me a sec." Ben whipped up a new drink and handed it to him with a flourish. "Hope it improves your day."

"Thanks!" He raised the cup in acknowledgement and breezed out the door. Ben grinned. There was a wonderful simplicity to his job—people came in tired, sad, depressed, and he made a little magic for them.

He made another fifty drinks, and the afternoon flew by. The line finally started to diminish. At last, there was one order left—a tall, non-fat latte with caramel drizzle. He grinned. Caramel was an underrated syrup, and he instantly liked anyone who ordered it.

He whipped it up, decorating the top with a heart in foam and caramel— yes, he was just that much of an artiste—and checked the name. "Tall non-fat latte with caramel for Ella." He set it down and looked up. His heart stopped.

She was about his height, with long red hair and brown eyes and a kind face. She wasn't beautiful in the cover-model sense, but she radiated warmth.

She was the girl of his dreams. Literally. The girl he had seen in his daydream at Ragazzi the day before.

She flashed him a smile as she took the drink. "Non-fat, right?"

"Yeah." His words failed him.

"For Ella?"

"Yeah."

She frowned slightly, and he realized he was staring. "Well, have a great day."

She turned to leave.

"Wait!"

She spun around, still looking more amused than annoyed. "What?"

"Um… you too. Have a great day. You're really pretty. Hope to see you again."

"You will. I just moved in down the street. See you next time." And then she was out the door.

Ben watched her leave. "'*You're really pretty*'? Seriously?" He was thoroughly disgusted with himself. "Ben, you're an idiot."

20.CHANGE

Carmelina pushed aside another stack of boxes, dusting off her jeans and sneezing at the cloud of fine powder that resulted. She hadn't been out to their storage unit in Rancho Cordova in forever. *I really need to clean this place out.*

She and Arthur had rented the unit ten years before, when they had cleared out their garage so he could park his new Jaguar there. Where it still sat, gathering dust.

He had wanted to sell all of this stuff at the time. "When are we ever going to look at this crap again anyhow?" he'd asked.

If she closed her eyes, she could still see him as clearly as if he were standing right in front of her, his bushy black eyebrows creased, his face caught somewhere between a frown and a laugh.

She put her hand on the stack in front of her and lowered her head, sadness overpowering her for a moment. *Why did you have to leave me so soon?*

It wasn't fair. Other couples got an entire lifetime together. What had she done to deserve this?

She wished he were still here.

If wishes were cannoli, we'd all be Mamma Cass, her mother used to tell her.

She laughed in spite of herself and resumed her search. It *had* to be here somewhere.

She moved another stack of boxes, refusing to be distracted by the labels: "pie tins, spatulas, and old silverware ." She didn't need any more kitchen implements.

The headboard to her mother's old bed, a heavy mahogany thing carved with vines and sparrows, leaned against another set of boxes. Taking a deep breath, she tugged on the weighty piece of furniture, pulling it out about six inches. Then it stuck.

Using her phone as a flashlight, she found the problem: it had snagged on pole from the metal swing set they'd stored at the back of the unit.

She kicked at the pole until it inched behind the foot of the headboard and tried once again to pull the wooden mass out. It refused to budge, but then it came free all at once, and she flew backward onto her ass on the pavement.

She stood up, mortified by her clumsiness, and looked around to see if anyone had seen her embarrassing fall, but the driveway was empty.

At last, she found the stack of once-white boxes marked "filing cabinet." They were in alphabetical order, five in all. She went through them one by one until she found the A-D box, which was, of course, at the very bottom. Her hands shaking, she opened the box.

And there it was.

The folder was labeled Catholic Adoption Services. She pulled it out and blew the dust off a stack of boxes at waist height. She lay the manila folder down and opened it carefully. The paper inside was curled and yellowed with age. She turned on the flashlight on her phone again and peered at the old form.

It was dated February 21st, 1975. And it carried her signature from when she had been just fifteen years old. She remembered the day like it was yesterday, when her mother had taken her into the offices of the adoption agency to sign away the rights to her child. The place had smelled like chalk dust, with green linoleum tile floors and sterile white walls. It had marked the end of her childhood.

And now?

Her mother was gone and her husband too. She felt all alone in the world.

She held the paper to her chest, fighting back the urge to cry. The vision she'd had in her cooking class had shaken her. It was as if her grandmother had reached down from heaven to rap her on the head. Somewhere out there was another human being of her own flesh and blood.

Now Carmelina just had to find her.

She managed to get the whole mess back into the storage unit, though she was tired and sweaty by the time she was done. She checked her watch. It was a quarter after four. By the time she got home, it would be too late to try to contact the agency—if they even still existed.

She pulled down the roll door and locked up the storage unit. It was past time to clear out all of this crap. And the Jaguar in the garage. It was time to make some changes in her life.

There was one person who might help.

She pulled out her phone and made the call. "Hey, I really need someone to talk to tonight. Are you free in about two hours? Sure. Let's meet at Downtown and Vine at about six?"

Carmelina arrived at the wine bar promptly at six thirty, just half an hour late. She was proud that she'd cut a full fifteen minutes off from the last time she'd seen Loylene.

It was a cute little place, modern but warm, with a wine rack just inside the lobby. It was also usually quiet—a great place to talk.

"You're fashionably late," Loylene said, kissing Carmelina's cheeks.

"I know. I am *so* sorry. I was out in Rancho Cordova looking for something...."

"You can get better drugs in town, you know," Loylene said with a sly smile. "Or so my kids tell me."

"I wasn't looking for drugs. Arthur and I have... had... well, *I have* a storage unit out there."

"Marjorie's still pissed at you for storming out during the club meeting, you know." Loylene looked over her menu.

"I'm sorry about that too. I just couldn't—"

"I know." Loylene patted her hand. "The first few months are the hardest."

Carmelina stifled a laugh. "Yes. *That* was it."

"Oh, I brought you the latest Tupperware flier. There's a really cool..."

This time it was Carmelina who put out her hand, forestalling her friend's enthusiasm for all things plastic. "Loylene, I need your help. Didn't you know someone in Catholic Services?"

21.MAMMA

MATTEO SAT IN THE DARKENED RESTAURANT, STARING OUT AT THE empty street outside. He glanced at his vintage Panerai watch, once his father's. It was a little after one a.m. Diego was still fast asleep upstairs.

Matteo had tossed and turned for hours before getting up. He was going to have to talk with Diego and soon. He pulled the chain from around his neck and stared at the golden cross. It was tiny in his palm. The cross from his mother, the watch from his father, anchors across time.

He closed his eyes, remembering the day, twenty years before, when everything had changed.

~

Matteo pulled his Fiat Ritmo into the driveway of his parents' house in Imola, a small village about twenty-five kilometers southeast of Bologna. It was a modest two-story home with a cement carport and a small, fenced-in front yard. Out back was his mother's prized vegetable garden, where she grew her famous, delicious *Cuore di bue* tomatoes, often as big as his fist.

He sat in the car for a moment, staring at the door to the house. Every nerve in his body was screaming at him to turn around, to run back home. He and Diego had talked about this and had decided it was time, but he could still change his mind. He could do this another day.

Then the door swung open and it was too late. His mother, Elena Bianco, stepped down onto the bare cement of the carport in her slippers and beckoned him inside, a broad grin on her face. He took a deep breath and turned off the car. He climbed out and put on a smile, and she threw her arms around him to give him a big hug.

"*Mio tesoro,*" she said, kissing both of his cheeks. "What a wonderful surprise. Come in! Come in! We were just about to have dinner."

Matteo shook his head. "I'm sorry, mamma, I didn't mean to interrupt. I can come back another time—"

She shushed him. "Don't be foolish. There's plenty for all three of us." She all but pushed him inside, pulling the door shut behind them. "We hardly ever see you anymore."

Oh my God, that smells good. "Is it…?"

She nodded. "Your grandmother's lasagna. Here, give me your coat."

He let her pull it off. She hung it on the old wooden rack by the door. He looked around. Nothing much had changed since the last time. The walls were the same soft yellow, the wooden window frames covered with white curtains. Photos of the family hung in the hallway—here a picture of his grandma Elsa, there a photo of Matteo and his sister in front of the Sagrada Familia in Barcelona, taken when he was twelve.

"Come on. Your father will be glad to see you."

Matteo's stomach twisted. *Maybe not for long. Well, it can wait until after dinner.* It was Nonna's lasagna, after all.

~

Matteo finished the last piece of his mother's wonderful lasagna, filled with meat, and eyed his parents. His mother got up to clear the dishes.

"Good to see you, boy." His father, Pietro clapped a hand on Matteo's shoulder. "You should come down to see us more often. Bologna's not so far from here."

In some ways, it's a world away. But he just nodded. He screwed up his courage. "Mamma, Papa, I have something I need to tell you."

His mother turned around, leaving the water running in the sink. "Is everything all right, *caro?*"

His father put a big hand over his. He worked in the shipbuilding trade up in Venice, and his hands were calloused and rough. "What is it?"

Matteo pushed down his fear. "There's… something I have wanted to tell you now. For a long time."

Elena sat down across the table from him. Strangely, she looked serene, as if nothing could faze her.

He glanced back at his father. Pietro was frowning.

"I'm… I like…" He tried to find a way to soften the blow, and failed. "There's no easy way to say this. I'm gay."

His father pulled his hand away as if he'd been burned. "Don't you say such a thing in this house," he snarled. His voice was a low growl. His mother put a hand on Pietro's arm, but he would have none of it. "It's not true. Tell me it's not true."

Matteo shook his head. "I can't."

"No son of mine is going to be a *finocchio!*" Pietro shouted, slamming his hand on the table, which shook like an earthquake.

For an instant, Matteo thought his father might strike him. Then Pietro spun around and stormed out of the house, the door slamming heavily behind him.

Matteo put his head down on the table with his hands over his forehead. "*Cazzo.*" He couldn't bear to look at his mother.

He heard the chair creak next to him as his mother came to sit next to his side. She pulled his hands away from his face gently.

He looked up at her, and was surprised to see her smiling. "Mamma?" He whispered.

She smoothed a stray lock of hair away from his face. "I am proud of you, *Tesoro.*"

"You're not angry?"

She shook her head, cupping his chin in her palm. "I've known this for a long time."

"But Papà…"

"He knows too. It's just… harder for him. He will come around."

"I hope so."

"I raised you to be strong. You never walk away from things just because they might be hard."

He hugged her and cried softly in her arms. It would turn out all right somehow.

Matteo looked around at the restaurant he and Diego had built together in this new city. This was their dream together, and he would not let it go. Not without a fight. He would talk to Diego that night after they closed. It would turn out all right somehow.

22.BACK TO SCHOOL

MARISSA STARED OUT THE PASSENGER WINDOW AT MCCLATCHY HIGH—
an imposing place, like the Parthenon or the US Supreme Court, with a big
banner strung up across its massive entry columns that said, "Welcome to the
Lion's Den." She frowned, not sure she was ready. She had never fit in all that
well at Bella Vista, but at least she'd had friends there.

One of the perks of being homeless, she thought wryly, was that you didn't
have to go to *fucking school.*

"You ready?" Marcos asked, giving her shoulder a friendly squeeze.

She glared at him. "Do I have a choice?"

He laughed. "We all do. I made mine, to try to help you. *Your* move."

She *did* like having a bed to sleep in while she figured things out. And it
wasn't like she was chained in her room. She could take off at any time if she
decided it didn't suit her. She'd be eighteen in a month, and then she could tell
them all to fuck off. "Yeah, okay. Let's go."

She grabbed her new pink backpack from the back seat, wrinkling her
nose a little at the color—Marcos had funny ideas what girls liked. She had
added a skull and crossbones with black nail polish on the back pocket, but if
he'd noticed, he hadn't said a word about it.

She checked her hair in the car window—still spiky and blonde like she
liked it. She'd applied some extra eyeliner—the only make-up she'd asked
Marcos to buy. "Okay, ready."

She turned to find him grinning at her like an idiot.

"What?"

Marcos just shook his head. He turned away, and she followed him into the new school with a heavy sigh.

Time to start her senior year.

~

Principal Laverne Krebbs beckoned them into her office.

Marcos smiled, happy to see the school staff was diverse. "Thanks for seeing us so quickly, Principal Krebbs," he said, taking a seat in front of her desk, which was covered with neat stacks of folders.

She reached out her hand. "Nice to meet the two of you…" She checked a sheet on her desk. "Marcos and Marissa. Are you the father?"

Marissa snorted. "Hardly."

"What Marissa means to say is that I'm her guardian. She's staying with me provisionally until Social Services can approve me for permanent foster care status."

"I see." Principal Krebs shuffled a few papers. "You live in the district. And Marissa previously attended Bella Vista in Fair Oaks."

"Yes. We've requested a copy of her transcript. She finished the previous school year there with good grades." *Well, good enough.* He wasn't sure why *he* felt so nervous. He wasn't the one enrolling. But this had been his school, and the kids back then had been nasty to him as a gay kid. "I… I have a question."

"Shoot." She folded her hands on the desk in front of her, giving him her full attention.

"Marissa is…" He looked at her, and she nodded, keeping her sarcastic comments to herself for once. "She's bisexual. I went to school here in the early nineties, and life was… *difficult* for queer kids back then."

The principal smiled. "Well, things are a little different here now, Mr. Ramirez. For one, the school has a married lesbian principal." She pointed to the picture of herself and another woman on the corner of her desk.

"Seriously?" Marissa picked up the photo. "That's so cool."

"And we have our own GSA here too."

"GSA?" Marcos asked.

"Gay Straight Alliance. A student group for LGBT students and their allies. The Westboro folks tried to protest here a couple years back, and the kids put up a counter rally to support LGBT rights. The WBC folks never even showed up."

Things really have changed. He remembered the time he'd had his head shoved in the gym toilet for a swirly by some of the football jocks. It still made him angry. "And if there is any trouble?"

"She can come straight to me."

He nodded. "When can she start?"

"Assuming I can verify your address, how about tomorrow? She can meet with one of our counselors today to choose her courses." She addressed Marissa directly. "You're a few weeks behind, but if you apply yourself, you'll catch up quickly enough."

"What do you think?" Marcos asked Marissa.

She was quiet for a moment, staring down at her black-painted nails. "I'll try," she said at last.

Marcos nodded. "Good enough."

"Danny, can you take Marissa Sutton here over to Guidance?"

The secretary popped his head through the doorway. "Sure. Come on. I'll show you the way."

She got up to follow him out. Then she turned and threw herself at Marcos. "Thank you," she whispered.

He wrapped his arms around her and squeezed her tight.

When she let go at last, she turned and left the office without another backward glance.

Marcos stared after her, stunned.

"Kids at that age are a bundle of contradictions," Principal Krebbs said with a smile. "You have any of your own?"

"Nope. First time."

She nodded. "It's going to be tough. She's already pretty much fully formed. Are you sure you are up for the challenge?"

"I hope so." He bit his lip. "She's so much like I was at that age. It's scary."

"We can help a little. The district has a program for transfers. We'll assign another student to shadow her the first couple days to show her where things are and to get her grounded."

"That would be great." He stared at his hands, wondering how he was going to manage all of this.

"And Mr. Ramirez?"

Marcos looked up into her eyes.

"I have two of my own, and they're a handful, even without the whole foster kid issue. Do yourself a favor and get some help. A friend with kids or some parenting books." She patted his hand. "You're doing a good thing."

23. NOW OR NEVER

DIEGO SLAMMED THE LAST OF THE DIRTY PANS INTO THE SINK, EARNING a stern look from Matteo from the restaurant floor. Dinner service was over for the night, and his stomach was churning. He'd put this off as long as he could. He had to tell Matteo *tonight*.

But Matteo had been acting strangely all evening. For days, really. His responses had been curt, and he wouldn't meet Diego's eyes. He knew Matteo like he knew his cooktop—where all the hot spots were and where things just simmered.

Matteo was hiding something.

Diego grunted. He had his own secrets.

He set to work on the dishes. They'd sent the help home early again to save money. He scrubbed the pans with a vengeance, trying to get them perfectly clean.

Matteo popped his head into the open kitchen. "Keep it down back here —we still have guests." He sounded more annoyed than usual.

Diego glanced out at the dining room. Two guys stared back at him, and he realized he must have been making quite a racket. He waved and flashed his best Italian smile. "Sorry!"

One of the guys grinned and waved back.

"I try the best," he said to Matteo.

Matteo looked like he might say something else, but then he just nodded and backed out of the kitchen.

It wasn't like him to hold his tongue. Diego was used to getting a tongue lashing, which he would return in true Italian style. But not this time.

Diego frowned, his sense of unease growing.

More than anything, he wanted to just close up the kitchen and run upstairs to bed. But he'd waited too long. It was now or never.

~

Matteo waited anxiously for the last couple to leave. They took their time, of course, ordering several bottles of Italian *vino*, for which he was thankful, along with *i contorni, i primi piatti, i secondi piatti*, and *le dolce*—a full four-course meal. It was their tenth anniversary, one of them had told him, and part of him was thrilled they'd chosen to spend it at Ragazzi.

But the other part, the one he locked carefully away behind the genteel smile and generous nature of the restaurant host, was practically screaming at them to get out.

Diego had calmed down a bit in the kitchen.

Matteo shot him a worried look. It wasn't like him to make such a ruckus with his kitchen tools. Something must have him really worked up.

At last, the couple finished and paid the bill, leaving with a ringing of the bell at the front door. The restaurant was empty.

Matteo locked up and carried the last few dishes into the kitchen, where Diego took them without a word and rinsed them, placing them in the dishwasher and starting the cleaning cycle.

Matteo looked around. The kitchen was spotless. "Wow, you worked fast tonight." Maybe he could manage to put this off just a little longer.

"Possiamo parlare in Italiano?"

"In Italian? Sure." There was no one around, and Diego had been practicing his English enough to earn a night off.

He sighed. It was now or never.

"Dobbiamo parlare," they both said at the same time. *We need to talk.*

Matteo laughed. "I guess we do," he said in *la bella lingua.*

Diego's face was grim. "Not here," he said, looking around. "Let's go upstairs where we can be more comfortable."

Matteo agreed. He followed his husband to their flat, wondering what Diego wanted to talk to *him* about.

~

Diego sank into the orange upholstered couch they'd found at Naturewood. It was hard to find *fashion* in this country—Americans were so afraid of color.

Matteo sat next to him, hands in his lap, his mouth compressed into a tight line. At last, he asked, "What did you want to talk about?"

Diego shook his head. He needed more time. "You start."

Matteo's eyes narrowed, but he nodded. "I've been keeping a secret from you." He sighed. "I'm sorry.… I should have told you. But I thought… I hoped I could fix it."

Diego's mind was racing. What had Matteo done? "Is it someone else?" he whispered, so softly that he wasn't sure Matteo would hear it.

But the pulling back and the horrified look that crossed his husband's face was enough of a denial. "No. Never! Is that what you thought?"

It was the first thing that had come to his mind. But Diego didn't want to tell Matteo that. "No, of course not. It's just the way you said it." He put a hand on Matteo's shoulder. "What is it? We shouldn't keep secrets." He kicked himself for being such a hypocrite.

Matteo looked away, his nostrils flaring.

"Come on. Tell me." Diego put a hand on Matteo's knee.

"We're almost out of money."

Diego snorted. "That's it?" He'd expected much worse.

Matteo stared at him as if he'd gone mad. "We can't afford more than another month's worth of expenses at this rate. We might lose everything."

Diego nodded. "You think I haven't seen the empty seats? It's only money. We'll work something out. We always do." He hoped that was true.

"I've already tried to get a loan. No one will help us."

Diego took Matteo's face in his hands. "Do you remember what happened in Italy, when your job was killing you?"

Matteo stared at him for a moment. "Uncle Beppo died and left us this place."

"Do you think fate brought us here just for failure and ruin?"

Matteo looked down, his eyes closed. When he looked up, there was new determination in his eyes. "You're right. You are always right." He pulled Diego into a tight hug.

Diego felt a stab of guilt. He really didn't want to tell Matteo his own secret, especially right now, when they felt so close.

"You had something to tell me too?" Matteo asked, letting go of him and staring into his eyes.

Diego sighed. It was time.

24. BREAKING POINT

"Tell me." Matteo was surprised how calmly Diego had taken his news, but he should have known Diego would figure it out. Matteo took his hand, squeezing it reassuringly.

Diego frowned. "I'm not sure how to tell you this…." Matteo could feel Diego's racing pulse. "I did… something bad happened. And I never told you."

Had he…? No. Diego could never do something like that. Matteo was as sure of that as he was of his own breathing. He took Diego's other hand. "Just tell me."

Diego closed his eyes. Matteo saw real pain etched in his suddenly lined face, as if Diego had aged ten years in a moment. "I lied to you," he whispered.

Matteo let go of Diego's hands. "About what?" His voice sounded thin and tight, even to his own ears.

Diego looked away. "Max contacted me and said he had found something out about me that I wasn't going to like." He sighed. "I put him off for as long as I could, hoping he would give it up—"

"Max… Cuccinelli? The immigration lawyer?" Matteo didn't understand. "What did he find?"

Diego got up and went into the bedroom. He came back with a sheet of paper and handed it to Matteo. "I met him on Saturday. He showed this to me, and this morning I found it slipped under the restaurant door." Diego wouldn't meet his gaze.

Matteo took it, his hand trembling. It was an Italian marriage license.

Moglie—Wife—Luna Mazzocco.
Marito—husband… Diego Bellei

He looked up at Diego. "What does this mean?"

Diego finally looked at him, his eyes red. "I was married to her. Before you."

Matteo's head was spinning "Okay. But that's not—"

"We're *still* married. Luna and I."

The paper dropped out of Matteo's hand and fluttered to the floor. "You *can't* be," he said. It made no sense. "*We're* married." The ground was shifting too quickly under Matteo's feet.

Diego shook his head. "She never signed the divorce papers. I didn't know."

"So you just found out." Matteo breathed again. "It's only been a couple days. You were afraid."

"I've known since your father died."

Those words struck Matteo like a frying pan. Since Pietro Bianco had died —that was eighteen years ago now. Diego had been lying to him for eighteen years. He picked up the fallen marriage license and stared at it blankly. Then he held it out at Diego like an accusation. "How could you not tell me?" His voice was tight with anger. "For almost twenty years?"

Diego reached out a hand, but Matteo pushed it away. "I wanted to tell you so many times—"

"Do you *know* what this means?" Matteo's voice was almost a whisper.

"I'm so sorry, Matteo—"

"It means we were *never married*, Diego. You can't be married to two people at once." Diego fell silent, and Marco knew he had scored a direct hit. But he was too angry to care.

The secret itself… *that* he could have handled. But the lying… "I have to get out of here. I am too angry to even look at you right now."

Diego said nothing, just stared at him with those puppy dog eyes.

Matteo grabbed his keys from the small walnut entry table and plowed down the stairs, red tinging the edge of his vision. *How could you do this to me?* ran through his head on a loop. He unlocked the door and pushed it open with such force that it shattered the glass in a crash.

You can clean up the mess this time, he thought blackly, and stormed off into the darkness.

∼

Diego watched Matteo go, powerless to stop him. All his excuses, all his rationalizations fell to dust in the face of that anger. He deserved it. Matteo prized loyalty and honesty above all else, and he had violated both. For years.

Crash.

The sound of breaking glass sent Diego running down the stairs. Had Matteo had done something stupid and stepped in front of an oncoming car? *Oh God, let it not be so.*

Instead, he found the front door broken into a thousand little shards, some still clinging to the frame. On the ground outside, the stickered word "Ragazzi" lay on the sidewalk, the glass behind it fragmented into pieces.

Diego stared at it for a moment, wondering how they would put it back together again. It was shattered beyond repair. Holding on to his emotions with a tight leash, he went to grab a broom and dustpan.

Diego had managed to clean up the worst of the shattered glass, dumping it into a plastic trash can from the kitchen. He wasn't sure yet what to do about the door itself. But at least it was something tangible, something he could fix.

Who knew where Matteo was? Diego had tried calling him, but he'd left his phone in their apartment when he'd rushed out. So Diego would have to wait and put back together what he could.

He dragged the trash can to the back door to take out in the morning. Then he found a box big enough to serve as a cover and taped it over the edges of the door. He looked outside, down the street, hoping to see Matteo returning. The sidewalk was empty.

Diego locked the door with his own key, for all the good that would do. He couldn't set the alarm. He'd just have to trust to luck until morning.

He sat up for an hour, watching the broken door, waiting for Matteo to return, and ran through what he could have done differently a hundred times in his head. It all came back to that one day, eighteen years before, when he'd withheld the truth.

Finally he gave it up as a lost cause and climbed the stairs to their empty bedroom.

In the morning, he was still alone. He found Matteo in their living room, fast asleep on the orange couch.

25. ENCOUNTERS

Marissa watched Marcos's Prius pull away, silent as a bicycle. She wasn't used to that. Everyone in her parents' circles drove SUVs—big, boxy black things that made mornings in their neighborhood look like the presidential motorcade. She snorted at the thought.

She was struck once again by how imposing the grand, colonnaded school entrance was. It was intimidating but less so than the thought of all the people inside. It was *so fucking unfair* that she had to start over.

Had her friends at Bella Vista even noticed she was gone?

She could still run if she wanted to. There was no one to stop her. She had Nathan tucked in the bottom of her pack, where no one could see him. Nothing else really mattered.

"Marissa?"

She spun around to find a geeky guy looking at her, one eyebrow raised. "Who's asking?"

"Jason." He extended a hand. "Principal Krebbs asked me to find you. She gave me this…." He showed her a picture of herself on his phone, taken at Ragazzi. Marcos must have given it to them, damn him.

"I don't need any help." He was kind of cute though, in a bookish sort of way, tousled brown hair and wire-frame glasses.

"Oh, I'm hoping you'll help me. Not the other way around." He grinned, his teeth covered in braces, sparkling in the sun. "Come on. School's about to start, and we have to get you settled." He beckoned her on. After a moment she followed, wondering what he meant.

What could he possibly want from her?

Carmelina went down the list of ingredients Diego had given her, working her way through the Corti Brothers supermarket. Her cart was filling up quickly with *prodotti di Italia,* and she started to question if this had been a good idea.

Arthur had never liked company. She had secretly wished he were more sociable. But now the grand cooking event was almost upon her, and she was picturing a ravenous horde descending upon her little kitchen.

Well, it wouldn't be as bad as all that. They were civilized folk—Marcos and Marissa, Sam and Brad, and Ben—just six of them altogether. Diego and Matteo had begged off, as they had the restaurant to run. If things went well with Daniele again tonight, she might invite him and make it seven.

She grabbed a few cans of crushed tomatoes and some of the vanilla tea she'd grown quite fond of and crossed the last two things off her list.

She was in line to check out when her phone rang. It was a local number but not one she recognized. She almost let it go to voicemail, but the screen seemed to sparkle. Like a sign. So she picked it up. "Hello?"

"Carmelina Di Rosa?" It sounded like an older woman.

"Who's asking?"

"This is Sister Clara at the Children's Home Society. Is this a good time?"

This was the call she had been waiting for. "Yes. Just a sec." She eased her cart out of line, banging the woman's cart behind her and earning a cross look. "I'm so sorry," she whispered, her hand over the phone. "It's an emergency."

She found a quiet corner in the wine section. "Sorry about that. I'm here."

"I understand," the nun said. "You have a busy life."

Carmelina thought she detected a note of jealousy there. "Again, I'm so sorry. You were saying?"

"Loylene Davies asked me to give you a call."

"Yes. I hoped to find some information about my daughter's adoption."

There was a long pause on the other end of the line. "Yes. That's what she said. Normally we can't provide that information, but…" That long pause again. She was making Carmelina nervous.

"Ms. Di Rosa, could you come to my office to speak about this?"

They must have *some* information for her. Carmelina started shaking. "I'm… Yes, of course. I can come right over—"

"I'm sorry, but I am booked until Friday. Would ten a.m. work for you?"

"Of course." She scribbled down the information on the back of her check register. "Thank you very much. I will be there." She hung up and stared blankly at the old, cracked linoleum tile. "Holy shit."

~

Ben was late to work again. He'd gotten lost writing his latest chapter, and even though he was sitting just twenty feet from The Everyday Grind, he somehow couldn't manage to make it in the door on time.

He threw his backpack over his shoulder, determined not to be *too* late. He ran down the boardwalk, twisting around a gay couple with a hurried "Sorry" and ran headlong into someone else.

"Hey, slow down there," a woman's voice said. "You almost made me spill my caramel latte!"

He looked up. It was *her*. "Ella," he whispered.

"Um, yes?" She pushed a loose strand of her red hair back behind her ear. "Do I know you?"

"Ben. From inside." He could have slapped himself—he felt like a total idiot around her. "From the Grind, I mean. I'm a barista."

"Not if you don't get your ass in here, you're not," Toby said, leaning out of the doorway.

"I'll be right in."

Ella laughed. "Oh, of course. You put a heart on my latte last time."

"Sorry about that. I like art."

"Me too." Her eyes almost sparkled. "It was nice to see you." She turned to leave.

Not again. "Hey!"

She stopped, looking over her shoulder. "What?"

"Would you… would you go out with me tonight?" He got it out, but it hurt like hell.

"I'm going to say no."

His heart broke, and he thought for a moment he might die of embarrassment right there. He turned to go inside, head down.

"Ben."

He looked up.

"Ask me again next time." She gave him a sly smile, then disappeared around the corner.

Ben went to work and found himself grinning from ear to ear all day long.

26. NO MATTER WHAT

DIEGO PULLED ON HIS WHITE CHEF'S JACKET AND BUTTONED IT UP, rolling up the sleeves. He had a fresh produce delivery coming in downstairs in a few minutes as well as a lunchtime rush to prepare for. Well, not so much a rush, but things had been busier the previous Wednesday. A student from a local Italian class had discovered them and had brought three or four of his classmates to order "authentic Italian food" and talk to a "real Italian." They had promised to return with more today.

Diego smiled at their enthusiasm for the language and country he was slowly leaving behind. The students confused their pronouns and verb tenses about as often as they got them right, but their love of his native tongue was still a beautiful thing to see. If things kept on as they were though, he might find himself back in the country he had fought so hard to leave behind, and all alone at that. It was a sobering thought.

Diego didn't know where Matteo had gone. He had been on the couch asleep when Diego had gotten up, but when he'd come out of the shower, the apartment had been empty.

He wanted to call Matteo, to sit him down and talk all of this out. But he knew his husband better than that. What he'd done was really bad. Matteo would need some time to sort things out before he'd be ready to listen to a word Diego had to say. Still, it was killing him not to make that call.

There was one good thing—his secret was out. The thing that had eaten away at him for years was no longer bottled up inside him.

But at some point, Max was going to call and demand his money. Diego had no idea what he was going to do about that.

He grabbed a little gel and ran it through his still-damp hair, styling it with his fingers. Satisfied, he headed downstairs to meet the delivery man.

~

It was depressingly sunny out.

Matteo wandered through the graves at East Lawn Memorial Park, not far from Ragazzi, wishing the sky would darken to match his black mood. He came here sometimes when he needed to think—it made him feel closer to his deceased parents. It was a little morbid and, he supposed, a little silly to be so sentimental. They were gone, and their spirits certainly weren't lingering here, almost ten thousand miles from their resting place. But still, it helped him put some distance between the everyday world and his thoughts.

He still remembered that Sunday in 1997 with a clarity that was breath-taking in its intensity. His father's body had been laid to rest in the cemetery just north of Imola. It had been a cool February afternoon, the white clouds scudding up from the Adriatic across the blue Emilia-Romagna sky, the smell of the sea carried far inland by the breeze. His mother stood to his left, all in black, sniffling behind her veil, and Diego to his right, clutching his hand tightly, as if trying to push all his own strength into Matteo. Matteo had been *broken*. Diego's love was the only thing that had gotten him through.

His gaze fell to one of the gravestones at his feet.

Elena Pestrin
3/26/1903-2/17/1997
Il Cuore della Casa

Matteo knelt, astounded. Elena was his mother's name, and 2/17/97 was the date his father had passed away. What were the odds?

He knelt down in front of the rose marble stone, brushing off the dirt and tearing away the encroaching grass. He set his hand on it, and a golden glow enveloped his hand. He yelped as it spread quickly up his arm, blocking out his sight.

~

Matteo sat next to his mother's bedside, the only sound in the room the slow but steady beep of the heart machine. It wouldn't be long now.

Her heart had been failing for years, but lately she had been weaker, barely able to walk on her own. That hadn't stopped her from living at home and diligently preparing a Sunday meal every week for "*la familia*"—herself, Matteo, and Diego.

The previous Sunday, when he and Diego had arrived, they'd found her on the floor in the kitchen, a plate of fresh-cut tomatoes scattered across the tiles.

The door to her hospital room opened a crack, and Diego came in, carrying a couple of cups of steaming coffee. "How is she?" he asked softly, handing one to Matteo.

"About the same." He took a sip and set it aside, leaning forward to put a hand on her frail arm. "I don't think I can do this, Diego," he whispered.

"I know." Diego touched his shoulder. "We will be strong enough together." His gaze strayed to Elena's bed. "Matteo, look!"

Matteo followed Diego's gaze. His mother's eyes were open, and she was staring at him.

His heart leapt. She hadn't been awake for days now. Maybe… just maybe… She opened her mouth to speak, but he couldn't hear what she was trying to tell him. "I'm here, Mamma." He leaned over her and kissed her cheek, taking her hand in his. "Diego is here too."

She nodded.

"It's okay. You don't have to speak."

She opened her mouth again, still trying to say something.

He leaned in.

"L—love… him," she whispered hoarsely. "No matter what."

Matteo pulled back, his eyes tearing up. She squeezed his hand, her eyes imploring him.

"I will, Mamma. I will."

She smiled faintly and closed her eyes, falling back into sleep. Three hours later, she was gone.

Matteo awoke, lying on his back in the grass, the blue bowl of the sky above him. It took a moment for him to remember where he was.

He missed her *fiercely*.

"I do love him, Mamma," he whispered. "I just don't know if it's enough."

27. LEFTOVERS

Carmelina wiped her hands on the apron that Arthur bought her last year, the one that made her look like a swimsuit model. The flour puffed into the air in little white clouds.

She glanced out the window at the driveway. It was still empty. Thank Jesus to Betsy that Daniele wasn't the type to arrive early.

She wasn't sure what had gotten into her, deciding to make a full home-cooked meal for the handsome Italian. Maybe she was just feeling sentimental for the days when she used to cook for Arthur. Maybe it was the magic the cooking class was working on her newly single life. Maybe she was just a glutton for punishment.

Whatever it was, her kitchen was a certifiable mess.

The pasta she'd made was laid out and drying on the small wooden table in one corner and was almost ready to go into the boiling water.

The vegetables were chopped, and the sausage was in a bowl ready to be cooked. She still had twenty minutes. She could do this.

Oh, and the parmigiano still needed grating…

~

Nineteen and a half minutes later, she poured the ragu pasta sauce over the just-drained pasta. The shredded parmigiano went on top, and she smiled as it started to melt.

And there was Daniele's car, pulling up into the driveway, just on time. Carmelina liked a punctual man.

She kissed her fingers and touched the brightly colored tile mosaic on the backsplash over the stove, sending a little prayer up to Arthur in heaven. Then she stripped off the dirty apron and threw it out onto the washing machine in the garage, checked her hair in the microwave window, and went to answer the doorbell just as it rang. "Well, hello," she said in her best sex-kitten voice, though it came out a little gruffer than she intended.

He was as beautiful as she remembered, dressed in casual business attire. He smiled back at her. "For you," he said, and from behind his back he pulled a dozen of the reddest roses she had ever seen.

"Oh, they're beautiful. Come on in! Make yourself comfortable." She accepted the flowers, and as his hand brushed hers, she remembered his touch the other night in the car after dinner. They'd only made it to second base, or was it third? She never had figured out the whole baseball metaphor. But she was hoping for a touchdown tonight. It had been way too long.

He followed her back to the kitchen, where she found a crystal vase for the flowers. "They're beautiful."

"Drop an aspirin in the water with them, and they will last longer."

"That's right, you're Mister Florist. You still sure that—"

"Still not gay." He laughed, and she got goosebumps.

"Have a seat. I was a little rushed today.… It was a crazy one." She pulled out a couple of her best plates and set them on the table.

"The pasta smells wonderful."

"One of Nonna Elena's recipes." She lit a candle and poured them each a glass of red wine from the bottle she'd opened before he'd arrived. "Give me a sec."

In the living room, she turned on the Bose speaker and selected her romance playlist. She'd gotten her neighbor's son to help her with that one, studiously ignoring his uncomfortable looks. Apparently nobody wanted to think about fiftyish women having sex. She supposed she could see their point.

Soon soft jazz filled the house.

She made her grand reentry into the kitchen and slipped on something, landing squarely in Daniele's lap. She stared up at him, mortified.

And closed her eyes as he leaned down and kissed her.

His lips were warm against hers, and her heart raced. When they parted, she opened her eyes and looked up into his.

"Are you hungry?" he said with a one-sided smile.

"Not in the slightest." Not for pasta, at any rate.

He lifted her up in his arms, and she laughed, feeling like a teenager again.

"Which way is the bedroom?"

She pointed.

"Are you sure you want to…?" he asked, looking into her eyes, searching for something.

She nodded. "I was hoping you'd ask."

~

An hour later, Carmelina sat against the fabric headboard, wrapped in the afterglow. Daniele's perfect, lithe body was stretched out naked beside her, not bad for a forty-year-old. She hadn't felt like this in… Well, she wasn't sure she had *ever* felt like this.

Daniele rolled over on his side to look up at her. "Was it okay?" he asked, his eyes sparkling.

Carmelina stretched out her arms above her head. "Darlin', it was a whole lot more than *okay*." She leaned over to kiss him, savoring his masculine smell.

She had loved Arthur. She truly had. But it had never been like this.

She pulled back and looked into Daniele's brown eyes. "Are you sure there's nothing wrong with you?"

She saw something on his wrist. Curious, she lifted it up into the light. It was a small tattooed cross. She raised an eyebrow.

He grimaced. "It's nothing." He pulled his hand away as if it had been burnt.

She smiled. "You don't need to keep secrets from me. I think we've moved past that stage, don't you?" Was he religious? He didn't seem to be, but then again, he *was* Italian.

"I should go," he said abruptly, and got up off the bed to retrieve his pants.

"You don't have to leave," she said, wondering what she'd done to push him away. She got up and pulled on her own nightgown, suddenly feeling naked and exposed. "There's still dinner. I can throw it in the microwave—"

"Another time." He finished buttoning up his shirt and gave her a quick peck on the cheek. "I'll call you tomorrow." He practically ran out of the room, leaving her speechless.

What the hell did I say?

It looked like she'd be eating leftovers alone.

28. LA LUNA

I found her.

Diego stared at it in disbelief. It was the night of the new moon, the apartment lit only by the streetlights outside.

He was dreading the inevitable demand from Max, his ex-immigration attorney, for the blackmail money. Instead, there was one from Valentina.

He checked the clock. It was just after eleven at night in California, or seven in the morning in Italy. Matteo was already in bed.

The two of them had worked side by side at Ragazzi all afternoon and evening, but Matteo had barely looked at him, let alone spoken more than three words. Now Diego sat by himself on the couch, afraid to go to bed.

He'd asked Valentina's advice the week before, and the words had come back with startling clarity. "You *have* to tell him." He'd put it off until he really had no more choice, and now he risked losing everything.

You found who? he texted back, his hands shaking, making it difficult to type out the words.

The three dots appeared on the screen for a moment, then went away.

He could picture his sister, perfect in her Valentino suit, getting ready for work, staring at the screen pensively while she decided how to tell him. Or if she should tell him at all.

What???

A moment later, the dots appeared again. And finally: *I found Luna. She wants to speak to you.*

He dropped the phone as if it had burned him. *After all these years…* Luna had been unstable, a live wire. There was no telling the damage she might do if he let her into his life again.

What did she say? he asked.

Three dots.

He waited, growling with anticipation. It was magic the way thoughts could be shared like this from the other side of the world. Magic and maddening…

She says she needs to see you…

The message trailed off.

What aren't you telling me?

There was a long pause. He stared at his phone as if he could will her to type whatever she was holding back. He started to call her when the dots appeared again.

"You have to sleep," Matteo said in Italian, from the doorway.

Diego looked up. "Are you talking to me now?"

Matteo frowned, his brow creased. Whether in anger or exhaustion, it was hard to tell.

Diego glanced down just as the message appeared from his sister. "Cazzo!"

She says you have a son.

~

Matteo poured the fresh coffee from the *moka* into two ceramic cups that said *Sacramento—the River City* with a photo of the Delta King on them. They'd been a part of his uncle's collection, and although they were a bit chintzy, he hadn't had the heart to throw them away.

He put down the pitcher and sat across the small kitchen table from Diego, whose hair was unkempt. There were dark patches under his eyes. He stared off to space, broken and lost.

"So you have a son," he said quietly, still unable to process it.

Diego shook his head. "I don't know. Luna says I do. But how can I believe her?"

"You don't. Find out if she is telling the truth, first."

Diego nodded, then looked at Matteo. "So you *are* talking to me."

Matteo smiled faintly. "I'm still angry with you."

"But do you forgive me?"

This time it was Matteo's turn to stare off into space for a moment. "When my mother died," he said at last, "she told me to just *love* you. No matter what it cost." He saw hope light in Diego's eyes and held up his hand. "I always will. But right now, I'm hurt."

"I know. I should have told you—"

"I have to wonder what other things you didn't tell me. What other secrets you might be keeping?" It killed him to say it. But there it was.

He expected Diego to argue. To promise there was nothing else. To beg.

"You're right," was all he said.

He looked back at Diego, stone-faced and staring at his hands.

"Everything you said is true. I lied and ruined everything." He looked down at his hand, turning his wedding ring around. "I made this into a lie." Diego slipped off the wedding band and laid it on the table between them. "I don't deserve you."

His words gutted Matteo. He tried to imagine a life without him and failed. In that moment, he *knew*.

Diego pushed away, but before he could get up, Matteo grasped his arm.

"Let me go," Diego whispered, almost a hiss.

"Diego, look at me!"

Diego slowly met Matteo's gaze.

"Yes, you *fucked up*. You lied to me, and that's going to take me a long time to forgive." He picked up the ring and held it in the air between them. "I gave this to you with a promise. For better *and* for worse." He took off his own ring and put them together on the table, side by side. "So maybe we're not married. I still meant what I said."

Diego eyed the rings doubtfully. "What are you saying?"

Matteo took his hands. "Do you remember what you told me yesterday, when I shared my own secret about our money?"

Diego shook his head.

"You said, 'Do you think fate brought us here just for failure and ruin?'"

Diego stared at him, dumfounded for a moment, and then burst into laughter that quickly turned to tears. "I am so sorry, Mattino," he said at last.

"It's gonna be all right," Matteo whispered. "We're gonna be all right." He pulled Diego close.

"What about Max? And Luna? And… my son?"

Matteo frowned, remembering the forces that were arrayed against them. "We'll figure it out," he said at last. "We always do."

As if in response to that thought, a new message flashed on Diego's phone.

Where's my money?

29. BETWEEN THE LINES

THE DOORBELL RANG. SAM GRUNTED. "CAN YOU GRAB THAT?" HE WAS right in the middle of an important scene in his second novel. Brad was working from home this morning.... Let him get it this time.

His character, Paolo Pausini, had just discovered how deep the rot went in the Italian embassy in DC. Sam was drawing on his high school Italian, textbook flung wide on his desk, to pull off at least partially realistic dialogue. Unfortunately, he couldn't remember how to form the formal imperative tense in *la bella lingua*.

Brad stomped by in the hallway behind him, probably annoyed at being called away from his own work.

Sometimes Sam thought Brad didn't take his writing seriously enough. Like it was more of a hobby, something he could be pulled away from at any time. Just because he worked at home didn't mean that he was free to run all kinds of errands or spend his whole day just keeping the place clean.

It had been bothering him lately, the little things Brad said to him. Hints, really, like his comment that morning about dust on the mantel. *Just come out and say it already....*

"Sam, come here!"

There it was again. The disregard for his time and his concentration. "I'm right in the middle of something," he called back.

"Seriously, you should come here."

Sam pushed back his chair with a loud scrape so hard it almost toppled over. "Really, Brad, you have to let me..." His words fell away when he saw what Sam was holding. "Oh my God, is that it?"

Brad nodded and held out the book to him.

Sam almost snatched it away from him. He turned it over to look at the beautiful cover, a photo of the state capitol building and a sexy-looking guy with that smoldering gaze. "Read Between the Lines, by Samuel Fuller," he read out loud. His first book.

"Samuel, huh?" Brad said with a grin.

"Holy crap, it's here," Sam said, still unable to believe it. He sank down into one of the leather armchairs in the living room and paged through it. It was real. He was an honest-to-god published author.

He thumbed open the dedication page. "This is for you," he said, holding it out to Brad, mouthing the words he knew by heart as Brad read them.

I knew the moment I met you. And you saw right through to my heart.

Brad looked up at him with a big grin, and he knew he'd done good. "I'm proud of you, *Samuel.*"

Sam brandished one of the couch pillows threateningly. "You're never gonna let me live that one down, are you?"

"Not a chance."

It was an epic pillow fight.

⌇

Joe, the restaurant manager for Zocalo, shook Ben's hand. "We'll let you know."

Ben had seen an ad for servers at the restaurant in the Sacramento Bee the night before and had decided to give it a shot. The pay was a bit better than the EG, and he hoped the hours might be a bit more regular. "Thanks. I've always loved this place."

Zocalo had been one of his first finds upon moving close to Midtown. An old car dealership from the early twentieth century had been transformed into a warm, light-filled space full of plants and beaten copper vases in the shape of armadillos and warm Mexican charm. He sat at the L-shaped bar, sipping his Diet Coke, and looked around. The place was fairly packed for a late Thursday morning, humming with chatter.

That's when he saw Ella.

She sat at a booth, half turned away from him, with a man a little older than she was, but there was no mistaking her profile.

Ask me again next time.

It looked like he was too late. She was seeing someone else.

He stared at her longingly, aware that he was being a little stalkerish, but he couldn't help it. Something about her had captured him.

She laughed at something the man had said. He had dark hair and brown eyes and perfect eyebrows. Something about him rubbed Ben wrong—he wasn't good enough for her. Ben was sure of it.

When the man got up to walk past him toward the bathrooms without even giving him a glance, Ben saw his chance. He got up and slid into the booth across from her.

Her eyes widened.

"Hi," he said shyly.

"Well, have a seat," she said, arching an eyebrow.

He blushed. "I'm sorry. I was here for an interview, and saw you…."

She waited for him to go on, silent.

"I'm Ben. From the Grind." This wasn't going well at all.

She cracked the slightest smile. "I know."

"You said to ask you again," he said in a rush, encouraged. "On Monday. Then I saw you here with him, that other man. He's not good enough for you, Ella." He closed his mouth, aware that he was babbling. "You must think I'm such a mess." He put his head down on the table, humiliated. Then he felt her hand on his and looked up.

She was laughing. "You're kind of cute, you know? Even if you were kind of stalking me."

He shook his head. "I wasn't, I swear. I really did have an interview. Then I saw you. It's fate." He produced Joe's card as proof. "So what do you say? Will you go out with me?" He put it all on the line. He didn't know what he'd do if she said no, and the other guy would be back soon.

She considered. "It *would* be unfair to say no, after all I put you through."

He grinned. "Are you serious?"

"How's Friday night?"

"Perfect!" He was working Friday night, but he'd find a way to get out of it. "How about seven o'clock?"

Someone had come up behind him and was hovering over his shoulder. Her date. He started to rise, ready to run.

"Ben? Meet my brother, Max."

30. THE OUTCASTS SOCIETY

Marcos looked around his small condo in dismay. Marissa had only been there for a few days and had arrived with little more than the clothes on her back. And yet, somehow, almost every surface in his once-pristine home was covered in something of hers.

The kitchen sink and counter were filled with enough dishes to have fed the cast of *RuPaul's Drag Race*, and that was just from breakfast this morning.

The dining room table was papered over with notes and half-finished homework assignments. English lit, from the look of things. He lifted up one of the papers, feeling like an archaeologist exploring some heretofore unknown ancient culture.

The couch in his living room was a nest of blankets Marissa had retrieved from the linen closet the night before, because she had been "colder than a penguin's butt," and then had never put away. He had refrained from asking why the butt was so much colder than a penguin's other body parts.

But the real *pièce de résistance* was the guest bedroom. She had taken it over and made it her own.

He looked at the pandemonium inside and shook his head. It was as if a fashionable spider had taken up residence there and strewn its webs about. Clothes of every shape and color were thrown across the bed. They hung from the ceiling fan, squeezed out of the closet door like rainbow toothpaste, and covered the dresser and nightstand. In the middle of it all sat Nathan, his glassy teddy-bear eyes looking up innocently as if to disclaim all responsibility.

Where had she gotten all those clothes? He recalled buying her a few things. Maybe he'd brought home a bag full of tribbles shaped like boyfriend jeans.

He closed the door tightly to prevent them from escaping, ignoring the stuffed bear's inquisitive gaze. He would have to talk about this mess with Marissa when she got home.

Meanwhile, he had a job to finish. The Center was paying him to upgrade their website, and he was already a few days behind.

He fired up his computer and glanced at his calendar.

Dinner at Carmelina's.

Damn, he'd forgotten all about that.

He really was enjoying the cooking class, and a part of that was this strange Italian-American redhead who just seemed to *get* him. They'd laughed their asses off together during the last class, and Marcos was looking forward to seeing her again.

He kinda liked her.

It was nothing romantic or sexual—shit, no. He was well and truly queer. And yet he found her brash sense of humor refreshing.

He glanced at the clock. It was a quarter to ten. If he pushed, he could get a good five hours of work done before Marissa came back home on the bus.

~

Marissa sat alone at lunchtime at a table in the corner of the cafeteria. Around her, everyone else was snapchatting or taking photos of each other. She missed her iPhone, but she'd lost it when her parents had kicked her out. Without a phone, she felt like a social pariah.

A shadow fell over her, and she looked up to see Jason standing there, lunch tray in hand. "Can I join you?"

She nodded. "Have a seat. We can start the official Outcast Society at McClatchy High."

Though she'd said it with a note of bitterness, Jason didn't seem to notice. He grinned and sat down next to her. "That's a great idea. We could make up a cool logo and some T-shirts and maybe a newsletter...."

It had become quickly apparent what Jason wanted from her: a friend, and maybe a shot at a little popularity around school.

He was a gay kid, but not the Gay Best Friend kind. He wasn't sparkly or fashionable like the popular gays or athletic like the sports gays. He wasn't even particularly witty like her street friend Ricky. It was hard for kids like him, gay or straight. She supposed she was one of those kids now, too.

"… and we could get together at Cafe Bernardo on the weekends like Marcy Minks and her friends…"

"Hey, slow down," she said. "It was just a stupid remark."

He frowned. "Oh, ok." He went back to picking at his spinach, and she felt like shit for shutting him down him. He was her only friend here, after all.

"What about the alliance?" she said after a moment, hoping to perk him up.

He shook his head. "That's all the popular kids."

She snorted. "Popularity in high school is *stupid*." She used to worry about that crap, but her time on the street had given her a new perspective. "You know, you're right. We should do it. Make our own little clique. One where we choose the members. We could call it the Outsiders. Or the renegades. Or…"

"I like 'The Outcasts Society.'"

"'The Outcasts Society.' I like it too."

Jason pushed back his glasses on his nose and smiled shyly at her. "Thanks, Marissa. I'm glad you're here." He looked around. "How do we get it going?"

The school bell rang, and the students in the cafeteria started to get up and shuffle out of the room.

"Like this," she said with a grin, and climbed up on the table. "Hey!" she shouted, and the room went quiet as five hundred other kids turned to look at her. "I'm Marissa, and this is Jason. If you don't know us, it's because you're too stuck up to look past your own nose."

"Get down from there, Ms. Sutton," Mr. Mitchell called, waving threateningly.

"If you're loners like us, come join us here tomorrow, at this table for the first official meeting of The Outcasts Society!" She climbed down before the teacher could chastise her again. He glared at her but didn't say anything more.

Jason was grinning ear to ear. "That was farking awesome." He frowned. "What if no one comes?"

"Cross that bridge tomorrow."

31.LUNCH WITH MAX

DIEGO WAS WAITING FOR MAX AT LUCCA IN MIDTOWN. JUSTIN WAS running the front of house back at Ragazzi, and a chef friend of Diego's had offered to cook for an hour. Who said they hadn't made any friends here?

The hostess had seated him all alone on the back patio. The place had a comfortable, relaxed vibe that appealed to him.

"Can I get you started with something?" the waitress, Lauren, asked.

He looked over the menu. "Beh, some of zucchini chips, please?" He pointed to them on the menu.

"Sure. Some water?"

He shook his head. "Save for the... how do you say it?"

"Drought?"

He nodded. "Some wine?"

"White or red?"

"Prosecco? Three?"

"Coming right up." She flashed him a smile.

As she left, the hostess appeared with another guest. "Mr. Cucinelli? Mr. Bellei is waiting for you."

"*Ciao*, Max," Diego said with a smile, standing and holding out his hand.

Max took it suspiciously. "Buon giorno."

"Have a seat," Diego said in Italian. "I've ordered us a little Prosecco and some zucchini chips to get started."

"About the money—"

"Have patience. if you're going to extort me, the least you can do is sit through a nice meal first." He took a deep breath, looking up at the clear blue sky. "It's a beautiful day, isn't it?"

Max just stared at him.

Diego pretended not to notice. Instead he studied the menu. Max was studying him with a frown on his face. Diego was enjoying this.

Their appetizer and Prosecco arrived. Out of the corner of his eye, Diego saw Max notice the third glass. "You'd better check your menu. Our waitress will be back any minute to take your order."

Max frowned and picked up his menu. He opened it and took out an envelope. "Finally, you've come to your senses." He opened the envelope and pulled out a piece of paper.

His face went white, then red with anger. "What the hell is this?" He held it up. It was neatly inscribed *Va' a farti fottere!* along with a smiley face.

"I think it speaks for itself," said another voice, over his shoulder. Max turned to find Matteo standing there. "But just in case... it says *go fuck yourself.* He flashed his brightest Italian smile. "We no longer need your services."

Max stood and threw his napkin down angrily. "So you know his secret. It doesn't matter. I can still call immigration on the two of you."

Matteo took him by the collar with one hand and pushed him up hard against the wall. "And I can report you to the state bar for extortion." He put his face right up against Max's. "Just try me." They stared at each other for a moment, then Max looked away. Matteo let him go, and Max scurried away.

Diego grinned at him. "That was amazing."

Matteo sat next to him, taking a sip of the Prosecco. "It felt fantastic, but he could still make trouble for us."

"Still..." He put his hand on Matteo's. "Thank you for doing this. I know I screwed up. But now—"

There was a loud screech, a thump, and shouts. Diego jumped up and ran toward the sounds, and Matteo followed. It couldn't be... He reached the front of the restaurant. A black SUV had run up on the curb, and Max was laid out in the street, unconscious. Or worse. *Oddio, I killed him.*

Carmelina had almost everything ready for the gathering. They'd be cooking the Italian recipes she'd learned from her class at Ragazzi. She'd left three messages for Daniele, but he hadn't returned her calls. *Screw him.* It was too soon to be playing the field, anyway. Her night of passion would have to tide her over until the next time Fleet Week came to San Francisco.

She grinned at the image of a bored Sacramento housewife of a certain age hanging around the docks, looking for a few good men. Or even just *one*.

She had set up two preparation stations: one for *passatelli* and one for *piadine*. It was a quarter to five, and her guests were due in just forty-five minutes.

She went over her ingredients. Flour, lard, milk, salt, honey, baking soda and baking powder for the *piadine*; parmigiano, dried bread, eggs…

"Oh crap." She'd forgotten to get eggs.

She checked the refrigerator. She had one egg left in the carton. She didn't have enough time to run to the store.

Dave. Her renter in the other half of the duplex always had a well-stocked fridge. She called his place, hoping he would answer.

"Hiya, stranger," he said. She could hear his smile.

"Hey there. You have any eggs I can borrow? I have company coming…"

"Hell, no, get your own damned eggs."

She grinned. "I'll be right over." She hung up and ran out, banging on Dave's front door.

"Who is it?"

"Open the damned door."

It swung open. "Come on in," he said with a grin.

"I wish I could. But I've got company coming." Despite being in his late forties, Dave was still really handsome, greying at the temples but with an appealing, boyish enthusiasm. It was true what they said—the best ones really were gay.

"So you said…. While I sit all alone in this little shack of a house." He handed her the carton. "Just use what you need and bring back the rest."

"I'll pay you later."

He waved her off. "Don't worry about it."

She had a thought. "Hey, are you busy tonight?"

"Just catching up on my binge watching. I'm almost through *Drag Race*."

"Why don't you come over? I'm teaching some friends how to cook."

"I don't know…."

"C'mon. It'll be fun, and I won't take no for answer."

"Can I come like this?" He was wearing old gray sweats—his "office" attire.

"Sure. But there's a cute single guy coming. You might wanna dress up."

She loved playing the matchmaker.

32. THREE TABLES

The phone rang.

Someone's canceling, Carmelina thought. Someone *always* canceled. She picked up the phone, pushing a strand of frizzy red hair behind her ear. "Hello?"

"Carmelina?" An Italian accent. For a second she thought it was Daniele calling to apologize for his abrupt exit the night before. She was about to light into him when the man said, "It's Matteo."

Her anger left her in a sigh. "*Ciao, bello. Come state.. come stai?*"

"*Bene*… it was a *difficil*… difficult day."

"Everything okay?" She'd only known them for a couple weeks, but her new Italian friends seemed relentlessly upbeat. It was strange to hear the strain in his voice.

"I hope so. I'm sorry to call. I wondered if it wasn't too late to say yes to your invitation?"

"Tonight?"

"Yes."

"Of course not. The more the merrier." Arthur would have had a fit to have such a ruckus in the house.

Arthur wasn't here anymore.

"Grazie mille. We just need a few friends tonight."

"Well, come on over."

"We will see you soon."

She hung up the phone, wondering what was going on with them. She was going to need to set up another cooking station. Maybe one of Nonna's old recipes.

Then the doorbell rang. *Showtime.*

~

Marcos looked around Carmelina's home. It wasn't huge, but it exuded warmth and comfort. The olive-green walls were hung with an eclectic collection of artwork running the gamut from classical to geometric modern. The brick fireplace sported a wooden mantel that held pictures of Carmelina with a handsome older man, presumably her recently passed husband. Albert? Archie? He couldn't remember. Maybe he was the old man.

The hardwood floors were polished to a luster, and the furniture blended traditional fabrics with a contemporary style.

"Where's the bathroom?" Marissa asked.

"Just down there," Carmelina said, directing her down the hall. "How are you doing with her?" she asked Marcos once the girl had closed the door.

Marcos shook his head. "It's not easy. The trial for her breaking and entering episode is next month. In the meantime, I'm trying to establish a bit of normalcy for her at home."

Carmelina arched an eyebrow. "She's taking over, isn't she?"

He nodded. He must have looked miserable, because she laughed and patted him on the shoulder. "I know what a handful a teenage girl can be. I was a menace."

"What did your mother do?" He could imagine the trouble she'd gotten into.

"She laid down the law. Kids need boundaries."

"Easier said than done."

"Maybe so. But she'll thank you for it later. Come on. I have a place for you to work on your piadine skills over here."

He glanced back at the closed bathroom door. "Marissa…"

"Leave her to me. I have plans for her tonight. You deserve an evening off." She set him down at a table at one end of the long kitchen. "Oooh, this surface is still filthy. Let me wash it off for you." Grabbing a rag, she glanced out the window. "Oh, I think your sous chef is here."

"Sous chef?"

But she was already off to the front door.

~

Dave reached toward the doorbell, but he hesitated. Usually he would come in the back way, but since Arthur had passed away, it had felt… intrusive to presume such familiarity. And truth be told, he'd been keeping more and more to himself in general. He ran a human resources consulting firm and had been able to conduct much of his business over the phone and the web. He felt safe at home.

It had been months since Carmelina had tried to play the matchmaker with him. Their cat-and-mouse game had been put on hold by her husband's death. But apparently it was game on again now.

He was glad to see her coming out of her own seclusion. But did it have to be at the expense of his own?

Five long years…

Carmelina had managed some spectacular failures with her purported matchmaking skills. Danny the Republican asshole had been particularly memorable.

Maybe I should just head back home.

The door burst open and Carmelina grinned. "I thought I saw someone lurking out here. Come on in!"

Dave sighed. He'd waited a second too long to change his mind.

~

Sam and Brad arrived next.

"Carmelina, this is Brad, my partner," Sam said, introducing a handsome man a few years his senior.

"You have a beautiful home," Brad said, stepping inside. "Thank you for inviting us."

"Glad to have you. Sam says you run the LGBT Center?"

"With the board. But yes, I'm there almost every day."

"Mister Weston!"

Brad turned just in time to receive a giant hug from Marissa.

He held her out at arms' length. "You look great. Marcos treating you okay?"

She nodded. "Mostly. Though he keeps his house too fucking cold…"

"Too what?" Brad raised an eyebrow.

"Too fracking cold."

"Better. Still, I bet it's warmer than the streets."

"I guess so."

Carmelina grinned at the girl's brash spirit. "Marissa, wanna wait for me in the kitchen? I'm going to show you how to make a special dish my grandmother used to make for me."

Carmelina sat Brad and Sam at the passatelli table in the dining room. She felt like a wedding planner with her seating chart all in order. They'd each work on their separate dishes, and then they'd eat dinner together at the long folding tables she'd set up out back. Fortunately it was unseasonably warm for the first of October.

Ben showed up next, and she put him with Sam and Brad. She had plans for Dave and Marcos, and she didn't want anything to disturb them.

At a quarter after six, Matteo and Diego arrived. Diego handed her a beautiful bottle of prosecco, which she accepted gratefully.

She picked up a glass and a fork, tapping one against the other loudly. "Okay, we're all here. The sooner we get started, the sooner we can eat!"

33. MAKING PIADINE

Dave decided he should have stayed home after all. Things had started out well enough. He and Marcos, who was actually really cute *and* a few years younger than him, had gone over the recipe Carmelina had provided, apparently from a cooking class they had taken together.

They'd mixed the ingredients—flour, lard, milk, salt, and the rest—talking as they went. Once, their hands had touched, and Dave had felt a momentary thrill at the contact. It had been a long time since he'd been with anyone or had felt a touch like that. But then things had stalled out.

They'd exhausted the usual list of topics: the weather, who was likely to win the presidential nomination, what they liked to watch on TV. It turned out they had very little in common on that side, with Marcos preferring *Supergirl* and *Green Arrow* and *The Flash*, while Dave liked *Project Runway*, *RuPaul's Drag Race*, *Top Chef*, and *Face Off*.

Now they worked together in stony silence, while at the other two tables, people laughed and chatted and generally seemed to be having a great time. So Dave concentrated on working the dough—getting the consistency just right, then rolling out each piadina on the table and sprinkling enough flour to keep it from sticking to the surface.

He glanced at his phone. It was close to seven on a Thursday night. He could have been home watching *Modern Family*. He could have made himself a nice mug of hot chocolate, put on his bunny slippers and robe, and settled in on his comfortable sofa in front of his comfortable TV in his comfortable house....

"Why do you live all alone?"

The question startled Dave out of his reverie. He turned to look at Marcos, wondering if this was just another conversational tact, one more topic to check off the list of social interactions. But Marcos looked serious.

"Why do you ask?" Dave was nothing if not good at deflection.

Marcos sighed. "Because I'm alone too. Well, except for my new ward over there." He nodded toward Marissa. "This is obviously a setup, right?"

Dave nodded. "I think so."

"I found the right guy once, but he got away, and I've been playing musical chairs ever since. I *shouldn't* like you. Blind dates never work, right? And then I thought, 'Why the hell not?' But I'm chickenshit at romance. So it was easier to ask about you."

Dave blinked. Had he heard right? "Me? You want to ask me out? Why?"

Marcos nodded. "You seem like a nice guy, and you're cute, and the fact that you're close to Carmelina speaks in your favor."

"Didn't you just meet?" He couldn't pull himself away from Marcos's brown eyes. It had been awhile, but he knew the signs. He was getting hooked.

"Maybe so. But we were twins, separated at birth."

Dave laughed out loud. "I can see that. You have the same big mouth."

Marcos threw a piece of piadina dough at him.

"Hey! Don't mess with the food," Carmelina called from the other side of the kitchen. "We have to eat that later."

Marcos grinned "That woman has eyes in the back of her—"

"I heard that!"

"And big ears too," Dave whispered.

Carmelina glared at the two of them.

Dave waggled his fingers at her, and she shot him a mock-serious look and turned away. *Maybe this guy isn't so bad, after all.* "He died five years ago," he said after a moment.

"Who?"

"John. Love of my life." He took a deep breath. "HIV Complications ."

Marcos whistled softly. "And you?"

"No. I was lucky. We found out he had it early on, and we were very careful after that. I took care of him in our home that last year." He sighed. Even five years later, it was hard to talk about it. There would never be another John.

Marcos put a flour-covered hand over his. "I'm sorry. I know what it's like to lose someone."

They sat together in silence for a moment, but this time it was a companionable one.

"So how about you?" Dave asked, starting in again on the piadine. He estimated they had enough dough to make about ten of the Italian flatbreads.

"What about me?"

"Why are *you* single?"

"Why do you ask?" Marcos's eyes twinkled.

"Because I want to ask you out, you idiot." His TV shows could wait—that's what the DVR was for.

This time it was Marcos who laughed. "I'd like that," he said at last. "Like a real date?"

"Yeah, a *real date*. What do I look like, some kind of trick you picked up at Faces?"

"Not in the least. It's just that…"

"What?"

"I haven't been on a *real* date in a long time. I'm afraid I might be a little rusty."

Dave smiled. "It's okay. I have lube. We'll get you greased up in no time."

Marcos snorted. "No, I'm serious. I'm out of practice. You'll have to go easy on me."

"I can do that. I'm a little rusty too. It's been five years since I was with someone, and that wasn't exactly a date." He closed his eyes, remembering those last few weeks. The drug cocktail had stopped working, and one after another, the opportunistic infections had shown up. He'd seen friends die of the nasty disease when he was in his teens and twenties. He'd never expected to witness it again. He had been alone for a long time, after.

John would want him to move on.

He opened his eyes, forcing a smile. "How about Saturday night?"

"Deal. Do you like Italian food?"

Dave nodded. "I'm here, aren't I?"

"You live next door?"

Dave nodded. "Carmelina lets me rent out the other side of her duplex."

"I'll pick you up at six."

"Deal."

He'd have time to go through his closet and see if he still had anything nice to wear.

34. MAKING PASSATELLI

"So how goes the Great African American Trans Novel?" Sam asked, grinning.

Ben shrugged. "The week's gotten away from me." He liked Sam—the guy was an open book. "And you? Anything new?"

"Oh, here we go," Brad said, rolling his eyes.

"I'm so glad you asked." Sam rummaged around in the backpack on the floor by his chair, pulling something out triumphantly. "I just got it this morning." He handed a book over to Ben.

"'Read Between the Lines.'" Ben turned it over. Sam's all-American-boy face smiled at him from the back cover. "That's fantastic!" Ben had a few short stories published in various journals, but nothing like this. Someday soon he'd finish his novel.

"It's the one I told you about. My political thriller, set in Sacramento."

Ben grinned. Sam's enthusiasm was infectious. "I'll have to get a copy," Ben said, holding it out.

"You have one. Check the title page."

Ben opened it.

To Ben: From one writer to another. Keep the faith! —Sam

"That's fantastic. Thanks, man! I'll start reading it later tonight."

"Great, make his head even bigger," Brad said, laughing.

"So Brad, what do you do?" Ben asked. If Sam was an open book, Brad was an encrypted one.

"Nothing important like writing," Brad said, rubbing Sam's back. "I run the LGBT Center."

"That's not nothing! I know lots of folks who've found help there. When I was younger…" Ben's phone was ringing. It was Ella. "Sorry, guys. I've got to take this."

"Go ahead." Sam waved him off. "We'll get things started here. I think our host has us making passatelli."

Ben stepped out into the front yard. "Hello?"

"Ben?" Ella's voice broke.

"Hey, what's wrong?"

"Can you get down to Sutter? It's my brother. There's been… an accident."

"Where are you?"

"Emergency. I'm so sorry to do this to you, but I hardly know anyone here."

"I'm only ten minutes away. Hang on. I'll be there as fast as I can."

"Thanks, Ben." She hung up.

She had called him. Something was wrong, and she had called *him*.

He found Carmelina in the kitchen, making dessert with Diego, Matteo, and Marissa. "I have to run," he said, kissing her cheek. "A friend's brother is in the hospital."

She gave him a hug. "Sorry to hear that. Can I send something with you? I'm sure I have leftovers in the fridge."

"No, thanks. But thank you! Gotta go."

He waved at his cooking companions and sped out the door.

～

"That was weird," Sam said.

Brad nodded. "One moment he's here, and the next he's gone."

Carmelina appeared from the kitchen with Matteo in tow. "Ben says he's sorry he had to go. A friend is in the hospital."

"Poor guy. I hope they're okay." Brad hated hospitals.

"In the meantime, I'm bringing you some reinforcements. Matteo here's going to join you to help you with the passatelli. I'm keeping Diego all to myself."

"Oh sure, you get the chef." Sam stuck his tongue out at her.

"Host's prerogative." She flashed them a smile and then vanished back into the kitchen.

"What are you guys making in there?" Brad asked.

"She swore me to secrecy," Matteo said. "How may I help?"

They divided up the labor between them. Sam grated the cheese. Brad tackled the bread, getting himself into a nice rhythm, while Matteo whipped the eggs. As they worked on the meal, they talked.

"So what's Italy like?" Sam asked. "I've always wanted to go. I'm writing an Italian character in my new novel."

"Don't get him started on writing," Brad warned Matteo.

Matteo smiled. "Italy is a beautiful country. But it's not the same country it was twenty years ago. The economy is bad, the European Union has made things worse in some ways, and taxes are very high. It's very duro… difficult to open a new business there."

"Surely it can't be so terrible," Brad said, though he'd seen how bad the Italian economy was when he'd worked for the senator.

Matteo frowned. "I had an accounting job in Bologna for fifteen years before we camed here. I didn't get a raise for the last thirteen."

Sam whistled. "So how do people get by?"

Matteo shrugged. "They move in with family. They don't pay their taxes. They leave."

He sounded sad. Brad changed the subject. "How's the restaurant doing?"

Matteo glanced up at the ceiling. "Beh, not well. It was my uncle's place, but after the remodeling, many people don't return."

"Damn. It's such a nice place." Sam turned to Brad, who was mixing the ingredients in a big bowl. "Why don't we support our own community?"

Brad shrugged. "It's because we're such a big, diverse group. The only thing we have in common is our differences." He blended the cheese and bread crumbs together and added the eggs, nutmeg, and lemon peel. "Sometimes the L doesn't understand the G doesn't understand the B doesn't understand the T. Throw in our asexual and intersex friends and the gender-fluid crowd, and it's a wonder we ever agree on anything." He put a finger into the dough and tasted it. "Damn, this is good."

Matteo grinned. "It was one of mia madre… my mother's recipes. And one of my favorites."

"I didn't think you two were coming tonight," Sam said, tasting the dough himself. "Damn. That *is* good."

"There was an incident this afternoon." The sad look returned to Matteo's face.

"Everything okay?"

"For us, yes. But it was upsetting. So we decided to take the night off. We didn't have reservations, in any case."

Marissa's laughter erupted from the kitchen. She seemed happier than he'd seen her in weeks. Brad looked at Matteo, considering. "It seems like this cooking class of yours has been really good for Marissa."

Matteo nodded. "I think so. Diego says she's a natural at the kitchen."

Brad smiled. The man spoke very good English but still got tripped up by prepositions. "I think I have an idea that could help us both."

35. MAKING APPLE FRITTERS

Carmelina shook her head, watching Ben's car pull away and hoping his friend was all right.

"Ben's trans?" Marissa looked up at her, hands wet.

"Yes. Does that bother you?"

"Why would it?" She went back to cleaning apples.

It's a different world. The school she'd attended had included boys and girls. White boys and girls. Well, there'd been the Johnson kid. He'd been the only person of color she'd seen until she was seventeen.

Now the schools here had every kind of child imaginable: kids from Russia, from Guatemala, kids who were gay and bi and intersex and trans. It was a wonderful thing, but sometimes she felt a little lost in this new world. She still didn't know what *intersex* was. Or *santorum.* Funny though—there was a right-wing politician by the same name. She should google it.

She sat down at the kitchen table with Diego and Marissa. Diego was showing her how to cut the apples into thin slices, dropping them into the marinade of sugar, rum, and lemon peels. "You're a good teacher."

He smiled. God, he was adorable. "Grazie," he said, and turned to Marissa. "You *arrotola*... how do you say..." He made a rolling motion.

"Roll," Marissa said.

"Yes. You roll it *così.*" He demonstrated.

Marissa was a lovely child too. How her parents could have thrown her out was beyond Carmelina's understanding. Sending her own daughter off for adoption had been hard enough.

Tomorrow, Carmelina would find out about the fate of that little girl. She'd been trying not to think about it all day long and had failed spectacularly. Annoyed, she pushed it aside once again and sat down to mix up the batter. "This is a recipe my nonna—my grandmother—taught me when I was about ten years old. She used to always make it for me when we went to visit."

"What was her name?" Marissa asked, concentrating on slicing the apples.

"Nonna Elena."

Diego smiled. *"La mamma di Matteo si chiamava Elena."*

Matteo's mother was Elena too? "It's a beautiful name. You don't hear it so much anymore. I love old-fashioned names." She put her hand on Marissa's, and the girl smiled up at her. She'd missed the whole growing up thing with her own daughter, but just maybe she'd get the chance to make amends.

Marissa felt an unexpected surge of affection for Carmelina. She had a warmth about her that Marissa's own mother had never had. For the first time in a long time, she felt *at home*.

Diego had told her she had a talent for cooking, A *dono*, he had called it, but the meaning had been clear enough. She'd never really been good at anything, something her parents had told her over and over. "Why can't you be like your brother?" Perfect Oliver. Athletic, intelligent older brother Oliver. Never-disappointed-the-parents-in-his-life Oliver. Sometimes she missed him.

Carmelina was asking her something.

"What?" she said, her eyes focusing on the woman's face.

"Do you like living at Marcos' place?"

She thought about it. "It's not bad. It's nice having my own room again. He doesn't like it when I vape."

"When you what?"

"Vape. You know, e-cigs. You buy this vape pen thing and some e-liquid in your favorite flavor. I like blueberry."

Carmelina laughed. "I have no idea what you just said. But aren't you too young to be smoking anything?"

Marissa frowned. "That's what Marcos says. But I wasn't too young to live on the streets."

"You were smart enough to take care of yourself," Carmelina chastised her. "That doesn't mean you weren't too young." She sighed. "When I was about your age, I thought I knew everything too. In high school, I slept with this beautiful boy named Jimmy Callahan. He was on the football team, and I was sure we were meant to be together forever." Her eyes took on a faraway look. "He told me he loved me, but then he moved away. And a week after he left, I found out that I was pregnant."

"You have kids?"

Carmelina frowned. "Yes, and no. I gave her up—my little girl. I was way too young to raise a child. At least that's what I told myself." Her eyes were moist. She wiped them with a dish towel. "When I look at you, though, I wonder if I made the right decision all those years ago."

"You would have been a good mom." She meant it.

Diego nodded. "*Una mamma bellissima.*"

"You could be *my mom*, for now. If you want." Her own mother didn't seem to be up to the job.

"I'd like that." Carmelina gave her a hug and didn't let go for a long time.

Diego watched the two of them together. They both had holes in their hearts.

He knew about family and broken hearts.

His own mother was still alive, living with his sister in Bologna. But her mind was almost gone. It had been leaking away for years, like water from a dripping faucet, a memory at a time splashing on the sink and then running down the drain.

The last time he had seen her, she hadn't been able to remember her name. Her frail hand had rested on his cheek. "Papà, is it you?" she had whispered.

And he had nodded and kissed her cheek. He knew about broken hearts. "We cook these now?" he said, pointing to the bowl full of rum and apples.

"In a few minutes. Give them time to marinate."

"Marinate?"

"Soak in the rum. For the flavor—the *sapore.*"

"Ah, I understand."

Tomorrow, he and Matteo would have to figure out what to do about his immigration status. Tomorrow would be hard.

But for now, it was nice just to be here, cooking in this beautiful kitchen.

Among family.

See the apple fritters recipe at the end of the book.

36. IN THREES

ONE OF THE PIADINAS WAS IN A HOT PAN. THE BROTH FOR THE passatelli was boiling on the stove, and they were about to start the apples when Carmelina smelled something. "Is that smoke?"

Her guests were all crowded into the kitchen, talking with one another.

"I smell smoke," she said more loudly. "Does anyone else smell it, or am I having a stroke?"

Sam, who was closest to the doorway to the dining and living room, peeked around the corner. "Oh crap. Your table's on fire!"

Without thinking, Carmelina grabbed a pot full of water that was sitting in the sink. "Outta my way," she said, and ran into the dining room, dousing the table with the contents of the pot.

The flames consuming the table cloth jumped higher. "Crap, that was the chicken water."

Brad grabbed the blanket that lay over the couch and used it to beat down the flames.

"Not that one!" she yelled, but it was too late. The flames were out.

The hand-knitted blanket her grandmother Elena had left her was a smoldering ruin.

Brad frowned. "Was this… special?"

She took a deep breath. "It was…. It doesn't matter. Thank you for putting out the fire."

Sam appeared with a roll of paper towels and started to sop up the mess. "Looks like the candle burned down and the wick set the tablecloth on fire."

At least the tablecloth was worthless. She retrieved a black plastic bag and shoved it and the ruined blanket inside, saying a quick prayer to her nonna.

"The table doesn't look too bad," Matteo said, wiping it off with a soapy dish cloth. "You can have it… how do you say? *Rifatto?*"

"Re-done." Truth be told, it was probably time to get a new one.

"Um, Carmelina?" Marissa's voice called her from the kitchen.

"What now?"

"There's something wrong with the oven. These piadini things aren't cooking."

Sam smiled. "Go. We've got this. Where's your cleaning stuff?"

"Under the bathroom sink." She lurched back into the kitchen. The oven was cold.

"That's all right. I can have it looked at later. Let's move the piadines to the lower one. Just means we'll be eating dinner a little later."

Marissa gave her a quick hug. "That's okay. Everyone understands."

"Thanks, love."

"Carmelina!" someone called her from the back of the house.

"Coming! Can someone open the windows to get rid of the smoke smell?" She ran to the hall bathroom.

"Lo farò!" Diego called.

"What's going on back here?" she asked Dave, who pointed at the toilet. Water was spilling over the edge.

"Did you turn off the valve?"

"I didn't want to touch it."

"Oh for God's sake." She waded into the small pool of water and shut it off. "Go grab me the plunger from the Master bath. It's under the sink."

Dave nodded sheepishly. He returned in a moment with the plunger, and she went to work. It was getting warmer in the house as the outside air flushed out the smoke.

She fought to bend the toilet to her will, pumping the plunger over and over again, but the damned thing wouldn't clear. At last she threw in the towel, literally, throwing a couple of old bath towels on the ground to soak up the water and then stuffing those into the bathtub for later clean up.

She shooed Dave out and closed the door. "No one uses this bathroom," she announced. "Use mine instead." She cranked up the air conditioning. It was too damned hot for an October evening. Through the open windows, she could hear her neighbors running theirs too.

She retreated to her bathroom and washed up as well as she was able, checking herself in the mirror. Disasters always came in threes, right?

"Everything else under control?" she asked as she returned to the kitchen.

"I think so," Sam said. "The table's all cleaned up."

"Thank God. And thank you all. This night couldn't get any worse—"

The house was plunged into darkness and silence.

"Fuck me nine ways to Sunday." She covered her mouth. So inappropriate. She had guests, after all. "Everybody stay where you are." Her eyes adjusted to the darkness, the three-quarter moon providing a little illumination. "I have some candles and a flashlight in a drawer." She navigated through the gloom, finding the drawer and pulling out the flashlight triumphantly. She flicked on the switch and was rewarded with a bright beam, which almost immediately fizzled out. "Lord love a duck!"

"Maybe this evening wasn't meant to be?" Dave said, putting a hand on her shoulder.

"Nonsense. Just give me a minute." She had saved worse gatherings than this. She found the matches and lit a couple candles. "There we go." She held one up to her face, and looked around at her guests. The place was getting decidedly warm now. "Everyone okay?"

There was general assent.

"Dave, can you go take a look and see if the whole neighborhood is out?"

"Sure. Give me a candle."

"Here you go. Hopefully the outage will be short, and we can get on with the evening," she said reassuringly.

"Carmelina!" Dave called from the living room.

"What now?" She worked her way through the crowd of guests and entered the living room.

"Don't come in here!" Dave said, just as she came face to face with a small, furry mammal. "There's a skunk in the house!"

She backed away slowly, ducking into the kitchen just as the skunk turned to spray its musk in her direction.

"Everyone out through the garage door!" she ordered, pausing only to turn off the stove and oven.

It was a total rout.

They gathered on the front lawn. The skunk had run away after it had done its damage. Carmelina had closed the door to her house on the whole sordid affair.

She surveyed the dark street and then the stars above. It was a beautiful night. The evening could still be saved. "Anyone want to order pizza?"

37. SISTER CLARA

She looked at herself in the unfamiliar mirror. She had aged a lot these last few years, the fine lines around her eyes spreading and deepening. Her skin had lost that youthful glow somewhere along the way.

She supposed it happened to everyone. Losing Arthur had done her no favors in the youthfulness department either.

She put on her makeup, taking a decade off her age in the process, and did her hair. She checked the mirror once more and decided she was presentable enough to go see a nun.

"Everything okay in there?" Dave called from the hallway.

"Yeah, I'm good." Her neighbor and tenant had taken her in after the disaster the night before at her own house. "Hey, where the hell is your toothpaste?"

"Middle drawer, right in front."

She loved teasing Dave. She'd seen the way he and Marcos had interacted at dinner before things had gone off the rails. She hoped…

No. she didn't want to jinx it. Dave deserved to be happy again.

In five more minutes, she was ready to go.

Her heart beat nervously in her chest. Part of her wanted to remain ignorant about her daughter. But a bigger part *needed* to know.

"I'll be back this afternoon to start figuring out what to do with my mess of a house." She kissed Dave on the cheek.

"Are you okay? Really?" They'd stayed up late after the party, talking about her decision.

She nodded. "I think it's time."

He pulled her in for a long hug. "Good luck," he whispered, kissing her on the cheek.

~

She drove across town in a daze.

She searched for the address along S Street, passing it three times before she realized it was in a drab old two-story brick building, tucked behind a row of half-bare trees, their yellowed leaves scattered along the sidewalk in random piles.

She parked on the street and entered the building through a golden archway, finding a young woman with blue-framed glasses and casual business attire seated behind an old wooden desk inside.

This wasn't how she had pictured this place at all. Nuns were supposed to wear black-and-white habits, live in beautiful white churches surrounded by green fields, and make cheese with their own hands. She grinned at the image.

This place looked and smelled like a high school admin office.

"May I help you?" Her name tag said Mary Elena. She had a nice smile.

"I'm here to see Sister Clara? I have an appointment."

"Up the stairs and down the hall. Room 201. I'll let her know you are coming."

"Thanks. I like the glasses." She climbed the stairs, wondering if stairs had gotten taller since she was younger. More and more, she appreciated the modern technology of elevators and escalators.

Room 201 had a wooden door with that old, obscuring glass they were so fond of fifty years before.

She tapped lightly on the glass.

"Come in."

Carmelina opened the door carefully. "Sister Clara?"

The woman nodded. "Let me make some room for you."

The tiny office was cluttered with paper, stacks of it in folders on the desktop, on the two chairs in front of the desk, spilling out of notebooks on the three bookshelves that were crammed along one side wall.

In the middle of the desk was a truly ancient computer, one with an amber screen that only showed numbers and letters and other characters.

"Please, sit."

Carmelina sat down on the hard wooden chair. "Thank you so much for seeing me. I was afraid you wouldn't want to tell me anything."

Sister Clara was dressed more traditionally, in a long black habit with a white scapular but without the veil. "Since *that film* came out… we have tried to change our image. We are not heartless."

Carmelina knew which film she meant. The one about the poor British woman who had lost her child when she had borne it out of wedlock. "I never thought you were heartless. Strict, sure. But not heartless." She rubbed her hip, remembering the spankings she'd endured in Catholic school. She hadn't been a model student.

Sister Clara smiled, just a little. Then her severe frown returned. "I went back into the church archives, and it's partly because of what I found that I decided to share this with you." She picked up a file in a manila folder and handed it to Carmelina. "That's everything we know."

Carmelina opened it. There was a copy of the adoption form, as well as a few old photos and some handwritten notes. "Her name is Andrea," she said in wonder. "Where is she now?"

The nun's expression changed to sorrow. "I am so sorry to be the one to tell you this." She looked out the window at the sky for a moment, as if deciding just what to say. "Andrea was killed by a drunk driver fifteen years ago, right here in Sacramento." She handed over a printout of a newspaper article.

Carmelina's heart stopped.

It wasn't true. It couldn't be true. Her daughter, the one she had given up to give her a chance at a better life with a good family…. "No."

"I'm so sorry. It must be terrible to learn about it this way. The article said it was instantaneous…."

"I have to go." She was trying not to cry. Not here. Not in front of the Sister. "Can I keep these?"

Sister Clara nodded. "They're yours. We have someone here you can talk to, if you want. Father Dyson is very good with these sorts of…"

Carmelina was already in the hallway, then careening down the stairs.

"Is everything okay?" Mary Elena asked.

"No," Carmelina managed and ran out the door to her car.

She made it inside before her control broke down altogether, and she sobbed like a baby, her heart broken in two.

38. TWO DATES

BEN LOOKED UP AT THE CLOCK. IT WAS A QUARTER PAST ELEVEN IN THE morning. He was seated in the hospital waiting area, and Ella had fallen asleep with her head in his lap. It was something that made him both enormously pleased and rather uncomfortable.

He'd catnapped on and off in the chair, and now his back ached, but he didn't want to disturb her sleep. This wasn't how he'd pictured their first date.

After a few minutes, Ella stirred, sitting up. She pushed back a lock of her long red hair and smiled sheepishly at him. "Did I fall asleep on your lap?"

"Yeah… kind of." Her voice flooded him with warmth.

"I'm so sorry." She brushed her wrinkled blouse. "I hardly know you. You really didn't have to stay."

"I don't mind." He was honored that she'd called him. And she had been really upset about what had happened to her brother. She had needed *someone*.

"Any news about Max?" She glanced anxiously at his hospital room.

He shook his head. "I just woke up. Should we go see?"

"Come on." She took his hand and led him toward her brother's room and pushed open the door quietly. Max lay there, unconscious. The left side of his face was scraped up, and his left arm was wrapped in bandages with a splint. He'd been really lucky that he hadn't been killed. And it had happened just a few blocks from the Everyday Grind.

One of the nurses was standing by his bedside.

"How is he?" Ella asked softly.

"You'll have to talk to the doctor," the nurse said, giving her arm a compassionate squeeze as she left the room.

Ella sat next to her brother's bedside, taking his hand. "I'm here, Max."

Ben felt uncomfortable witnessing such intimacy. "Maybe I should go...."

"Please, stay. It helps to have someone here."

They sat in silence for a few minutes, then there was a knock on the door.

"Mrs.... Jackson-Cucinelli?" The doctor poked her head in the door.

Ella stood. "That's me. How is he?"

But wait, was she *married*?

"I'm Doctor Bashari." She picked up the chart. "Your brother is doing well. There was some internal bleeding, but we addressed that in surgery. It's too early to say for sure, but he is likely to make a full recovery."

Ella threw her arms around Ben, hugging him tight. "Oh God. I am so relieved."

He held her tightly. He hated to even think it, but he hoped Max would stay unconscious just a little while longer.

Brad looked around the little Italian restaurant. It was a bit modern for his tastes. He liked things a little more mid-century than twenty-first century. But it was cute and clean, and the aroma coming from the kitchen was tantalizing. "I'm surprised there aren't more people here."

Sam nodded. "Diego's amazing with the food, and Matteo is the consummate host, but I don't think they know much about marketing."

A nice place like this in the Fabulous Forties should be bustling for lunch on a Friday afternoon. Instead there were only ten guests.

Matteo arrived carrying two plates. "Here we have a specialty of the house. *Le piadine di Diego Bellei.*"

The piadina was a warm, fresh flatbread whose aroma made Brad's mouth water. It was folded and filled with melted cheese and prosciutto.

"Eat it like a sandwich," Matteo advised, miming the action. "Would you like some wine?"

"Nothing for me. Just some iced tea."

Matteo nodded. "And for you?"

Sam shook his head. "Water's good."

Brad took a bite of the piadina. It was fantastic. They'd never managed to eat the ones the night before. "Oooh, that's delicious. And Diego's good with Marissa?"

"He's amazing." Sam bit into his own piadina. "Mmm. That *is* good. Yeah, he's great with everyone, but I think he has a soft spot for her."

Matteo brought his iced tea.

"Can you sit with us for a moment?" He wanted to get Matteo's take.

Matteo nodded. "Let me check in with our other guests, and then I can sit with you."

He returned a couple minutes later and pulled up a chair. "What did you want to talk about?"

"That idea I had last night. We have a lot of kids at the Center who have been kicked out of their homes, like Marissa. Their families don't understand them."

Matteo nodded. "This happens also in Italy."

"We try to find transitional housing for them. But they also need work experience. I just got a grant that I want to use to fund a pilot program. Do you know what that is?"

Matteo shook his head. "*Boh*… A program for pilots?"

Brad laughed. "No. It's a test. And if it goes well, it may become permanent."

"Oh, *sì*. I know what you mean."

"I'd like to send some of the kids, the ones who have an interest, over here to work for you. We would pay for the program."

Matteo's eyes lit up. "That would be fantastic."

"And the Center could help get the word out to the community about this place having gay owners, right?" Sam looked at him expectantly.

Brad nodded. He'd been thinking about that. "One of the roles of the Center is to support gay-owned businesses in Sacramento. Have you joined the Chamber?"

"The Chamber?" Matteo shook his head.

"It's a group of LGBT-owned businesses. It's a great way to network. To meet other people in the community."

"Ah. Yes, I would like that."

"Perfect. I'll put together a proposal, and we can set up a meeting next week. I'd like to move quickly on this. These kids are falling through the cracks all the time."

"Through the cracks?" Matteo looked at him quizzically.

"Getting lost in the system."

"Ah, I understand. It's a great idea. Let me talk to Diego this weekend."

"Perfect." Brad grinned. He'd been hoping to expand the Center's reach since he'd become its director, and now he had his chance.

39. OUTCASTS AND VAGABONDS

MARISSA TRUDGED DOWN THE HALLWAY TOWARD THE LUNCHROOM, LOST in her thoughts. The night before at Carmelina's had been *nice*. Like having a home again, at least until things had gone all to hell.

There'd been a *fucking skunk* in the house! Like that *ever* really happened.

And Carmelina's kitchen…. It reminded Marissa of the place she'd gone in her head when she'd helped Diego make the piadines. Warm. Friendly. Home.

Marcos was sweet, but his place was impersonal. It was good to have a bedroom, but it wasn't really hers.

Sometimes she missed her mom. Her *adopted* mom. Even if she was a coldhearted bitch sometimes. She missed vaping too. Marcos wouldn't let her do it, like she wasn't already almost an adult. Maybe Jason had a vape pipe.

She turned the corner into the lunchroom and stopped dead. The table she and Jason had chosen had a huge, hand-lettered banner over it that said, "The Outcasts Society." Jason himself stood below it, a huge grin on his face.

He wasn't alone. He bounded up to her like a puppy. "Look, 'Rissa! It's great, right? I made it last night with my Mom."

Underneath the makeshift banner was a collection of kids—short kids, skinny kids, fat kids, kids with tats, kids with pierced noses, kids with big glasses—and they all turned toward her expectantly. *Lead us*, their wistful gazes said.

It was all too much. She hadn't bargained on this.

Marissa turned and ran, Jason's voice trailing after her.

He found her ten minutes later in Ms. McCluskey's English classroom, eating her sandwich all alone. She saw his face at the door and turned away. She didn't want to talk to him, not right now.

The door opened.

"Marissa… you okay?"

"Leave me alone." She felt like she was five years old again, and that just embarrassed her more.

Jason sat down at the desk next to her and was silent for a few minutes.

She finished her sandwich, ignoring him. Marcos had packed her carrots and a bag of gummi bears. She set aside the former and tackled the latter.

"I'm not going away," Jason said at last.

"I wish you would." She regretted it almost immediately. He was a sweet kid. He didn't deserve her anger.

But he didn't seem offended. He put a hand on her shoulder.

She shrugged him off. "Hey, don't do that! I might hit you."

He actually laughed. "You wouldn't do that. I trust you." He gave her a big grin.

He trusts me. It took a minute for that to sink in. This silly gay kid *trusted* her. She'd done nothing to earn it. In fact, she'd done exactly the opposite. She'd run away from him and his silly banner. Yet here he was.

Maybe she could try to act more than five years old. Just this once. "You know you're an idiot, right?"

He nodded. "Been told so many times. Will you at least come and meet the Society?"

"Do I have to? I'm not big on leading."

He laughed. "Who stood up on the table yesterday and called all the misfits together?"

He had a point. "All right. I'll come. But I'm not promising anything."

In the end, she found she had twelve new friends and allies. And she hardly had to lead at all.

Carmelina pulled into her driveway, feeling numb.

Someone had parked their Mercedes in front of her house.

Daniele was sitting on her front step.

"What the hell are you doing here?" she asked, getting out of the car. She was irritated and in no mood to deal with his shit.

He stood and smiled sheepishly. "Good afternoon to you too. I came to apologize."

"Apology accepted. Now leave me alone. I've had a bad day, and it's about to get worse." She had to deal with her house issues and was not looking forward to the mess inside. She pushed past him, but he took her arm gently and stopped her.

"*Bella donna*, I am so sorry. I reacted badly when you asked me about the cross tattoo on my wrist. It has… a lot of personal significance to me."

His accent melted her.

She tried to resist. Really, she did. He had acted like a total bastard two days before, when he had pulled a wham-bam-thank-you-ma'am and left in a huff.

And yet, he was *so beautiful*. And he liked her.

She owed him a hearing. Didn't she?

"Well, come on inside. But I gotta warn you, it's like Dante's Inferno in there." She opened the door and let him in.

The pungent smell of skunk lingered in the air, making her eyes water.

She opened the living room windows. "Want to get the others? I need to air the place out."

Daniele grimaced at the smell. "What happened in here?"

"It's a long story. I think I have a vengeful ghost."

She'd meant it as a jest, but he nodded, looking around at the damage. "I think you may be right. Your husband…"

"Arthur?" She snorted. "You think Arthur's haunting me?"

He nodded. "It's possible. My mother believed in the spirit world—curses, and ghosts, and the paranormal. When I was five, one of my uncles haunted our house for a month. Did he die here?"

She closed her eyes, remembering that dark day three months before. "Yes."

"Maybe he's not ready for you to move on just yet."

"I don't know if I believe in that sort of thing. But if I did… how would you get rid of it?" Or should she? If it was really Arthur…

"You have to have an exorcism."

She stared at him, her mouth hanging open. "An exorcism? That's just batshit crazy."

She looked around the room. It smelled of skunk, the walls were coated in flour, and the bathroom was a terrible mess. The burned spot in the center of the table glared back at her.

Nothing ventured, nothing gained.

"Where do I find a good priest?"

40. FIRST DATE

Ben prowled through the hospital florist shop, looking for the perfect flowers, something he could afford. He glanced at his watch. It was a quarter to six—dinner time.

Being a barista was a wonderful job. It left his mind free for his writing—plotting poor Jesse's next steps—and he loved the people he got to meet, but the pay left something to be desired.

The woman behind the counter was frowning at him over her thick glasses. Ben knew that look. The cashier was trying to *read* him. He knew he passed pretty well these days, but every now and then, something he did or said or maybe even something undefinable about him that he was unaware of tripped something in someone else's brain.

He picked up a bouquet of pink roses—roses for romance, pink because red just didn't seem appropriate, under the circumstances—and plopped them down on the counter. They weren't *too* expensive.

He'd been very careful with his funds these last six months. His meagre Everyday Grind salary and his severance package from Intel had to tide him over for another six months so he could finish his novel and see it published. After that... well, he was trying really hard not to think about what came next.

"That all?" Katia the cashier asked, her voice just a little lower than he might have expected, her face a little fuller.

And Ben *knew*. He could *read*, too.

"Yup, that will do it." He grinned, and she smiled back at him, the shared secret between them.

"Fifteen Thirty-Six," Katia said.

He handed over a credit card, wondering once again just how many others like them there were in the world. How many people slipped through life in their new roles, mostly unnoticed. What it would be like to be someone who couldn't *pass*? He signed his receipt.

"Hope they like them," Katia said.

He winked and tucked the roses under his arm and his wallet in his back pocket.

He started back through the halls of the antiseptic facility. He tried to forget how much he hated hospitals. His father had spent his final days in one, as his body slowly shut down. Alzheimer's was an asshole of a disease. In his father's case, his body had simply forgotten how to breathe.

His own mother had told him to leave. She'd said his father didn't need to see what a "shemale bitch" his own daughter had become. So Ben had taken to sneaking in at night to spend time with his father.

She had banned him from the funeral too—the last straw. They hadn't seen each other or even spoken since, going on five years now.

Five minutes later, he eased open the door to Max's hospital room.

Ella sat there, beautiful as ever, holding Max's hand, a perfectly silent tableau. A frown creased her forehead.

He cleared his throat softly.

She looked up at him, and a smile lit up her face. "Hey."

"Any change?"

She shook her head. "He's stable. That's all they will tell me."

He nodded. "That's something, at least. Are you hungry?"

"I don't know. I should be, I guess. I haven't eaten hardly anything today."

"You need to keep your strength up. He gestured to her. "Come on."

"I hate hospital food."

"I know, but we'll find something we can eat." He took her hand and pulled her gently out into the hall after him.

"What are you up to?" She glanced back at the door to Max's room.

"You've had a hard day. Trust me." He smiled encouragingly.

Soon they arrived at the hospital cafeteria, which was bustling at this time in the evening. He led her to a table in the corner. When she saw it, she laughed. "What have you done?"

He'd borrowed a white bed sheet and had set up the little table with a couple candles from the gift shop and the flowers. "Tonight was supposed to be our first date, after all."

The room around them erupted into applause. He blushed. he hadn't intended for this to be a public spectacle.

For the meal, he'd run up the street to Centro to snag her a burrito and himself a plate of beef tacos. "I figured you liked Mexican food—I did catch you at Zocalo, after all." He pulled out the chair for her and handed her a paper napkin. "Okay, so this is not quite how I pictured it—"

"It's beautiful." Her eyes were wet.

He hastened to lighten the mood. "Well, it's not Zocalo, but it's pretty good. For *Sacramento* Mexican."

She laughed. "I guess I *did* promise you a date. But Max—"

"Is going to be fine." He took her hand, trying to push love and support from his hand into her skin. "You're staying with him? Eat! Before it gets cold!"

She picked up her burrito. "Yes, for a couple months until I find my own place." She took a bite. "Damn, that's good."

He nodded. "You really need someone to show you around the city. You can get a lot here without spending too much money." Except for rent. He was lucky. His had been the same for the last couple years. "So what brought you to Sacramento?"

Her expression darkened. She looked away across the room, frowning. When she spoke again, her voice was dull. "A bad divorce." She set her half-eaten burrito down on the plate.

"Hey, I didn't mean to upset you," he said, seeing her slipping away from him. "We can talk about something else."

She shook her head. "I'm sorry. I'm not really hungry. I shouldn't have left Max alone." She stood and kissed his forehead. "This was really sweet of you, Ben. Thank you."

He watched her leave, befuddled by what had just happened. Clearly he'd hit a nerve.

Was her ex a real asshole? Shit, did he die?

He dropped his taco and ran after her. Their first date was *not* going to end in ruin.

41.SECRETS SHARED

Ben caught up with Ella just outside of Max's room. "Hey," he called, a little out of breath. "You forgot these." He handed her the pink roses.

"They're so nice," she said, taking them and holding them up to smell them. "You must think I'm a total mess."

"No more than I am."

She snorted. "Not likely. Just moved to a strange city, brother in the hospital, crying at the drop of a hat. Tell me one thing about your life that's crazier than mine right now."

Ben took a deep breath. "I'm a trans guy in love with a cis girl."

She looked up at him, her eyes wide. "You're trans?"

Ben sighed. "Yes. I'm sorry. This is probably the worst time to tell you."

"Why would you say that?" She put a hand up to his cheek. It was warm and soft.

"Because… because it's *always* the worst time. Look, I'm sorry. I'll take off. You have your brother to take care of." He started to turn away. "I never should have—"

"Ben." Her voice was firm and stopped him in his tracks.

"What?"

"I don't mind."

"About what?"

"I don't mind if you're trans." She sank down on the bench against the wall and pulled him down with her. "My moms is trans too."

"Your moms?"

She nodded. "Lexi. She used to be my dad, Alex. She transitioned about ten years ago."

Ben took a moment to absorb that.

"I thought you might be. Oh, not 'cause you're effeminate or anything. But I've learned to spot the signs. I think it's one of the things I liked about you when we first met."

Ben was at a loss. This had literally never happened to him before. Girls he liked always freaked out and ran when he told them. "Sorry. I'm speechless."

"Stop saying 'sorry'." She leaned in and kissed him quickly. It only lasted a second, but it opened up a world of possibilities in Ben's head. "You should go home; get some rest. I'll be okay here now. I can call you if anything changes."

Ben nodded. "Can I come back to see you tomorrow?"

Ella grinned. "You'd better. After all, your first date wasn't exactly a smashing success, was it? You owe me another one."

Someone was banging on the front door. Irritated, Dave paused his DVD player. It was just a rerun of Gilmore Girls. It could wait. "Who is it?"

"Your annoying landlady."

Dave grinned and pulled the door open. "What the hell do you want? Come on in."

Carmelina settled into an oversized leather armchairs in the living room and sighed. "I finally got the mess cleaned up at home, no thanks to you."

"Sorry. I've been busy," he lied.

She looked around. "I can see that!"

Magazines were strewn around the living room, and his favorite blanket was on the couch next to him, along with an oversized coffee mug half filled with melting Tin Roof Sundae ice cream. "It was a long day. I was working with a client in midtown who wanted advice on how to fire his staff and move all the jobs to China."

"Fucking capitalist bastards."

Dave snorted. "About right. So what's up?"

"Do you mind if I stay with you for a couple more days?"

"Of course. You don't even have to ask. This is your house, after all."

"I know, but I don't like to impose." She looked out the window into the darkness, toward her own place. "It'll just be until Sunday morning."

"What's happening Sunday morning? Plumber coming?"

She shook her head. "He's already gone. I'm having some work done."

He nodded. "No problem. Hey, what happened at Catholic Charities? Any leads on your daughter?"

Carmelina immediately started to tear up. She hardly ever showed her emotions, not even to him. Dave jumped up and sat next to her on the edge of the chair. "What happened?"

She shook her head. "It's stupid. It's been decades since I let her go. She probably didn't even think about me."

"What?"

She looked at him, and her eyes were red from crying. "She's gone. Some drunk asshole killed her sixteen years ago, and I didn't even know it."

"Crap." He hugged her fiercely. "Oh God, I'm so sorry."

She cried on his shoulder, squeezing him tight. She had been so hopeful. *First Arthur, and now this.* "I don't even get to see her," she said through sobs. "To tell her I loved her."

"I'm sure she knew."

At last she let him go, wiping her eyes. "You don't know what it means to have you here. When Arthur died, I thought I'd never sleep in that bed again."

"I know. I remember." Those last few months with John, when he'd had to do everything—from feeding him to wiping his ass—had been long, and brutal. And precious beyond words. When he'd finally gone... "I know," he repeated.

Carmelina blew her nose. "I know you do." She got *that* little gleam in her eye. "So... Marcos?"

Dave stared at her. "Seriously? From mental breakdown to matchmaker in sixty seconds?"

Carmelina shrugged. "It's what I do. It makes me feel better. Now spill."

He sighed. "We have a date tomorrow night."

"Oh my God, that's fantastic!"

"Well, don't get your hopes up. I am a little rusty at the whole dating thing. He'll probably take one look at me, turn around, and run away."

She took him by the chin. "Listen to me. You are a wonderful, fantastic, loving man, and Marcos would be lucky to have you. Got it?"

"Yes, ma'am." Carmelina could be frightening when she got too serious.

"Good. now do you think he'll still be around Sunday morning?"

"Will you be?"

She ignored him. "Answer the question."

"Um... I hope so?"

"Good. You can both come to my exorcism."

42. FAST FOOD AND LATE NIGHTS

Sometimes the words just flowed. Every author knew how it was. There were moments when it felt like you'd tapped into some other place, some real *thing* that was happening as you typed, and the words just poured out onto the page as if you were the conduit for a greater story.

And then there were times like this.

> *Cody stared at the file…*
> *Cody glared at the file…*
> *Cody shot a glance at the file…*

"Cody doesn't know what the fuck he's doing." Sam was on a self-imposed deadline to get his next novel out to the publisher by the end of October— twenty-nine days and counting. But at this rate, he'd be lucky to have half of a first draft. Maybe he should have waited for NaNoWriMo. The National Novel Writing Month always inspired him to plow ahead, forcing him to ignore his inner critic.

He glanced at the clock. It was a quarter after nine already. *Crap, where did the time go?* He hadn't eaten anything since lunch, and his brain was refusing to cooperate. He was sick of looking at the screen.

As if on cue, Brad popped his head into the den. He was in his bathrobe, which he still managed to make look sexy. Brad, at thirty, looked great. He made each one of those years look good. "You almost done?"

Sam nodded, closing the laptop. "I'm packing it in for the night. I'll go grab something to eat from the fridge…"

Brad was shaking his head. "Follow me."

He led Sam out into the living room. The lights were out, but there were candles all around. One of their blankets was spread on the floor, and a stack of Chinese takeout boxes adorned the center.

"When did you do all of this?" That's when he noticed a fire flickering in the fireplace.

"I ran out about half an hour ago for the food. I know how hard you're working on the book, and I thought you could use a break."

"You're amazing," Sam said, pulling Brad in for a kiss. "So what do we have?"

"Um, orange chicken, Thai basil noodles, and some yellow curry chicken." He popped open the boxes and handed Sam a pair of chopsticks. "Oh, and some brown rice."

Sam picked up one of the boxes and pulled out a big piece of orange chicken. "It's fantastic," he said between mouthfuls. "Here, try." He put a piece in Brad's mouth.

"Holy crap, that's good."

"Where did you go?"

"PF Chang's. It's a chain, I know. But the food's good."

"Oh my God, I'm hungry." Sam wolfed down half the box. "I still remember the day we moved in here together last year," he said between bites. "When this place was brand new to us."

Brad nodded. "It's been a year already?"

"Last month. Oooh, you have to try the noodles." He held out a chopstick full, and a few of them fell onto Brad's chest. "Sorry." But he didn't *really* feel sorry about it at all. Instead, he leaned forward and licked them up off Brad's furry pecs.

"Don't get me started, unless you plan to finish me off too," Brad said, giving him the *look*.

In response, Sam pushed him gently onto the blanket and spilled noodles onto his own chest.

Brad grinned and pulled Sam down to kiss him, laughing as the noodles got stuck between them, skin to skin. Maybe it would be a good night after all.

~

Matteo growled at his computer screen. He and Diego had sat down together to analyze their business, finding places to make cuts and save a little money.

They'd have to let one of the expediters go. Diego would simplify the menu to cut down on the ingredients they needed to stock in the restaurant's kitchen. And they would forgo their own salaries for a while. Combined, the changes would buy them another month. Maybe two, if they were careful, long enough to give this new plan with the Center time to kick in.

It looked good on paper, but now his PC was acting up.

Diego had told him he should have bought a Mac. But Macs were *so* expensive. *Next time*, he thought. If they had any money left to their names.

It was late. Diego had gone to bed a couple hours before, but Matteo had tossed and turned, worrying that they hadn't done enough. That there was something he was overlooking, some key that would turn it all around.

If there was, he couldn't see it.

There was a loud crash behind him.

He jumped up, looking wildly around the room.

A photo album lay open on the floor where it had fallen off one of the bookshelves that lined the little den.

He peered back toward the bedroom. Diego seemed to have slept right through the noise.

Matteo stooped to pick up the album.

It was full of pictures from his childhood, photos of trips the family had taken around Italy and Europe. School photos. The old house in Imola where he had grown up. "'*I*' is for '*Imola*'..." he whispered, thumbing through the pages. How had it fallen? Everything else was neatly in place.

Then he saw it.

The photo was from a trip to Rome when he'd been eight years old. They'd stopped by a *tavola calda*—the Italian equivalent of a McDonalds, but so much better. The fast food there had been amazing, well made, and cheap to produce.

He stared at the grainy image for a long time.

Maybe it could work here.

There was a big University campus close by, and legions of cars passed by every morning and night. If they sold good Italian food, quickly, at reasonable prices...

He turned back to his computer and started searching for hard data. He needed to know if this was viable before he presented it to Diego.

43. IS SOMETHING BURNING?

"I thought you two were going out." Marissa sat at the dinner table, working on her math homework. She was clearly more interested in Marcos's love life.

"I thought *you* had a test to prepare for," he shot back as he checked the pasta sauce. He was far more comfortable making Mexican cuisine than a simple Italian dinner. Give him a sack of pinto beans, some chicken, and a couple hours, and he could whip up a dinner to rival his mother's own. She'd told him so herself.

He'd promised Dave Italian though, so Italian it would have to be.

"I've got all weekend to study. So what happened?" She came over to see what he was making. "Smells good."

The water was boiling. He poured in the whole-wheat pasta—Trader Joe's was magic for decent, healthy fare—and checked the garlic bread in the oven.

A quick glance at the clock showed he had a good fifteen minutes until his guest arrived. "*You* happened. I realized it wasn't a good idea to leave you unsupervised on a Saturday night."

Marissa snorted. "Like I have anything to do."

"I thought you made some new friends?" He tasted the sauce. Not bad. It needed a little more garlic.

"Jason and the Outcasts? They're not real big on the social scene, if you know what I mean."

He laughed. "I don't have a clue. Hey, as long as you're not studying, could you set the table?"

"Sure." She put her books back in her bedroom. "Which dishes?"

"The blue-and-white ones."

"Oh, fancy. You must like this guy." She stared at the table for a minute. "What am I going to do for dinner?"

"Eat with us, of course."

"On your date?" She screwed up her face. "Isn't that kinda… weird?"

"You're a part of my life now. Besides, I want to take things slow with this one."

"Whatever." She set the table for three. "How come you aren't *with* someone?"

"I'm with you."

"You know what I mean."

It was a question he'd asked himself before, but there was no one good answer. "I guess I just wasn't ready. I liked going out to the bars. Meeting new guys, being forever young." He sighed. "I'll be forty next year. I don't turn the heads of the cute guys like I used to."

"Damn, you *are* old."

He flicked her with the kitchen towel. "Wait until you're my age and alone." He smelled something.

"Um… I think the bread is burning."

"Dammit." He opened the oven and a burst of smoke filled the kitchen. "It's not too bad." He peered at the darkened pieces of bread. "Maybe I can scrape off the worst of it."

"Forget it," Marissa said, looking over his shoulder with a frown. "It's a lost cause."

"At least the pasta is all right.…" He tasted the sauce and spat it out into the sink. "Crap. I think I used too much garlic."

She tried it. "Um, yeah, that's pretty bad." She glanced at the boiling water. "At least the spaghetti looks okay."

"He's going to be here in ten minutes. I don't have enough time to start over from scratch!" He dumped the sauce down the drain and went to open the living room window to let out the smoke. *This* was why he hated dating.

"Calm down. Give me your phone."

"It's on my desk. What are you going to do?"

"Get you Caviar."

"I don't see how that'll help. The stuff is vile. And where would you even find it?"

"It's a delivery app. We'll have dinner here in no time—I'll get something from Paesanos. Just clean up this mess, fast."

~

Dave knocked on the door. Marcos's condo was in a nice building—one of those refurbished older ones.

He hoped Marcos liked the flowers he'd chosen. He'd stopped by the Safeway on R Street to pick some up and had chosen this batch of daisies because it was dyed in rainbow colors. Now he was second guessing his choice. Rainbow—how cheesy was that? Frantically, he looked around for a place to stash them, but the hallway was bare. Maybe if…

The door swung open, and Marissa, Marcos's foster child—he thought, but he really wasn't clear on that—opened the door.

"Hi Dave. Come on in." She ushered him in side. "Your date is here!" she shouted. "He brought flowers!"

Dave sighed.

Marco's place was a lot like the man—sleek, modern, and warm. Shelves against one wall were filled with books, mostly biographies, from the look of them. A copy of Justin Trudeau's biography sat on the living room table. Dark leather furniture gave the place a loft feel, and the scraped hardwood floors finished the look.

Marcos appeared from the kitchen. "Sorry to keep you waiting."

"For you," Dave said, holding the bouquet up with a weak smile. "I hope you like flowers…."

"They're beautiful." He took them and rummaged up a vase from the kitchen, depositing them neatly inside. "Have a seat."

It smelled a little like smoke. "Is something burning?"

Marcos flashed a rueful smile. "I ruined dinner. I was doing too many things, and it got away from me."

"We can go out, if you'd rather." *Nice to know he's human.*

Marcos shook his head. "Marissa used an app to order dinner. I hope you like Paesano's."

"I'll be in my bedroom," Marissa said with a smile. "Call me when dinner gets here!" Her door closed behind her.

"She seems like a good kid," Dave observed.

Marcos looked unhappy.

"What?"

"I *really* like you," Marcos said after a moment.

Dave laughed. "I like you too. What's wrong with that?"

Marcos fidgeted. "I… *don't* want to sleep with you."

Ouch. "Okay. I get it. You don't think I'm attractive." He started to get up.

"No. I mean, I do want to. I think you're *really cute*. I haven't been able to stop thinking about you since Thursday."

Dave sat back down on the leather couch. "Ah, okay… so?"

"I have a bad habit of jumping in bed with guys I hardly know and then finding out we're incompatible the day after." Marcos looked him in the eye. "I think we could be something together. I don't want to make that mistake with you."

Dave grinned. Here he'd been nervous about jumping back in the saddle again, but taking it slow suited him just fine. "I think that could work for me." He leaned forward to kiss Marcos.

It was sweet, and it made his heart thump a little harder.

The doorbell rang.

Marco's eyes sparkled. "Dinner is here."

44. A PROPOSAL

Diego put away the last of the dishes and mopped down the floor of the restaurant kitchen. They'd had almost forty diners over the course of the night. Fantastic news, but coming just after they'd let go of Justin, it had made for a long night for the two of them.

"It'll be easier once we've been at it a few months," Matteo had told him before they'd embarked on this mad adventure together. "We'll hire a good manager, take nights off. You'll see."

Well, he'd seen, all right. Here he was at a quarter after eleven, cleaning up after a long day in the kitchen. And where was Matteo?

Upstairs, on the computer.

Not that he could complain, really. Matteo had forgiven him for something far worse.

He stashed the cleaning supplies, took one last look around the kitchen, and headed upstairs.

Matteo was in his little den, as expected, his face bathed in blue light from the computer screen.

"*Cosa fai?*" Diego complained, shucking his apron and shirt.

"In English," Matteo chided.

"*Sono troppo stanco per l'inglese.*"

Matteo gave him a pitying look, but switched over to speak in Italian. "Everything cleaned and locked up downstairs?"

Diego nodded. "That was some rush we had today. If every day was like that…"

"…we could hire some more help."

"If only!" He pulled down his pants.

Matteo glanced over and whistled. "My sexy Italian boyfriend."

"Husband."

"Not at the moment. Besides, it's kind of a turn-on to think of you that way." Matteo closed his laptop and stood, stretching.

After all these years, he still looked good to Diego.

"Wanna hop in the shower with me?" Diego asked, swinging his underwear around playfully on one finger.

"I thought you'd never ask."

Afterwards, they lay together on the bed, still wired from the day and their shower together. Matteo ran his hand along Diego's back.

"Oooh, yes," Diego said, arching his back. "Scratch *right there*."

Matteo scratched up and down Diego's back lazily.

"Damn, that feels good."

Matteo climbed on top of Diego and began to massage his shoulders. "How about that?"

"Yes, please."

Diego's back was spotted with little freckles, but they were almost hidden by his all-over tan. Matteo had always liked those freckles.

He knew that Diego slipped up to their rooftop to take a little sun whenever he had the chance. Matteo had no idea where he found the time.

He'd called the hospital earlier in the day. Max still hadn't woken up.

"I made an appointment with an immigration attorney for Monday," he said. Matteo could feel Diego stiffen under his grip.

"Are you sure that's a good idea?"

"I think we have to. If we get caught… if Max wakes up… we could get thrown out of the country and never be allowed to come back in."

"I guess…."

"It will be all right. Brad recommended this one."

"You told him?" Diego twisted to look up at him.

"No. Just that we needed some advice." He kissed Diego's forehead, eliciting a deep sigh.

"I'm sorry I got you into this mess."

Matteo leaned down to kiss him. "Done is done. We'll figure it out. Speaking of which… I had an idea."

"About Max?"

"About Ragazzi." Time to make his pitch. "What if we could cut our costs and maybe make a little more money?"

Diego turned over, and Matteo lay down next to him. "How? I am not cutting corners on the ingredients. A job worth doing—"

"Is worth doing well. I know, I know. Here, look." He pulled out the photo he'd found the night before and handed it over to Diego.

Diego looked at it and smiled. "You were so cute back then."

"I'm not cute now. I'm fat. And hideous."

"You're *handsome* now." He touched Matteo's face gently. "How old were you?"

"About eight, I think."

"I wish we'd known each other then." He turned it over. "So what does *this* mean?" He held up the photo.

"I was going over the accounts when one of the photo albums fell off the bookcase. This photo popped out. I remember this trip. It was the first time I ever visited Rome, and they had this amazing restaurant there. The food was really good, and they served it pre-prepared so you could get it to go."

Diego frowned. "I'm not sure I want to serve prepared food."

"Think about it. The University is just a couple miles from here, with a huge student market. And what about the folks on their way home, out there on Folsom Blvd?"

"Maybe…"

"I found the owners of this place on Facebook. They're still there after all these years." He took back the photo and stared at it, remembering that day as clearly as if he'd just been there. "They wrote me back this morning. They said they'd be willing to give us some advice. And with the kids from the Center— Diego, I think we could really make this thing work."

Diego yawned. "I'm too tired to think about it tonight. Maybe we can talk about it more in a day or two?"

"Sure." He leaned forward and kissed Diego. "Wanna turn out the light?"

Diego reached out and flicked the switch on the bedside lamp. He snuggled up next to Matteo, putting his head against Matteo's shoulder.

Time enough to have a bigger discussion tomorrow. At the moment, Matteo was content just the way things were, with Diego in his arms.

45.BAGGAGE

Ben stared at his cell phone. On the plate next to it, a half-eaten slice of Eatuscany's pizza was quickly growing cold.

"What's wrong? You do not like the pizza?"

Ben looked up. Stefania, the restaurant's owner, looked at him quizzically.

"It's good," he said. "Really. I'm just not in the mood today, I guess."

She held out her hand "Want me to heat it up for you again?"

"Nah, I'm good. I might try some of your gelato in a bit though.…"

"Just come in when you're ready." She gave him a pat on the shoulder.

Ben liked this place, and he found Stefania's Italian accent charming. The food was good too. He sat at one of the sidewalk tables, watching the people go by, carrying chocolate treats from Ginger Elizabeth next door or frozen yogurt from the place on the corner.

In his mind, he went over the events of the previous night. Things had gone off the rails when he'd arrived at the hospital for his second "date" with Ella.

~

Ben held a dozen red roses in one hand, pressing the third-floor button impatiently with the other. She hadn't responded to his texts, but maybe her cell signal was weak in the hospital. Or maybe she was just too busy.

The doors opened, and Ben stepped out into the antiseptic halls of the third floor. They had moved Max out of the emergency room. Ben double checked the room number he'd gotten from the hospital operator.

He hesitated at the door to Max's room. What if she had changed her mind? What if she didn't want to see him anymore? Maybe this was all a bad idea. Maybe he should just leave her alone for a little while. Back off.

The decision was taken away from him as the door opened and he came face to face with a tall brunette woman. She was probably in her fifties, but she had Ella's features.

"Ah, you must be Ben." She didn't smile.

If he guessed right, this was Lexi, Ella's "moms." Ella must have told her about him. "Yes, I am. I came to see how she was doing. Are you her mother?"

Lexi smiled. "Yes, you could say that. Listen, Ella's asleep in there." She closed the door quietly behind her. "I was going to get some coffee. Would you like to come with me?"

"Um… sure?"

She pulled him gently away from Max's room by the arm. Ben looked over his shoulder at the closed door. He'd been *this* close.

"It's so nice to meet you. Ella told me all about you when I got to town this morning."

All about me? "How… how is Max doing?"

"He's still out. But the doctors are encouraged. Thanks for asking."

They arrived at the cafeteria. "The coffee here's fairly abysmal, but it does have caffeine in it to keep me awake. It's late, back where I came from."

"Where is that?" Ben grabbed himself a Pepsi. As a barista, he didn't think he could stomach hospital coffee.

"A little town in the Hamptons. Long Island."

Ben nodded like he knew what that meant. Closest he'd ever gotten to the Hamptons was watching *Royal Pains*.

They paid for their drinks and found a table in one corner of the cafeteria.

"I wanted to start off by saying how grateful I am to you for being here for Ella, when all this happened." She put a hand on his. "It was a relief knowing she wasn't facing this alone."

He nodded. "I was happy to. Ella's an amazing woman."

"Yes, she is. I assume she's told you about me?"

"Yes." No point in denying it. "She seemed very proud of you."

That made her smile. "It's mutual. You know how hard it is to transition. I spent the first fifteen years of my life in turmoil. Back then we didn't have a name for how I felt inside. Then another thirty-three years trying to live as someone else. You know how that is."

Yes, Ella had told her moms *everything*. "Yes, I do." He wasn't sure where she was going with this. "I lost a lot of family members when I transitioned. It was painful, but the alternative was worse."

"Yes." She sipped her coffee. "God, this really is awful today."

Ben laughed. "I work at the Everyday Grind. I can bring you something better tomorrow, if you'd like."

"I don't think that's a good idea, Ben."

"It's not a problem. Really! And trust me, I make far better brew than that swill."

"I mean, I don't think you should come back here. Ella's got a lot going on right now, and we're both worried about Max."

"What?"

"Look. We both know being trans comes with a lot of baggage. I'd rather see my daughter end up with someone… a little less complicated."

Ben couldn't believe what he was hearing. He looked down at the bunch of flowers on the table. They were already wilting from lack of water. "You don't want me dating your daughter… because I'm trans?"

"I wouldn't put it like that, but essentially, yes."

"But you're trans!"

She laughed, and this time it was a bitter sound. "Yes, yes, I am. So I'm in a good position to know what I'd be letting my daughter in for, aren't I?" She finished her coffee with a grimace and stood, holding out a hand. "I take it we understand each other?"

Stunned, he refused to shake it.

She shrugged and walked away. "It was nice to meet you, Ben."

Now he stared at the phone, trying to decide what to do.

Being trans comes with a lot of baggage.

The more he thought about it, the angrier he became. Sure, he had baggage. But who didn't? The trans community certainly hadn't cornered the market on baggage. He was supposed to leave Ella alone because her own mother was internally transphobic? *I don't think so.* Not unless he heard it from Ella herself.

He picked up the phone and sent her a text. *Can I meet you?*

A minute later, she replied. *Tomorrow. 12 PM. EG.*

It looked like they'd be having a second date after all.

46.EXORCISING THE PAST

Father Murphy, the priest who'd arrived with Daniele, reminded her of no one so much as the actor Emmet Walsh. He was short, with wispy tufts of silver hair and an air of utter certainty about himself and his place in the world that seemed—she felt bad for thinking it—sorely misplaced.

They were outside. It was a beautiful Sunday morning. "And you're… retired now?" she asked.

He nodded solemnly. "I do weddings, baptisms, blessings, and exorcisms to keep me busy. Frankly, I rarely get a good house exorcism anymore. What leads you to believe the house is haunted?"

"There have been strange things happening since my husband passed away."

Dave and Marcos had shown up for the grand event too. "I see a redheaded monster walking around inside sometimes," Dave said with a serious face.

"Redheaded monster. Interesting."

"Shut up!" Carmelina mouthed at him.

Dave stuck his tongue out at her behind the priest's back.

"What they mean to say," Daniele said, glaring at Dave, "is that there were a number of strange incidents this last week. I think her husband hasn't gone on to rest after his untimely passing."

"What sort of events?" Father Murphy raised a bushy white eyebrow.

Daniele looked at Carmelina.

"Well, let's see. A clogged toilet. Burned piadine. A power outage. Oh, and a skunk came in and smelled the place up."

"These all seem like normal things…."

"Not when they take place over less than half an hour."

He reached for something from behind his ear that wasn't there. "Where did I put that pencil again?" He looked around, confused.

"It's in your hand, Father." *Where did you find this guy?* Carmelina mouthed at Daniele.

"Ah, there it is." He smiled happily. "It's often difficult to tell if a house is haunted. Perhaps we should start with a simple exorcism and see if that helps?"

Carmelina shrugged. "You're the expert."

"And really, why overcomplicate an exorcism?" Marcos asked.

Father Murphy seemed to miss the sarcasm. "Yes, I agree. Shall we go inside?"

"Of course. I have to warn you, it smells a bit." She'd cleaned up most of the mess, but the skunk smell was still strong. She ushered everyone inside.

"Yes, it is rather pungent, isn't it?" Farther Murphy said, wrinkling his nose. "Ah well, sooner started, sooner finished." He pulled out a bottle of Kirkland water. "Consecrated it myself," he said with a kind smile.

"If you need any more, I have a case at home," Dave whispered.

Carmelina shushed him.

The Priest opened the bottle, taking some in his palm. "Is this where the worst of it occurred?" He looked around the living room.

Carmelina nodded. "The skunk attack was right about here."

He nodded and proceeded to splash the floor, the walls, and most of her furniture with flicks of Holy Costco Water.

"Not the Baumgardner!" Carmelina grabbed the watercolor painting off the wall just in time—a carousel horse she'd bought in a little gallery in Carmel the year before. "I'll put this back in the bedroom."

When he was done, he splashed each of them in turn.

Carmelina wiped the water from her face, scowling.

The priest opened a big leather-bound book and began to read. "In the Name of the Father, and of the Son, and of the Holy Ghost. Amen. Most glorious Prince of the Heavenly Armies…"

"This is a bunch of malarkey, you know."

Carmelina turned to find Arthur—her Arthur—sitting in his favorite chair, looking up at her through his coke-bottle glasses.

"If you wanted me to go, you could have just asked."

Carmelina stared at him. It wasn't possible. He'd been dead three months now.

None of the others seemed to notice the strange and somehow absurdly normal apparition in their midst, in his brown corduroy slippers and blue bathrobe. His pipe lay in an ash tray on the small table next to his chair, a lazy trail of smoke drifting up from the bowl.

"You're not really here," she said, frowning. "This is some kind of fever dream. I must be sick, or out of my mind—"

"Suit yourself. You always were right, after all."

It wasn't a dig. Arthur had told her, soon after they married, that as far as he was concerned, she *would* always be right.

She needed to sit down.

She took a seat next to him on the little couch they'd chosen together ten years before, with its embroidered upholstery—flowers—and Chippendale legs.

"He really does know how to ramble on, doesn't he?" Arthur said with a grin, glancing at the priest.

"…bind him and cast him into the bottomless pit, that he may no longer seduce the nations…"

She smiled in spite of herself. "I know, right? I'm only doing this because Daniele convinced me it was a good idea." Of course. She felt like an idiot. "Daniele. That's why you're angry."

Arthur chuckled. "I'm not angry. I want to see you happy."

"I wish you were still here," she said, putting a hand out on his. It felt warm, alive.

"You and me both. But when the Good Lord calls…"

"…you should have let it go to voicemail."

He laughed, that heartwarming and slightly nerdy guffaw of his, and her heart melted.

He put his other hand on hers. "Promise me something."

She nodded. "Anything." *Just stay with me a little while longer.*

"Ask Daniele about September twenty-third."

She raised an eyebrow. "What do you mean?"

"Just promise you will." He pulled her close to him and kissed her lightly on the lips. "Farewell, *caramia*. I loved you full and well."

"Don't go!" She tried to grab him, but her hand touched only air.

"…to keep us safe and sound. We beseech Thee through Jesus Christ Our Lord. Amen."

Water splashed on her face. Carmelina blinked, wiping it away from her eyes. She was standing next to Dave and Marcos.

"That should do it," Father Murphy said. "That'll be a hundred dollars."

"Excuse me?"

"Check or cash is fine. And here…" He handed her a card.

"Weddings & Exorcisms Unlimited—Hitch'em and Ditch'em. Very clever."

Dave snickered.

"Turn it over."

She looked on the back of the card. "Services rendered: weddings, funerals, blessings, baptisms, and exorcisms… buy two, get the third free." She glared at Dave. "Not a word."

"If you need me again—for a repeat performance, or if someone passes on —you'll get the next thing at no charge."

"Um… thank you?" She ushered him out the door, closing it behind him.

"That was educational," Dave said, smirking.

"Get out, all of you!" She pushed Dave and Marcos out the door. "I'll see you two later at Ragazzi."

She pulled Daniele back inside. "Dinner tonight?"

He nodded. "Sorry about that. He's a friend of my mother's."

"It's all right. It was… enlightening."

He kissed her lightly, and her mind flashed back to Arthur. "Seven o'clock?"

"Here?"

"Pick me up. This place isn't ready for public consumption." She'd gotten accustomed to the smell, but she was going to need a shower.

"Deal." Then he was gone.

September twenty-third.

She drifted over to the mantel, looking for Arthur's photo. She picked it up and laughed.

He was no longer scowling but was winking at her instead.

She held it to her chest and smiled.

47.SALT TO TASTE

Diego had prepped the chicken early for his Sunday afternoon class. He enjoyed being the teacher, sharing with others some of the dishes his mother had passed down to him.

It was one thing to make them in the Ragazzi kitchen alone or with the help of a sous chef. But it was quite another to pass them on to a whole new group of people who would take them home and make them their own.

Today, he planned to teach the class how to make an Italian classic: Chicken Cacciatore, or *Pollo alla Cacciatora con Patate alla Contadina*, as the Italians called it.

He had prepared three chickens, figuring that would be enough for his small class.

The bell on the front door chimed.

"*Ciao, bella*," he called out to Carmelina.

"*Ciao, bello*." She gave him a peck on each cheek.

Marcos and Marissa followed shortly after, along with the new guy, Dave, who'd been at Carmelina's disastrous dinner party.

"What are we making today?" Marcos asked.

"*Cosa?* Ah… What are we making?… *cosa facciamo*." He searched for the right words. "Kitchen… no, *chicken* alla cacciatora."

"Oooh, I love Chicken Cacciatore," Carmelina said. "My grandmother used to make it, Southern Italian style."

"This is Northern… *versione?*"

"Version."

The bell chimed again. This time it was Sam with Brad in tow, and following the two of them was Ben.

Diego smiled. "I think we all here…"

The bell chimed again. And again. Another group of people came in the door, three couples, two gay and one lesbian, from the looks of things.

Carmelina and Marcos jumped up to grab a few more chairs.

The bell chimed again.

Where were all these newcomers from?

"I may have told a few friends to stop by for the class," Brad said with an impish grin.

All told, they ended up with twenty faces, more than half of them new. Diego was going to need some more chickens.

"*Salve, amici vecchi e nuovi.…* Hi, friends new, friends old." He held up one of the chickens. "Today we make *Pollo all Cacciatora. Cacciatora* means… how hunters would… *preparano?*" He glanced at Carmelina.

"Prepare?" she whispered.

"Yes. Prepare foods. With *cipolle, odori, pomodori…* I mean, onion, herb, tomato, and for sure, wine."

He proceeded to show them how to sear the chicken.

～

Marissa poured white wine into the pan, laughing as it sizzled and started to evaporate. She loved cooking, which was kind of weird.

"You're a natural at this," Carmelina said.

Marissa blushed. "You think so?" Her parents had never told her she was good at anything. Just the opposite, in fact. Her mother was always complaining about how lazy she was, how she never finished anything. Marissa had seen no reason to try to change her mind.

"Yes. Not everyone can cook. For a while there, some folks thought it was a feminist badge of honor to not cook at all." Carmelina chuckled. "I've always enjoyed it, myself. That's the key. Do the things you enjoy."

It *was* fun. "But I'm not a feminist. I don't hate men."

Carmelina put the chopped tomatoes and thinly-sliced onions in the pan. "You have a lot to learn about feminism, and you need to show us feminists some respect," she said, frowning. "We fought for everything you have now. There was a time women couldn't even vote. When I was young, women were expected to marry a man and settle down. Your career was at home, raising kids."

Marissa stirred the pan gently. It smelled *delicious*. "I'm not sure I want kids."

Carmelina put a hand on her shoulder. "You can do whatever you want with your life. If you want to stay home and have kids and cook for them every night, that's an option. But if you want to have your own restaurant and become a top chef, you can do that too."

"Or become President?"

Carmelina nodded. "If we're lucky, even that too." She snorted. "Though why anyone, man or woman, would actually want that job—"

"To change things," Marissa cut in. "So kids can afford college and don't end up homeless on the streets." There were so many things wrong with the world.

Carmelina looked at her appraisingly. "You're going to make a difference. I don't know how, but I can feel it."

Marissa blushed. "I hope so."

"I know it."

~

At the counter, Dave and Marcos were just getting their chicken prepared.

"I'm terrible at this kind of thing," Marcos said. "I usually buy the whole breasts at Nugget."

"It's not that hard. My mother showed me how to cook from scratch. She was really good at it. She had to be, with four kids." He took the knife. "You just cut here and here and here. Want to give it a try?"

Marcos shook his head. "You go ahead. I'll watch." He loved looking at Dave's hands. The man had beautiful skin, and those hands moved with grace and precision.

"There we go. What's next on the recipe?"

"How are you doing?" Diego said, looking over their shoulders. "Nice cuttings."

"Thanks," Dave said with a grin. "Your English is getting better."

"Matteo *mi fa…* make me practice, every day." He rolled his eyes.

"Maybe we'll teach you Spanish next," Marcos said. "I'll bet it would be a lot easier for you."

"It is as Italian. *Forza!*" He patted them on the back and moved on.

Marcos stared at his partner. Dave really was handsome. A little older than the twinks Marcos was used to bringing home. But solid. *Real.* He imagined what Dave might look like under his red T-shirt, under his Levis—

"Hey, are you gonna help me or not?" Dave was glaring at him, but his eyes twinkled.

"Sorry! What do you want me to do?" *Yes. Tell me, please....* His imagination took hold of him once again. Those beautiful lips—

"What does the recipe say?"

"Just a sec." Marcos fumbled for the paper. "Okay. Put the chicken in the pan with the sage, rosemary, and mashed garlic clove, and salt to taste..." *Taste.* He imagined licking Dave's neck.

Yeah. He had it bad.

48. A LITTLE ADVICE

BEN PEELED THE POTATOES, WORKING THROUGH THE LARGE SACK WITH trained efficiency. His mother had taught him how to cook when he had still been a child.

"Alice, you hold the potato like so and grate the peel away from yourself like this." She'd demonstrated for her daughter, flicking the peels away into the sink with practiced skill. In seconds the potato was bare. "You have to watch your fingers though. Don't want to skin yourself, do you?"

Ben closed his eyes. He'd *hated* the name Alice. Not only was it a *girl* name, which he most certainly was not, but it was *old fashioned*.

His mother had loved traditional things. She'd been proud that Ben's father earned enough at the meat packing plant to pay for everything they needed, so she could stay at home and raise her two children, Ben and his brother Mason, traditionally. She'd been proud of her traditional Victorian home in Mansion Flats. And she'd been proud of her traditional family—the perfect husband, boy, girl, and golden retriever.

It still stung Ben to the core that his own mother had disowned him. He wondered from time to time how she was doing. His brother called him now and then with status reports, but sometimes he just missed his mom.

This whole thing with Ella's moms had really thrown him, bringing up his own mother's rejection as if it were fresh.

"*Come va?* How's it goes?" Diego put a hand on his shoulder.

"Almost done." He pointed at the big bowl of peeled potatoes he'd amassed.

"You make a good… how do you say…" he mimed stirring something in a pan.

"Cook?"

"*Sí!* A good cook!" Diego patted his shoulder and gave him a big grin, then moved on to the next group of students.

"You almost done there?" Sam called.

"Yeah, just a couple more." He'd been paired… or, he supposed, throupled, with Sam and his husband Brad. He finished the last of the potatoes, and brought the bowl back to their corner of the counter. Diego had suggested they prepare them all at once to save on cooking space on the stove.

They each grabbed a paring knife and set about quartering the pile of potatoes, piling them in a large bowl.

"I can't believe there are so many people here today," Sam said, looking around.

"I put the word out at the Center," Brad said with a grin. "There are a lot of folks who like supporting queer-owned businesses."

"You okay, Ben?" Sam asked, shooting him a concerned look. "You seem a bit quiet today."

"I'm… yeah. I'm okay."

"Come on. Something's bugging you. Spill." He looked at Ben like an expectant puppy dog.

He shook his head. "It's stupid."

Sam laughed. "If you knew half the stupid things I've gotten worked up over recently…"

"Maybe we should leave poor Ben alone," Brad said, frowning.

"No, it's all right." Ben sighed. "I just started dating this girl, Ella, and her mother doesn't want her going out with me because I'm trans."

"Ah." Sam shook his head. "People can be so narrow minded."

"Would you date someone transgender?" Ben asked.

Sam looked thoughtful. "Um, I think so? It's never come up. I guess it would depend on the person?"

Lots of gay guys *said* that, but it felt like Sam meant it. "When I transitioned, I built up this whole fantasy around it—that I would be just another guy. Just like all the other guys. That people would look at me and see someone physically *male*."

"And?"

"Mostly, I pass. But just when I forget about being trans, when it slips my mind for just a moment, someone steps in and reminds me."

Brad nodded. "Being gay's like that too. You forget, sometimes, that you're a guy who likes guys, that society's still not a hundred percent on board with that. And then some homophobic jerk reminds you."

Ben nodded. "Weird thing is, Ella's mother is transgender too."

"Huh." Sam rubbed his chin. "Did she say why she didn't want you seeing her daughter?"

"She's afraid of all the baggage I'll bring into the relationship. And I guess she would know, right? Maybe I'm being an idiot—I should just date other trans folks. It would be easier."

"But then, wouldn't there be twice the baggage?" Sam said with a grin.

"Yeah, well, there is that." Ben cut his last potato.

"How old is she?" Sam asked.

"Who?"

"Ella."

"I don't know… maybe thirty?"

"Then what her mother wants really doesn't matter, does it? You're both adults." Sam finished his stack and set down the knife. "You have to do what's right for the two of you."

"I guess so."

Sam put a hand on his. "Ben, you're an amazing guy. Just because you got there a different way than Brad or I doesn't diminish that in any way. You're not an asshole, and I have a lot of experience with assholes."

Ben grinned. "That's a little too much information."

"Hey, are those potatoes ready yet?" Carmelina shouted from the stove.

"Just finished. There in a sec." Ben grabbed the bowl. "Thanks, guys."

Diego closed the door behind the last student. The whole thing had gone really well, despite the extra people. They'd actually turned a profit this time, and he'd had an idea of his own to share with Matteo.

"*Caro*," he called up the stairs.

"Coming."

Diego gathered the dishes and pots and pans and stacked them in the kitchen. He'd just started washing them when he heard the telltale patter of Matteo's feet coming down the stairs. "All clear?"

"All is gone," he affirmed.

"Everyone's gone," Matteo corrected him. "How did it go?"

How did it go? Com'è andata. "Good!" He handed Matteo a dishrag, and they worked on dishes together. "We were twenty today!"

"There were… Oh, never mind. That's fantastic!"

"I had an idea," he said in Italian. "What if we did classes several afternoons a week? Close the place two until five. That's our quietest time anyhow."

Matteo nodded, thoughtful. "That could work."

"With takeout service at lunch and dinner as usual. We could really improve our cash flow. Look!" He dried his hands and held up his earnings for the afternoon.

"Cash flow? Someone's been listening."

Diego grinned. "Yes, *caro*. When you're not boring me to death."

"Hey, I'm not boring!"

"Of course not." Diego pecked him on the cheek. "So what do you think?"

"Flirting will get you everywhere."

See the chicken cacciatore recipe at the end of the book.

49. JUST A SECOND

third full, not unusual for a Sunday night.

Carmelina smiled graciously at Daniele as he pulled out her chair. It was nice being on the receiving end of someone's gentlemanly urges again. She saw a flash of the cross tattoo on his wrist and frowned. It was an unwelcome reminder of another evening that had gone less than ideally between them.

He slid into the booth seat across from her and flashed his most charming smile.

She wasn't ready to slide back into things so easily with him. "I haven't been here in ages," she said, studying the menu. The stuffed peppers looked especially inviting.

"I'm so sorry about this morning," Daniele said. "My mother recommended that priest. Apparently he's done some great feng shui for her before."

She chuckled in spite of herself. "He does eastern religion too?"

"As I said, I am most apologetic."

"At least we got a good show out of it." She looked over the rest of the menu. "Mind if we start with the zucchini chips? They're really good."

"Sure, why not?"

Their waiter, a cute young guy in a crisp white shirt who could almost have been her grandson, stopped by the table. "Good evening. My name is Jason. Can I get you started with something to drink?"

Carmelina smiled at him. They were so cute at that age, but Lordy, he was young. "Sure.... Do you have anything from Six Hands?"

"Yes, I think we have Cabernet Sauvignon and Chardonnay in the cellar."

"I'll take a glass of the Cab." She set down her menu. "Daniele?"

"Nothing for me. Well, maybe a bottle of Perrier?"

The waiter nodded. "Back in a minute with those drinks."

Curious. "Don't you ever drink?" she asked Daniele.

He shook his head. "I learned a long time ago it's better for everyone if I don't."

"A mean drunk, huh?"

"Something like that."

They placed their order when Jason returned, and Carmelina sat back, examining Daniele from across the table. "I'm not sure if I have forgiven you yet."

"For the exorcism? I know. It was a bad idea—"

"For running out on me after we had sex."

"Ah." He blushed. "I know. You just caught me off guard."

"About the tattoo?"

He nodded. "It represents a really dark time in my life."

She put her hands on his. "Daniele, what happened on September twenty-third?" She felt him tense up and heard his sharp breath.

"Who told you about that?"

She'd scored a hit. "Let's just say you weren't entirely wrong about the whole 'ghost of the dearly departed husband' thing."

He stared back at her for a moment, then he seemed to deflate, like one of those car dealership balloons when the pump is turned off.

"Hey, it's okay. You can tell me. No judgment." She squeezed his hands.

"I do bad things when I get smashed," he said at last.

She nodded. "I'd guessed that. Go on."

"I used to go out on the weekends with my friends from Sac State and get really stinking drunk, but we were smart about it. We'd take a taxi to the club together and then take another home."

"That's sensible." She had a bad feeling she knew where this was headed.

He looked away, his vision unfocused. "One night it was just Jeff and I. He wanted to check out this new place in Davis by UCD, and it was too far to cab. So I drove." He wiped his eye with the back of his hand. "We were there for four hours. We had a blast. And I didn't think I was all that drunk. I *felt* fine. We drove home a little after two in the morning." He paused, and the side of his mouth twitched. "We were coming through midtown—down J Street—when this car pulled in front of us, going really slow. I got angry and tried to get around him, but he must have been drunker than I was, because he was weaving all across the—"

"Here are the zucchini chips." Jason set them in the middle of the table. "You two doing all right?" He was far too perky.

"We're fine, thanks," Carmelina said, shooing him away. "Go on," she said to Daniele.

He took a long sip of his Perrier. "I passed him on the right as we were coming up on Marshall Park, just before Business 80. But I misjudged it and ended up riding on the curb for just a second—" He choked up and put his hand over his eyes.

She squeezed his hands. "It's okay. I'm right here. What happened then?"

"It was just for a second, but this woman had come out of one of the bars, I guess, and she was there in front of me, and..." He looked up at her, and his eyes were wet. "I've thought about that moment every day since it happened. Replaying it in my head. Thinking about what I could have done differently. If I just had stayed home. Or hadn't drunk anything. Or had taken Highway 50 instead of J Street."

"Did she...?"

He nodded. "Almost instantly. I got this to remember what happened. What I did."

She touched the tattooed cross, running her fingers across it. So much pain.

"They ruled it an accident. I was just below the legal limit, so they let me go. But I've never forgiven myself—"

"Hello there. Who had the stuffed peppers?" an expediter asked, bringing their food.

"Those are mine," Carmelina said, clearing a space. Restaurant folk always managed to show up at the worst times.

"And you must have the Chicken Saltimbocca."

Daniele nodded. "Thank you." He wiped his eyes with his napkin, and then they were alone again.

"So that's why you don't drink anymore?" *What a terrible lesson to have learned.*

"I haven't had a drop since that night." This time he took *her* hand. "Can you forgive me? For my rude behavior the other night? And for what I did?"

"We all make mistakes." She drew her hand away with a little smile.

She glanced down at her dish. It looked delicious. "Let's eat before it gets cold." She took a bite. It *was* good, but her mind was elsewhere.

50. THE TIME WE HAVE

Ben glanced nervously at his watch. It was a quarter past twelve in the afternoon, and Ella was late. Maybe she'd decided not to come. Maybe her moms had found his texts and had forbidden her to see him.

She was in her thirties. Why did her parent still rule her life?

It was a warm, early October afternoon in River City. He sipped on a chai latte under the shade of the huge old oak tree in front of the Grind, watching the passersby. He had to work later, but for now he was free.

He'd been neglecting his writing over the last week, but he was so close to the end. He just couldn't seem to focus on it properly. Not with Ella taking up most of his mental energy.

"Hey, sorry I'm late!" Ella's hand was on his shoulder. "I couldn't get away. Moms and I were having lunch at Cafe Bernardo. I finally told her I needed a little alone time. That I wanted to take a walk."

She came. He grinned and gave her a big hug. "It's all right. I was just enjoying the day."

"So you want to?"

"Want to what?"

"Take a walk with me? I've been cooped up in the hospital for days."

"Um… sure! Where do you want to go?" He got up and slipped his backpack over his shoulder. "I don't need to be back here until two-thirty."

"Capitol Park? It's such a beautiful day."

"Sounds good." They strolled down the boardwalk that fronted the MAARS Building. Ella looked a little withdrawn. "Thanks for coming to see me."

"Moms told me what she said to you. I was really angry with her. But she had her reasons."

He frowned. Moms' 'reasons' were that he was trans and that she didn't want her daughter dealing with all of his baggage. "What did she tell you?"

They turned the corner, descending the stairs to the sidewalk. "Let's stop at Devine and get some gelato," she said with a wan smile. "We can take it to the rose garden at the park and talk there."

They stopped by the gelato place, which was busy as usual on a Sunday afternoon.

"What's your favorite flavor?" Ella asked, her hands on the glass.

"Hmmm… probably the *stracciatella*. Or the honey lavender. But not together."

"I've always been a big chocolate fan myself."

"Then you can't go wrong with the double chocolate."

In the end, he got her a waffle cone with three flavors of chocolate, and they made their way down to the park. They found a sunny bench facing the center of the rose garden, where water trickled over a white fountain surrounded by a quartet of heart-shaped planters. They sat in silence for a few minutes while they finished their gelato. She was staring at the fountain, and he was staring at her.

"She told me I was too much trouble for you," he said at last. "Your moms."

She turned to regard him for a moment, and nodded. "It was probably easier for her to tell you that."

"What do you mean?" Ben's brow furrowed. "*You're* the one who doesn't want you to see me anymore?"

She looked away again, silent.

"I'm sorry—I don't know what I did to upset you? Did I say something I shouldn't have? I thought things were starting out well between us—"

"Ben, I'm dying."

That knocked the wind out of his sails. "What do you mean?" It made no sense. She was here, whole, vivacious—and beautiful. She was more alive than anyone else he knew.

"I have a degenerative neurological condition called Fahr's Disease. It's been in my family for a long time." She sighed, and turned to face him again. "I was living with my moms in Chicago, waiting to die. I finally got tired of hiding."

"So you moved here?"

"Yeah. Max is here, for starters. I thought I could make a new start with whatever time I still have." She sniffed and wiped her nose with the back of her hand. "He told me he'd found this experimental treatment at UC Davis, but the trial was already full. He said he had some way of getting enough cash to buy me a way in."

"Ella, I'm so sorry." He ached to see her like this.

"It's all right. I've known for a couple years now. Sometimes I have a hard time controlling my movements. It comes and goes. But it pretty much only gets worse from here." She put a hand on his arm. "You don't want to be with me, Ben. It will only bring you sadness."

She started to get up, but he gently pulled her back down.

"I saw you, Ella. In a vision."

"What?" She frowned. "That's not funny."

"It was the day before I met you. I had this vision of you, with me, in this adorable little kitchen in a house that belonged to the two of us. When I saw you, I just *knew*."

"Even if I believed you," she said, staring at him, "it would never work. I'm sick, Ben. I'm never going to be the girl of your dreams."

"Don't you get it? You already are." He pulled her to him and kissed her.

She resisted at first, but then she kissed him back, putting her arms around him and pulling him to her tightly.

At last, she let him go. "We shouldn't be doing this," she said softly. "It's not fair to you."

"Let *me* decide what's fair and what's not." He cupped her chin in his hand gently. "Ella, I want to be with you for whatever time you have left, if it's a year, a month or even just a week."

She bit her lip. "Are you sure?"

"Surer than I've been of anything in a long time."

"I don't know—"

"You don't have to decide right away. I'm patient." He took her hand and lifted her up off the bench. "Come on. You promised me a walk, right?"

He called in sick to work, and they spent the rest of the afternoon walking through town and talking.

51. 'DOPTERMONSTER BLUES

MARCOS THREW HIS KEYS INTO THE BOWL ON THE SMALL GLASS-AND-metal table by the front door. Marissa wasn't home yet. He had the place all to himself. He'd been cramming code at Temple Coffee, trying to finish up a job for a new client. The guy was nice, but he had no clue how programming or Wordpress actually worked. Marcos had spent the last week trying to manage expectations and had done so much custom coding he was afraid the whole thing would come crashing down with the next developer update.

He liked being out in the real world when he was coding. He'd spent too much time crammed in a small cubicle when he'd worked for Intel out at their complex in Folsom, before he'd been replaced by someone cheaper with an H-1B visa. But never mind all that. He preferred working for himself, even if the pay wasn't steady. He'd established a good network of clients and had about as much as he could handle.

He sank down on the couch and sorted through the mail. Costco was selling a bunch of crap, as usual. He'd weed through that later. There was a money beg from the food bank. He'd given the last Christmas and probably would again this year, or maybe for Thanksgiving, but that was still a month and a half away. Then he ran across a letter from the Sacramento County Juvenile Court. He opened it and stared at the contents. Then he folded it up and put it neatly into the envelope.

Marissa got home a half hour later. "You here?"

"Yes. In the kitchen."

She'd made herself very comfortable here in the past nine days. "Oooh, that smells good. What is it?" Her head popped up over her shoulder.

"Ancient Chinese secret," he said with a grin.

"What?" She pulled herself up to sit on the island. She held a paper bag.

"Old commercial from the seventies." He chuckled. "No, it's something called *calabacitas*. It means *zucchini* in Spanish. My Mom always makes it this way, with a broth and tomatoes and lots of cheese. What's in the bag?"

She held it open to show him. "I stopped by the Freeport Bakery and got us a couple pastries for dessert."

"Oooh, I love that place." He tasted the broth. It still needed a bit of seasoning. *Maybe some garlic salt?* "Hey, how did you get home, then? Bribe the bus driver to wait for you?"

"Nope. Jason's mom gave me a lift. She was stopping at the bakery, and vee-oh-lah."

"It's pronounced 'vwah-lah.'" He frowned. "Who's this Jason guy? Should I be worried?"

"I told you about him. He's the gay kid they assigned to me. You know, to keep me out of trouble."

Marcos laughed. "I imagine he has his hands full."

"I have no idea what you mean." She beamed innocently.

"Hey, want to grab a couple bowls, some silverware, and chips and salsa? We're just about ready."

"Sure. The Fiestaware?"

"Whatever you want."

"Hey, what's this?" She was holding the envelope from the court.

"Let's sit down first. Then we can talk about it." He was worried she'd be upset. He served a couple ladlefuls each of the aromatic soup. It wasn't quite how his mother had made it—he'd added some chicken—but the smell always reminded him of her. He hadn't seen his parents since the holidays in Palm Springs, where they'd retired a few years before.

Marissa took a sip of the soup. "Oooh, it's good."

Marcos dipped one of his tortilla chips in the plastic bowl of TJ's salsa in the middle of the table. "So."

"The letter?"

"Yeah. You probably already figured out what it is."

"It's about the 'break-in', isn't it?" She used air quotes.

Marcos nodded. "The court date's in about three weeks."

"Fucking Jessica—"

"Hey, have a little respect. She's *still* your mother."

"Adoptermonster."

"Even so. You can't go flying off the handle like that in court, you know."

Marissa frowned.

"There must have been a time when things were better between you two."

"When I was little, she used to take me to the zoo on Sundays. We'd go feed the giraffes, and then we'd have a picnic lunch together out on the lawn."

"See? That's nice."

"Just wait. When I was seven or eight, she told me I was adopted. It was at Raleys, and we were in the checkout line. I wanted some peanut M&M's, and she wouldn't let me get them, and I threw a fit. I guess I wouldn't stop crying."

"You were a kid."

"Maybe so. But she said, and I still remember it word for word: 'I wish we had never adopted your sorry little ass.'"

Marcos whistled. "That's terrible."

"After that, she'd tell me that whenever I did something wrong. And I think I started doing things just to dare her to say it again. Because if it was true, maybe that meant I wasn't like her. That I wouldn't grow up to be mean and spiteful like she was."

Marcos put his hand on hers. "Marissa, you're nothing like that. A headstrong, pain-in-the-ass teenager, to be sure. But look what you've done for all those outcast kids at school."

"That was mostly Jason's idea—"

"Maybe so, but you ran with it." He sat back, remembering his own teen years. "One thing I've learned: each of us is responsible for the person we become. When my parents threw me out, I could have been bitter. I could have let it ruin my life. But I chose to move forward. To be who I was in spite of that." He frowned. "I'm still learning. I've lived most of my life on the chase, looking for the next party, the next guy. I don't want to live like that anymore. You came into my life, and I started thinking about things… differently."

"You mean, like you and Dave being together?"

"Yeah, like that." He was already looking forward to their next date on Wednesday. He picked up the envelope. "Look, we'll get through this together. Then you can figure out what you want to do next, and I'll support you." He smiled wryly. "And who knows? Maybe your 'doptermonster will come around."

Marissa snorted. "Fat chance."

"Anyhow, let's eat before it gets cold. My mother would never forgive me if I ruined her signature dish, and I can't wait to try those pastries."

52. FIFTEEN MINUTES

MATTEO LOOKED AROUND THE SMALL BUT TIDY LAW OFFICE. IT WAS painted a bright yellow with white trim, and the light streaming in from the window facing J Street made it seem bigger than it actually was. Behind the large mahogany desk that took up half the space, shelves held a preponderance of legal tomes. A bright-green fern in a blue pot sitting on a pedestal by the window did its best to relieve the dark, staid tones of the furniture.

The door swung open next to him. "So sorry to keep you two waiting." Dana Pearce was dressed impeccably in a gray pinstripe pantsuit. She was short, and her hair was close-cropped and a vibrant red. She sat down at her desk, leaning back in her chair. "I've been prepping for an upcoming case, and the judge just denied my motion for a delay. I've got about..." she looked at her watch, "... fifteen minutes. What can I do for you two gentlemen?"

"Brad at the Center referred us to you," Matteo said, a little taken aback by her brusque manner. "We wanted a gay or lesbian lawyer...."

"Hold up right there. Common misconception, but I'm bisexual. Go on."

He nodded. "That's good too. We just wanted someone who would understand the position we're in."

She leaned forward and put her elbows on her desk with her chin on her hands. "Why don't you tell me exactly what that situation is?"

"Well, you see, we were married two years ago here in the US..."

"Twelve minutes."

"We're married, but Diego was married to a woman in Italy before, and she never divorced him."

"Ah, there we go." She sat back, considering the two of them. "Did you know you weren't divorced when you married Matteo?" she asked Diego.

"Cosa…? Divorced…?"

"Sorry, his English isn't very good yet." To Diego, he said *"Sapevi che Luna non aveva firmato le pratiche per il divorzio quando mi hai sposato?"*

"No. No!! *Dopo*. Later."

"Okay, so there was no intentional fraud." She thrummed her fingers on the desk. "And does Immigration know about this? I'm assuming you're here on a visa?"

"I am," Matteo said. "He's here as my spouse."

"Ah. There's the problem, then."

Matteo nodded. "So what do we do?"

"Well, the easiest thing is to invest. Do you have a business?"

Matteo nodded. "Ragazzi, over on Folsom Boulevard in East Sac."

"Oh, I've heard of that place. Brad said it was really good." She took out a legal pad and wrote a few notes. "Okay, your fastest option is to invest in the business. You can get what is called an EB-5 visa. Matteo, you're already covered, so Diego, you'd need to invest. What kind of assets does he have?"

Matteo shook his head. "Not so much. What would he need?"

"At least five hundred thousand, and you'd have to hire ten employees."

Matteo blanched.

"Porco cane!" Diego said.

"Ah, so he understood that." She flashed him a smile and glanced again at her watch. "Eight minutes."

"So what are our other options?"

"Honestly? Since Immigration hasn't brought it up, he should get his divorce taken care of first, and then we can get you two legally remarried. After that, we can approach Immigration. Is his wife willing to go through with the divorce now?"

Matteo looked over at Diego. *"Vuole sapere se ora Luna ti concederebbe il divorzio."*

Diego shrugged. *"Spero di sì."*

"He hopes so."

"Then I'd suggest getting a quick divorce. Then we can talk again."

"That… might be a problem." Italy didn't do things quickly. Especially divorce.

"How so?"

"They just approved a new law that allows quicker divorces in Italy."

"Perfect. What's the problem?"

"'Quick' means six months instead of three years."

"Ouch."

"After a three-year separation."

"Ah."

"So?"

"So you don't have much of a choice, do you?" She picked up a photo off her desktop and showed it to them. She was in it, along with a handsome man in a Hawaiian shirt and jeans. Behind them, the Grand Canyon was spread out in all of its glory. "That's my husband, Ken. We met when I was in London on a one-semester student exchange. We're married now, but it took three years to get through all the immigration bullshit."

"That's… encouraging."

"Do you love him?"

He nodded. "More than anything."

"Does he love you?" She glanced at Diego.

Diego nodded. "*Naturalmente.*" He grinned.

"My point is, it will all be worth it if you can stick together no matter how hard it gets." She glanced at her watch. "Time's just about up. Anything else?"

"Any other advice for us?"

"Keep your heads down. No traffic stops, no speeding, no petty theft. Remember, right now you're living on borrowed time." She grinned at Diego. "Especially you. You look like trouble."

"*Cosa? Che ha detto?*" Diego looked hurt.

"*Un momento.*" He patted Diego's leg.

"Fortunately for you two, Immigration is focused on Latino undocumented workers these days, so if you don't make waves, you can probably ride this out."

"Thank you so much. What do we owe you?"

"Brad's a good friend, so this little session is on the house, but if you hire me, I charge $300 an hour. I *do* have a sliding scale, if your income is low enough." She glanced at her watch once more and nodded. "And with that, we're done for today." She stood and shook their hands. "Pleasure to meet both of you. When the divorce is finalized, come back and see me, and we'll talk strategy." She gathered up her briefcase and was out the door with a quick smile and a wave.

"*Allora? Che ha detto?*" Diego asked.

Matteo sighed. He had been hoping for something easier. "You have to go to Italy and get a divorce."

53. WHERE THE TRUTH LIES

Carmelina browsed through the beautiful selection of fresh flowers at Fiori Amorosi, the flower shop owned by Daniele's family. Daniele wasn't there, but she had wanted to see the shop again. It had been years since she had been there.

It was a beautiful place, with dusky-yellow Venetian plaster walls that lent it an Old World feel and thick wooden shelves covered with flowers and vases and other knickknacks.

"Can I help you?" The young woman behind the counter, probably all of nineteen years old, flashed her a braces-filled smile.

"Yes, I want to buy a hundred flowers. Something… bright. Colorful."

"Hmmm… Is it for a party?"

Carmelina frowned. "Not exactly. It's… for my daughter. She passed away a long time ago. It's complicated."

Braces flashed her a sparkly smile. "I understand. We have a lot of carnations on hand. They come in lots of colors—"

"No *carnations*." They reminded her of her senior prom, a dismal night that had ended in tears.

"Hmmm… How about some mums?"

"No. Too frilly."

"Hmmm…"

The constant humming was starting to annoy Carmelina. She looked around the shop and selected a bundle of yellow daffodils. "How about these?" She had always liked daffodils. Arthur had wooed her with them for a month before she had said yes to going out with him.

Every day he would send her more. One the first day, two the second, three on the third, until finally she'd received a bouquet of thirty yellow daffodils with a note. "Please. Say Yes. I'm running out of money."

Braces frowned, an annoyingly cute expression. "Hmmm… Let me check."

"Yes, please do." Carmelina tried not to grind her teeth.

Thirty minutes later, she walked out with a hundred yellow daffodils.

She drove the fifteen minutes to St. Mary's Cemetery. It was a Tuesday afternoon. She parked the car, looking out at a funeral party gathered around an open grave.

She sat in her car for a few minutes, watching the mourners, wishing she had known when her daughter, Andrea, had been put to rest. She *should* have known. Should have felt it *in her bones* when her own flesh and blood had been taken from this world. Instead she'd probably been working at the County Welfare Office, maybe stopping to get a coffee or having lunch with Loylene and laughing about the latest office affairs.

At last, she pulled out the map Jenna at the cemetery office had faxed to her. She got out of the car and started walking among the graves. The lawn was yellow—another sign of California's severe ongoing drought.

It took her about fifteen minutes, but she finally located the marker. It was a simple stone plaque embedded in the ground. "Andrea Smith, 1975–2000." She sat down next to the stone, tracing it with her fingers. "I'm here, baby. Fifteen years too late. But I'm here."

Why had she ever given up her beautiful child? She had hoped the little girl would have a better life with a loving family. Her mother had convinced her it was for the best.

If only she had fought harder. Maybe she could have prevented this from happening. She wiped her eyes with a Kleenex from her purse and blew her nose.

She lay the bundle of flowers on the adjoining gravesite and undid the ribbon that held them together. There was no can to place them in, so instead she set them over the grave, one at a time, laying them out below the grave marker.

"There are so many things I wish I could tell you," she said as the flowers started to pile up. "It wasn't your fault that I couldn't take care of you. I was so young and scared. I was only fifteen when I had you, and I didn't know what to do." She knelt and kissed the gravestone. "I am so sorry, my love. I wish to God I had been there for you." She put down the last flower and laid down with her head on the pillow of blossoms.

It was a beautiful day in early October; not a cloud in the sky.

When she'd set off to find her daughter, she'd never imagined it would end like this. She had hoped coming here, to this final resting place, would give her some closure. Instead, she felt guiltier than ever.

Her cell phone rang. She pulled it out, feeling a little disrespectful at having not silenced the ringer. Fortunately she was all alone in this part of the cemetery. She got up to walk away from the grave.

Caller ID said "Catholic Svcs". "Hello?"

"Hello? Is this Carmelina di Rosa?"

"Yes it is."

"Hello. This is Sister Clara. You came to see me this last week?"

Carmelina sniffed, wiping her nose with the back of her hand. "Yes."

"Good. I wanted to let you know that I was going through our files. I found an interesting notation about Andrea. Where did I put it?" There was a shuffling of papers. "Ah, here it is. About a year before she died, she had a child. She was put up for adoption when Andrea passed away."

Carmelina's breath caught. "I have a grandchild?"

"It appears so, yes."

She felt too heavy for her legs to hold her. She sank down to the ground, shaking. "What… Was it a boy or a girl?"

"I don't know. But the county might be able to tell you more. It appears they handled the adoption through the foster care system."

"Thank you. Oh my God, thank you. I mean… I'm sorry, no disrespect to God."

Sister Clara laughed quietly. "I understand, under the circumstances."

"Could you email me the information you have?"

"Of course."

"Thank you so much."

"God bless."

Carmelina hung up the phone. She stood unsteadily and made her way back to Andrea's grave. "You had a child," she whispered. Then it struck her.

"I have a grandchild."

54.'RISS AND TRIS

MARISSA SHOVED HER BACKPACK IN HER LOCKER AND SLAMMED IT SHUT. It had been a shitstorm of a day, starting with the fact that she'd left her math homework at home. Jason was out sick too. Strangely enough, she kinda missed his puppy-dog presence. And now *this*.

She stared at the note that Mr. Davis had slipped her during English class. Mrs. Dominguez, the school counselor, wanted to see her after lunch.

She didn't need to see a counselor. What did they think was wrong with her? She came to McClatchy every day, did her homework (even if she forgot it at home sometimes), and she'd even made a few friends. She wished they would just leave her well enough alone.

She got into the lunch line, staring morosely at the offerings. Today's meal was just great—a perfect shit topping on a shitty day: boiled cabbage, corned beef sandwich, and a side of steamed broccoli. What did they think this was, St. Patrick's Day? Though she didn't think broccoli was usually associated with Guinness and four-leaf clovers. It *was* green though.

At least they still had chocolate milk, and she could probably drown the rest in ketchup. She took ten packets. *That oughta do it.*

She slipped into her seat at the Outcasts table, hoping the rest of the group would ignore her. No such luck.

"Hey 'Riss," Caity said, grinning, eyes big as an owl's behind her coke-bottle glasses. "We were just arguing over which of the Reds we should tar and feather first." The Reds were the school's three most popular girls, Tabby, Shalisha, and Hayley, who all wore matching bright-red nail polish.

"Tabby," Marissa said without hesitation. "She'd scream the loudest." She emptied one packet after another of the strangely orange ketchup over her meal. She took a bite of the cabbage. Not bad.

"Shalisha would be better." Clark's gay flame burned bright. He was adorable. "She'd *die* if she had to wear anything not runway appropriate."

"I don't know.... Those girls don't seem so bad," a new voice said. "Mind if I sit with you guys?"

Marissa looked up to see a newcomer standing next to her. He was six foot two, at least, skinny with a mop of dark hair and a large black plug in each earlobe. Both arms were covered in tattoos. He was cute and totally her type. "Sure. Have a seat." She scooted over to make room.

"Thanks. I'm Tristan." He offered his hand.

"Marissa." She looked at his lunch. "How'd you get a burger and fries?"

He grinned. "My mom's one of the lunch ladies."

"OMG. I have to get to know you better."

He laughed. "Want some?"

"Please." She snagged a few fries from his tray. "How come I've never seen you around here before?" she asked through a mouthful of fries.

"We just transferred in last week from Santa Cruz." He stared at her. "You really like fries, don't you?"

She blushed, her hand over his tray with her third handful. "Sorry. Um… want some of these?" She held up a piece of broccoli covered in ketchup.

He wrinkled his nose. "No thanks. Sweet of you though!"

She laughed. "You do realize this is the Outcast Society, right?"

"Yeah, someone told me. Right where I belong." He took a big bite of his burger and winked at her.

His right arm was covered with a flame-breathing dragon. "I love the tats," she said. What's this one represent?"

He blushed. "I love sci fi. It's a bronze dragon and his rider. From Pern."

"Pern?"

"Anne McCaffrey. You should really check them out."

She nodded. "I will." She glanced at the time. "Sorry, gotta run. Appointment with the school counselor." She chugged her chocolate milk and got up.

"That can't be good. Antisocial tendencies?"

"Almost certainly. Nice to meet you!"

"Likewise."

The day was getting better already.

❧

She knocked on the counselor's door.

"Come on in." Mrs. Dominguez's voice beckoned her inside. She was stocky and kind of old... maybe forty? Her short-cut hair and no-nonsense demeanor practically shouted *lesbian*. "Take a seat, Miss Sutton."

Marissa did as she was told. "Am I in trouble?"

Mrs. Dominguez looked up with a frown. "No, not at all." She turned to her computer. "It's just that we've had a rather... unusual request. Your mother has asked to meet with you."

Marissa's blood ran cold. "She's *not* my mother."

"Sorry? It says here—"

"I'm adopted."

"Ah. I see. In any case, she's asked if we can facilitate a meeting. Technically, she's still your legal guardian. I wanted to talk to you first, to see how you felt about it. Were you... were there problems at home?"

Marissa snorted. "Do you mean, did she beat me?"

"Well, yes. Was there any abuse?"

"Nothing physical. But she threw me out when I told her I liked girls."

Mrs. Dominguez frowned. "Well, that was judgmental of her, wasn't it? Okay. So you don't want to see her?"

"She can see me in court."

"What?"

"She said I broke into my house. I have a court date, end of the month."

Mrs. Dominguez frowned. "That's absurd. She ought to be ashamed. Alright. I'll tell her I can't facilitate a meeting, but you may have to see her anyway."

"Thank you. Can I go?"

"Yes. But Marissa..."

"What?"

"If you ever want to talk, my door is always open."

Marissa nodded and darted out of the room.

Tristan was waiting for her outside. "How'd it go?"

She shook her head. "My mother wants to see me."

"Which is not good?"

"Long story."

He nodded. "Wanna tell me after school?"

He was cute *and* sweet. What did she have to lose?

"Sure. See you at three."

55.EMPTY

Carmelina entered the central branch of the Sacramento Public Library System—a beautiful structure inspired by the Italian Renaissance style—through its gorgeous, light-filled gallery. The morning sunlight streamed through the tall arched window at the street side to lend the long hall a warm amber glow.

She had tried to get online to look for articles about her daughter's death, hoping to find a clue to her grandchild's identity, but the newspaper archives had been glitchy, and she hadn't been able to access the articles for the year 2000. She'd turned to the library website, but they wanted her to have a library card first before she could access the information. So she decided it was just easier to go down there directly.

She waited in line at the reference desk, looking around the brightly lit space while she waited. Sunlight shone through windows above rows and rows of wooden bookshelves, and the smell of paper and ink took her back to when she used to go there often for her studies in college. Libraries seemed so quaint in the age of Amazon and the internet and e-book readers. Yet here this one was, still standing, still full of books, knowledge, and the aroma of *literature*.

"May I help you?" The librarian was not at all what she'd expected: a young woman of maybe twenty, with one side of her head shaved and the other in a short bob cut. She had a tattoo of red roses streaming down her left arm.

"Yes, Brianna," Carmelina said, reading the woman's name tag and putting on her friendliest voice. "I'm trying to find some articles from the Sacramento Bee from 2000."

"Of course. I can help you with that." She flashed Carmelina a warm smile that went a long way to resolve any misgivings Carmelina might have had about her looks. "Follow me."

She led Carmelina to a long bank of computers and sat her down in front of one of them. "Just click here to access the Bee archives," she said, pointing over Carmelina's shoulder. "You can put in a search term and choose a year."

Brianna's body was warm next to hers. Carmelina wondered if her grandchild was anything like this woman. Strong, independent, with her own stubborn sense of style. She nodded. "Got it. Can I print out anything?"

"Of course. There's a printer down there." She gestured to the end of the table. "Just try to keep it short. You can choose which pages to print in the pop-up window. We're a little short on paper this month."

"Got it. Thanks so much!" She waved Brianna off and dove in, Typing "Andrea Smith" and "obituary."

She found it almost immediately.

Andrea Smith, Kindergarten Teacher
August 15th, 1975–September 23rd, 2000

Andrea Smith passed away at Mercy Hospital after being struck by a drunk driver in the early hours of the morning outside a Midtown Sacramento nightclub. Ms. Smith was a beloved teacher at the Caleb Greenwood Elementary School in River Park.

Carmelina gasped as she read the obituary. Her daughter had been a teacher, and Caleb Greenwood was just down the street from her house. How many times had she passed by that school? Had she seen her daughter outside once, twice, maybe a hundred times, and never known it?

She read on.

She is survived by her two-year-old daughter, Mary Smith.

So Andrea had a daughter! And Carmelina had her name: Mary.

Carmelina closed her eyes for a moment, trying to imagine her granddaughter. Would she have red hair like her grandmother?

She stared at the black-and-white photo of her daughter. Would she have Andrea's turned-up nose?

She wished she could reach into the photograph and pull her daughter back through it into her embrace. To never let her go again.

With a heavy sigh, she printed the article. Sister Clara had said that the county had handled the adoption. Now that she had the name, she could contact Loylene and see if her friend still knew anyone from their time at the County Welfare offices who could help.

Then she searched the archive for "Andrea Smith" and "drunk driver ." Several articles came up, but one in particular caught her eye.

Local Woman Killed by Drunk Driver

Andrea Smith was killed by a drunk driver as she came out of Harlow's Restaurant and Nightclub at 2:15 a.m. A car traveling eastbound on J Street jumped the curb and struck Ms. Smith, injuring her. She was taken to Mercy Hospital, where she passed away from blunt-force trauma.
The driver's name has been withheld pending identification. He was taken into custody on suspicion of driving over the legal limit....

Carmelina's hands started to shake.

Daniele had told her about an accident just like this, an accident he had been responsible for. She had felt sad for the woman at the time, but... it couldn't be. Oh Lord in heaven, it couldn't be. Not Daniele. Not her baby girl.

She scrolled up to check the date at the top of the page. September 23rd.

Arthur had tried to tell her.

She pushed away from the desk, nearly toppling the monitor, and ran toward the bathroom, her stomach cramping as a wave of nausea rolled through her.

Carmelina made it to the stall just before the contents of her stomach came spewing out.

She retched until her stomach felt as empty as her heart and mind.

Then she sat there on the cold tile of the bathroom floor, miserable and alone, one thought running through her head over and over again.

He killed my baby girl.

56. THE ADOLESCENT ARMY

Matteo looked up from the Square app on his iPad. *"Dici sul serio?"*

Diego grinned. "English, please."

Matteo laughed. "Are you serious?" Now Diego was calling *him* on his language skills.

Diego nodded. "No more lunches." He gestured to the new cooler case they'd installed, borrowed from one of Diego's chef friends while they gauged if the new idea was going to work. *"Le piadine…* the piadines is the best popular."

"Fantastic." Students from Sac State had made up most of the lunch rush, but a few of the neighbors had popped in to say hello too. "We made…" he checked his app. "…four hundred dollars after expenses today. Almost enough to pay for your ticket."

Diego put his hands down flat on the counter and sighed. *"Ho paura."*

"I know. Me too." It was natural for Diego to be afraid. He was going to confront his ex. What if she said no? Even if she said yes, how long would the divorce take?

What if Diego couldn't get back into the US?

They'd found a temporary chef, but would he work out in the kitchen?

All this to deal with, just as things were finally starting to work themselves out at the restaurant.

He said none of those things. Instead, he reached forward to rub Diego's strong arm and say *"Tutto sarà buono." Everything will work out all right.*

Diego started to say something, but the door chime rang out.

"Hey, did you guys save anything for me?" Marcos asked, looking around the restaurant. "Today's the big day, right?"

"Nothing left," Diego said with a sly grin. "But I make you something."

Matteo gave his friend a big hug. "They cleaned us out. Must be Diego's good cooking."

"Or the handsome host." Marcos settled into a chair at the bar. "Thought I'd stop in and check on things before I go to pick up Marissa after school. You two ready for the adolescent army that's about to flood the place?"

"Adoles…?" Diego asked as he fired up the grill and put some pasta on to boil.

"*L'esercito di adolescente*," Matteo explained. "Our new helpers."

"Ah. *Sì*! I am… *eccitante*? Excited."

"We'll see how you feel by the end of the evening." Marcos smirked.

"Something to drink?" Matteo asked his guest as he turned the closed sign around and locked the door.

"Sure… a beer?"

Matteo slipped him a Peroni.

Marcos squinted at it.

"It's kinda like the Italian Budweiser."

Marcos shrugged. "Things are finally going well for you two. That's great. Cheers!" He took a sip of the beer and made a face. "At least it's cold."

"And cheap." Matteo shared a look with Diego. Diego nodded. "Diego's leaving for Italy Saturday."

"Just Diego? You two aren't…?" He looked back and forth at the two of them.

"Oh no, not at all." Matteo chuckled. "Quite the opposite. We haven't told anyone this. We just found out Diego's first marriage never ended."

"Holy shit."

"*Certo*. Oly shit." Diego smiled grimly.

"It could cause problems for us if the authorities found out. So we have to be careful until Diego can resolve the situation with his ex."

Marcos nodded. "Not a word." He got up and gave Matteo a big hug, which he returned a little awkwardly. These Americans and their unexpected displays of emotion. Then he hugged Diego too.

Marcos checked his phone. "Gotta run to pick up Marissa. See you guys in a few."

Matteo let him out and waved as the man ran down the street.

"*Forse non era un buon'idea di dirglielo?*"

"Maybe not. But I had to tell someone. And I trust him."

Diego nodded. "Need to make ready now for the army *adolescente*."

~

Marcos pulled up in front of McClatchy High to wait for Marissa.

She appeared at the steps of the school a moment later, walking with a tall, lanky dark-haired boy.

Marcos leaned forward.

The boy looked like a walking skateboard ad.

Then she kissed him.

Marcos sat back in the seat, flummoxed. *She has a boyfriend.*

He wasn't ready for this. Truth be told, he still didn't feel entirely ready for Marissa, but that ship had sailed. He certainly wasn't ready for Marissa to have a boyfriend. Or a girlfriend, for that matter.

The passenger door swung open, and she settled into the seat next to him. "Hey!" She gave him a peck on the cheek.

"Hey. So, anything exciting happen at school today?"

She shook her head. "Same old boring shit. Come on, let's go! I don't want to be late!"

He shook his head and pulled the car out onto the street.

Marissa had a boyfriend.

Was he supposed to do anything about it?

And if so, what?

~

Diego lined up his new staff, the teenagers who the Center was paying to work at the restaurant from four to seven p.m. three days a week. There were five of them, including Marissa, who had shown some talent for cooking in the Sunday classes.

He read his prepared English speech. "Each of you will learn all aspects of the restaurant business." He wasn't sure if he was pronouncing it all correctly —was it bizniss or busy-ness?—but they seemed to get the drift. "We'll start with Marissa in the kitchen with me as sous chef, Danny at front of house with Matteo, and Meghan, Ricky, and Q as bussers. Understand?"

Marissa winked at Ricky. *Must be friends.*

Matteo and Diego spent the next hour walking the kids through their duties. They reminded Diego of himself when he was first learning the trade.

Matteo showed the bussers where to get the dishes, silverware, and napkins and how to keep an eye on each client without being intrusive. He also showed Danny how to check in guests with a smile and how to keep track of the tables.

In the meantime, Diego worked with Marissa, showing her what they would be making and how they needed to prepare the pasta, vegetables, and sauces.

"You make your own pasta here?" she said, as he demonstrated the process.

"*Sì*. It's necessary. Best flavor. Here, let me show you how."

Marcos watched Marissa with a bemused smile. She was attentive, excited, and *engaged* with Diego. It was a wonderful thing to see her blossom, but it wasn't the only blossoming she was doing, apparently.

They'd have to have *the talk*. He was so not looking forward to that.

In the meantime though, he had to run home to get ready for his hot date.

57.RICE AND ROSES

Dave checked the Spanish rice. It was never as good as when his mother made it. She had a true gift in the kitchen. A pinch of this, a spoonful of that, and her recipes always came out the same. And always delicious.

The *calabacitas*, as his mother called the cheesy zucchini soup she used to make, was almost ready, and the chili verde, his favorite of all her dishes, was practically falling to pieces.

He had cheated on the tortillas, picking up a bag of Micaela's from Nugget. They were just about as good as the real thing and a hell of a lot less messy.

It had been ages since he had cooked for someone else, but it had come back to him as easily as if he had been preparing banquets all year long.

His mother would be proud.

For dessert, he had prepared something decidedly not Mexican—an angel food cake topped with a slathering of whipped cream, strawberries, and bananas. It wasn't *traditional*, but it was a family tradition.

Maybe he was overdoing it. With his luck—which was almost always bad —he'd scare Marcos away with his overabundant table.

Better to be who he was than pretend to be something else.

~

Marcos pulled into the driveway of Dave's place, a cute little brick-and-wood-slat bungalow painted a cheery yellow. It was just around the corner from Carmelina's. In fact, they were attached at the garage.

He parked the Prius and got out of the car, grabbing the bundle of red roses and a bottle of wine from the front seat.

He waved at a man and woman going by on bikes. They waved back and were followed in quick succession by a young boy with a dog, a father trailing three little girls, and a green Karmann Ghia roaring by from the other direction.

It was like that old movie *The Truman Show*, where the kid grew up on TV in this weird dome thing, and the same six sets of people circled by on a loop in front of his window, over and over.

Marcos waited a moment to see if the couple on the bikes came back around.

No such luck.

He shook his head and went to knock on the door.

Dave opened it, flashing him a big grin. "Hi!"

"Hey there." He kissed Dave's cheek. "Um, nice apron."

It was the statue of David, from Florence. Dave glanced down at David's tiny cock. "Well, that's unfortunate." He grinned again. "Hey come on in!"

Marcos followed Dave inside the house. The place was cozy; the walls were painted in a nice Tuscan gold, and candles flickered all around the room. "Very nice. And it smells heavenly in here. Oh, these are for you." He handed Dave the bouquet.

"They're beautiful." Dave took a deep breath of their perfume. "Come on into the kitchen. I'll put them in some water."

The kitchen was *old*, with white cabinets and white tile and grout.

"Sorry. The landlady hasn't redone the kitchen yet."

"Carmelina?"

Dave laughed. He had a beautiful laugh. "I keep telling her it's not a big deal. I'm only here for a little while." He sighed. "At least, that's what I thought five years ago."

Marcos glanced down at the linoleum floors. "Uh huh. Anything I can do to help?"

Dave was trimming the rose stems. He plopped them into a glass vase full of water and handed it to Marcos. "Want to take them out to the dining area and put them on the table? I think we're about ready to eat."

Marcos did as he was told.

A seemingly endless selection of Mexican dishes followed. Chile verde. Rice. Some kind of zucchini soup. Tortillas. Chips. Fresh made pico de gallo. Guacamole.

"Hey, are we expecting other guests or something?" he asked, eying all the food.

Dave stopped, a bowl of refried beans in his hands, and actually blushed. "It's too much, isn't it?"

Marcos laughed and shook his head. "Not at all. It's just a lot of food."

"Have a seat." Dave put the beans down on the table on a trivet. "It's my mother's fault. It's just how she is. You stop by her house and she says to sit down, she'll make you a little something. And the next thing you know, it's Mexican dinner service for six."

Marcos sat. "My mother was the same way. She was constitutionally incapable of cooking a meal for less than eight people."

"Was? Oh Marcos, I'm so sorry—"

"Oh, no, not like that." Marcos grinned. "She lives in Palm Springs now, and she and my dad have a chef who cooks for them most of the time. Now she only goes into the kitchen on the holidays, when the family gets together."

"Got it. Go ahead. Get started." Dave gestured at the food. "You're probably starving."

Marcos was. It had been a long day of coding and then running Marissa around. He scooped up some rice and beans and a helping of chili verde. He took some of the salsa too. He used a tortilla to scoop up a bit of each thing. "Damn, this is good," he said through a full mouth.

Dave wrapped his own food up burrito style and wolfed it down.

"The soup is amazing." He fished out a spoonful of broth and zucchini and cheesy, gooey goodness.

"It's called *calabacitas*—one of Mom's specialties."

"She must be a great cook." There was something else he wanted to say, but he was a little scared to bring it up. "I've… been thinking about you, a lot," Marcos said at last, afraid to look up at Dave lest he be disappointed by his response.

"Me too."

Marcos looked up. "Maybe we could… take things a little faster?"

Dave's face lit up. "Yeah?" He reached out to touch Marcos' hand. "I'd like that." He glanced at all the food. "This will all keep for a little bit—"

knock knock knock

Dave laughed. "Foiled again. Just a sec. I'll go get rid of whoever it is." He jumped up and ran to open the front door, while Marcos took another bite. He'd need to keep up his stamina, after all.

"I'm so sorry to bother you."

Marcos knew that voice.

"Not at all," Dave said. "Come in."

Carmelina entered the house. Marcos could see she'd been crying, even from a distance.

Her gaze registered the candles and the table. "You guys are on a date, aren't you? I'm interrupting you. I'm so sorry. I'll talk to you later." She started to leave.

Dave looked at Marcos, who nodded. "Don't be ridiculous. Come sit with us. We have plenty of food."

She sniffed. "Are you sure? I don't want to be a pest."

Dave nodded and guided her to the table. "Here, have a seat. I'll get you some sparkling water."

"Thanks."

Soon they were all together around the table.

"Now," Dave said, putting his hand on Carmelina's. "Tell us what happened."

As she began to recount what she'd discovered earlier in the day, Marcos turned to look at Dave. He was fully engaged with their friend, the look on his face a mixture of care and true concern. He set everything aside in an instant to help a friend in need.

That was the moment, Marcos would realize much later, that he started to fall in love.

58. THE BOX OF HOPES AND DREAMS

Carmelina hung up the phone. Making that call had been one of the hardest things she had ever done in her life. Asking Daniele to come over so she could… could…

She didn't even know what she wanted from him.

Someone to blame, to yell at, to absolve her of her own guilt.

Hers was the original sin, after all. If she hadn't given that beautiful little baby girl up for adoption so many years before…

There were no answers. Only gnawing guilt, anger, and more questions.

Did Daniele know it was her daughter he'd killed?

She didn't think so. Why confess to her a half-truth if he knew she'd eventually learn the rest?

Her anger flared anew, a blaze of red that momentarily blinded her. She staggered, catching herself against the wall of her kitchen. That was followed by an equally strong wave of sadness.

Breathe, Carmelina, breathe.

She took a deep breath, then another, then another, counting each one in and out. *One. Two. Three. Four. Five. Six.* At last, she reopened her eyes.

She had held so many secret hopes and dreams for her daughter once. She needed to reconnect with them, lest this despair overwhelm her.

She went to her bedroom and opened her closet door. Surely it was still up there somewhere. She grabbed the stool from her bathroom and turned on her phone flashlight, searching the closet shelf.

She found it soon enough, half-buried under a stack of Arthur's clothes she had set aside for donation to the Salvation Army. Putting them on her nightstand, she pulled down the box.

It was a bright-blue hat box that used to belong to her mother. She sat on the bed and laid it next to her, pulling up the lid.

After she had given her daughter up for adoption, she had borrowed this box from her mother, and over the next several years, she had added things to it for the girl, one item at a time, tying each one to a wish or dream.

She picked up the little pair of pink-and-white shoes on top, bought when her daughter would have been a year old. She had hoped that day that Andrea, as she had come to call her daughter, would walk and dance and run and climb and explore all the world in shoes just like these.

Next to the shoes was a plastic unicorn. She'd wanted her daughter to see the wonder and magic in the world around her, to never lose that sense of *possibility*.

There was a Harvard shirt that she'd bought on a visit to Cambridge, when her daughter was approaching college age. She had hoped Andrea would be smart, would get a good education, and would be successful in her life.

The next thing in the box struck at her heart. It was a baby rattle—a plushie ring with a pink bear on top. Bought in the hopes that Andrea would one day have a son or daughter of her own and make a different choice than her mother had.

She held it tightly to her chest with one hand and put the other to her mouth, suppressing a sob. *I'm so sorry, Andrea.*

Marcos and Dave had been so sweet, hugging her and telling her this wasn't her fault. That she had done what she had to do to give her daughter a better life. Her Catholic mother had made it clear that there was no place for an unmarried mother in the family.

The boys next door had taken the time to comfort her instead of kicking her out when they were clearly on a date.

Nevertheless, it all rang hollow.

She should have been there for her daughter, no matter the cost. She should have *known* when Andrea died. Somewhere deep inside her heart, she should have known.

The doorbell rang.

❧

"*Ciao, bella.*" Daniele kissed her on both cheeks. "You said to come over right away, so here I am...." He looked at her face and frowned.

She had been crying on and off for hours. She knew she must be quite a sight.

"What's wrong, *cara mia?*"

This is too hard. She closed her eyes and steeled herself. "Please come in and take a seat on the couch."

"Of course." He did as he was told, still frowning. "What's this all about?"

Carmelina sat in her armchair and picked up a manila folder, handing it over to him wordlessly.

"What is it?" His brow knitted in concern.

"Just read it, please." Even to her own ears, her voice sounded dull and lifeless.

He opened up the folder and started to read. She saw the moment the recognition dawned on his face. "This is…"

She nodded, feeling a strange sense of calm descend over her. Her left hand, the one closest to Arthur's chair, suddenly warmed, as if her dead husband had put a hand over hers.

Daniele finished reading the article and closed the folder and set it down on the glass dining room table. "That was a long time ago," he said softly, looking up at her. "We talked about this, remember? I was a different person then."

She nodded. "Yes. Yes, I'm sure you were." She pulled the little rattle out of her sweater pocket, holding it in her hand. *I'm so sorry, Andrea.* "She was my daughter, Daniele."

Daniele looked at her, at the folder, and then back again. "I… I don't understand."

"The girl you killed, that night you were drunk off your ass." She tried to keep the bitterness from her voice, setting the rattle down on the table next to the folder. "Her name was Andrea. I gave her up for adoption, forty years ago."

"*Porco cane.*" It struck him like a blow, knocking him back into the couch. "I didn't know." He put his hands on his cheeks, his whole body shaking.

Carmelina's calmness was unraveling, consumed by anger, guilt, and sadness. She struggled to keep it together. "I think… I think it's best that you leave. Now."

Pain twisted Daniele's features. "I didn't know," he repeated, sitting up and reaching out toward her. "I am so sorry, Carmelina. Please let me help."

She recoiled from his touch. "I can't be near you right now," she said, her voice brittle as glass.

"It can't just be over. Not like this." The pain on Daniele's face matched her own. "Just talk to me. *Please.*"

She closed her eyes. "I don't know. Maybe later, once I've had some time. Right now, I need you to leave. *Please.*"

He looked up at her once more, like a dog who had just been kicked in the gut. He nodded and got up to leave. "I am so sorry," he whispered once more from the doorway. Then he was gone.

Carmelina locked the door behind him, picked up the rattle, and fled to her bedroom. She gathered all of the things from her box—the shoes, the unicorn toy, the shirt, and the rattle—and held them tightly to her chest, sobbing uncontrollably for what she had lost.

What she had never had.

59. GREEN LIGHT

the days since she and Tristan had met.

They planned to hang with some friends at Sweets and Sugars after school. She was going to try something called a *mangonada*.

It wasn't a date. Not really. But it was with Tris.

She sat through her last class of the day, bored to death, staring at the clock as it ticked down the minutes. It seemed to go slower the closer to three it got. In the background, Mrs. Markham droned on.

Marissa stared at the second hand. Each second seemed long enough to sing the chorus to "Can't Feel My Face" between each *click* of the old clock.

Finally the bell rang, and she leapt out of her seat in her eagerness to get to Tristan. She turned to find her adoptive mother, Jessica, waiting for her. Marissa snarled under her breath.

"Hello, Marissa."

Jessica was *perfect*. She wore a tight pink sweater and a matching pink skirt, gold bangles inlaid with pink coral on her wrists along with matching earrings, and pearls. *Pearls*. Her blonde hair was fresh from the stylist. Jessica Sutton wasn't *on fleek*. She *was* fleek.

"Hello, Jessica."

Her adoptive mother frowned, creating delicate lines around the edges of her lips. "Please don't call me that. I'm your mother—"

"You're *not* my mother." Jessica hadn't earned the right to be called that.

"I *am* your mother," Jessica insisted, "and I don't want to fight with you anymore."

"That's rich, coming from you," she said, shriller than she'd intended.

"Everything all right over there?" Mrs. Markham called from her desk.

"Yeah, we're good, Mrs. Markham," Marissa said. To Jessica, she said, "What do you want?"

Jessica looked uncomfortable, massaging the arm of her sweater between her fingers. "We want you to come home."

"We?" Marissa looked around. "I don't see Phillip and Oliver here."

"Your father's at work. And your brother is in school at Bella Vista. Where you should be."

"I'm perfectly happy here at McClatchy." Marissa picked up her backpack and brushed past Jessica.

"I'll drop the charges," Jessica said.

Marissa stopped, hand on the door knob. "What?"

"I'll drop the breaking-and-entering charges."

Marissa turned around slowly. "In exchange for what?"

"I miss you." She wore a sad pout like an accessory.

Marissa wanted to believe it. She *really* wanted to. But she knew Jessica too well. "In exchange for what?" she repeated, her voice dangerously low.

"I just want you to come home. The neighbors and the folks at the club are talking—"

And there it is. "Unbelievable. You're here because of what other people think? After you threw me out on the street for being… oh, what did you call me… a *disgusting lez?*" She was surprised, but she shouldn't have been. This was a new low, even for Jessica.

"Your counselor said you have a boyfriend now," Jessica said hopefully, ignoring Marissa's anger. "I'm sure the whole *lesbian thing* was just a phase. Come home, and we can put all of this behind us."

Marissa felt her anger building inside. Lesbian thing? *Just a phase?*

She took a deep breath, calming herself down. No good would come of shouting at Jessica, at least not in public. "I can't even… I'm *done.*" She stared at the woman who should have been her mother and saw only bitterness and disappointment there. "I'll see you in court. *Jessica.*"

She opened the door and left the room, closing it firmly behind her.

Then she ran down the hall, eager to be away from that horrible woman.

～

Tristan was waiting for her in front of the school. "Hey there," he said with a grin. "You, um, look a little shady."

"Yeah." They walked toward the street together. It was a warm, sunny Thursday, especially for early October. "Jessica came to see me."

"Jessica?"

"My adoptive mother person."

"I thought you lived with a guardian?"

"Yeah, Marcos. He's a good guy."

"Must be." He scratched his neck. "What did she want?"

"She wanted me to come home. She wants me to go back to being her good little porcelain doll in her perfect little world."

Tristan laughed. "You don't look like a doll to me. So what happened? Why aren't you living with her?"

Marissa sighed. She had hoped to keep her new life less complicated. But her old one kept sticking its nose in where it didn't belong. "She caught me with a girl. She wasn't happy about it, so she kicked me out."

"You're… bi?"

"Yeah."

He nodded. "Cool."

They were at the corner. Marissa looked across the street at Sweets and Sugars. Their friends were waiting for them. She didn't much feel like hanging. "Hey, would you mind if we just walked together for a bit?"

"Sure. Whatever you want."

It was the right answer. They made their way down Freeport, under the shade of the old oak and elm trees, and she told him all about her upbringing in the Sutton household and how she'd finally broken free. Or been pushed out. Somehow it seemed less painful when she talked with him about it. He listened to everything, nodding and interjecting the occasional 'yeah,' 'sure,' or 'that's crazy' at appropriate times. Somewhere along the way he took her hand.

By the time they reached the freeway underpass, she felt really comfortable with him. "It won't matter, anyhow. In a couple more weeks I'll be eighteen, and I can do what I want."

He squeezed her hand. "That's good."

They stopped at the corner, waiting for the light.

She looked him over. He was cute, sweet, a good listener, and with his gauges and tattoos, he was *exactly* the kind of guy Jessica would hate.

She pulled him down for a kiss, and he didn't resist. Their lips met, and she felt good, really good, for the first time all day.

The light turned green, but she didn't even notice.

60. WHIPLASH

"Hey there. You made it!" Sam gave Ben a big hug. "Glad you could come on such short notice. I just thought it might be something you'd enjoy." The space on the sidewalk in front of the convention center doors was packed with people waiting for the conference to start.

Ben grinned. "For a queer writer's con in downtown? How could I say no?"

"We writers gotta stick together." Sam pulled his fleece jacket off. It was warm out for mid-October, and he was already starting to sweat. "Technically it's a diversity con—DiverSac." He frowned. "It sounds kinda dirty, doesn't it? So of course, there's a large queer contingent."

Ben snickered. "Whatever. I'm *this close* to finishing my novel, but I need a little free head space before I tackle the ending."

"How's it going with Ella?" Sam knew things were complicated.

"Um… better? We had a long talk on Monday. She wanted to talk with her mother about me. Her mom's trans, but she doesn't like trans guys, or something? Plus she's been spending time with Max, her brother." He shook his head. "I thought I'd check in with her after I finish the book this afternoon."

"God, I know how that goes. I get so nervous at the end of the story. After all the weeks and months writing the rest of it, can I deliver? Will the ending work? Or will it all fizzle out into a sad pile of wet noodles?"

"Exactly." Ben slapped his arm. "Hey, at least you've gotten one published."

"Yeah, it just ratchets up the pressure for the next one." The gathered crowd shifted forward. "I think they're opening the doors." They followed the crowd into the convention center.

"What are you going to after the welcome breakfast?"

Sam pulled a folded sheaf of paper out of his pocket. "I went through the schedule and made a list. The first one is called 'Politics 101: Writing the Law.' I know it sounds boring, but it's really about how to make legal drama work in books and screenplays. One of the *Law & Order* writers will be there, along with Roald Stone, the guy who writes the *Legally Blind* series."

"Is that the one with the blind detective who 'sees' better than the cops?"

"Yup. They're a little cheesy, but I love how he finds these obscure bits of the law and twists them to his own ends." The latest one was on Sam's Kindle, about half-read.

"Sounds like fun. Mind if I tag along?"

"Mind? I'd love it." It was nice having a writer friend in real life. They registered and grabbed something to eat at the welcome breakfast. Afterward, they went off in search of room 105. They found it at the end of the hall, arriving just in time. The only seats left were in the front row.

"So how many *Law & Orders* and *CSIs* are there now?" Ben asked. "I used to watch the original *CSI*, back when it had the one guy with the hair—"

"Hello, everyone." A young man strode to the front of the panel table, mic in hand; likely one of the con volunteers. "I'm sorry to tell you that we've had to make a substitution on the panel today. Professor Hans Satterlee has been delayed en route from Seattle. In his place, we have Professor Jameson Cort from the University of Arizona English Department."

"That's rich." Ben chuckled. "Professor Court on a panel about writing and the law."

Sam was *transfixed*. There he was, the man he'd left Tucson to escape, looking just as handsome and self-confident as ever, his blond hair neatly swept back and his fine gold-rimmed spectacles layering a gloss of sophistication over his beautiful tanned skin and stubble. His gray sports coat and jeans made him look like the poster guy for "cool literature professor."

"You okay?" Ben asked, waving a hand in front of his face. "You look a little pale."

Jameson's gaze swept the audience and stopped at Sam. The man smiled and then looked away.

Sam shook his head. "I think I'm going to be sick."

"What's wrong?"

"He's my ex."

Sam managed to get through the next hour of the panel discussion, mostly by refusing to look at Jameson. When the man spoke, Sam looked down at his hands in his lap. When Sam closed his eyes, he could almost feel the man's touch—Jameson's hand on his face, his kiss on Sam's neck. The cruel, almost offhanded way he'd treated Sam that paradoxically had only seemed to make Sam want him more. Then, when he'd grown tired, there'd been others....

"Sam, wake up. It's over." Ben was shaking his shoulder gently.

"Huh?" He looked around. Everyone else was getting up and heading to their next panel. "Is he gone?"

"Sam Fuller. What a pleasant surprise."

Sam looked up into Jameson's blue eyes. They were fixed on his, and he felt the electricity between them.

"Hi, I'm Ben." Ben held out his hand, interrupting the connection. "I'm Sam's boyfriend. Nice to meet you, Professor Court. How do you know Sam?"

Sam started to breathe again, and mouthed a silent *thank you* to Ben. "He was my professor in my last year at the U of A. I didn't know you were going to be here, *Professor* Cort."

"It was a last-minute thing," Jameson said, staring at the two of them uncertainly. "It certainly was a surprise to see you here, I must admit. Though I did read your book. It was quite good."

"Thanks," Sam said, uncertain how to respond to that.

"Say, I'm going to be here for a couple of days. If you have time, maybe we could get together and get some coffee and... catch up?" His tone left no doubt as to what he meant.

Bastard. "I'll see. I'm pretty busy this weekend—"

"Here's my card. Call my cell if you find the time." He shook Sam's hand, then Ben's. "Nice to meet you, Ben."

When he turned to talk with someone else, Sam gave Ben a big hug.

"What was that for?"

"For stepping in like that." He raised an eyebrow. "My boyfriend, huh? I thought you didn't play for my team."

"Not usually. But sometimes you need a pinch hitter at the bottom of the ninth."

"I'm not even gonna pretend I know what that means."

"So what's next?"

Sam pulled out his schedule. "Let's see. There's a session on world building I wanted to check out."

"Sounds good." Ben looked at his own copy of the schedule. "Looks like it's in 102. Let's go. I want to get better seats."

Sam followed him out of the meeting room, looking back at Jameson once more.

The man was chatting with a couple of women from the session.

Sam could still *feel* Jameson's touch.

He shivered and followed Ben out of the room.

61. TEQUILA COURAGE

Ben lifted his hands off the keyboard. It was done. For better or worse, his book was done. He sat back, staring at the computer screen. Six months he'd worked on this novel. Six months, this time, since he'd taken his sabbatical. In reality, it was more like six years since he first put metaphorical pen to paper.

I should feel *something.* A surge of excitement. A profound sense of relief. Or even a deep-seated sense of worry that his writing wasn't good enough.

Instead, he was numb.

He printed out the final chapter and stuck it into an envelope to send it off to Sandy. He stopped in his kitchen for a celebratory glass of tequila. He almost never drank, but when he did, he liked the good stuff, and maybe it would loosen him up a bit. He sat down at his little kitchen table and sipped it, savoring the taste. A warm glow slowly suffused his stomach, spreading out into the rest of his body. He sat back and closed his eyes, and Ella was there with him, her beautiful smile beckoning him.

After their long walk on Monday, he'd let her be. She'd told him she was dying with little hope for reprieve. She didn't want to be a burden on anyone. It had all made sense at the time, but tequila had a way of undoing his ordered and logical thoughts. It dredged up all the things that he buried when he was sober, trotting them out for him to see like a cat with a dead mouse.

Ella was beautiful. She liked him. More importantly, she *understood* him. She was totally comfortable with him as a trans guy. He'd seen enough of the world in his thirty-five years to know what a wonderful gift that was.

I love her. The thought surprised him. *What the hell?* He'd known her all of a week and a half. He *couldn't* love her—he hardly even knew her. The whole idea was absurd.

Yet the idea ate at him, worming its way into his head. *I love her.*

He reminded himself of the facts. *Her mother doesn't want me anywhere near her.* And *she's dying.* It made no sense to fall in love with someone who might not make it past Christmas. Simple emotional self-preservation dictated as much. They had no future.

I love her. Nothing good ever came from emotional entanglements. People always turned their backs on you, sooner or later. His parents, his old friends, his last girlfriend… you only opened yourself up for heartache if you let someone get too close.

I love her. He *had* to go see her. He put away the tequila and the used glass and grabbed the envelope for Sandy. He hopped into his trusty old powder-blue VW Bug—the car was sixteen years older than he was—and set off toward Midtown. He'd drop off the package for Sandy at the post office and then head across the river into town.

He knew where to find Ella. He just hoped she'd be happy to see him when he arrived.

～

He pulled into the hospital parking garage and took the first spot he found, screeching into the spot. A man walking to his car glared at him, and he waved back sheepishly. "Sorry!"

He was going too fast. He would scare her off if he kept this up. He closed his eyes. *Think, Ben, think.*

He needed to shake off the effects of the tequila, first and foremost. There was an Everyday Grind kiosk in the hospital. Coffee first, then make a plan.

He found the coffee shop and ordered a regular coffee, black. He needed it to be strong. Then he sat down at a table and drank it in one long drag, slamming the cup down onto the table.

He tried to work out some kind of grand speech, typing it into his phone, but between the tequila and the caffeine from the coffee, he felt hopelessly muddled.

Maybe this had been a bad idea after all. Maybe he should just go home; try this another time.

He got up and headed for the elevator and ran smack into someone, knocking both of them to the ground.

"I'm so sorry!" He got himself untangled and found himself face to face with Ella. "Hi."

"Hi. You need to watch where you're going." Her tone was sharp, but her lips curled up in a slight smile. She was dressed in jeans, a white sweater, and a matching wool cap.

"I was hoping to run into you," he said with a wicked grin of his own. *That* might have been the tequila talking.

"Ouch. That was *bad*." She laughed. "*Really bad*. Help me up?"

He got up and extended a hand to her, lifting her off the floor.

"Were you really here looking for me?"

He looked into her warm brown eyes, and his fear melted away, along with his grand imagined speech. "Yes. I missed you," he said simply.

She shook her head. "We can't do this." She looked away, her face lined with sadness. "You *know* we can't do this. I'm sick, Ben—"

He cupped her chin and lifted her face gently toward his. "I don't care. I'll take whatever you've got. I missed you."

Her eyes searched his. "I don't want to be a burden. I've already asked too much."

"Ella, you are without a doubt the most beautiful girl I have ever met, inside and out. You could never ask too much of me. I just want to spend time with you. Please don't take that away from me."

She closed her eyes.

She looks like an angel.

At last, she nodded. "All right."

He pulled her into his arms, and she hugged him back tightly.

He didn't know what he'd just gotten himself into—just that there had been no other choice.

62. AT THE ZOO

"So why are we here?" Dave looked up at the peaked entrance to the Sacramento Zoo. He hadn't been there since he was a kid. Marcos had called him out of the blue and asked him to get to the zoo as quickly as possible.

Marcos grinned. "There's something I want to share with you." He handed Dave a ticket and looked at his phone. "Come on, or we'll be late."

"Oooh, mystery. What, are the lions in season? A little gay penguin mating going on? Or maybe the seals are putting on a show?"

"Better."

They turned in their tickets and went through the gate into the zoo.

It was a small zoo by national standards, but big enough that you could still kill an hour or two seeing all the animals. Dave's mother used to bring him there after school with his siblings. They didn't have a lot of money, but she'd sprung for the annual pass so they could come whenever they wanted.

Marcos led him past the tigers and lions but not past the bears. Though he did spy a couple of human bears staring avidly at the big cats. "Lions… tigers…"

Marcos laughed. "Too easy."

They veered left, past the river otter enclosure. Marcos was pulling him along now, practically running.

"Where the hell are you taking me? There's not much zoo left."

"You'll see!"

They came around another corner, and there was a short line in front of one of the displays. Dave craned his neck to see what was in the zoo paddock beyond. It craned its neck back to look back at him.

"Giraffes?" Marcos had brought him all the way down to Land Park to see *giraffes*?

Marcos nodded, grinning like a little kid.

"Okay, I don't get it. I've seen giraffes before, lots of times. I mean, they're cool and all—who wouldn't want to have a twenty-foot neck? But…"

"Just be patient." Marcos gave him a quick peck on the cheek. "Oh, and turn around and face this way. I don't want you to ruin the surprise too soon."

What, are we going to take one home? Dave shook his head, but he turned around as instructed and faced away from the paddock. It made things a little difficult as the line moved forward, but he soon mastered the foot-over-foot side step.

Behind him, he heard "oohs" and "ahs." He started to turn but Marcos glared at him. He felt like a five-year-old child waiting to open a present.

"Two?" a zookeeper named Marcie asked them when they reached the gate.

"Yes please," Marcos said, handing her a few bucks in exchange.

"Is he a first timer?" she said, glancing at Dave with a smile.

"Yup. He's a virgin."

"Ouch! Just blurt it out loud, why don't you?" Dave glared at Marcos.

Marcos laughed, then frowned. "Wait… you're not… are you?"

"Are you kidding?" Dave squeezed Marco's ass. "I've had plenty of experience."

"You guys are cute together." Marcie grinned encouragingly. She waved them through the turnstile and up a small flight of stairs, which Dave navigated backwards, slowly. "Have fun!"

Another zookeeper, Carlos, handed them a couple of branches.

"Interesting."

"Okay, you can turn around now."

Dave looked over his shoulder and gasped.

There were two giraffes, one adult and one baby, just five feet away, their heads straining over the wooden railing toward him. "Oh my God." They were beautiful. Their spots were the softest velour, a lovely deep, rusty brown.

He'd never seen a giraffe up close like this.

"Go ahead. Feed them. They're hungry." Marcos pushed him forward gently.

"Just hold the branch out toward them. Keep your fingers back," Carlos suggested. "They won't hurt you, but they get a little eager sometimes."

Dave did as he was told.

The younger giraffe reached out toward him, and he held up the leafy branch like a sword. "Is it a boy or a girl?"

"A boy."

The giraffe took the branch in its mouth, chewing on it and pulling Dave forward in the process. "Hey, slow down, boy. Can I touch him?"

Carlos shook his head. "They're wild animals, and they can get a bit skittish if they are touched."

"Fair enough." He grinned at Marcos. "I'm gonna call him Spot."

"Very creative," Marcos said, handing his own branch to Dave as the baby finished the first one. It snorted loudly, and Dave fell back into Marcos's arms in surprise. Marcos laughed out loud. "He's not gonna hurt you," he said at last. "Go on. Give him the other branch."

Dave inched forward, branch held out in front of him.

The giraffe sniffed it and turned away.

"Oooh, snubbed by a baby giraffe."

"Yeah, funny…. Hey!" As he'd turned to stick his tongue out at Marcos, the other giraffe reached for the branch and pulled it up out of Dave's hands.

She chewed on it sedately, staring down at them with what Dave could only describe as a lazy smile. "And you're Swindler."

Swindler didn't seem to care.

"This is amazing," Dave said as the baby giraffe sniffed in his direction. He'd never realized giraffes were such beautiful, magnificent creatures.

"Worth the drive?" Marcos asked as they exited the platform.

For his answer, Dave pulled Marcos against the railing, wrapped his arms around him, and kissed him.

Marcos held him tight. Dave felt safe. Loved. Desired.

"I take it that's a yes?"

"A definite yes. This was… I've never experienced anything like this. Thank you."

"You're welcome. Hey, we already bought the tickets…. How about we go and explore the rest of the zoo? You said you hadn't been here in a long time?"

"Not since I was a kid."

Marcos took his hand and led him down off the platform.

Dave glanced back at the giraffes, the older one bobbing its head to take a branch from a little girl, who squealed in delight.

What an extraordinary, unexpected thing Marcos had shared with him.

That was the moment, Dave would realize much later, that he started to fall in love.

63. DESCENDENTS

Diego sat in coach, waiting for the plane to taxi and take off. Matteo had dropped him at the curb, hurrying back to the restaurant to get Diego's replacement up to speed with the way Ragazzi's kitchen worked.

Diego stared out the window glumly at the line of planes waiting ahead of them.

Going home should have been a joyous occasion, a chance to see his family—his sister and his mother especially—and all their old friends.

Matteo should have been here with him.

Instead, Diego was on a one-man mission to try to change Luna's mind. To find some way to get out of a decades old marriage before it ruined his new life.

And Matteo's.

Though reforms had been enacted earlier in the year to cut down the time it took to get a divorce, it still meant at least a six-month delay under most circumstances. Far too long. If the immigration authorities caught on before he and Matteo could fix things, he might be thrown out of the United States for good.

Diego cursed the Italian legal system.

He had no idea how he was going to pull this off. He just knew he had to try.

I have a son. That was one more thing to face up to. If Luna were telling the truth—and with her, one never knew—there was a grown man waiting to meet him. Diego had been with Luna in 1987 for a brief time, so that would make his son what… twenty-seven?

It was hard for Diego to absorb—that he might have a son who was already almost into his thirties whom he had never met.

Did the man know about Diego? Did he hate him? Did he wonder why his father had never come to see him, had never been a part of his life?

Luna should have told him. Should have let him make his own choice when it came to the boy—the man.

Diego had sent his sister a long email, explaining everything that was going on with Matteo and Luna. He'd asked her to set up a meeting with Luna after he arrived, so he could… hell, he had no idea what he planned to do or say. But he had to try.

His phone buzzed. He'd forgotten to put it into airplane mode.

Remember, I love you, no matter what.

Diego smiled. Matteo was thinking about him, even in the midst of the rush at Ragazzi. Diego was doing this for the two of them, putting something right that he should have done a long time before.

He had to remember that.

He turned his phone off and shoved it in his pocket as the plane finally turned onto the runway and the engines powered up, pushing the jet down the runway and up into the late morning sky.

Carmelina sat in the comfy chair in the nook by the doorway at the Everyday Grind location closest to River Park. Across the street, the old House of Fashion building sat empty. It was a gorgeous old white building, a bit worn and tattered with age, one that had seen the coming and going of so many seasons that it had approached a sort of timelessness.

Carmelina could relate.

She'd had two days to try to digest what she'd discovered about Daniele and her daughter. She felt shaken to the core.

Why would God do this to her? Play this wretched trick? Send a man into her life, only to break her heart with a cruel twist of fate's knife?

Dave waved at her through the window.

"Hey there," he said as he entered the cafe. "What the hell are you doing here, sitting all alone and moping?"

"Hey, darlin'." She kissed him on both cheeks.

Dave pulled off his jacket and sank down in the chair across from her. "So what's up? Are you doing all right?"

"Thanks for coming. Go get a coffee first, and then we'll talk." Dave always made her smile.

"All right. But I want you to tell me everything when I get back." He squeezed her shoulder on his way to the counter.

Dave had been her go-to guy ever since Arthur had died. He was a rock and always found time for her, no matter how busy he might be.

He was back in a minute with a decaf Americano and a plate of assorted lemon and chocolate scones. "These are for you, too" he said, sitting down and taking a sip of his coffee. "Now tell me. What happened?"

"I told him."

"Oh shit."

Carmelina nodded. "It was the hardest fucking thing I've ever done. After burying Arthur, that is. But I had to hear it from his own lips."

"What did he say?"

"He admitted it. Everything. But he didn't know she was my daughter—at least, that's what he *said*." She closed her eyes, picturing her daughter's face from the newspaper article. "She was a beautiful girl."

"I have no doubt. Look at her mother."

She gave him a wan smile. "He begged me—-did everything but get down on his hands and knees—to let him stay."

Dave stared at her intently. "What did you *do*?"

"I kicked him out. It hurt too much to have him there." She sipped on her mango sunrise tea.

"God. I can't imagine."

"So."

"So." He reached out and put a hand on hers.

She fought it, but she couldn't stop the tears. *God, I'm a mess.* She'd been a regular waterworks these last few days. "I don't know what to do."

He got up and gave her a hug, enfolding her in his warm arms. "I know."

It felt good just to be held by someone who had no claim on her. Who wanted nothing in return.

After a moment, he let go and pulled his chair over to sit down next to her. "What do you *want* to do next? If there's anything I can do to help, you know I'm here."

"I know you are." She thought about it. There was only one thing she wanted. That she needed. "I want to find my grandchild."

64. PEOPLE HAVE IT OFF

MARCOS SAT AT THE DINING ROOM TABLE IN HIS CONDO, WORKING ON his laptop, keeping one eye on the bathroom door. He'd heard stirrings in Marissa's bedroom an hour before, and then she'd popped out briefly, only to vanish into the bathroom before he had a chance to say more than "Marissa, I'd like to speak to—

She'd been in there now for thirty-seven minutes—not that he was counting.

Sooner or later she'd have to venture out, and then they would have *the talk.*

He was dreading it.

He'd never had to give *the talk* before, and truth be told, no one had ever really given it to him either. His father had sat down with him once to tell him "about the whole sex thing." By that time, he'd already been doing the "whole sex thing" for a few months with a cute guy from school named Russ, but his parents hadn't figured out that he was gay yet. So his father's awkward descriptions of vaginas and over-the-bra action and how to treat a lady fell on deaf ears.

He much preferred the AbFab version: "Sweetie, people have it off."

Now here he was in the adult role, one he felt particularly unprepared for this day, but somebody had to do it.

The bathroom door flew open. Marissa emerged from her cocoon.

"Hey there…" he tried, but she was almost too fast for him again.

"Gotta run. See you tonight for dinner!" She flitted past him like a butterfly, kissing him on the forehead.

He grabbed her hand and pulled her gently back. "Wait just a minute, little speedster. I need to talk with you before you go. I've been waiting for you all morning. Please have a seat."

She sank down into one of the other dining room chairs reluctantly. "What is it? I'm already running late…"

"Did you do your homework?" Damn, he felt just like his father.

"Half of it. I'll finish the rest tomorrow. Is that all?" She started to get up again.

"No, wait. I saw you with someone the other day."

She smirked. "You'll have to be more specific."

"With a boy. I saw you kissing a boy, out in front of the school." *Damn, this was hard.*

She laughed. "Yeah, that's one of the things high schoolers do."

"I know." He sighed, exasperated. "Look, please don't make this any harder than it already is. I know you probably have a lot of urges—"

"Eeeew. Wait, are you giving me the sex talk?" She wrinkled her nose.

"Um… yeah? Why, am I doing it badly?"

"Not sure yet. Keep going."

"Okay, so I don't know if your parents—"

"*Adoptive* parents."

"—*adoptive* parents ever talked to you about sex. I'm going to assume you know that when a man and a woman have sex…"

"Baby. Yeah, clear on the whole procreation thing. You know, we have Sex Ed in school now."

"Right." His own Sex Ed had been a series of horror films shown to his class in freshman year. What all manner of venereal diseases would do to you and your privates. He still had pustule-filled nightmares sometimes. "Okay, I want to lay down a few ground rules."

"Got it."

"One, I want you to feel free to talk with me whenever you have questions about it. I'm always here for you."

"Okay."

"Two, I don't think you're ready yet for sex. Sex… it changes everything. You can learn all about it in Sex Ed class and still know absolutely nothing about what sex really is. And once you try it, you can't go back. You haven't tried it yet, have you?"

She stared back at him. "Do you really want to know?"

"I… um… if you want to tell me. Or talk to me about it. I'm trying here."

Marissa nodded. "I know you are." She looked thoughtful. "I haven't yet with the guy you saw. His name's Tristan, by the way."

"Tristan. Okay."

"But I have. Done it. In the past."

"Gotcha." He reached under the table. "I know you're a teenager, almost an adult. I know I can't stop you if you decide you two want to… you know."

"I know."

"But if you do, here is some… protection." He handed her the sack of condoms and lube he'd picked up at the Center.

"You are so much cooler than my adoptive father," she said, laughing. She pulled out the lube. "You know I don't need this, right?" Then she pulled out a condom, turning it over. "Wait, where did you get these?"

"The LGBT Center. They give them out free. Why?" *Maybe they're not the cool kind.*

"I know. I used to go there, remember? You aren't using these, are you? Tell me you haven't used any of them."

"No, I haven't. Why?"

She rolled her eyes. "Maybe we do need to have *the talk*, after all. These condoms are *expired.*"

"Oh shit." *God, I'm a terrible parent.* "Let me see." Sure enough, they were six months out of date.

"You two are having safe sex, aren't you?" She sounded really serious. "You know you can catch all kinds of things if you don't play safe."

"What?" Wait, now she was giving *him* the sex talk?

"You and Dave?"

"We're… we haven't… No. We decided to wait."

"Thank God. I don't think you're ready yet. But when you are, I want you to feel free to talk with me whenever you have questions about it." She kissed him on the cheek. "I'm always here for you." She got up and headed for the door.

"I'll get you some better condoms from the drug store," he called after her.

"Don't bother. I have my own. See you tonight!"

The door slammed behind her.

Marcos stared at it for a long time, wondering how she had suddenly become the adult in the relationship.

65.IN HIS COURT

Sam sent the text and waited anxiously for Jameson to respond. In the meantime, he checked himself again in the bathroom mirror. He had his best *come-fuck-me* clothes on; his black button-down long-sleeved shirt, undone halfway to his waist; his worn Levis that showed off his ass to perfection; his cowboy boots; and the piède de résistance: his black cowboy hat.

He looked damned fine. And fuckable.

He couldn't believe he was actually going through with this, but he needed it. He sent the text.

Yes, I am free. Glad you decided to contact me.

This was going to work.

*See you soon. *cucumber emoji**

"You sure about this?" Brad poked his head into the bathroom, looking a little worried.

Sam nodded. "I need to do it. I'm so glad you understand."

"Not entirely?" Brad gave him a raised eyebrow. "But I'll be okay. Just come back home to me."

Sam kissed Brad on the cheek and called himself an Uber. In five minutes he was on his way.

He was a bundle of nerves: scared, excited, a little nauseous. He'd only decided to do it a half hour before. It had been almost two years since they'd lasts seen each other. The man had preyed on him, using his position as a teacher to take advantage of him. *And yet...*

Now he was here.

Sam's knee bounced up and down in the back seat of the Prius.

"Exciting plans tonight?" his driver, a man named Hector, asked, smiling at him in the rearview mirror.

"Yeah. You could say that."

"It's just… you look a little nervous."

"Yeah." He stared out the window at the buildings along 16th Street. "Meeting an old friend." A bump in the road almost sent his nervous stomach into revolt.

"Hock Farm's a nice place. Took my girlfriend there once."

"Oh yeah?" Sam closed his eyes, trying not to think, to feel.

"You gotta try the burger. You like bleu cheese?"

"Not really." Just the thought of bleu cheese made him uncomfortable at the moment. He drew a long, slow breath, trying to calm his nerves.

"Get the mac and cheese then. They get all their shit locally…"

"Sorry, not in a talking mood."

"I feel ya, man."

Hector went quiet, but Sam had the feeling he'd offended the poor guy. "Look, I'm sorry—"

"Doesn't matter. We're here."

"Look, I'll give you five stars." He pulled out his phone.

That earned him a smile. "Appreciate that. And good luck with your ex-girlfriend!"

"He's not my ex-girlfriend…"

Hector was already gone.

Sam closed his eyes. *Am I sure about this?* There was still time to back out.

"Sam!" Jameson waved to him from half a block away. He was probably coming directly from the convention center. He gave Sam the once-over. "Damn, you look good. All this on my account?"

Sam blushed. "You look pretty damned good yourself." Sam had always had a thing for older guys, especially literary types.

"Thanks. Shall we go inside?" He held open the door, and Sam allowed himself to be escorted in.

"Cort, party of two," Jameson said to the hostess. "Hey, I was kind of surprised to hear from you," he said to Sam. "You and your boyfriend… Ben, is it?"

"Br… Ben. Yeah, right."

"You seemed pretty tight at the con."

"Ben's busy tonight."

Jameson winked at him. "Clearly."

The hostess led them to a table by the window. Sam tried not to stare at Jameson.

"This looks like a nice place," Jameson said approvingly.

"It's one of my favorites. The food's really fresh. Sacramento's a big farm-to-fork town." He looked over the menu and decided on the pork sliders. "So… you seeing anyone?"

Jameson shook his head. "Not really. There was a guy over the summer, but… things didn't work out." He stared at Sam over the menu. "I have a confession to make."

"You're not just here for dinner?"

Jameson laughed. "No, I'm not." Jameson stared at Sam for a moment before continuing. "But I'm not just in Sacramento for a conference, either. I was hoping to find you here."

Sam's heart began to race. "What? Why?"

"You're the one that got away."

Sam stared at him. Here in front of him was the man he'd fallen in love with in college, had hoped to spend the rest of his life with, before… and Jameson was apparently here to apologize to him. "You hurt me pretty badly, you know."

Jameson nodded. "I know. And I'm sorry, I really am." He put his hand on Sam's. "Look, I'm not really all that hungry. Want to… go back to my room? I'm at the Hyatt. It's just next door."

Sam hesitated. Did he really have the guts to go through with this? That touch brought up all the old feelings again. In the end, that was what decided him. He nodded. "Let's go."

Jameson grinned and took his hand. They brushed past the waitress. "Sorry, emergency. Gotta run." Then they were outside.

In the elevator on the way to the seventh floor, his ex reached over to brush his hand across Sam's crotch.

Sam pushed him away gently. "Not yet. Be patient."

"Oh my God, I've missed you." He kissed Sam's neck.

Sam's pulse started racing. He wasn't ready for this.

They reached Jameson's hotel room, and the man pulled him close for a kiss.

Sam turned away. "Let me clean up a little first," he whispered in Jameson's ear. "Why don't you wait for me on the bed? I'll be out in just a second." He closed the bathroom door behind him and shivered.

This was harder than he'd thought. He looked at himself in the mirror. Was this what he wanted?

"I'm ready for you," Jameson called from the bedroom.

He nodded to himself. He *had* to do this. "Coming." He pulled out his phone. Opening the door, he found Jameson spread out on the bed wearing nothing but a condom. "Smile," he said. He snapped three quick pics.

"What the hell are you doing?" Jameson demanded, pulling the bedspread over his naked body.

"Just a little well-deserved revenge. What you did to me was wrong. You took advantage of a much younger student who was stupid enough to believe all your lies and bullshit. Then you cast me aside and started out all over again with someone else." He held up his phone. "Now I have these. If I ever hear that you have taken up with another student, these and my full story will go to the Dean of the U of A's office." He slipped his phone into his pocket. "Good night, *professor*." He left the room, letting the door slam in the face of a sputtering, indignant Jameson Cort.

A young writing student from Sac State Sam recognized from the conference was standing outside with a key card.

Sam rolled his eyes. "I wouldn't, if I were you," he said with a grin. "Unless you like crabs."

"Hell no! Thanks, man!" The guy turned and almost ran back to the elevator.

Jameson had them lining up in the halls. *Came to Sacramento for me, my ass.* The man was the same cheating, lying sack of shit he'd always been.

Sam had been worried he would feel guilty about all this, but he'd been wrong. It felt damned fucking good.

He took another Uber home.

"Did it go okay?" Brad asked.

"Yeah, it did." Sam grinned. "He'll never pull that bullshit again."

Brad sighed with relief. "You had me a little worried."

"You're the only guy I need." Sam pulled Brad close to him, right where he belonged.

66.HOME

Diego pulled his suitcase down from the luggage rack and stared out at the airport through the little oval window. It was a gloomy day in Bologna, and it suited his mood perfectly.

Really, he should be happy. His sister Valentina would be here to pick him up, and he'd get to enjoy some of his mother's home cooking when they reached Bertinoro.

He smiled at the thought. He'd missed his mamma's homemade passatelli —a recipe passed down to her from his grandmother. It had been a real treat sharing it with his students at Ragazzi.

If that made him a *mammone*, so be it. There were worse things than being a mamma's boy.

The line finally started to move, and he nodded at the stewardess as he passed. "*Grazie mille.*"

"*Buona giornata,*" she replied with a bright smile. "*Benvenuto in Italia.*"

At last he was free of the plane's claustrophobic embrace. Fourteen hours was way too long to be cooped up like that.

He looked around for Valentina and was disappointed not to see her waiting for him. He'd just pulled out his cell phone to call her when he heard a shriek.

"Diego!"

He grinned and turned just in time to take his sister into his arms. She squeezed him hard, earning disapproving looks from some of the other disembarking passengers. "You're home! You're here!" She kissed him on both cheeks.

"Yes, I'm here." He couldn't help but smile at her infectious joy. She looked a little harried, her black hair wild with static electricity, but as he remembered, that was her normal state of existence.

"Come on!" She disentangled herself from him and took his hand, dragging him down the concourse. "Do you have any checked bags?"

"Just this one and my backpack."

After nine months in the United States, it was strange to be surrounded by Italian signs, Italian speakers, by everything Italian once again. For once, he was in the majority. *Damn, I've missed this.* "Why are we in such a hurry?" he complained.

"I don't want to pay for a full hour in the parking garage."

"Where are Bianca and Dante?" He'd been expecting to see her kids here with his sister. He'd brought them each a Ragazzi T-shirt.

"They're at home with Mamma." They burst into the fresh, cool air outside, and she led him onward to the parking garage.

It was a good hour's drive home from Bologna's airport, time he was looking forward to spending with her to catch up. "I see you still have the same old beat-up Fiat."

"It still works," she said, swinging open the hatchback so he could stow his suitcase. "Unlike my ex-husband."

Diego snorted. Roger had been in Italy as an exchange student from the US when he'd met Valentina. They'd had a short, sweet romance, a longer, bitter marriage, and an acrimonious divorce.

Diego hopped in the car with her. "You ever hear from him?"

She shook her head, starting up the Fiat. "Not since 2012, when my lawyers tracked him down. He still doesn't send the payments like he's supposed to." She jammed the car in reverse and backed out with the briefest of glances behind her, getting a sharp honk from an oncoming Peugeot.

She gave him a rude gesture and sped off.

Diego laughed.

"What?" She glared at him.

He shook his head. "Nothing. It's just good to be home again."

Soon enough they were out on the autostrada, zooming past farms and wide, open golden fields. After the niceties, their talk turned to the reason he was there. "So this man, Max… he tried to blackmail you?"

"Yeah. He found out about Luna, somehow, and the fact that we'd never gotten a divorce. I should have told Matteo. But I didn't think it would matter. It's not like they let gays marry here anyhow."

"And now you could be in a pile of trouble with Immigration if they found out?"

"Yeah. I have to get Luna to agree to a divorce. Even then it might not help."

She nodded. "My divorce took three years, and that was after he left the country and his own children."

"I know." He sighed, watching the passing countryside go by. He had no idea what the answer was, but he had to try. For Ragazzi. For Matteo.

"Luna has agreed to meet you on Tuesday. I thought you could use a couple of days with the *famiglia* first."

Diego nodded. "I'm looking forward to Mamma's—"

"*Passatelli.* I know." She laughed, and the sound did his soul good. "It's all you ever talk about it. She's making some for lunch."

He grinned. "How are the kids?"

"In trouble, as always." She handed him her phone. "Check the photos."

He flipped through them. Bianca was wearing her soccer clothes and had a skinned knee. Dante looked more reserved, as always—quiet kid, but so smart. "What did they do?"

"Bianca slipped off her bike in town and got a couple of nasty cuts. Dante brought some rats he trapped to school in his backpack, and they escaped."

"Damn. That must have been interesting." How was he missing all these things?

"He got suspended for three days."

They pulled off the autostrada and climbed up into the hills. Diego got a lump in his throat as they approached the village. He'd grown up here, in a little house on the outskirts of town. It was a small place, maybe ten thousand inhabitants all told.

Soon Valentina was pulling into her driveway on Via Giovanni Bovio. The car jerked to a halt. "We're here!" She climbed out of the driver's seat and slammed the door.

"Ciao, Valentina," a woman called from across the street.

"Ciao, Mrs. Ricci! Diego's home!" She pointed at her brother proudly.

"*Benvenuto a casa,* Diego," Mrs. Ricci called, beaming, her floral-print dress and gray hair flapping in the breeze. "You have to come over and see me when you have a chance."

"I will, Mrs. Ricci. I promise."

Diego grabbed his luggage. He looked up at the two-story white stucco building with its signature red tile roof. It looked like it needed a new paint job.

He shrugged and followed Valentina inside, where he was immediately assaulted by the most wonderful smell. *Passatelli.*

He dropped his bags and ran into the kitchen. "Mamma!"

His mother, well into her sixties, set down her spoon and turned, a look of joy creasing her features. She opened her arms to him. "My Diego. Oh how I have missed you!" She hugged him tight, sending up puffs of flour from her apron that made him sneeze.

He didn't care.

He was home.

67. THE ACCIDENTAL CHEF

"WHAT DO YOU MEAN, YOU CAN'T COME IN TODAY?" MATTEO STARED AT his cell phone, on speaker mode, rubbing his temples.

"Sorry," Phil, their fill-in chef, said. "Like I said, I'm sick. Cough cough."

Matteo looked up at the clock. "It's a quarter to nine on a Sunday. In two hours, we're opening for lunch. How am I going to find someone so fast?"

"Not my problem, boss."

Things had gotten off to a rocky start between them the day before. Phil had seemed like an odd fit to Matteo from the beginning, but Diego said his resumé was perfect, and he'd come highly recommended from his last job. Which Matteo imagined must have been at a low-rent burger joint, the way he'd splattered grease and flour around the kitchen. They'd had words afterward, and Matteo had spent two hours cleaning up after the man had stormed out.

Now he was without a chef for Sunday service and for their weekly cooking class.

"We hired you to do a job," Matteo said testily. "I need you here in half an hour."

"No can do. *Maybe* I'll be able to make it in tomorrow. If I'm not sick anymore. Cough."

"Get here in thirty minutes, or I'll find another chef!" He hung up. Pushing a little colored button on a screen was a hell of a lot less satisfying than slamming down a receiver.

Ten till now. He needed a chef, and he needed someone fast.

He made half a dozen phone calls to friends of Diego's. Everyone was booked or out of town.

At last he reached Dyson Clay, the handsome chef down at Forked. "Yeah, I can help you guys out. But I have to be out of there by one thirty, one forty-five latest."

"Thank you so much! *Oddio*, you don't know how much that will help."

"Happy to help. Be there in an hour."

Matteo hung up and took his first real breath of the morning. Lunch was covered. That was the most important thing.

Now he just had class to worry about.

"Well, that's it, then." Dyson washed his hands at the kitchen sink after they'd finished loading up the dishes in the dish washer. "Nice crowd today."

The expediters had already been sent home.

Matteo nodded. "We've been getting good… *come si dice*? Mouth words?"

Dyson laughed, deep and heartily. Though he was in his late sixties, the chef was handsome still, what they called a silver fox. Or maybe a silver bear. "Word of mouth. That's really good. Anytime I can lend a hand—"

"How about tonight?" Matteo said hopefully. He had no desire to call Phil back again.

"Ah, wish I could, but I have a chef's table thing at the restaurant tonight." He dried his strong, hairy arms. "You a Kings fan?" Handsome though he was, the man was also terminally straight.

"Not really."

"Too bad. It would be fun for you and Diego to come with me and Alyson to a game sometime. And when the new arena opens next year…"

"We'll get a lot more business out our way after your downtown parking rates go up," Matteo said with an evil grin.

Dyson snorted. "You're probably right." He pulled off his apron as he headed for the door. "See you!"

"Thanks again." Matteo glanced at the clock. He had about fifteen minutes to get things ready for the class. He was no chef, but there was one thing he knew how to make.

Dessert.

Carmelina was the first to arrive at Ragazzi.

She'd almost decided to stay at home. The last few days had been bleak, as if the world had tipped sideways and all the color had drained out, but she wasn't one to wallow in self-pity.

Matteo stood behind the counter, looking forlorn. "*Ciao, bello.*"

"*Ciao, amica!*" He perked up at the sight of her, flashing her a big smile.

"Where's Diego? Is he running late today?"

Matteo shook his head. "He's in Italy. He… he had some family business to take care of."

"Well, then, we'll just have to get to know each other a little better, then, won't we?"

Matteo laughed. "I guess so."

"What are we making today?" She eyed the counter, which was covered with fruit and stacks of chocolate bars, both white and dark. "I like what I see so far."

"I'm not a chef, but I do make a good dessert. It's one of Diego's preferreds."

"Favorites?"

"Favorites. Thank you. It's called *Spiedini di Frutta al Cioccolato.*"

She grinned. "Oooh, sounds sexy. What does it mean?" As long as it had chocolate in it, she was sure to love it.

The bell on the door rang, and Marcos and Marissa arrived. "Oooh, chocolate," the teenager said as she plopped herself down at the counter. "Can I?"

Matteo nodded. "Sure. We have extra."

"Hey there," Marcos said, kissing her on the cheek.

"Hey darlin'."

"In English? Fruit and chocolate stick?"

"Stick?" The lightbulb went off. "Oh, skewers." On one side of the counter there was a stack of metal skewers. "So, what do we need to do?"

"You want to start cutting up the fruit? We'll serve these for dinner tonight too."

"Sure thing." She washed her hands and grabbed a kiwi and a knife and started cutting.

It felt good to be busy.

~

After class, Matteo pulled Carmelina aside. "I need your help."

She read the distress in his eyes. "Sure. What can I do?"

"We lost our chef for dinner tonight. I think I have someone for tomorrow, but people will start arriving in an hour."

"You need a chef." Why was he asking her?

He nodded, looking miserable.

"Matteo, I'm not a chef—"

"But you *know* how to cook."

She shook her head vehemently. "There's no way I can run a restaurant. I've never done it before."

"You've cooked for your family, right?"

"That's different. It's just one or two dishes." The man must be off his meds.

He nodded. "Perfect. That's all we need. We'll call it a special event. Just make what you know best."

"I don't know—"

He took her hand, looking into her eyes with his big brown eyes. "Please? I don't know what else to do."

She thought about it. She did have a couple of dishes her nonna used to make, that she knew how to prepare without a recipe. And it *would* keep her mind off Andrea. And Daniele. "All right. I'll do it."

"Thank you."

"But you have to stay and help. You can't leave me here all alone."

Matteo nodded.

"Okay, I need some flour, eggs, tomatoes… where do you keep your biggest saucepan?"

A neatly hand-lettered sign appeared in the front window half an hour later:

Special Event!
Il Menu Presso Fisso:
Mamma Carmelina's Homemade Ravioli
Red Wine
Spiedini di Frutta al Cioccolato
$12.99

See the spiedini di frutta recipe at the end of the book.

68. TRIBES

Marcos stood on the sidewalk outside Capital Stage, staring at the passing cars on J Street. It was still warm out, too warm for a mid-October evening, but he didn't mind.

People brushed past him, entering the nondescript one-story building to collect their tickets. Nondescript except for the brightly colored mural painted on the red outer wall of the place. The season had just begun, as had the signature mural Cap Stage commissioned every year along its front wall, adding a new panel for each of its six plays.

Marcos wasn't much of a theater goer, but Dave was, and apparently seeing plays was one of the things couples did when they were dating. Marcos preferred movies, with their slick soundtracks, big buckets of popcorn, and seat-shaking effects.

Then again, Marcos was a little rusty at the whole dating thing in general. For most of his adult life, he'd been more of a pickup guy, master of the one-night stand.

Look where that had gotten him: alone and lonely at forty.

Time to try something different. And so here he was at a play on a Sunday night in Midtown.

He glanced at the tickets. The show was called *Tribes*, and it had something to do with a deaf kid and his family. Beyond that, Marcos didn't have a clue.

"Hey there. Sorry I'm late." Dave gave him a quick kiss. He was adorable in a bright-blue cashmere sweater and black jeans, though he must have been warm.

"Just happily waiting for you."

Dave grinned. "It's nice to be waited for. Ready to go in?"

Marcos opened the door and ushered Dave inside, taking advantage of the opportunity to admire Dave's backside.

The woman behind the counter waved at them as they came in. The place was clearly in an older building, vintage fifties like much of this stretch of J Street, but it had been nicely remodeled. A long hallway led back to a modern industrial-style lobby, complete with a small snack bar.

"Feel like a coffee?"

Marcos grinned. "I'd love one. Oooh, these cookies look good too."

"So get one!"

Marcos shook his head. "It'll make me fat."

Dave laughed. "I don't think it would hurt. You look great to me."

"Because I never eat cookies."

"Well, I'm going to have one. I've been good today. Fruit for breakfast and a salad for lunch." Dave stuck his tongue out at him. "Do what you want."

Marcos weighed the calorie risk versus the solidarity of sharing one with his date and gave in.

"You two are adorable together," the guy behind the counter said with a grin.

"You hear that?" Marcos said, giving Dave a quick kiss. "We're *adorable*."

"Yeah, don't let your head swell up."

Marcos held out a twenty.

Dave pushed his hand out of the way. "I invited you, so I'm going to pay for it."

"But *you* paid for the tickets."

"Don't take his money." To Marcos he said, "Put that away. It's no good here."

Marcos shrugged. Another first: letting the other guy pay for him. This whole dating thing was going to take some getting used to.

They wandered into the courtyard behind the theatre, and Marcos was struck by the fountain. It was a green piano, but where the keys should have been, a waterfall poured out. "This is amazing." He walked around it to see how it had been put together.

"It is. I love what they've done with this patio. It used to be just a bare slab of concrete."

They found a couple of chairs, sipped their coffee, and nibbled at their cookies.

Marcos felt awkward. He'd exhausted his small talk at the fountain. What the hell did guys talk about when they weren't trying to get each other into bed? Not that he would have minded....

He'd picked up a new box of condoms just in case. He had a serious case of blue balls, but Dave was worth the wait.

The courtyard lights flashed.

Power outage? "What the hell?"

"That's the five-minute warning." Dave pulled him out of his seat. "Let's go take our places."

They found their seats in the front row, and Marcos settled in to see what this whole *live theatre* thing was all about.

~

Two hours later, the lights came up; the actors took their bows.

Marcos sat there, stunned.

"So what did you think?" Dave looked at him anxiously.

"It was… oh my God, it was like looking at my own family up there." The play had touched him viscerally. The story and the immediacy of live theatre. He could almost have reached out to touch the actors as they passed by left and right, spinning their tale.

It had been like watching his own childhood.

Dave raised an eyebrow. "You're not deaf." They got up and followed the crowd out of the theatre.

"I don't know. It's hard to explain." He looked up and down J Street. "Feel like going to the Grind for a coffee? Maybe talk a little?"

"Sure." Dave took his hand, and they walked down the street together. Such open displays of affection in public still made him a little nervous, but Dave's gesture brooked no argument.

They walked in silence toward the coffee shop, each lost in his own thoughts.

Once they got their drinks, they sat outside on the boardwalk under the giant oak tree. It was a perfect evening.

"The play really got to you, didn't it?" Dave asked at last, cocking his head to the side.

Marcos nodded. "Yeah. I… I never liked theatre. I mean, I never really *tried* it. But it always seemed so pretentious to me."

Dave laughed. "It can be. But it can also be gut-wrenching, frightening, or enlightening. Sometimes even transformative."

"Transformative. That's a good word." The way Billy, the deaf character, had been such an alien in his own family. How they'd never bothered to learn sign language or even teach it to *him*. How they turned away from him so he couldn't tell what they were saying and wouldn't bother to let him know what was said. "It was like he was an outsider in his own home."

"Ah."

"My parents never understood me when I was a kid. To my father, playing with dolls and painting my nails red at ten were things that needed to be beaten out of me for the sake of my manhood." He thought about it. "When Billy finally found someone to teach him sign language, when he found a whole community of people out there like him…"

"It was his coming out."

"Exactly." The play seemed like a metaphor, intended or not, for queer kids. For his own teen years even. "I never thought about it like that. I was an outsider in my own tribe."

Dave put a hand on his. "You have a new tribe now."

Marcos looked up into Dave's eyes. They were full of warmth and compassion.

And love.

He pulled Dave to him and kissed him for a long time, earning applause and cheers from a couple of passersby. "Want to come over?" Marcos asked, his voice hopeful.

"Is Marissa home?"

"She's staying with a school friend tonight. We'll have the whole place to ourselves."

Dave grinned. "I brought a change of clothes."

Marcos stood and left his coffee to cool on the table. He pulled Dave up with hi, and took him home.

It turned into a perfect night too.

69. OFFICE HOURS

Carmelina sat at a table for two at Temple Coffee, clutching a Post-it nervously and staring at her phone.

Eleven-thirty a.m.

Her cup of coffee was going cold beside her, untouched.

She'd spent the better part of the morning at the Sac Bee's offices, convincing the nice young woman at the obits desk to help her find Andrea's obituary. She'd tried online first, but the Bee's site had failed to turn up anything.

Now at last she had a copy of it, and with it the names of Andrea's adoptive parents: Susan and Darryl Smith.

Smith was a tough nut to crack—there were so damned many of them—but she'd managed to find a Darryl Smith. He was a Professor of Archaeology at Sac State, just minutes from where she lived, and she had his office number.

Sac State.

Carmelina closed her eyes, wondering how often her little girl had been there with her father. So close.

She used to walk the school grounds daily, wandering the sidewalks under the beautiful trees, enjoying the youthful energy that abounded there. How many times they might have crossed paths, maybe even have seen one another.

She was filled with guilt.

Wasn't a mother supposed to *know* her children? Shouldn't there have been some spark of recognition, some kind of instant rapport? She'd searched her memory, trying to recall an instance when she might have seen Andrea being pulled along behind some stranger. When their eyes would have met, when she might have *felt* that connection.

There was nothing.

Somewhere out there though, she had a grandchild. Somewhere in the world there was a little piece of her still, and a piece of her daughter too.

That decided it.

She picked up the phone and dialed Professor Smith's number.

It rang three times.

"Hello?" It was a man's voice. He sounded vaguely annoyed.

"Professor Smith?"

"My office hours are from two to five. Please call me back at that—"

"I'm so sorry to bother you. I'm not a student." She took a breath, then plunged ahead. "Are you the Darryl Smith who's married to Susan Smith?"

There was a sharp intake of breath on the other end of the line, and then a long pause. "Who wants to know?"

"I had a question—"

The line went dead.

Carmelina sighed. She supposed she might have reacted the same way if someone had called out of the blue, asking for private family information.

But his reaction told her one thing. *This is the guy.*

And he had office hours starting at two p.m.

She was waiting in one of the hard wooden chairs outside of his door just after two when an older man approached. He was probably in his mid-sixties, with a full gray beard and a balding head.

"Hello," he said as he unlocked the door. "Can I help you?"

"Professor Smith?"

"Says so on the door."

She laughed, but he didn't. "Ah, um, might I have a moment of your time?"

He looked her over and apparently decided she didn't look dangerous. "Come in. You can put those books on the floor over there."

The books he was referring to were stacked on one of two additional wooden chairs which sat on one side of a desk covered with them, as were bookshelves on all four walls, crammed with books old and new. She lifted the stack from the indicated chair—*Ancient Rome, Dwellings and Detritus, The*

Hidden Pompeii—and placed them carefully on the ground. "You have a lot of books," she said, forgetting momentarily her reason for coming.

"You said you needed a moment?" He settled into his old green leather chair, which squeaked in protest. "I'm afraid I don't have much more than that. I have a student appointment at two-thirty, and I need to check my email."

Carmelina stared at the books that covered his desk. There was a computer somewhere under there? Shaking her head, she jumped right in. "I called earlier about Andrea—"

He snarled, "You reporters, always looking for an angle. She was killed in a car accident, and she's dead and buried. That's all I have to say. Now if you'll excuse me." He stood and pointed to the door.

"I just need—"

He lifted her up and pointed her to the exit. "Please don't bother me again." He gave her a little shove and started to close the door behind her.

She had no time to be offended at his rude behavior. "Professor Smith… Darryl… please. She was my daughter!"

The door stopped.

He stared at her through the opening for a moment. "What do you mean?" His voice had a dangerous edge.

"She… I gave her up for adoption. in August of 1975. I just found out that she died. Please… please talk to me."

He looked down at the ground, and for a moment she was sure he would turn her away. The air around him seemed to shimmer for a moment

Carmelina shook her head. She was imagining things.

At last he nodded and opened the door again. "Come in."

She sat again across from him. "Thank you."

"I always thought this day would come. When you adopt a child, you wonder why someone would ever give up such a precious thing."

"I was very young." She pulled a manila envelope out of her purse and handed him a copy of Andrea's adoption paperwork. "So you know I'm not lying."

He took it and looked through it. "Fifteen. You *were* young." It didn't sound like understanding. "So what can I do for you, Ms.…"

"Di Rosa. I was hoping to talk with you and Mrs. Smith—"

"Mrs. Smith passed away fifteen years ago, not long before Andrea."

"Oh, I'm so sorry. What happened?"

"Cancer."

Oh God. She nodded. "I am so sorry. I lost my husband just a few months ago."

"My condolences."

She realized she was crying, just a little. Arthur, then all this…. It was too much.

"Here, take a Kleenex." The professor handed her a box, and she took one gratefully, wiping at her eyes and blowing her nose. "What can I do for you? Please understand, I'm not trying to be an ass. That part of my life was very painful, and even now it's hard for me to reopen those old wounds."

She nodded. "I'll keep it brief, then. I understand that Andrea had a child."

"Yes. Her name was Mary. She was almost two when Susan passed away." He looked away, his face turning red. "It was just the two of us. Neither of us had any family. That's why we adopted: to give a home to someone who didn't have anyone else. When Susan died, I couldn't… I just couldn't." He was shaking.

Mary. She felt horrid for bringing all this up for him again. But she had to know. "So you gave her up? For adoption?"

He nodded.

"She *has* family, Darryl," she said softly. "She has me. You and Susan did everything for Andrea. Now I want to find Mary and give her that too." Wherever she was, she probably had a family already. But she'd deal with that reality later.

He nodded. "Give me your email. I'll see what I have and will send it to you tonight or tomorrow." He looked her in the eye. "Did you miss your daughter, after?"

She sniffled, her tears dangerously close to the surface. "Every day."

"Me too. If you find her… can I meet her?"

She nodded. "I'd like that." She reached out a hand, and he shook it.

"I'll email you soon."

"I'll be waiting."

She left him, and for the first time in days, she felt a ray of hope.

Her name is Mary. I have a granddaughter.

70. WEEKIVERSARY

Marcos stared morosely at the lawyer across the desk from them.

Mort Zimmerman was an old family friend, someone his mother had referred him to when he'd called to tell her what was going on with Marissa and her parents. The man didn't hold out much hope. *It's never fucking easy.*

Marcos had picked Marissa up after school and brought her to the consultation, but he'd hoped the news would be better. "So… just so I have this straight. Even though she is taking her own daughter to court, there's nothing we can do to show she's an unfit mother? I mean, she's taking Marissa to court."

Mort shook his graying head. "I didn't say that. Let's just take one thing at a time. The first thing we need to do is to deal with this charge of breaking and entering." He turned to Marissa, looking at her over gold-rimmed glasses. "Did you take anything from the house that wasn't yours?"

She shook her head. "Only some clothing. My teddy bear. Some cash I had saved—"

This was new to Marcos. He wondered what else he didn't know.

"Where was the cash?" Mort asked, his voice kind.

"In my sock drawer, inside a music box my aunt gave me."

Mort sighed. "*That* could be a problem. They might claim the money belonged to your parents." He typed in some notes on his laptop, the keys clacking loudly in the silence of the room. "When did you see your parents last?"

Good question. "When they found her in her bedroom—"

Mort held out a hand to silence him. "I was asking Marissa."

Marcos looked over at his charge. She squirmed uncomfortably in her chair. "Thursday," she said at last.

"What???" Marcos was half out of his chair before he realized he was moving. He sank back down, his face hot. "*Where* did you see her on Thursday? And why didn't you tell me?"

Her face drained of color as she stared at her entwined hands. "She… she came to school to see me. She told me that if I came back to live with her, if I dropped the whole 'lesbian thing,' that she would drop the charges." She looked up at him. "I'm sorry I didn't mention it. I just wanted to forget it had happened."

"What did you tell her?" Knowing she'd kept this from him was making him acutely uncomfortable.

"To go to hell."

Marcos snorted. "I'll bet she didn't appreciate that." Jesus. It was just like when he was a teenager, and his parents had thrown him out for being gay. He'd hoped the world had changed, and yet here they were. And yeah, he might have kept it to himself too, at that age. "So what do we do?" he asked the lawyer.

"It's a first offense. We'll argue that she didn't do any harm or really steal anything at all, since they were all her possessions to begin with. We point out that the parents were the ones who put her out on the street in the first place, so they bear some of the blame. Marissa, you turn eighteen on the day after the hearing?"

"October 28th."

He nodded. "Technically you're still a minor. We'll use that. Mr. Ramirez, are you willing to take on a more permanent role as Marissa's guardian? She'll legally be an adult soon, but the court might be more comfortable letting her off the hook if it's clear she has mature adult supervision."

Marcos took a deep breath. He hadn't planned anything of the sort when he'd reached out to Marissa that first day outside Ragazzi. It was a lot of responsibility.

He looked over at Marissa.

She was staring at him, waiting for his answer.

He looked down at his hands.

"It's okay. If you don't want me." Her tone belied her words. She *needed* him. "I can take care of myself."

He almost laughed. She was so much like he'd been at that age that it hurt sometimes. *That* was what decided him. "Of course I want you," he said, looking up at her. "You're a part of my life now, as much of a whirlwind as that's been."

She stared at him as if trying to judge the sincerity of his words. Then a grin spread across her face like wildfire. She *leapt* at him, throwing her arms around his shoulders. "I love you, Uncle Marcos."

Uncle Marcos. He chuckled. He could live with that.

~

"That was something back there." Marissa got into Marcos's Prius. She was still a little in shock that he'd agreed to act as her permanent guardian.

"The lawyer?"

"No. What you said. About me."

"I meant it. You can count on me to be there for you, 'Riss." He gave her a quick hug.

She loved how those warm arms made her feel.

"You gotta not be afraid to tell me things. Okay?" He let her go, and she wiped her eyes before he could see the tears.

She nodded. "I'll try. Can you drop me off at Rick's?" she asked, suppressing a sniff.

Marcos started the car and pulled out onto I Street. "Have a sweet tooth, do you?"

"Kinda." It was her weekiversary with Tris, and they'd decided to hang and share a piece of chocolate cheesecake.

"You meeting some friends there?"

"Yeah, something like that."

"One friend in particular?" He grinned at her.

"Maybe."

Marcos shook his head. "I don't see how you can eat so much sugar. It'll rot you from the inside."

"I'm young and beautiful." She said it with a dramatic flailing of her arm. "I can handle it."

He laughed. "And don't think I'm not onto you with this whole 'Uncle Marcos' thing."

"I don't know what you're talking about." Marissa pulled out her phone and texted *almost there* to Tris.

"Look, I know our 'talk' didn't go so well the other day." They pulled up at the curbside in front of Rick's Dessert Diner. "Just be careful, whatever you two do."

"I will." She kissed him on the cheek and started to get out.

"Hey."

"What? He's waiting—"

"I want to meet him."

She turned to stare at him. "Why?"

"It's what we uncles and parental figures do. How about dinner? Friday?"

She bit her lip. "I'll think about it."

"Be home by eight. It's a school night!"

She blew him a kiss and shut the door, waving at him as he drove off.

Tristan was waiting for her inside, looking gorgeous in a black Brain Dead T-shirt, black beanie, and jeans.

She slid into the booth next to him and gave him a kiss. "Happy weekiversary!"

He laughed. "That's the dorkiest thing I've ever heard."

"How about this? My… Marcos wants me to bring you over for dinner."

"Sure, why not?" He pushed a loose lock of hair back behind her ear.

"You don't mind?" That surprised her. Her dates always *hated* meeting the parents.

He shook his head. "Has to happen sooner or later. Hey, does this mean we're getting serious?"

She thought about it. "I don't know. Maybe? We don't have to—"

"I'd like to." He whispered in her ear. "Real serious."

She shivered. What his voice did to her, inside. "Maybe—"

"One slice of chocolate cheesecake a la mode." The server dropped off the plate and a couple of forks and put an end to the discussion. "Enjoy!"

Tris offered her a forkful of chocolate cheesecake. "Think about it?"

"I will," she said, and bit into the cheesecake. It was delicious.

Sinful things always tasted the best.

71. NOW I KNOW

SAM SCANNED THE ROOM.

Temple was one of Brad's favorite hang-outs. Just two blocks from the Center, the local coffee shop was a work of art. Its floors were plastered with rows upon copper rows of pennies, all laminated into the floor and up the sides of the counter. 532,000 of them, as Brad was often fond of telling him. He found Brad sitting on the cafe's brown leather couch, perusing a copy of Outword, the local gay paper.

"Hey there." he gave Brad a quick kiss.

"Hi!" Brad put the paper down. "I got you a mocha. Hope that's okay."

"It's perfect." He took the cup and snuggled into the other end of the couch. "You called?" Brad didn't usually bother him at home unless it was urgent. It was his work time.

Brad nodded, setting down his own cup. "Yeah, sorry. I know you were writing. It's just—"

"That's okay." Sam sipped at the mocha. It was good. He'd been dying for a little coffee. He stared at Brad for a moment, trying to puzzle out what was going on. "I hit a sticking point, anyhow. It's good to get out for a few minutes. What's up?" *Still upset about Jameson?*

Brad didn't answer for a moment. He picked up his coffee again and took a sip. "This is hard for me to ask." He stared at Sam over the top of his coffee.

Sam reached out and put a hand on Brad's shoulder. "Just spit it out. It's about Jameson, isn't it?"

Brad nodded.

"I knew I should have left well enough alone." Sam sighed and sank onto the couch to stare at his hands. He'd screwed things up with Brad. He knew it.

"Yeah, it's about Jameson. I need to know something. Be honest."

"What?" Sam's face felt numb.

"You and him. He was your first, right?"

Sam nodded. "First relationship. Not my first guy."

"God, I'm gonna screw this up. Forget I even—"

Sam laughed halfheartedly. "I thought I was the one screwing things up here." He looked into Brad's eyes. "Just *ask*." He *knew* what Brad was asking.

"Do you... still love him? Or have feelings for him?" Brad looked like his whole heart was balanced on the end of that question.

"No, I don't." He had once. Maybe. But not like what he felt for Brad. He tried to find the right words, feeling clumsy and awkward. "What we had... when I first met him, I was flattered that such an accomplished professor would take me seriously. He was handsome, refined—I mean..." *Some word-smith I am.*

"Older." Brad's eyes narrowed. "You never talked about him before."

"I know. When we broke up, it almost broke *me*." He thought back on those sun-filled October afternoons when Jameson had taken Sam under his wing. "It started out innocently—brushing his hand past mine, accidentally bumping into me when we got up. Then one day, I noticed... how interested he was in me. In a different way." Those tight jeans had hidden nothing. "I made a mistake. He was my teacher. I shouldn't have—"

"It wasn't your fault." Brad's voice was calm and reassuring, the edge gone.

Something had shifted, but Sam wasn't sure what it was. He forged on. "Anyway, we were together for three years. I *thought* it was real. But he'd been cheating on me the whole time." He'd come home from class to the house they shared, early one Monday afternoon, to find Jameson in bed with a fresh-man, someone from his English 101 class. He wasn't sure what hurt more: the betrayal itself or the fact that his lover had chosen someone who shared none of their love for the written word. "You can't erase the past. When I saw him at the conference..." He looked back at his hands. There *had* been a spark there, an attraction. It killed him to admit that, even to himself.

Brad took his hand. "Do you still have feelings for him?" he asked again.

Sam sensed something at work here, as if Brad saw right through him, knew what he was thinking. "No. There was a moment of... I don't know... lust? Chemistry? A fleeting remnant of what I thought we had. But there's nothing else there." He looked up again.

Brad's eyes were wet, and he seized Sam up in a tight hug. "I love you so much. You have no idea how much."

Sam returned the hug. "What's this all about?"

Brad sniffed and pulled away, holding Sam at arm's length. "I needed to hear you *say it*. When you walked into my life last year, you made me a different man. A better man. But then Jameson showed up, and I was so scared I would lose you." He squeezed Sam's hands in his own. "Now I *know*." Brad let go of Sam's hands and eased down on one knee next to the couch, put a hand into his pocket, and pulled out a small black velvet box.

The whole place went silent.

Brad looked up at Sam, and his eyes shone. "Sam Fuller, will you marry me?" He opened the box to reveal a flawless white-gold ring.

Sam almost choked. His own eyes blinded with tears. "Holy shi— Oh my God. Yes! Of course! You just… there's a ring… oh my God!" He pulled Brad up into his embrace, putting his arms around his love's waist, his thumb wrapping around Brad's belt loop.

Brad kissed him deeply. The onlookers exploded into cheers.

After a long moment, they separated, just a little. Brad put his chin on Sam's shoulder.

"I love you, Brad Weston," he whispered. He was stunned. How did that just happen? Only a moment earlier, he'd been afraid he was losing Brad.

Now we're engaged!

Brad pulled back to look at him. "I don't want to wait any more. Let's get married today. Tonight! We could fly to Vegas and—"

Sam laughed. "What's the rush?"

"I'm ready. I've been ready for a long time, but now… I don't want to wait. Aren't you?"

"Yeah. Yeah, I am. But let's at least take a breath here. I want my mom to be there. I want to invite our friends"

Brad nodded. "All right. Let's plan it. How about November 1st? It's our anniversary."

Sam frowned. "Our anniversary is April 10th."

Brad grinned. "November 1st is the anniversary of the day we met. The day you walked into my office for the first time."

"You remember the exact date?" Sam was impressed.

"Like it was yesterday. I knew even then that you'd change my life. I just didn't know how much." He kissed Sam again. "So what do you say?"

Sam hugged him tight. "I do."

72. SCREW ALL THE REST

Ben waited for one of the restaurant managers. He leaned against the wall and watched the buzz of activity as servers and expediters whizzed by carrying plates of enchiladas Guanajuato—his favorite—and empanadas.

Zocalo was never *not busy*. It was one of his favorite restaurants in Midtown, as much for the casual decor and bright lighting as for the great Mexican food. The televisions above the bar showed some kind of basketball game, the squeak of rubber and the occasional roar of the crowd creating a steady background noise to the sibilant whisper of the patrons, couples and clumps of people having a late lunch.

Ben's stomach was performing motions it should have been incapable of as he tried to keep a zen attitude about the job. He needed it. His bank account balance was slipping inexorably toward zero.

He did *not* want to go back to Intel.

He looked down at his phone, hoping to distract himself. Ella smiled up at him from his home screen wallpaper, her quirky expression sending a shiver through him. The last few days with her had been amazing.

She would touch his hand or laugh and throw her red hair back, and his world would shimmer and change.

He hoped to have some good news to give her on their next date.

"Hey, Ben." Carlos, the manager, shook his hand, offering him a small smile that gave away nothing. "Thanks for coming back in."

"Glad to. I'm hoping you have a job for me?" The EG had been great for his writing schedule, but now that his novel was done, he needed some extra income. Ben knew how unlikely it was that his book would hit it big. With his remaining savings and a decent salary, he hoped he could squeeze by while he started to write the next one.

"Yes, if you're willing to work here." They sat down together at a long table in the events space at the back of the restaurant. "I was very impressed by your resume. But to be blunt, you seem a little overqualified?"

Ben laughed. "You mean because I used to work at Intel and have a master's degree?"

Carlos nodded. "Yes. So tell me, why do you want to work in the restaurant business?"

Ben sighed. "Honestly, the tech world sucked all the life out of me. At the end of the day I wanted to kill myself."

"And now?"

"Now I channel all that creative energy into writing. A job like this… it would give me benefits and a good schedule to go with my writing career."

Carlos considered him for a moment. "That makes sense. But I don't hire anyone who's not passionate about food, especially Mexican food. You'd have to start at the bottom as an expediter and work your way up."

"I can do that. I love Mexican food. Your Enchiladas Guanajuato is one of my favorite meals in all of Sacramento, and Mayahuel has a cream of poblano soup that's to die for."

Carlos laughed. "You know you're not supposed to talk about the competition at a job interview, right?"

"Maybe not. But you did say you wanted someone who was serious about his Mexican food."

Carlos grinned. "Fair enough." He held out his hand. "So when can you start?"

~

Ella was waiting for him at Cafe Bernardo, a couple of blocks from the hospital. She looked a bit drawn. The time spent waiting for Max to wake up seemed to be taking its toll.

Ben was concerned. It couldn't be good for her health.

"Hey!" he said lightly, covering his concern with a warm smile.

"Hi, handsome." She kissed him, lingering a little longer than normal. They sat down at a table by the window in the brightly colored place.

"How's Max?" he asked as casually as he could manage as he thumbed through the menu.

"No change." She picked up her own menu and stared at it vacantly for a moment before setting it down again. "How did your callback go at Zocalo?"

Ben loved that she thought about him even though she had so much to worry about on her own. He grinned. "I got the job!"

"That's great!" Her own grin matched his, briefly lighting her tired face as she reached out to squeeze his hand. "When do you start?" Her hand twitched, and she pulled it quickly away from his to hide it under the table.

"Day after tomorrow." He frowned. She shouldn't be ashamed. Not with him.

"Thash great." She coughed to cover her slur and looked away, pulling her red hair behind her ear reflexively, her Fahr's Disease rearing its ugly head.

He put out a hand to touch her cheek. "You're having symptoms tonight, aren't you?"

She nodded miserably. She wouldn't look at him.

"You don't have to hide them from me," he said gently, stroking her cheek. "You know that, right?"

She looked up, her eyes moist. "It's so frustrating. I jush want to forget about it for the night." She gritted her teeth. "Just," she said carefully, "I want to spend a happy evening with you and not think about it."

He got up and slid into the booth next to her. "Give me your hand."

She held it out to him hesitantly.

He took it in his. It was warm and soft. His stomach jumped again, but in a distinctly different fashion than it had at Zocalo. "Look, it's perfect."

Ella laughed in spite of herself. "Hardly." But she let him pull it up to his lips.

Ben kissed it gently and let it go.

She picked up her water. "To a happy evening, and screw all the resh."

And somehow it was.

73.MOONSET

Diego stared at Luna's apartment door, shivering in the predawn cold, his breath coming out in visible puffs tinged yellow by the old porch light.

Valentina squeezed his hand. *I'm here.*

He nodded and reached up to knock on the door.

He was still half asleep. Valentina had woken him at two in the morning, telling him someone had called her from Luna's number and had urged that they come to Bologna posthaste. More of Luna's usual drama, he supposed. And yet…

The door cracked open.

"Come in." The man looked like he was in his mid-twenties and was wearing a priest's collar. "Diego?"

"Yes." Could this be his son? The age was about right. Fate was a cruel mistress sometimes. "I was told Luna wanted to see me."

"Come with me. I'm Father Roberto."

"Are you… Why are you here?" He followed the man down the hallway, and his sister trailed after him, looking as confused as he was.

"I'm her priest. She asked me to come administer the last rites. It won't be long now."

Diego stumbled. "What?"

"She's in her bedroom. Here." The father opened the door at the end of the hall.

A woman lay on a small bed, comforters piled up over her and a nest of pillows behind her head. The skin on her arms was yellow and bruised, and she seemed to be asleep.

"What's wrong with her?" he whispered to the priest.

The man stared at him. "I'm so sorry. I thought you knew. She has end-stage liver disease."

There was someone else in the room too. A boy, maybe sixteen or seventeen, sat in a chair in one corner, staring morosely at Luna. The boy looked up at him briefly and looked away.

Did she have a second son? *Odd*. "So what am I supposed to do?"

"I'm told she wanted to see you before…"

Diego swallowed and nodded. "Thank you." He sat in the chair next to the bed, taking in Luna's face. It was lined as if with great age, her skin almost transparent, a sickly yellow. She looked so *old*.

His anger and resentment toward her faded away like melting snow.

Luna must have heard him. Her eyes opened, and she fixed her gaze on him. "You came." Her voice was thready, much reduced from the lively one he remembered.

She was a faded copy of her own life.

"Ciao." He brushed the back of his hand across her cheek. "You look as beautiful as ever."

Her lips pursed in an attempt at a smile. "Liar."

His own smile was lopsided. "Never." He leaned forward to kiss her forehead. "Luna, I'm so sorry I didn't come sooner. I didn't know."

She nodded and closed her eyes. For a moment, he thought she'd drifted back to sleep. Then she opened them again with apparent effort. "I want…" She pursed her lips again, and then licked her lips. "I want you to take care of Giovanni."

"Giovanni?"

Luna nodded. "Your son." She pointed across the room, and he turned to meet the youth's angry gaze.

"You're *not* my father." The boy stood, pushing the chair back against the wall with a screech. "I don't care what she says." He ran out of the room.

He's my son? Diego watched him go, his mind spinning. It wasn't possible. He and Luna had been together more than two decades before, and the boy was clearly still in high school.

Oddio. That one night.

Luna had come back into his life, eighteen years before, demanding money to keep quiet about their marriage when Matteo had been beside himself over the death of the father. When Diego had tucked his lover into bed and gone out to get badly drunk.

He'd dreamed about Luna, how it had been when they had been together.

He thought it had been just a dream.

Diego looked down at her, a mere shadow of her former self.

She nodded, seeing it in his eyes. "So sorry, Diego." She reached a frail arm to him, resting her hand against his cheek. "Should have told you."

He'd been preparing himself to meet his adult son, to see his wife, and to insist she finally give him a divorce. To yell and rage and shout, if he had to, until he got what he needed to fix his life with Matteo. But this…

What the hell was he supposed to do with this? How could he rage at someone who was dying?

He said the only thing he could think of. "It's okay, Luna. It's okay." He lay her hand back on the comforter and brushed back her hair behind her ear. It was brittle and sparse.

She smiled this time, her eyes saying what her lips couldn't. Then they closed, and she slipped away into sleep once more.

Diego sat there for a long time, watching her chest rise and fall, his mind numb. How was he going to tell Matteo about this? How was he going to raise a son?

His sister tapped him on the shoulder and gestured for him to follow her.

The priest took his place, watching over Luna.

Valentina led him to the apartment's small kitchen, all gray cabinets and white tile. She'd prepared tea and had set up two cups on the wooden chopping block. "Pull up a stool."

"Thanks." Diego sat and picked up the cup to drink some tea. It was warm and strong.

Valentina sipped from her own cup, watching him over the rim. "I spoke with the priest while you sat with her. He filled me in."

He nodded. "How long does she have?"

"Hours. Maybe." She closed her eyes. "These things are never certain."

He shivered, trying to process the finality of it all. "How did this happen to her? She's so young."

"She has hepatitis. She's apparently had it for a long time, and she's been sick these last few years." She took another sip. "Diego, I have to ask you something."

"Giovanni?"

Valentina nodded.

"I didn't know about Giovanni until you texted me two weeks ago. I swear it."

"So you think he really is yours?"

He knew what she was asking. He hated having to answer it. "The last time I saw her… when she demanded money to keep quiet. I was very drunk that night. I think I… It's certainly possible."

Valentina looked away. "He looks like you. He has your eyes, and the fire there reminded me of you when you were that age."

"She wants me to take care of him." Diego closed his eyes, picturing her aged and tired face again. "I don't know if I can. And Matteo, how do I tell him?" His eyes teared up, and his nose started to run. He hadn't asked for any of this, and the boy already hated him. He'd already put Matteo through so much. "I don't know what to do."

Valentina set down her cup and hugged him. "Oh, Diego, what have you gotten yourself into this time?" She rocked him back and forth and kissed his cheek. He rested his head against her chest, tears running down his face. "It's ok, *Polpetto*. We'll figure it out."

God, he hoped she was right.

Someone cleared their throat.

Diego looked up to see the priest standing at the doorway. "Sorry to interrupt, but I think it's time," he whispered.

How does he know? Diego stood and followed the man out into the hallway.

Luna's crazy life was drawing quickly to a close.

For some strange reason, he'd been called here to watch her moon set for the final time.

74. TELL ME WHEN

Carmelina looked around the P.I.'s office. It was neat and impersonal, with standard Ikea furniture in soft wood tones and grays. A lone ficus stood by the window for color, where vertical blinds let in a diffuse light through the mottled amber glass.

She picked up the sheet of photo paper once more. It was already well worn, despite the fact that she'd printed it out just two days earlier. She couldn't stop looking at it. A baby's face stared up at her with beautiful brown eyes, a little child named Mary. Her granddaughter, a little piece of her own life, cast out into the cold, hungry world. She had a beautiful smile.

Darryl had been true to his word. The professor had sent over a few baby pictures, including this one, and the name of the agency that had handled the adoption, a place called Happy Homes in Rancho Cordova.

Carmelina sighed. *That* had been a dead end. She had no easy way to prove her relationship to the child, and the adoption records were sealed, in any case. Zondra, the woman she'd talked to at the agency over the phone, had been unmoved by her tale and had refused to provide any information about the adoption.

Maybe the universe was trying to tell her to give the whole thing up, to just let it go before someone got hurt. Maybe her intrusion into Mary's life, whatever it was like now, would only bring the girl confusion and pain.

And yet, Carmelina had to *know. Arthur, what would you do?*

Her dead husband's spirit was uncharacteristically silent on that point.

"Mrs… Di Rosa." The private eye was nothing like she would have expected. She was young, professionally attired in a tailored suit jacket and skirt, her blond hair pulled back in a neat bun. "I'm Emily Stamp." She held out her hand, and Carmelina shook it.

Emily sat down behind her desk.

Carmelina grimaced. Emily had a firm handshake.

"What can I help you with today?"

"I'm trying to find my granddaughter. And I suppose it's *Ms.* Di Rosa now. My husband passed away a few months ago." She handed over the manila folder with copies of everything she had collected so far.

"I'm sorry to hear that, *Ms.* Di Rosa."

Carmelina thought she heard a hint of admiration there for her choice to move on. "No one gives you a course in how to handle these things once they're gone."

Emily nodded. "So did she run away? Your granddaughter?" She leafed through the documents.

"No. Not exactly. I gave up my daughter Andrea for adoption in 1975." It still hurt to say that out loud. "I've just learned that she was killed in a car accident some years ago and that she had a daughter before she died." Her stomach hurt.

"Ah."

"Her daughter was also given up by her family. It seems to be a sad fact of life in my family."

"You're adopted?"

"No.... I just meant... sometimes I think I started Andrea off down a difficult road, and her daughter has paid for my mistakes."

Emily put the file on her desk. "I was adopted too, Ms. Di Rosa. My mother was a drug addict, and giving me up was probably the best decision— maybe the only good one—she ever made. Don't beat yourself up." She sat back, considering Carmelina. "These adoption agencies can be hard to crack," she said at last. "I presume you've already contacted..." She leafed through the folder. "Happy Homes?"

Carmelina nodded. "They were less than helpful."

Emily snorted. "I'd imagine. Listen, I've dealt with these kinds of cases before. Getting information through official channels can be expensive, time consuming, and difficult."

"I understand."

"I've had more luck in these cases with less... orthodox means."

"I don't want you to do anything illegal." *But if it meant finding Mary...*

"I said unorthodox, not illegal."

"Do I want to know?"

Emily grinned. "Probably not." She lifted the folder. "May I keep these?"

"Of course. What will it cost me?"

"Hmmm. Give me five hours, ninety dollars an hour?"

"I can do that." Carmelina shivered. *Mary, I'm going to find you.*

"You won't be able to use this information in court, and I can't advise you to make contact based on what I will provide to you. That decision, and any consequences that may follow, are yours and yours alone."

"I understand. How long will it take?"

"A few days. I'll contact you when I know more. I'll just need your credit card. I charge a $250 retainer for cases like this."

It was worth it. It was all worth it if it meant Carmelina would find the missing piece of her heart, if she would have a chance to give to this girl what she had stolen from Andrea.

She handed over her Visa.

"Give me just a moment." Emily disappeared into the adjacent room.

Carmelina's cell phone buzzed.

It was a text from Daniele.

Can we talk?

Carmelina closed her eyes. She wasn't ready to see him again. She wasn't sure if she would ever be. The man who had killed her daughter. *If only I hadn't given you up, Andrea.*

There was more than enough guilt to go around over Andrea's death.

I can't. Not yet.

She wanted to hate him. She wanted to burn with righteous wrath when she saw his name. She wanted to want to rip his eyes out, to claw at him until he bled and hurt like she did.

Instead, he only made her feel empty and dead inside, especially when she thought of the *now* that had come to be because of the *then* that she had chosen.

"Okay, that does it," Emily said, returning her Visa to her. "It was a pleasure to meet you, Ms. Di Rosa. I'll be in touch in a couple of days."

Carmelina stood and shook the woman's hand again. "Thank you. I'll wait to hear from you." This was going to be the hardest few days she'd spent in a long time. She wasn't good at waiting.

Emily showed her to the door. As Carmelina descended the steps to the ground level, her phone buzzed one more time.

Tell me when.

75.ALONE WITH A BOY

Marissa followed Tris into his dad's house. School was over, and she had a couple of hours before she had to be home. She was supposed to be at the internship at Ragazzi, but she'd called in sick for the afternoon.

The house was a brick mansion on 46th in the Fabulous Forties, set back from the street by a wide lawn with a gorgeous old elm tree. Marissa had never seen such a big home. "It's really beautiful." A pair of grand staircases led up from the open foyer to the second floor.

"Thanks. When my dad bought this place, it was half this size. He and my stepmom tore most of it down and built this instead. Just a sec. I'll grab a couple of sodas, and we can go up to my room."

"You don't live with your mom?"

"I go back and forth."

"Is your stepmom home?" she called after him, looking around. The floor was tiled in white marble, and there were four large gray vases filled with white lilies placed at intervals around the edge of the entryway. Mirrors reflected back the colorless room, making her feel like she'd stepped into a black-and-white film. She hadn't realized that Tris's dad was *rich*. Or that the home would feel so *cold*.

"Sorry. She's out with her friends at some cultural event or other. She's hardly ever here." He kissed her and handed her a Pepsi and then beckoned for her to follow him upstairs. "Come on." He smelled good, like really good —some strange combination of soap or cologne and… What was it? Whatever it was sent a shiver down her spine. She hesitated at the base of the stairs.

Was this *it*? If it was, was she *ready*?

"What are you waiting for?" he called from the top of the stairs. He grinned, his floppy black hair framing his face, his tattoos making him a work of art.

If this was it, maybe she *was* ready. She wanted to kiss him. To have him hold her. To do things to her she wasn't ready to admit to herself. *Calm down, Marissa.* "I'm coming." She tried to look casual. If Tristan was going to get lucky with her today, there was no sense in letting him know ahead of time. She'd make him work for it.

Tris opened the door to his room like a gentleman. She went inside and found it wasn't at all what she expected after the chilly entryway.

One wall was filled with albums. Not CDs but actual honest-to-goodness record albums. Her dad had a few of them. Something about the music sounding better on vinyl. She'd never been able to hear the difference herself.

The room was cozy. The windows were framed by earth-toned curtains, the hardwood floor half covered by a thick, shaggy rug just calling out for the touch of bare feet. His bed, neatly made, had the thickest comforter she had ever seen, with an African pattern that added texture to the general decor. The room was warm, like Tris.

"Have a seat," he said, patting the bed. "I want to play something for you."

She sat on the bed and slipped off her shoes, luxuriating in the soft rug.

He flipped through his albums, pulled one out, and freed the album from inside. He handed her the cover. It had a seductive picture of a woman with eyes like drops of turquoise set against a lush red background. It said "Diva."

"You trying to tell me something?" she asked, admiring his arms as he put the record on a turntable and lifted the needle.

"You don't know Annie Lennox?"

Marissa shook her head.

"That's one of the best records ever. And it sounds so much better—"

"—on vinyl. I know, I know. My dad's a true believer too."

He laughed. "Marcos?"

"No. My real… my adoptive father." She still missed her parents sometimes. Missed what they had been like together as a family.

The music started. It was rich, earthy, enchanting.

Tris took her hand and mouthed. "Whyyyyyyy."

She laughed. "It is beautiful."

In response, he kissed her.

Her heart pounded.

She put her hands around him and pulled him closer, and they fell back on the bed together, his warm body on top of hers. He kissed her neck, making her shudder again.

"Do you *want to?*" he whispered in her ear.

The world stood still as he waited for her to answer. The room was filled with music and expectation.

Oh God, she *wanted to.*

She wanted Tris more than she'd wanted anything since… well, since she'd begged her parents to buy her the little teddy bear she'd named Nathan.

They were all alone. No one would know.

Her phone chirped in her pocket.

Tris frowned.

"I'm sorry. It might be Marcos." She pulled herself out from under him awkwardly and took out her phone. It was a message from Meghan, one of her friends from the LGBT Center youth group.

Ricky's in the hospital. Beaten pretty bad.

"Oh shit."

Ricky. She'd almost forgotten about him since she'd gone to stay with Marcos. They only ever saw each other anymore at Ragazzi. Ricky Martinez, the guy who was always her ray of sunshine and bullshit. Who'd found himself a sugar daddy. Who thought he was invincible.

"What happened?" Tris lifted the needle, and silence returned to the room.

"One of my friends is in the hospital.…" She messaged back to Meghan. *Where?*

Sutter on L Street.

"Are they okay?"

"I don't know. Listen, I have to go." She pulled on her shoes. "I'm sorry, Tris, but I have to see if Ricky's okay. I don't know how I'm going to get there. I can walk, I guess. It's not that far.…"

"Hey, slow down." He took her hand. "Let me take you."

"You don't have a car."

"Yeah, but my dad does. Lamborghini or Porsche?"

"Are you sure?"

He nodded. "Dad's gone back East for a conference."

"Okay." She kissed him. "I love you." She meant it.

76. BRING HIM HOME

"I'm here to see Ricky Martinez," Marissa told the nurse on duty in the emergency room.

"Are you family?" The woman frowned at her over thick-rimmed glasses. She looked more like a librarian than a nurse.

"No. He's a good friend."

"Family only. Sorry. Wait over there." She pointed to a bank of green chairs.

Marissa glared at her but decided against making a scene. *For now.*

She sat with Tris, staring at the door to the treatment rooms. She texted Meghan.

Here. Where r u?

Be there soon.

"I can try talking to her," Tris suggested, shooting a glance at the nurse. He was being such a gentleman.

She squeezed his hand. "It's okay. Let's just wait a little bit." Maybe once Meghan got there, they could tag team her.

"Sure."

Tris went to get them something to eat from the vending machine.

Marissa glanced at her phone. It was almost five o'clock. Marcos would be expecting her home soon.

"I'm here to see Richard Martinez."

Marissa perked up. There was a man at the nurse's station with his back to her.

"And you are?"

"He called me. I'm his emergency contact."

The nurse checked her screen and nodded. "You can go right on in, Mr. Weston. Dana here will take you back."

"Mr. Weston?" Marissa called.

Brad turned to find her standing there. "Hey, Marissa. What are you doing here?"

"Meghan texted me. I needed to come see him."

Tris returned with a packet of powdered donuts and two cups of coffee. "Best I could find on short notice." He gave her an embarrassed shrug and kissed her cheek.

"Mr. Weston, this is Tris, my boyfriend."

"Call me Brad. And nice to meet you, Tris. Marissa, you want to come in with me to see him?"

"Is he okay?"

"He will be. But he got beaten up pretty badly. I talked with him on the phone for a few minutes before I came over."

She sighed, relieved. "Okay." She remembered how hard it was on the street.

"Let me go in and see him first, and then I'll send someone out for you if he wants to see you."

"Thanks!" She gave him a quick hug.

He disappeared behind the door.

Marissa stuck her tongue out at the nurse when the woman wasn't looking.

"That's good news, right?" Tris said, handing her a coffee and a donut. "That he's awake and talking?"

"I hope so." Marissa wondered who had done it. Why Ricky hadn't called *her*. Why she had almost forgotten about *him*.

Two minutes later, Nurse Dana returned to take her back to see him.

Brad watched the two kids—that's what they were, as much as they tried to pretend otherwise—reunite.

Ricky was a mess. His cheek was bruised, he had a black eye, and apparently a couple of broken ribs too. The kid seemed deflated.

"What the hell happened to you?" Marissa asked with all her usual tact.

Brad cringed. Ricky was in bad shape. "Marissa, maybe we shouldn't…"

"It's okay," Ricky said, managing a slight grin. "She's right. I was stupid." Some of the life seemed to flow back into him.

"Did your sugar daddy do this to you? I'll *fucking* kill him…"

"No. He dumped me a couple of weeks ago." He wheezed, having a little trouble breathing. "Found someone younger." He sighed. "Been back on the streets again." He looked up at her, his left eye half opened above the dark bruise. "What about you?"

"Tell me what happened." Marissa sat on his bedside, taking his hand.

Ricky sighed again. "I needed cash. I heard there was a cruising spot down in Land Park. This guy picked me up." He paused for a painful breath. "We did it in the bathroom. When I asked for my money, he… wasn't happy. He did this."

"I'm guessing you didn't report it to the cops," Brad said.

Marissa shot him a look.

Ricky shook his head. "They don't care about street trash like me."

That broke Brad's heart. These poor kids had nowhere to go, no one to help them. Sometimes he wanted to kill the parents who kicked beautiful kids like these out.

The Center did everything it could to support them, but there were limits to what they could offer—an afternoon hangout, food and a hot shower, and help connecting with other services.

Sacramento desperately needed more housing for its homeless youth, especially the queer kids like Marissa and Ricky. *We need to get these kids off the street. This kid.*

He had to do *something*. "I'll be right back."

Marissa and Ricky nodded.

"Tell me about you," Ricky was saying as Brad stepped out into the hallway and closed the door behind him.

Nurse Dana called him. "Mr. Weston, there's someone else here to see Richard. His… her name's Meghan. Can I send her in?"

He nodded. "Please. Ricky will be glad to see *her*."

She nodded. "Understood."

"Call Sam at home," Brad told his phone. He almost hung up. This was too much to ask, especially right now.…

"Hey, handsome." Sam's voice sounded bright and cheerful.

"Good writing day?"

"Yeah, so far. Just got off the phone with an officiant. I can tell you about her when you get home. What's up?"

Brad took a deep breath. "Look, I know this is a big ask. With the wedding coming up, and our lives being already complicated enough—"

"What's going on?" Sam sounded suspicious. "You're not getting cold feet, are you?"

"Of course not! Being married to you is all I think about."

"Then what?"

Brad hesitated. "There's this kid. His name's Ricky. One of the Center kids."

"What happened? I know that tone."

"He got beaten up pretty bad." He was shaking with anger. "Oh God, Sam, you should see the poor kid. How can anyone…" He stopped himself. Getting emotional wasn't going to help matters. "I can't save them all, Sam. I wish I could, but I can't." His eyes were wet, and his chest felt hot. "I know it. I know I can't save them."

"It's okay, Brad. Bring him home."

"What?" Surely Sam couldn't be okay with this crazy plan.

"If you can work things out with foster care, bring him home."

"But what about the wedding? Your writing?"

"We'll figure it out. Bring him home."

"You sure?"

"Yeah."

Brad sniffed. "Okay. I'll do some checking and let you know what happens."

"Okay."

"Sam?"

"Yeah?"

"This is why I want to marry you. I don't think I've ever loved you more than right now."

Sam was quiet for a moment.

"You still there?" Brad thought he heard a sniffle on the other end of the line too.

"Sorry. Just getting myself together. You got me crying too." He laughed softly. "You're the one with the big heart here. I'm just along for the ride."

"Sweet *and* self-deprecating." Brad smiled. "In two more weeks you'll be stuck with me for good, you know."

"Can't wait."

"Love you."

"Love you too."

Brad hung up and reentered Ricky's room to find Meghan and Marissa both sitting with the patient. "You guys doing okay?"

Ricky nodded. "Marissa was just telling me about her run-in with the 'doptermonster."

Marissa grinned.

"I don't even pretend to know what that means. Ricky, I'm going to make some calls to see about getting you a place to stay, okay?"

"I can't stay here?"

"Maybe for the night."

"Okay. I *don't* want to go back to foster care."

"I'll see what I can do. Back in a bit. You guys take good care of him, ok? I'll let Tris know you may be awhile, Marissa."

"Thanks Mr. Weston."

"Call me Brad." Jesus, these kids made him feel old.

He ducked out of the room again to make a few calls. He had a lot to get done if Ricky was going to be their houseguest.

77. THE AFTERMATH

"Leave me alone." The boy's petulant voice set Diego on edge.

Diego took a deep breath. He'd spent the morning and early afternoon with the priest and his sister, mapping out funeral plans for a woman he'd never expected to see again in his life. The ceremony was planned for Sunday, just four days away—which was pretty fast by Italian standards, but there was no family to worry about other than his son, and Diego needed to get home.

My son. He was having a hard time accepting it, especially the fact that the boy was still in high school. Matteo was going to have a fit when he found out, and rightly so. And how was he going to take care of another human being? He knocked again, more forcefully this time.

"I said *go away.*"

"Sorry. I can't. I need to talk with you." He opened the door and stepped inside, looking around at the boy's room. It was small, with a simple wooden desk and chair against the wall under a dirty window and an armoire and double bed with a threadbare white bedspread taking up the rest of the space. A couple of tattered Bologna FC posters graced one wall, handsome, athletic soccer players in striped blue and red jerseys staring down at Diego in disdain.

Not too different from the glare Giovanni was giving him from the bed.

The boy wore white ear buds, a matching Bologna jersey, and his knees and gangly legs stuck up out of a pair of board shorts. He was reading the Sports Gazette.

Sports. Diego shook his head. Could they have any less in common? He sat down on the bed.

Giovanni closed his eyes and ignored him, bobbing his head to the music.

Diego frowned. He reached forward and plucked the ear buds out of Giovanni's ears.

"Hey! I was listening to those!" Giovanni grasped for them, but Diego set them on the desk out of reach.

"I need to talk to you. You *don't* have to talk back, but you *do* have to listen." *Was I this much of a pain in the ass when I was his age?*

Giovanni crossed his arms and glared at him again.

"Look, I am so sorry, Giovanni. Your mother and I knew each other a long, long time ago. I had no idea she was sick—"

"Gio."

"What?"

"I'm not Giovanni. Everyone calls me Gio." As if that should have been obvious to anyone besides a total idiot.

Good to know. "Okay, *Gio*, then. I'm so sorry about your mother. She was… unique in the world." He looked away, not sure what to say next. "We're planning a beautiful ceremony for her, on Sunday."

Gio didn't respond, staring back at Diego blankly.

Diego tried another tack. "You don't have to like me."

Gio snorted. "Good thing."

"Hey! Enough!" He looked Gio right in the eyes. "Look, I didn't want this any more than you did. I had absolutely no fricking idea I had a kid. You think I woke up one morning and thought, 'Oh, wouldn't it be great to have some snot-nosed teenager in my life?' Nevertheless, here we are. I'm stuck with you, and you've got no one else but me. Luna's gone." He regretted it as soon as he said it, seeing Gio's bravado crumble and tears fill the boy's eyes. "Oh Gio, I'm sorry. That's not how I wanted to say it."

He tried to pull the kid in for a hug, but Gio pushed him away. "I hate you!" He ran out of the room.

Diego jumped up to go after him, but his sister met him in the hall and held him back gently. "Let him go, Diego. He's upset. He needs to get some of it out of his system."

"I guess." He heard the front door slam. "I hope he comes back."

She patted him on the shoulder. "He will. Come into the kitchen. I've made us some lunch."

He was *starving.* "I will. But I have to skype with Matteo first."

She nodded. "Have you told him?"

"About Gio? Weeks ago, when you texted me."

"I meant about the boy's age."

He shook his head. "I have to. I thought he'd be older. I didn't realize—"

She hugged him. "*Forza*. I'll be in the kitchen when you're ready."

Diego wandered back to the living room, pulling out his phone. It was about three in the afternoon in Italy, so it would be six in the morning in California. Good thing Matteo was an early riser.

Matteo answered after a few rings, shirtless with a towel around his waist, still dripping from the shower. "*Ciao, bello! Come stai?*"

"I'm fine. It's been a rough twenty-four hours." Diego sank down on the old leather sofa, which creaked in protest, and stared up at the photos of Luna and Gio that adorned the mantel. "Luna's gone."

"What happened?" Matteo ran a hand through his hair, as he did whenever he was agitated.

"She's been sick for a long time. That's why she wanted to see me."

"Ah." Matteo sat on their bed. "Oh my God."

"I know."

"When? How?"

"Last night. Her priest called us to come over."

"I'm so sorry, Diego."

Matteo's eyes narrowed. "That doesn't sound good."

"I met my son. Gio."

"Is he nice? You'll have to invite him to come see us."

"He's seventeen."

There was silence as Matteo worked out what that meant. "*Cazzo.*"

"Yeah. Matteo, I'm so sorry—"

"Not now." Matteo's expression hardened. "We can discuss it when you get home. Are you bringing… Gio?"

Diego nodded. "Luna got him a travel visa."

"Smart. When?" He was all business now.

"The funeral's Sunday. I hope to be home early next week."

"Let me know. I will pick you up." His hand made repeated passes through his hair. "I have to go. I have a lot to do today."

"Okay." Diego felt queasy. "I love you."

"Talk to you tomorrow." Matteo cut the connection.

Diego sat staring at the blank screen for a long moment. "*Cavolo!*" He had a mess to sort out when he got home. He went to find Valentina in the kitchen. With his stomach tied up in knots, he didn't feel like eating, but he did need a little sisterly love and advice.

78. ALWAYS RIGHT

Matteo set down the phone.

He stared out the window at the street below for a while, his emotions in turmoil. He'd just started to get past the news Diego had given him a few weeks before. That he had married a woman. That he was still married. That he had a son.

All of that was understandable. Digestible. He even accepted why Diego had waited so long to tell him.

But this…

The boy—Gio—was seventeen.

The only time Diego had seen Luna, after he'd met Matteo, at least as far as Diego had told him, was that one week when she had come back to blackmail him for money.

The week of Matteo's father's death.

Matteo closed his eyes. *He slept with his ex.* He exhaled heavily. How was he supposed to deal with that?

The phone rang, the business line for the restaurant. "Ragazzi. How can I help you?"

"Matteo?"

"This is Matteo." The voice sounded familiar.

"Hi there. It's Sam. From the cooking class."

"Sam! how are you?" Matteo smiled despite his uneasiness. It was good to hear a friendly voice.

"Good. Hey, I need to ask a favor."

"What's going on?" Matteo was proud of his mastery of English idiom.

"Brad and I are getting married!"

"*Oddio*, that's fantastic! When?" They seemed like such a sweet couple.

"On November 1st. It's our anniversary."

"Anniversary?"

"Of the day we first met."

"Got it. So what can I do for you?" Matteo closed his eyes, remembering again the day he and Diego had married on the beach in Hawaii. How little he'd known then.

"We'd like to hold the wedding at Ragazzi. It's about the right size, and we've made some good friends there. I think it would be perfect. And to be honest, most of the other venues are already booked. Do you guys ever do weddings?"

"Here?" It wasn't something they'd ever really contemplated, but why not? "Sure. I think we could arrange that. How many people?"

"About twenty-five."

"Yeah, we can accommodate that many." He'd have to check the reservation book and figure a few things out, but it was doable. "You wanna come in and talk details?"

"Sure. When?"

"Sunday? After class?" Class. *Cavolo*, he'd forgotten about the next class. Three days. He had three days to prepare.

"Perfect. See you then. Brad will be thrilled."

"Glad to be able to do it for you."

"Thanks, Matteo!" Then he was gone.

Matteo sat back in his chair, bemused. *A wedding. Here.*

For a moment, he'd even forgotten about his problems with Diego. He sighed again. They'd have to have a long talk when Diego got home.

In the meantime, he had some interns arriving downstairs to corral.

Diego stirred the gnocchi in the big pot on his sister's stove.

She was busy making the sauce, and the crushed tomatoes and fresh-cut basil were sending up a heavenly smell.

Gio was in the living room, attached to his phone.

"Thanks for letting him stay here with us until we go home," Diego said, peeking out to make sure the boy—his son—was still there. That was going to take some getting used to.

"Bianca!" Valentina called.

"Yes, Mamma," the girl said, presenting herself.

"Get Dante and set the table. Dinner will be ready in about ten minutes."

"Yes, Mamma."

"You have them well trained."

His sister laughed. "They're on their best behavior. There's company for dinner."

Diego smiled. "I remember how Papa would talk to us before the guests came over. 'If you two do anything to embarrass me in front of the company, I'll spank you so hard you won't be able to sit down for a week.'"

His mother chuckled. "Diego's just like you, Dante." She was grating parmesan cheese at the table.

Diego and his sister shared a look. Mamma had been more and more forgetful, but only lately had she started confusing him for Dante Sr., his late father. "I'm Diego, Mamma."

She squinted at him. "Of course you are. That's what I said, Diego."

Diego sighed under his breath. "Of course you did, Mamma." One more thing to worry about.

His sister stirred the sauce next to him. "So how'd it go with Matteo?"

Diego pulled out one of the gnocchi and nibbled on it. Almost. "*Boh…* okay? He's angry."

"He has every right to be." She gave him *the look*, the one that said he knew she was right.

"I know. I've screwed everything up. Thing is, I don't even remember sleeping with her."

"Sleeping with who?" His mother looked confused.

"Luna, Mamma."

"Ah."

Valentina set the sauce on the back burner and wrapped her arms around him from behind. "It will all work out, *Polpetto*."

Diego nodded. "I hope so. I don't know if I'm ready to be a father."

She snorted. "No one's *ready* for it. *I* sure wasn't, and yet here we are. But you don't have much of a choice, do you? You'll do okay." She kissed him, and he got a whiff of her perfume. It was the one his mother loved, too—Roberto Cavalli.

We really are becoming our parents.

"I just hope Matteo doesn't throw me out when I get home. Or before."

"Matteo loves you. He'll get past this. Is the pasta ready?"

"I think so."

"Drain it and put it in here." She pulled down a big ceramic dish from the top of the refrigerator, one that was covered in hand-painted lemons.

He poured out the water in the sink and then parceled the pasta carefully into the bowl.

Valentina covered it with her marinara sauce and then sprinkled on some fresh basil leaves and a bit of the parmesan Mamma had grated for them.

"It looks delicious," he said, taking in a deep breath. "I may have to steal it for Ragazzi."

"I'll email you the recipe." She kissed him on the cheek and whispered, "Everything will work itself out. You'll see." There was a little shock where her lips touched him, and Diego saw a sparkle in the air around her. Then it was gone.

She picked up the bowl and swept into the dining room with it, calling out, "*Mangiamo!*"

Diego followed with the salad, comforted by her words.

Valentina was always right.

79. FIRST DAY

"The tables here are all numbered. When the food comes up, get it out to the guests as quickly as possible." Carlos showed him the floor map. "We want food to arrive at the table hot and fresh."

"Got it." The map was a swimming jumble of colors and numbers. Not for the first time, Ben wondered if he was dyslexic.

"You're the eyes and ears of the restaurant," Carlos was saying. "In between expediting, you should be circulating through the floor, refilling drinks, and bringing fresh chips and dips. If we do our job right, our guests should never be looking around, wondering where their food is."

"Okay. Makes sense." Ben was nervous. He'd never done this before. At least at the Everyday Grind, he had a counter and an espresso machine between him and the clients. Here, he was totally exposed.

He took a deep breath. *You can do this.* "Where do I get refills?"

"Good question." Carlos showed him where the chips, dips, and drinks were. "You'll be working with Luis tonight."

One of the waiters looked up from behind the bar and waved at him.

"Luis, this is Ben. Ben, Luis."

"Nice to meet you." Luis shook his hand. He looked about Ben's age, with a shaved head and a serious demeanor. He had tattoos on both arms. "You work hard, you'll do well here."

"I always work hard."

"Good to hear. Just follow my lead. Got it?"

Ben nodded. "Got it."

Luis grinned. "Hey, relax. You'll be fine, man." He handed some glasses and a pitcher of water to Ben. "Take these to that table—number four."

Ben consulted the map. "Four. Got it."

He hustled over to the table by the big garage-door-style windows. The afternoon sun slanted down into his eyes.

There was a party of four women there, probably in their thirties. If he'd had to guess, he'd say they were taking an early day off work together. They already had a pitcher of margaritas on the table, and from the raucous conversation and laughter, they'd gotten the party started somewhere else before they'd come in for dinner.

"Water?"

"Yes, please," said the woman closest to him, a blonde in a lime-green strapless. "Hey, you're kinda cute."

"He is cute," said one of the other women, a brunette in a white blouse and jeans. She blew him a kiss.

"Water, ma'am?" he asked the third woman, trying to ignore the first two.

"Yes, please."

"I think we have a newbie here, ladies," the blonde said, whistling.

"He must be."

The blonde batted her eyelashes at him. "We come in every Thursday, and I don't ever remember seeing you here."

He overextended, trying to reach one of the water glasses, and the pitcher flew out of his hands, soaking the redhead in the blue blouse and slacks seated by the window.

Ben blanched. "I'm so sorry...." What had he done?

"You spilled it all over me," she said, frowning. She was soaked from head to toe. "That better be water." She sniffed her soaked blouse.

He backed away from the table, hands out in front of him. "I'm so, so sorry. Let me get you a towel."

"Ladies... I am so sorry. Ben's new." Luis inserted himself smoothly between Ben and the table. He handed the redhead a towel.

"He needs more training."

"Yes, we're working on it. He literally just started five minutes ago. What if I get your drinks tonight for the table, and Linny, I'll pay for your meal tonight?" he said to the redhead.

"I suppose that would help," Linny said. "Thank you."

"Done. It's so sweet of you to cut the guy a little slack. That's one of the things I love about you ladies: your kindness and generosity."

They looked at each other, and then the table exploded in laughter.

"Don't worry. I'll have words with our new expediter here." He turned to Ben. "I'll see you in the kitchen," he said ominously.

Humiliated, Ben almost ran to the back, grateful to be away from the women.

How had he managed to fuck things up at his very first table? He *needed* this job. *I'll do better next time.*

Luis came through the double doors a minute later. The waiter's grim expression shifted almost immediately to amusement. "First time out, man. That's rough. You okay?"

"What?" Ben was confused. He was expecting to be dressed down. But *this*?

"First days are always rough, and that group can be a little rowdy. I had to put on a show to make them happy. Don't worry, you'll get the hang of it. You got the touch, man."

"Wait. So you're not pissed off at me?"

Luis shook his head. "You'll learn. Next time just go a little slower."

"I thought you were going to have me fired."

"You're all right, Ben. Why don't you shadow me for the next hour, and I'll give you the lay of the land?"

"I'd appreciate that."

He followed Luis out into the dining room.

"First thing to remember," Luis said as they approached the next table, "always keep the customer happy. You do that, and you've got it made."

The rest of the evening passed in a blur. By the time he was ready to go home at midnight, he'd learned what times were busiest, how to tell when a client was going to be a pain in the ass, three ways to defuse a tense situation, what the hell *ceviche de guaymas* was—cold fish soup—and how to keep 'em smiling.

That last skill came in particularly handy with a table of gays who called him over at the end of the night to personally give him a ten-dollar tip.

He left happy.

Ella had taken to staying at his place. He slipped into bed at a quarter to one, snuggling next to her warm body.

"How'd it go?" she mumbled.

"Good. Go back to sleep. I'll tell you tomorrow."

He breathed a happy sigh of relief to be home. To be with her.

He had survived the first day.

80. WEIRD

His kitchen was a mess, filled with mixing bowls and cutting boards and piles of chopped peppers and sliced onions. The stove was crowded with pots and pans, and there was flour everywhere, dusting the kitchen as if someone had slaughtered the Pillsbury Doughboy. *Why in the hell did I decide to make homemade tortillas?*

His *abuela* used to make them for him, shaping the dough by hand into perfectly formed circles before cooking them to perfection on the *comal*—she always called it a *plaque*—the flat, wrought-iron skillet she used bare-handed with a breathless skill. He still remembered her warm, fresh tortillas with great fondness.

He looked at his with genuine regret. They were lumpy, misshapen things, more like Dali's melted clocks than the puffy, perfect circles of his grandmother.

Still, they tasted *good*.

He dipped his thumb into a glass of ice water again to cool the burn he'd sustained on the comal. Apparently he didn't have Abuela's dexterity with it. At least he'd managed not to slice off a finger preparing this meal.

Marissa would be home in about half an hour. He'd have to hustle if he wanted to have things ready for the Big Meeting. Marcos wished Dave were here, but he'd begged off at the last moment. Something about a "work emergency."

He jerked his thumb out of the freezing water, pulled on his 'Ove'-Glove, and threw the vegetables into a hot skillet. A comforting aroma filled the room, and he was once again in Abuela's house when he was seven years old.

~

Marissa pulled Tris away from the door to the condo building and into her arms. She leaned back against the rough brick, and he leaned in to kiss her.

He pulled away and searched her eyes. "What's wrong? Your… Marcos is waiting for us."

"I know." She shrugged. "I'm not ready to go inside just yet."

His eyes narrowed. "You're not ashamed of me, are you?"

"No!" She startled herself with her vehemence.

"Well, okay." He frowned. "Then what is it? Did you wanna vape first?"

"Nah. I'm kinda sick of that stuff."

"Well?"

She frowned. "It's just… He's gonna get all weird with me about you. About this."

"About us?"

"Yeah. And the whole sex thing."

"But we haven't—"

"I know. But he gave me 'the talk' last week. Well, he tried to."

Tris laughed. "Seriously? Doesn't he know about Sex-Ed class?"

"Yeah. I guess he feels responsible for me. It's sweet. But I ended up giving *him* some tips."

"Ewwww."

"Yeah. So weird."

Tris rested his hand on the wall above her shoulder. "Listen. He's your parent now. Basically, right?"

"I guess."

"Parents are *supposed* to be weird. It comes with the position."

"You promise you won't let him freak you out?"

"Scout's honor."

"You were a boy scout?" She had a hard time picturing it.

"Yeah. Five years. I still have the uniform."

"Ooooh… the possibilities." She snaked a hand around his neck and pulled him close for one more kiss.

"Um, no. It hasn't fit me since I was thirteen."

"*I* could try it on." She winked at him. "Come on. I'm hungry." She pulled him toward the door.

"Oh my God, you're… you're…"

"Perfect?"

"Yeah." He grinned. "Sure. Let's go with that."

Tris was smart. She liked Tris.

~

Somehow Marcos managed to pull it off. When the door opened, thankfully five minutes late, he had a dinner on the table his mother and grandmother would have been proud of:

Calabasitas, a delicious cheese-and-zucchini dish his mother had always made him when he was down. Fajitas—chicken and steak—served with a heaping side of sautéed vegetables. A big bowl of homemade pico de gallo he'd made the day before, so all the flavors could combine properly with one another. A bowl of Spanish rice. And finally, his *pièce de résistance*: the stack of crazy-shaped tortillas tucked away in a ceramic warmer.

"We're here!" Marissa called from the doorway. "Ooooh, something smells amazing."

She was followed by a boy who was at least a head taller. "Hi Mr. Ramirez. I'm Tristan." The boy held out his hand.

Good manners, at least, but Marcos couldn't help but stare at the tattoos running up and down his arms. "Tristan. Do you have a last name?" It came out a little sharper than he intended.

"Dayton, sir."

Marissa glared at him.

"Well, great. Come in. I just put the food on the table."

"It smells wonderful," Tristan said. "Are you a trained chef?"

Marcos turned away and rolled his eyes. The boy was a flatterer too. "Nope, just learned how to cook from my mother and grandmother. Have a seat."

They passed around the dishes, and soon everyone's plate was full. Marcos heaped some rice, veggies, and fajitas on one of his little tortillas and folded it over, taking a bite. It was really good. He wondered why he didn't cook more like this. Mexican food was one of his favorite things. His grandmother would have been proud of him in spite of the tortillas. "So, Tristan… Marissa's told me almost nothing about you."

"Well… I just moved here with my mother from Santa Cruz." Tristan looked at Marissa, who nodded. "My dad lives here too… over in the Fab Forties."

Marcos whistled. "Must be rich."

Marissa took his hand and squeezed, her nails digging into his palm.

"He does all right."

"Nice tats." Marcos winced as Marissa's nails threatened to draw blood, but he couldn't help himself. Any boy who wanted to date her better be worthy.

Tristan didn't seem to notice. "This one symbolizes my Sioux heritage," he said, holding up his left arm. "It's a *wakinyan*, or thunderbird. I'm one-quarter Sioux."

Marcos pried his hand away from Marissa to take a closer look. It was a beautiful piece of art, and it said that the kid respected his ancestors. At least some of them. Marcos's respect for him went up a notch. "What's the other one?"

"It's a tree. When my grandmother had breast cancer, she lost one of her breasts. She had a tree of life tattooed over it. When she passed away, I had the tree tattooed on my own arm." He held it out for Marcos to see.

The roots started at the base of his fingers, and the tree itself wound up from his wrist to his shoulder. So the kid had respect for his elders too. "What are your plans after high school?"

"I'm hoping to get into USC. They have a great engineering college there."

Marcos grinned. "I like this guy," he said to Marissa.

She rolled her eyes.

"I think you're supposed to disapprove of me," Tristan whispered.

Marcos laughed. "Sorry. Too late. If you want to date him, you're gonna have to do it knowing you have my full approval."

Marissa shot Tristan a look that clearly said *I told you so.*

Marcos grinned. "Get used to it. I only get more embarrassing from here."

81. NORMAL

"Okay, so that takes care of the photographer. Jenni and Sarah say they'll do it for free." Sam grinned. "Or at least in exchange for a pizza and small donation to WEAVE."

"Sounds fair." Brad frowned. "Are we sure about these invitations though?" He held up one of the RuPaul Signature Edition invites from the pile on the kitchen table. "I mean, I love me some drag queens as much as the next guy, but Sharon Needles is some seriously scary shit."

Sam laughed. "She does have a certain *unique* aesthetic. But they're fun. And we love Pandora Box, right?"

"Yeah, I guess so." He went back to addressing the invitations by hand, another thing Sam had insisted upon. At least the guest list was blessedly small: twenty or so of their closest friends and family. Sam's mom was even coming up from Tucson. "Just so we're clear, I'm *not* dressing in drag."

"Yeah, about that…"

"Not going to happen."

"I had an idea."

Brad had started to get a little wary of Sam's wedding *ideas*. "What?"

"My friend Kate… you met her last month at her wife's birthday party?"

"Yeah, I remember. Short dark hair, cute smile?"

"That's her wife, Catie."

"Kate *and* Catie? Ah. Okay."

"Anyhow, she's a licensed officiant. And she does this really cool drag king thing."

"I don't know—"

"Here, I've got some pictures." Sam held his phone up so Brad could see it. Kate was wearing a suit. Her blonde hair was cut short, and she was holding a wine glass. She looked like Niles from Frasier.

Brad pushed the phone away. "Why can't we just do this like everyone else?"

Sam put his phone down. "What do you mean?"

Brad couldn't help himself. This had been building for *days*. "Oh, come on. We have rainbow carnations, pink bowties, and drag-queen invitations. And now a drag-king officiant? Next you'll be putting me in fairy wings and setting the wedding march to 'I Will Survive.'"

"I was thinking 'Born This Way,' actually." Sam took his hand. "Where's this coming from? You didn't complain before."

Brad sniffed. "I don't know. I just wanted to have an elegant, *normal* wedding." He regretted it as soon as he said it.

"*Normal?*" Sam's voice was cold.

"Yeah, you know, like my parents had."

"So you want me in a wedding dress?"

"No. Come on. You know what I mean."

Sam shook his head. "I'm afraid I don't."

Brad forged ahead. "You know, matching tuxedoes. Solemn wedding vows. A minister to lead the ceremony, maybe in a church or a boring reception hall. I just..."

"What?"

"This all just feels so... *gay.*"

"Ah."

"Yeah."

Sam sighed. "When my mother married my father, they did it in a church, with a minister, and a tux and a white dress. And you know what? They were divorced in three years." He squeezed Brad's hands. "But this isn't really about the wedding, is it?"

"You're from a whole different generation—"

Sam laughed. "Yeah, right. You're only seven years older than I am. You mean to tell me that you Reagan babies didn't have drag queens or rainbow flags?"

"Of course we did. But I've always been more on the conservative side of things. I left the party when I realized how they fought against LGBT rights, and when I realized how much many of them loathed me personally. And I love the Pride Parade as much as the next guy. But it's still hard for me. I just want to fit in. Sometimes it feels like we go out of our way to be different."

Sam surprised him, leaning forward to kiss him. "Hey, I get it. You've made some big strides this last year." He sat back and put his hands behind his head. "Thing is, there is no such thing as *normal*. Everyone is different." He closed his eyes. "I remember the first time I went to San Francisco Pride. I was eighteen, and it was my first time in the City. I was there with my friend Jack, and we found a place on Market Street, just in front of one of the BART stairways."

Brad nodded. "That's a good spot."

"Right? No one right behind you. And in the shade until noon." He opened his eyes, but they were focused somewhere in the distance. "There were so many people there, so many *kinds* of people. Black, white, Asian, Latino, lesbians, drag queens, bisexual folks, leather, people in animal costumes—you name it, they were there. For the first time in my life, I was in a place where *I* felt normal. Where I wasn't the odd kid out, the sissy, the faggot."

"I guess I can see that. I didn't come out until I was twenty-three." Brad tried to imagine what it must have been like to be openly gay in high school.

"In school, kids would rough me up, or sometimes they just shut me out, which was even worse. Every single day, someone reminded me I was *different*. That I didn't fit in. That I wasn't *normal*." His eyes focused on Brad. "Then one day, it hit me. *No one* really fits in. They all pretend, but everyone is different. Anna Ortiz was bulimic. Jeff Handler was dyslexic. One of the Cooper twins had an affair with the band coach. Being gay wasn't the problem. Being in high school was." He took Brad's hands again. "So I get it. You want to be *normal*. Like everyone else. But I didn't grow up being like everyone else. I didn't get to be normal until I found my community. Until I wrapped myself up in the rainbow flag."

Brad stared at him for a long moment. It had never occurred to him that all these things that Sam suggested for their wedding were anything more than gay props—Sam's way of giving the rest of the world a not-so-subtle *fuck you*. Instead, they were part of *Sam's* normal.

Sam looked away. "I gotta remind myself, this wedding is for both of us. If you want something a little more toned down, I'm okay with that. I just want to get married to you. I don't care how."

Brad squeezed Sam's hands. "Hey, why can't it be both? Elegant *and* over the top? We've both got the gene, right? Why can't we make it both beautiful and gay as hell?"

Sam's eyes lit up. "Really?"

"You made a good case." Brad chuckled. "Besides, I bet you'd look great in a white wedding dress."

Sam burst into laughter. "Sorry. Not gonna happen. Two tuxes, or you're coming home a single man."

"I can live with that. On one condition."

"What's that?"

Brad held up the invitation. "Ms. Needles has to go."

"Deal. I think there's an extra Jujubee at the bottom of the box we can use instead."

Brad grinned. "So we're getting married."

"Looks like it." Sam leaned forward and kissed Brad again for a long time.

Brad really was the luckiest boy in the world.

82. SOMETHING TO LOOK FORWARD TO

Dave sat on the rug on his bedroom floor in his pajamas, holding the photo frame in his hands, rocking gently back and forth.

It had been an accident.

He'd been rooting around his garage, looking for an old notebook, when he came across *the box*. It was a standard banker's box, a white box with a white box top that was covered in dust. He recognized it instantly.

Two years before, on the third anniversary of John's death, he'd packed up all the remaining things that reminded him of his love. He'd put them out here up on the top shelf in the garage, out of the way. Out of mind. Not that he ever really forgot.

But life went on. Every day, every week, every month was a little easier.

Until he'd opened the box.

Now he sat on the floor of his bedroom in his pajamas, staring at a photo of the two of them together on their trip to Venice, posing in front of the Bridge of Sighs. The dusty glass was stained with tears.

He'd called in sick to work on Friday and then had cancelled on Marcos for dinner.

He'd tried to sleep through the night but had tossed and turned, his mind spinning through all his past moments with John. Dave knew he was being irrational, that he should snap out of it, that John was gone and wasn't coming back.

It made no difference. He was in relapse. Knowing this had happened to him before didn't make it any easier to climb out of now.

Someone knocked on the front door. Dave looked up but made no move to answer it.

They knocked again. "Dave, you in there?" It was Carmelina.

If he just stayed quiet, maybe she would leave.

She knocked one more time. Then silence returned.

He pulled a shirt out of the box and held it up. It was a plain gray T-shirt. Dave held it up to his face, burying his nose in it.

It still smelled like John.

"Why don't you get something more colorful?"

John laughed. "I look good in gray and black."

"How about this one?" Dave held up a bright-red button-down short-sleeved shirt.

"No way. I can't wear red."

"I bet you'd look great in red."

"Nope. It brings out every zit and blemish on my face."

Dave grinned "You're crazy. I wear red all the time."

"You have beautiful Mexican skin. You can wear anything. I'm a winter."

"You don't even know what that is."

Dave stuck his tongue out. "I know what looks good on me." He kissed Dave and pulled two more dark gray T-shirts off the shelf. "Here, I'll get one of these." He held up another shirt.

"That one's gray too!"

"But it's a blue *gray."*

Dave sat there holding the shirt for a long time while a bar of sunlight through the blinds chased dust bunnies across the floor.

Something woke him up. The jangle of a key in a lock. He looked up.

His front door creaked open. "Hello?"

"Dave, it's me." Marcos' voice. "Are you okay?"

When had he given Marcos a key? "Yeah. Okay. Just leave me alone."

Marcos poked his head through the doorway. "There you are." His tone changed. "Hey, what happened?" Marcos knelt beside him. "I called you all day yesterday, but you never responded."

"I... I just... I can't." He wished Marcos would just leave him alone.

"Hey, hey there... It's okay. It's me." He sank down next to Dave and picked up the photo in the black frame. "Who's this?"

Dave squeezed his eyes shut. "John," he whispered.

"John, the one…?"

Dave nodded. "He died five years ago."

Marcos' hand slipped around Dave's shoulders, drawing him into an embrace.

He felt nothing. He was dead inside.

Marcos held him for a long time.

At last he said, "Come on. Let's get you cleaned up."

Dave let himself be led to the shower. Marcos undressed him and got him under the warm water. It felt… not comforting, exactly. *Comfortable.* That was a good word.

Afterward, Marcos toweled him dry and led him back to the bedroom.

He climbed into bed, and Marcos joined him, spooning him, his chest warm against Dave's back.

Something about that touch, about the warmth of Marcos's skin, calmed him. He closed his eyes, content to just be still, to be warm and safe.

Tomorrow. I'll deal with life tomorrow.

~

Something buzzed.

Marcos opened his eyes, looking blearily around the room. It had to be late afternoon, from the light slanting in through the blinds onto the olive-green walls. Carefully, he detached himself from Dave, trying not to wake him.

He picked up his phone. It was a text from Carmelina. A *bunch* of texts.

Need to talk.

Are you there?

It's important. Need to talk with you.

And ten more besides. He texted her back.

Sorry, taking care of Dave.

…

Is he okay?

…

I think so.

…

Can I meet you for coffee? Tomorrow morning?

. . .

Marcos glanced over at Dave, who was sleeping soundly. They'd talk things over when he woke up. Besides, he could always cancel the coffee date if he had to.

I think so. 10 AM, the EG on J and 38th?

…

Perfect. see you there.

He wondered what was so important.

~

Dave awoke to the sound of pots and pans. He sat up and swung his feet over the edge of the bed. *What the hell?* Then it all came flooding back. The box, the picture. The emotional paralysis. He hadn't felt like that in… in five years. And then… Marcos.

He padded out of the bedroom through the tiny living room with its over-loaded bookshelves and into the kitchen. Marcos was cooking eggs. "Hey, stranger."

Marcos jumped. "Holy shit. Don't do that to me!"

"Sorry." Dave sat at the kitchen table. "I must have been pretty out of it when you got here."

Marcos nodded. "I was worried about you. You didn't return my calls."

"How did you get in?"

"You showed me the key under the rock. Remember?"

"Oh, yeah."

"You hungry?"

Dave thought about it. "I'm starving, actually."

"Here you go." Marcos filled half of a plate with eggs and plopped down a couple of tortillas too. They were warm. "When I don't have a comal, I cook them on the burner like my dad taught me. Orange juice?"

"Yes, please."

They sat down together and attacked their plates. By the look of it, Marcos was as hungry as he was. The eggs were really good—fluffy with lots of cheese, just like Dave liked them.

"So… what happened?" Marcos asked at last, chewing his last forkful of eggs.

"It's hard to explain. Sometimes everything's just too much."

"Like when you find a photo of your deceased partner?"

"Yeah. Sometimes I just shut down. My grandmother was like that too."

He looked out the kitchen window at the evening glow. "It's happened to me four times before. The last one was right after John died."

"I can imagine."

"I get it if you want to run."

"Run?"

"Away from me."

Marcos shook his head. "I *like* you, Dave. I'm not going to run just 'cause you sometimes go into power-saving mode."

Dave smiled. A little. "You *do* know this entitles you to a little of your own craziness."

"I'll keep that in mind."

Dave grinned and squeezed Marcos's hand. "Something to look forward to."

Marcos squeezed back. "I think I'm falling for you." The expression on Marco's face was naked and vulnerable, and it touched Dave.

In that moment, he felt *alive*. "Me too."

83. BROKEN WING

Sam and Brad wrestled the heavy, solid wood desk out of Sam's den. They'd cleared a place for it in the living room. *At least I'll have a nice view of the street while I'm working.*

It was a beautiful mid-October day. He'd barely had a chance to look outside though. After they'd wrapped up their wedding planning in the morning, he'd spent a solid four hours working on his second book, *Across the Line.* He was on deadline, and he had enough time—barely, if he managed to get a chapter done every three days. That was going to be harder now, with the inevitable distractions of the wedding and their new house guest, but it would all be worth it.

"Why did I let you talk me into getting this monstrosity?" Brad asked, setting his end of the desk down in the doorway to the den.

"Because it's a *genyouuwine* antique? Because it only cost twenty-five dollars?"

Brad crossed his arms. "Nope, I don't think so."

"Because you love me and put up with all my writerly eccentricities?"

"Bingo. Let's get this thing moved into place." Brad tried to pick up his end of the desk again with a grunt. "Damn." He set it down again with a heavy *thunk.* "We need help."

"I can see if Jim's home."

"Good idea. He's a strapping guy." Brad whistled. "I wish I were still that nimble."

Sam climbed over the desk into the hallway. "Damn, you're only thirty. You're not an old man, for God's sake."

Brad laughed. "There's a lotta years between your twenty-three and my thirty."

Sam kissed his cheek. "You'll always be young to me. Be right back."

He swung open the front door and bounded down the stairs. It felt good to be outside.

Jim lived in the blue Victorian next door. He was a nice guy—bit of a silver fox, if Sam was honest. He liked sexy older guys, though he'd never tell Brad that. Not again. Made the poor guy feel old. Sam knocked on the door.

There were footsteps inside, and then Jim Oberkrom opened the door. "Hey Sam. What's up?"

Sam grinned. "Moving a bit of furniture. We've got a houseguest coming and needed to make some room."

Jim scratched the silver stubble on his chin and smiled. "Need a hand?"

Sam nodded. "Yes, please. If you're not busy."

"Nope. Just getting ready to go down to Fox and Goose for dinner with a couple of friends."

"It'll only take a moment."

"Let me grab my keys. I'll just leave for the restaurant from your place."

"Perfect." Sam watched him disappear down the hall. Yup. Good-looking guy. He and Brad really ought to find someone to fix Jim up with.

"Okay, all set." Jim pulled the door hard to close it and locked it behind him.

Sam couldn't help but notice the apple keychain. "You a farm-to-fork enthusiast?"

"What? Oh, this." He held up the keychain. "Nope. Used to be an elementary teacher in South Sac. See?" It said, *World's Greatest Teacher*.

"High praise." Sam bounded back down the stairs. "Come on. Let's get this over with."

Back at home, he held the door open for Jim.

"Hey, Jim!" Brad shook Jim's hand. "Thanks for the assistance. This desk of Sam's is made out of gold bars or something."

"Gold bars, huh? That's a helluva retirement plan you've got there. What do you want me to do?"

Sam chuckled. "You must have been popular with your students. Bet you always made them laugh. Let me climb over into the den." Sam clambered over the top of the desk. "Okay, if you can help Brad with that end? It's the heavier side."

"Sure. Happy to help." He ran his hand along the smooth, polished wood. "This is a beautiful piece. Where did you find it?"

"Estate sale out in Granite Bay. Brad hates it."

"No, I don't. I just wish it didn't weigh a ton."

"Next time you go estate-sale shopping, let me know. I love hunting for hidden gems at those things."

Sam grinned. "See? He gets it."

"Well marry him, then," Brad grunted.

They lifted it together on the count of three and managed to free the desk from the den.

They baby-stepped it forward together, then around the corner into the living room. Of course it was backwards, so between the three of them, they managed to turn it around, barely missing taking out a lamp and the corner of the dark leather sofa on the way.

Finally they backed it into place.

"You sure this is going to be okay?" Brad asked, worried. "He's a writer," he said to Jim.

Sam nodded. "Ricky can't make it up the stairs for now. And maybe a change of scene will inspire me." He was a little stuck on one of his protagonist's motivations. But usually those things worked themselves out. Eventually. "Thanks, Jim, for the help. If we can ever return the favor—"

"I'm sure I'll need it. Let's grab some coffee sometime. You guys have been here for months, and I hardly know you."

"We'd love that." Brad put out his hand, but Jim gave him a hug, then Sam too. "Welcome to the neighborhood, about a year late."

"Have fun at Fox and Goose!"

When he was gone, Sam spent the next half hour moving the rest of his things out of the den.

He looked around at the empty room a little sadly. It was *his* space. he was going to miss it. But it was for a greater cause.

∾

There was a knock at the door.

Brad opened it to find Ricky with his social worker, Connie Jenson. "Hey, Connie."

"Hi, Brad. Mind if I come in and take a look around?"

"Sure. We have his room all ready. Sam, want to show her?" He'd set up a bed and a dresser they'd borrowed from some friends. The rest would come later.

"On it. This way." Sam led the social worker to the new bedroom.

"Hi, Ricky." Brad reached forward to hug the boy, then stopped. "Broken ribs. Right."

"Hi, Mr. W." Ricky stepped inside and looked around the entry way and living room. "Nice." The bruises around his eyes were still an angry dark purple, but the edges were fading a little to green and red.

"You're looking better. Are you hungry?"

Ricky nodded. "They fed me lunch, but that was six hours ago."

"Where are your things?"

"The john took it all. I didn't have much."

Brad shook his head and sighed. These poor kids went through so much. "Come on into the kitchen. We have dinner ready. Hope you like hamburgers."

Ricky nodded. "Yes, sir."

Connie popped her head out of the bedroom. "The room looks good, but you'll need to get him some clothes and basic necessities. And he needs to be in school within the next seven days. This is a provisional placement. I'll be stopping by a couple of times a week and unannounced times to check on him. And Ricky?"

"Yes, ma'am."

"If you need anything, call me." She gave him a card. "Brad, can the Center help get Ricky a phone?"

Brad nodded. "We'll take care of it."

"Okay. Let me know the number when you do." She leaned forward and kissed Ricky lightly on the cheek. "Sam and Brad are good people. They will take care of you." Then she was gone, leaving only the faint smell of perfume like flowers in the air.

"Let's eat."

"Yeah, I'm starving," Sam said, giving the kid a reassuring smile.

Brad went to put a hand around the boy's shoulder, but he flinched away. "Hey, it's okay. You're safe here."

Ricky nodded, but he looked a little spooked.

There was more to heal here than a little bird's broken wing.

84.LORD LOVE A DUCK

Carmelina stood in front of the store window. On display was the most adorable pair of baby shoes, patent leather in pink and white. A little hand-lettered card next to them said "12 months." It was August 15th, 1976, one year to the day after Andrea's birth. One year to the day after Carmelina had done the most painful thing she could imagine: giving up her baby girl to a stranger.

Carmelina closed her eyes, holding out her hands and imagining Andrea in her arms, her voice gurgling, her brown eyes looking up at Carmelina. Andrea didn't have a clue what was coming next; she trusted her mother completely.

Despite Carmelina's own mother's assurance that she had done the right thing, she knew it would haunt her forever. That little face she might never see again.

Carmelina opened her eyes. Maybe this idea was foolish. Maybe she'd be better off finding a way to let go.

She pulled out her pocketbook and leafed through it. She had just enough to pay for the shoes if she skipped lunch the next couple of days. She would put them in the little blue box, and someday, maybe, she would give them to Andrea herself.

Decided, she pushed open the shop door, the bell announcing her intentions.

"Sorry to keep you waiting." Emily Stamp closed her office door behind her, her voice startling Carmelina out of her reverie.

"That's okay. I'm not sure I'm ready for your news, to be honest." What if Emily hadn't found anything? *What if she had?*

"I understand. This must be difficult for you." She sat down behind her desk and leaned her chair back, entwining her fingers over her stomach. "Before we get started, can I ask you something?"

She's pregnant. Carmelina wasn't sure how she knew it. "Sure."

"If your daughter had come looking for you, would you have wanted to meet her?"

"Absolutely." It came out with a vehemence that surprised Carmelina, but there was really no doubt in her mind. "Why? Are you thinking of looking for your own mother?"

Emily looked out the window, a wistful expression on her face. "Maybe," she said at last. "Dani and I are becoming parents ourselves, so motherhood has been on my mind a lot these days. I'm not sure I want to meet her though. She was an addict, from what I've learned. Do I want that in my life? In my child's life?" Emily shrugged. "Anyhow, enough about me." She sat up and pulled a folder out of one of her desk drawers.

"You know who she is?"

Emily nodded. "One of the perks of the job. I'm my own personal PI."

Carmelina leaned forward and took her hand. "I can't tell you if it's a good idea or not to meet her. I can only tell you that I would give everything I have for the chance to see my own daughter just *one more time*."

Emily sniffed and wiped the corner of her eye. "I… Yes, good to know. I'll think about it. Now, should we talk about your granddaughter?"

Carmelina sat back, a trickle of sweat running down her spine. "You found something, then?"

"More than something. I have her name and her adopted parents' phone and address. I also pulled some public records. There are photos in there too." She slid the folder across the desk. The tab said "Mary."

Carmelina picked up the folder and held it to her chest. This was it. Her hands tingled, and she was suddenly suffused with an almost overwhelming anxiety tinged with joy.

She opened the folder. The first thing was a school photo of a beautiful blonde girl maybe seven or eight years old. "She's beautiful." Carmelina could see her own face in the girl's features. She smiled and closed her eyes and kissed the photo, then set it aside. The next thing was a junior high transcript.

"I'm afraid I do have one bit of bad news."

Carmelina looked up with a frown. "What?"

"She's been placed in temporary foster care. I don't know with whom. If you want, I can try to find out more."

"What happened to her?" Was she a juvenile delinquent?

"Some kind of dispute with her parents."

"Okay." That was all right. One thing at a time. She turned back to the school transcript and started to read it. Carmelina's heart raced. "That's her name?"

"Yes. They changed it when she was adopted."

She flipped through the file, searching for a more current photo. At the very back, there was a newspaper clipping dated August 2014. *High School Junior Wins Race.*

"Lord love a duck." It was *her.*

Emily frowned. "That's a reaction I've never seen before. What's it mean?"

Carmelina closed the folder. "It means I think I know where to find her."

"Well that's a first."

Carmelina laughed. She was *this close.* She thanked Emily and gave the woman a big hug. "You have no idea what you've done for me," she said, squeezing her tight. "I hope you go see your own mother. Regardless of what might happen."

"Thank you. I hope your reunion is everything you hoped for." She closed her office door with an encouraging smile, hand on her stomach.

Carmelina let herself out of the lobby and descended the stairs to J Street.

Marcos. She needed to talk to Marcos. He would know what to do next.

She grabbed a coffee at the Everyday Grind on 20th. Then she sent him a text. *Need to talk.*

There was no response. She sipped her coffee out on the boardwalk under the great oak tree, watching a cyclist in neon-green spandex cycle by.

Are you there?

So many things she wanted to say to her granddaughter. So many questions to ask.

It's important. Need to talk with you.

She lost track of how many times she texted him as the afternoon slipped by. She was just about to give up and head home when her phone *dinged.*

Sorry, taking care of Dave.

Is he okay?

… I think so.

Can I meet you for coffee? Tomorrow morning?

She waited anxiously for his response.

… I think so. 10 AM, the EG on J and 38th?

Perfect. see you there.

She'd waited forty years for this moment. Another seventeen hours wouldn't kill her.

85. THE LINK

Diego put his hands on the coffin. He remembered the last time he'd seen Luna, the night she died.

She'd looked like an angel, her eyes closed in perfect peace, her pale white face and blonde hair perfectly arranged as she left this Earth.

She's already gone. The pale, stiff wraith inside the coffin was as much Luna as he was George Clooney. Still, one respected the dead, and one followed the forms.

He stretched in his borrowed suit. Valentina's friend Paolo was a little skinnier than he was, but Diego had been loathe to buy a brand-new suit for just this one occasion.

He stepped back to let Gio have some time with his mother.

Diego's sister Valentina put her arm around him and hugged him. "You okay?"

He nodded. "I'm ready to go home." He missed having Matteo to talk to, to figure all this stuff out.

Gio stood next to the coffin for a long time, his hand on the closed lid.

"It's been good to have you here, even under such dire circumstances," Valentina said softly. "Mamma's not getting any better."

He nodded. "I am lucky to have you here to look after her. I wish Claudia and Cinzia lived closer."

They shared a glance at their mother, dressed in her funeral-day finery, the same dress and veil she'd worn to his father's funeral years before. "I remember when we were all kids, and she would make us dress up for church. You never wanted to wear those frilly dresses."

She laughed. "And you had always skinned a knee—and your trousers—by the time we got home again. We were troublemakers."

As if on cue, little Dante chased Bianca past them, laughing and screaming.

Valentina caught Dante by the collar and hauled him backwards. "*Comportati!*" she hissed, depositing him on one of the pews. "Sit there and be quiet. You're embarrassing your family."

Dante sulked and fidgeted.

Diego stifled a laugh. Their family members were about the only people here, so it would be hard for the boy to embarrass them. Luna had had no one, and only a few others, maybe friends and neighbors, had bothered to come.

At last, Gio turned away from the casket. "It's not her in there," he said flatly. "I'll be in the car." He brushed past Diego.

Valentina rubbed Diego's arm. "He's hurting. He'll come around."

"I hope so. Are we ready to go?" Diego just wanted to get this day over with.

"Sure." Valentina kissed his cheek. "*Forza.* Come on, Mamma. Time to go to the cemetery."

Diego took one more look at Luna, and then helped his mother up from the pew. He threw his arms around her and hugged her tightly. "*Ti voglio benissimo, Mamma.*"

"What's this for?" She squeezed him back.

"Just because."

~

They followed the hearse to the cemetery, driving past the white towers of the crematorium and onto the grounds, to Luna's final resting place inside a white marble mausoleum.

It was a bright, sunny day, at odds with the sobriety of the ritual being enacted by the bereaved. Valentina parked as close to the mausoleum entrance as she could manage.

Diego helped his mother out of the car.

Gio sat in the back seat, playing a game on his phone.

"You coming?"

The boy looked up and nodded. He turned his phone off and joined Diego at the curbside.

The two of them helped the other pallbearers carry the casket to the mausoleum. The grass was soft from rain the day before, and Diego had to place his feet carefully with each step as they crossed the field to the tent. The last thing he needed was to trip and send Luna's casket flying.

They entered the building, and Diego was struck by how serene and lifeless the place was. They set the casket down carefully, and the priest rose to speak.

"Luna Mazzocco was a wild spirit, one that passed from this Earth too soon. Her surviving family member, her son Giovanni, has provided roses. If you are so inclined, please take one and place it on the casket and take a moment to say your final goodbyes." Diego stood and followed his sister to pay his last respects. He took a rose and laid it on top, whispering, "I'll take care of him for you." Then he stepped aside to let the others have their chance.

Diego closed his eyes, remembering the summer they had gotten married, when he was still young. When almost anything had seemed possible. As crazy as Luna was, she'd had a light in her. It had been her brilliant smile and uncensored laughter that had drawn him to her in the first place. It was still hard for him to believe she was gone.

He looked up. Everyone had gone to pay their respects except for Gio. "Gio," he whispered. "It's time."

"I can't." The boy looked up at him, and his eyes were red and wet.

"Come on." Diego held his hand out. "I'll do it with you."

Gio stared at him for a moment and then nodded, putting his hand in Diego's. He stood and walked slowly to the casket.

Diego handed him a rose. "Here. Say what you need to say."

Gio took it, and then threw it at the casket. "Why did you have to die?" he said, his voice raising to a scream. "Why did you leave me?" He hit the casket with his fists. "Why did you die?" His voice trailed off into a whisper.

Diego sighed. "Come on, kiddo. Let's take a walk."

Gio's face was red, but he nodded. He kissed the coffin and whispered something and then turned away, stone-faced.

Diego's heart broke for him. He put his arm around Gio's shoulder, and they exited the mausoleum into the sunlight. They walked down the road between the grassy sections of the cemetery. The sun was warm on Diego's shoulders, a bit of a breeze blowing the Italian cypress that lined the edge of the place. "You're right, Gio," he said at last, glancing sideways at his son. *My son.* "It sucks. The whole world sucks right about now."

Geo nodded. "It does." His hands were in his pocket, and his face was gray,

"When my *papà* died, I cried for weeks." Diego took a deep breath. "Luna was a beautiful woman, and she loved you fiercely, you know. I see a lot of her in you—she'll always be a part of you. The best part of you."

"You do?"

He chuckled. "Yes. She was defiant, like you. She never let life keep her down for long. And you have her features."

"I wish she was still here."

Diego nodded at a man laying flowers on an old, crumbling headstone. "I know, Gio. I know." He squeezed the boy's shoulders. "Listen, I know I'm not her. But I'm here for you, and I'm not going to let you down."

Gio turned and threw his arms around Diego and began to cry, ugly sobs racking his whole body.

Diego rubbed his back. "There there. It's gonna be okay, son. It's all gonna be okay."

He remembered his own father saying just those words to him when his nonna had died. He was part of a chain, a link between his parents' generation and the next.

In that moment, he believed his own words. "It's all gonna be okay."

86. THREE FOR COFFEE

Marcos waited anxiously at the Everyday Grind for Carmelina. He'd left his boyfriend at home. Dave seemed more himself this morning, and they'd spent a couple of hours chatting at breakfast. Now Marcos sat in the alcove by the front door, watching the traffic pass by along J Street.

A woman in pink-and-black spandex with gray, curly hair sat under a patio umbrella just outside the cafe, intent on her laptop screen. Was she writing a romance novel? Or a letter to a long-lost love? Or maybe a paper on particle physics? Two handsome young men walked by with a golden retriever on leash, talking and laughing, at the same time that a Harley roared by in the opposite direction. It was a gorgeous, sunny day. One more day without rain in the midst of the drought, but nice all the same.

He glanced at his watch. It was five after ten. Carmelina was late. What did she need to talk with him about? Was there something wrong? Then Carmelina walked past his window, a look of grim determination on her face. So it was something serious. Marcos got up to greet her as she came in. "Hey gorgeous," he said, giving her a hug. "I grabbed a latte while I was waiting."

"Oooh, that looks good." She managed a smile that didn't reach her eyes. "I'll get myself one too. Be right back."

Marcos looked around. It was usually quiet, and today was no exception. The EG had a warm, friendly vibe, from its African wall art to its warm earth tones and friendly staff. He'd come to think of this one as "his" Everyday Grind. It was closest to home, and the baristas all knew him by name.

Carmelina returned a moment later with a steaming mug of coffee and a biscotti. "Were you waiting long?" She sat down in her chair, putting her over-sized blue-and-gold shoulder bag on the table.

"About ten minutes."

"I'm not taking you from work, am I?" She frowned.

"A little, but that's okay. It can wait."

"You sure?" She nibbled on her cookie.

"Yes."

"Dave okay too?"

"Yes! Enough stalling. What's this about? You have me all worried."

For her response, she took a sip of her coffee, staring at him through the steam for a moment as if judging his mood. She set down the mug. "You know I've been looking for my granddaughter?"

He nodded. "Your daughter was adopted, and something happened?"

"She was killed by a drunk driver."

"That's right. I'm so sorry."

She smiled wanly. "Thank you. It's an old pain. The loss. I didn't know she was killed until recently…. I guess I always hoped she would come find me, one day. When she was ready."

"Of course. That must have been terrible news to hear." He put his hand on hers. "Are you okay?"

"Yes. Mostly." She pulled her hand away and put her palms around the coffee cup as if soaking in its warmth. "I hired someone to find my grand-daughter."

He nodded. He would have done the same. "Did they find her?"

She nodded. "Yes. I just met the investigator yesterday."

"That's amazing! Oh my God, I'm so thrilled for you." Marcos grinned from ear to ear. "I was so nervous about this whole meeting thing. You had me really worried, being all secretive and shit. Will you get to meet her soon?" He tried to imagine it, meeting someone you'd thought was lost forever.

"That depends on you." She reached her hand inside her bag. pulling out a manila folder and handing it to him.

Uncomprehending, he opened it. Inside, there was a picture of a little girl. "She's beautiful, but I'm not sure what this has to do—"

"Keep going."

Next was a school transcript. He picked it up. *Not bad, all in all, grade-wise.* "So her name is…" He froze.

"Marissa."

He looked up at Carmelina, a torrent of emotions running through him: incredulity, disbelief, shock, and anger. "She can't be."

"Keep going."

He turned back to the folder. Further on, there was a news article and a few more pictures. It was her, *his* Marissa. "Is the investigator sure?"

She nodded. "As sure as she can without DNA. She has the records."

Marcos shook his head. This couldn't be happening. He and Marissa were a family now. She'd become an inseparable part of his life in the last month. Sure, he'd known the court might see things differently when her adoptive parents were in the room. But this… this was something he'd never expected.

"I know this is a lot to process. I was as shocked as you. I don't want to come between you two. You've been just what Marissa needed."

"Then what *do* you want?" He would fight for Marissa if he had to.

"I want to talk to her." She stared at him, unblinking. "She's my blood."

He closed his eyes, feeling the moisture gathering at the corners of his eyes. "I'm sorry. I'm thrilled for you, I really am. But Marissa and I…" *Marissa and I are what?* He had no parental rights here. He was a foster parent to her, no more.

"Marcos, look at me." Carmelina took his hands in hers, squeezing them tight. "I don't want to take her away from you. Hell, I don't want to raise a child. I know what a pain in the ass they are." She let go of his hands and sat back, her smile fading. "I just want her to know she has family. I want to be her grandmother. Her nonna. My own family is all gone."

He blinked. For just a moment, his own grandmother Consuela sat there in Carmelina's place, smiling at him, her salt-and-pepper hair looking like she'd just come from the salon, her gold-rimmed glasses framing her face. "I love you, Mijo," she whispered.

Marcos blinked again and she was gone, but he knew what she meant. He took a deep breath. "You *should* be a part of her life. You both deserve that."

"Are you sure? You're okay with this?" Carmelina's hands trembled in her lap.

"Yes. I am. I will be." He exhaled, letting go of his fear. "Oh my God, you're Marissa's grandmother!"

She laughed. "I am, right?" She got up and gave him a bear hug.

He hugged her back. "When do we tell her?"

"This afternoon at Ragazzi?"

"Too many people. Let's take her somewhere after." Marcos closed his eyes, missing the sparkle that enveloped them both for just a moment, but he felt its magic.

87. HOW TO MAKE A GOOD SAUCE

He'd let Sam talk him into coming to this cooking class for their *big reveal* —Sam's words—and now he was kneading enough potato dough to make what seemed like a hundred thousand gnocchi.

"You're cute like that." Sam kissed his cheek, possibly the only part of his body not powdered with flour. Sam had been in charge of boiling the potatoes and had gotten off scot-free in the flour department.

Carmelina was kneading the dough next to him, attacking it with a single-minded ferocity.

"Hey, go easy on that. That dough didn't do anything to you." Something was eating at her.

She laughed, but it was a bit strained. She kept looking at Marissa and Tris, who Matteo had put to work making sauce. Ricky was there too, but he hung back a bit from the pair. He was worried for the kid.

"Something wrong?" Brad whispered, indicating the couple.

"No." She wiped sweat from her brow with the back of her hand. "Just thinking."

Brad glanced down at his own dough. It was still a floury mess, while hers looked like it was ready to… to cut? To bunch up in little balls? He had no idea how one actually made gnocchi from the stuff.

"You ready?" Sam whispered in his ear.

"Now?" Seriously, Sam wanted to do this while he was covered in flour?

Sam laughed. "Why not?"

"Um, sure." He'd thought to do it around the dinner table, but this did feel like a *family* moment. "You want to?"

"You go ahead. You're the one who proposed."

Brad grinned. He had a hard time believing this was all going by so fast. He cleared his throat. "Excuse me, everyone… Sam and I have a bit of an announcement." He looked over at Ricky. "Well, two, actually. Ricky Martinez, the handsome young guy standing there with Marissa and Tris, is coming to live with us."

Ricky blushed, but he managed a bow and a side grin that just made him more adorable.

"And second, Sam and I have decided to get married."

Carmelina grabbed him in an unexpected hug that sent a cloud of flour into the air. "Oh my God, I am so thrilled for you guys."

Brad coughed, waving flour away from his eyes as he struggled to breathe. "Thanks."

She let go of him and squeezed his arms gently, her eyes getting a little teary around the edges.

"The wedding's in two weeks—on Sunday the first. Matteo and Diego have agreed to let us hold it right here, at Ragazzi."

Matteo held up a glass of wine in salute. "*Siamo contenti di avervi.*"

Brad grinned. "I'll pretend to know what that means."

"Who proposed?" It was Marcos, who had brought his partner, Dave.

"I did."

"Did you get down on your knees and everything?" Carmelina's eyes were shining.

"Well, one of them." He looked around the room. "Some of you we have known for a long time. Some of you are new friends. But you all have become our family. Sam? The invitations?"

"Oh, right." Sam dug into his backpack and pulled out the brightly colored envelopes. "One for each of you, courtesy of RuPaul." He handed them out. "We hope you all can make it. We know it's short notice. Matteo, when does Diego return?"

The usually affable Italian frowned. "This week."

The room went back to work, and one by one, their friends came up and gave each of them a hug. Last of all, Sam hugged and kissed him again. "I can't wait to marry you," he whispered in Brad's ear.

When Sam let go, he was covered in flour, as was the rest of the room.

"Looks like it's gonna be a white wedding," Dave said dryly, dusting flour off his black shirt.

~

Carmelina washed her hands off in the sink, glancing over her shoulder now and again at Marissa. Now that she knew Marissa was her granddaughter, she could see the resemblance; the curve of her nose, the way she pushed her hair back behind her ear. So what if they said mannerisms weren't inherited?

Was that what Andrea had looked like at her age?

Carmelina had missed so much in the last forty-odd years. She was anxious to tell Marissa who she was. To not miss anything else.

"Hey."

Marcos's voice in her ear made her jump, and she splashed him with water.

"Hey!" He wiped off his face.

"Sorry. I'm just… you know."

He followed her gaze. "Yeah. I know. We'll talk to her this afternoon together."

She nodded. "I know the waiting shouldn't matter. It's just a couple of hours. But still…"

"You want to run over there and throw your arms around her."

Her face was hot. "Yeah. I do."

"So? Go help her with the sauce."

"Yeah?"

"Why not? You two are friends." He gave her a playful shove.

"Sure we are," she muttered, not entirely convinced. She dried off her hands on her apron, picking up a little more flour, but she didn't care.

She tapped Tristan on the shoulder. "Mind if I cut in?"

He smiled. "Sure, why not?" He kissed Marissa. "I'm gonna go keep Ricky company. He looks lonely."

"Good idea."

"How's it coming?" Carmelina picked up a wooden spoon and dipped it into the sauce to take a taste. "Oooh. Not bad. Needs some more basil."

"But Matteo said…"

Carmelina put a hand around Marissa's shoulder. "We're the cooks, right?" she said with an impish smile.

Marissa laughed. "I guess we are."

"Hand me some of that fresh basil."

Marissa grabbed a handful.

"I prefer to tear the basil leaves by hand. It smells so wonderful, and you know you've been cooking when you're done." She demonstrated. "Smell." She held her fingers under Marissa's nose.

"Oooh, that smells good."

Carmelina nodded. "Doesn't it? You can never have too much basil." She tasted the sauce again. "Needs a bit more garlic too, I think. Garlic you have to use a knife for." She slammed the garlic down on the cutting board and it popped into a dozen cloves. Then she showed Marissa how to chop it.

"How do you know how to do this? Make a good sauce, chop the garlic just right, all of it?" Marissa asked, dropping the garlic into the sauce by hand. She tasted it and a broad grin split her face. "It's really good."

"My grandmother taught me everything she knew about Italian cooking." Carmelina kissed the girl on the forehead.

Just as I plan to teach you.

See the potato gnocchi recipe at the end of the book.

88. IT'S KINDA NICE

WHILE THE GNOCCHI WERE COOKING, MARISSA SLIPPED AWAY TO SIT down with Ricky and Tris. She hadn't seen Ricky since the day at the hospital four days earlier.

Ricky and Tris were sitting alone in a corner of the restaurant. Ricky's broken ribs made it difficult for him to exert himself much, even for cooking.

The two guys were deep in conversation. Marissa slipped into the chair next to them. "Hey, Ricky, how are you?" she said when there was a pause in the conversation.

"I'm okay. Better, I think. The doctors say it will be a couple of months before I'm all healed." He tapped his rib cage gently.

"Did they find the guy who did it?" She was still angry with him for taking a chance like that, but you couldn't say anything when someone was injured.

Ricky shook his head. "Not yet."

Tris took her hand. "Did you know Ricky used to be a… what did you call it?"

"Hustler."

"Yeah, that. That he had sex for money?"

Marissa nodded. "Yeah, I did." She had to remind herself that Tris had no experience with homelessness. Or the homeless. "There are a lot of kids on the street who don't have any other way to survive. Ricky was luckier than most. He had a steady guy."

"A *sugar daddy*, right?" Tris looked inordinately proud of himself.

Marissa laughed. "Yeah. That. Until he got dumped and then picked up the wrong guy." She glared at Ricky.

"Hey, I didn't *know* he was the wrong guy," Ricky protested.

She sighed. "So how's the new place?"

"With Sam and Brad?" Ricky smiled. "Not bad. I have my own room, and Brad's a decent cook." He shrugged. "I just keep waiting for it all to go away, you know? It always ends."

"Brad's a good guy." But she knew what he meant. Ricky had been through a dozen foster homes before going it alone on the street. Some had been decent. Some… some he never wanted to talk about.

She glanced over at Carmelina. The woman waved back at her.

"She's being really weird today." Marissa liked Carmelina, but this was starting to verge on stalking. Still, there was something about her that Marissa felt drawn to, something warm.

"Tell me about it," Ricky said, looking over at Sam and Brad. "They're insta-parents. Every five minutes they're checking in on me. Am I okay? Do I want some water? Something to eat? How do my ribs feel?" He snorted. "It's annoying."

"It's kinda nice though, right?" Marissa liked having her own room again, a bed, and a place to shower that wasn't shared with a hundred others.

Ricky sighed. "Yeah. Yeah, it is."

～

"Dinner is served." Matteo held up the wide, shallow platter painted with yellow lemons that he and Diego had bought in Amalfi together. The gnocchi were piled up high, covered in fresh basil and the sauce Marissa and Carmelina had made.

Matteo had arranged the tables together into one long one in the middle of the room, enough to seat sixteen. He set the gnocchi in the middle, and Carmelina brought out the fresh, hot garlic bread and a green salad. He still wasn't used to the whole bread-and-salad-first nonsense, but when in America…

Everyone gathered around the table and took their seats. The salad, bread, and pasta went around, and a soft chatter filled the room, the sound of good friends getting reacquainted after a week's absence.

Matteo was reminded of his own family meals—his grandparents, aunts and uncles, and cousins all gathered around the dinner table *la tavola*—for a communal meal in his parents' tiny dining room. Always full of so much life and activity.

"It's nice, isn't it?" Carmelina said.

He nodded. "In Italian, we say, '*A tavola non si invecchia.*' At the table, one doesn't age."

"Oooh, I like that." Carmelina shuffled some salad onto her plate and handed him the bowl. "We have our own little Italian family here."

Our own little family. She was right. Somehow, they'd created a family out of nothing here on these foreign shores.

Only one thing was missing. His Diego.

He took a spoonful of gnocchi for himself and a little bread.

"Hey, are you okay?" Carmelina was staring at him.

"It's nothing."

She squeezed his arm. "I'm really good at listening."

He knew that look. She wouldn't give this up until he gave her an answer. Matteo sighed. "I just found out that Diego has a son. Gio." It weighed on him.

"Damn. And you didn't know?"

"No."

"Was it while you two were—"

"Yes. Gio's seventeen." He shook his head. "I should be supportive of him and Gio, but it's hard. What Diego did—you probably think I'm a terrible person."

She gave him a hug. "Not at all. I understand better than you know," she whispered.

"Thank you." He felt a little better having told someone, but he wondered what she meant. "Would you excuse me a moment?"

"Sure. If you ever need to talk, I'm here."

He kissed her cheek. "*Grazie, bella.*"

He made his way upstairs and pulled out his cell phone. It was midnight in Italy, but he needed to talk to Diego. He was a night owl, anyway, so he'd probably still be awake.

"Pronto," Diego said. He sounded half asleep.

"Ciao, Diego. It's Matteo."

"What time is it?" Diego asked in Italian, not English.

Matteo let it go. Diego was in Italy, after all. "About midnight, where you are."

"Is everything okay?" He sounded alarmed. "Is the restaurant—"

"Everything's fine. I just wanted to call and tell you I love you."

"Gio—"

"I'm still angry with you. But we'll work it out." *We always do.*

"Okay."

"Go back to sleep. I'll see you at the airport on Tuesday."

"*Ti amo.*"

"*Ti amo di più.*"

He hung up the phone and stared at it for a moment. It was good to hear Diego's voice, but they still had a lot to talk about when he came home.

Matteo slipped the phone into his pocket and went back downstairs to rejoin his new family.

89.NEWS

She put them on her lap under the table where no one could see them. *Deep breaths.*

She should have ordered a decaf. The caffeine in her espresso was doing nothing to help calm her nerves. Besides, she really shouldn't be so nervous. She'd known Marissa for a month now. Well, twenty-eight days was close enough. Five Sundays.

But she *hadn't* known that Marissa was her granddaughter.

The door to the Everyday Grind swung open.

Deep breath.

"Hey there," Marcos said. His eyes darted back and forth, as if he was planning his exit, just in case.

"It'll be fine," she whispered in his ear as she hugged him, projecting a confidence she didn't feel. "Hey, Marissa."

"Hey." The girl gave her a diffident hug and settled into a seat with her phone, texting with one hand.

"I'm going to grab us a couple of drinks. Marissa?"

"Skinny Mocha, please." She didn't look up.

Marcos shrugged and went to fetch drinks.

Carmelina sat back and tried not to stare at the girl. Marissa had already seemed a little uncomfortable at their closeness back at Ragazzi. Carmelina didn't want the girl to think she was a stalker.

Marissa finished her text and put her phone down on the round marble table. She looked up at Carmelina and gave her a half smile. "What?"

"Oh, nothing. It's just that… you remind me of someone."

"Oh yeah? That's weird." Her phone buzzed, and she picked it up again and glanced at the screen, then started another text.

She looked so much like Carmelina had at that age.

"Is that Tristan?"

"Yeah. He wants to do something tonight."

"He seems like a nice kid."

"Yeah. I like him." Her hand raced across the screen.

Carmelina envied her that. Texts always took her a long time to type, even on a smartphone. And she was always screwing things up, losing emails, deleting apps. It all made her feel terribly old.

"Here we are." Marcos reappeared with a couple of paper cups. "One mocha for you." He handed a cup to Marissa. "And a double grind for me." He sat down next to Marissa, stretching his legs. "Did I miss anything?"

Carmelina shook her head. "Marissa has been busy."

"Sorry." She put her phone in her pocket and looked up. "Okay, done. Marcos said you wanted to talk to me?"

Carmelina had a whole speech practiced. How sometimes adults made bad decisions and lived to regret them. About Arthur's death and her search for connections. About how sometimes what you were looking for turned out to be right under your nose after all.

She threw it out the window. It was now or never. "Marissa, I'm your grandmother."

～

How about dinner at MD?

Marissa could *feel* Carmelina staring at her.

Marcos had been really sly about what she wanted to talk about. Maybe she needed someone to house sit, or something?

Sounds good. I'll text you later.

"Sorry." She put her phone in her pocket. "Okay, done. Marcos said you wanted to talk to me?"

Carmelina reached out to take her hand. "Marissa, I'm your grandmother."

What the hell? "Um… What do you mean?" Her mother was dead. Her stepmonster had told her so. Some kind of car accident. How could Carmelina think they were related?

"I… I gave away my daughter—your mother—for adoption four decades ago. I just found out that she was killed in an auto accident just after you were born and that you existed. I didn't know...."

Marissa pulled her hand away. All her life, she'd wished her *real* mother would find her. That she'd be alive, and that she would sweep in and take Marissa away from that awful, stuffy home in the suburbs. But *this*? "Where were you? All those years? And why should I believe you, anyway?"

Carmelina nodded, her eyes wet. "Look, I know it's hard to accept. I had a private investigator look into your identity. She gave me these...." Carmelina handed her a manila folder.

Marissa took it, leafing through it. There were pictures of her, including an old article about a track race she'd won the year before. She stared at them in disbelief. *Why now?* Why after all these years, when her life was finally going right? She liked living with Marcos. She hardly knew Carmelina at all. "I don't... I can't." She threw the folder back at Carmelina, getting up so fast she knocked the chair over backwards.

"Marissa!" Marcos looked angry and embarrassed at her behavior.

She couldn't stand it. Not *that*. Not from *him*. "I'm sorry. I have to go." She ran out the door, past a startled woman reaching for the handle. "Sorry," she mumbled, and ran down the street, her eyes nearly blinded by tears.

~

Marcos got up to set the chair upright and started to run after her.

"Let her go," Carmelina said, her voice sounding tired.

"Are you sure?" Marcos sighed. "I'm sorry," he said, sitting down. "Maybe I should have talked to her first. Prepared her somehow."

Carmelina snorted. "How do you prepare someone for news like that?" She took a sip of her coffee. "Besides, she's right to be angry. I *should* have gone looking for my daughter earlier—much earlier. Maybe then I would have found *her*."

Marcos stared at the door, still not entirely convinced he should have let Marissa go. "Why didn't you?"

"Oh, I don't know. I guess I had myself convinced it was for the best. That her life was better without me." She set down her cup. "And there was Arthur too. He never knew."

"Are you sure she'll be all right?"

Carmelina nodded. "Give her time. She needs to process it. When she's ready, she'll come back."

"How do you know?"

Now she smiled. "She's a lot like me."

"Wait, I have that Find Friends app thing." He unlocked his phone and opened the app. "I can see where she's going. See?" He held up his phone triumphantly. At least he could keep an eye on her from afar.

"Looks like she's heading for midtown. Wait…. Where'd she go?"

Marcos looked at his phone. Marissa's dot was gone. "That's weird." He closed the app and reopened it. Nothing.

"She doesn't want you tracking her."

"Shit." Carmelina was right. Marissa had an independent streak. She must have turned it off.

She was like a daughter to him. The thought of her coming to harm…

He'd give her a couple of hours, and then he would call her.

If she didn't answer… well, he'd cross that bridge when he came to it.

He had a good idea where he would find her.

90. SCARS

Marcos stared at his watch and then at the door to his condo. It was nine p.m. already, and Marissa hadn't come home. She had school the next day.

"I'm sure she's okay." Dave wrapped his arms around Marcos from behind and gave him a hug. He'd come over to keep Marcos company and to keep him from chewing his nails off while he waited. Neither effort had been wholly successful.

"I hope so. Maybe we shouldn't have ambushed her with it." How had he gotten so attached to her in such a short time?

"You had to tell her someday." Dave shook his head, whistling. "Never would have guessed Carmelina had a grandkid."

"She never talked about it?" The two were close.

"Nope. I guess it's something she kept buried deep."

Nine-oh-five. This was getting ridiculous. "I'm going out."

"Want me to come with?"

Marcos shook his head. "I need to find her and talk to her alone. She trusts me." He shook his head. "Well, she did. Before…" Now he was second-guessing his decision to tell her the way they had, to not break it to her more gently. "Anyhow, I think I know where to find her."

Marcos stood in front of Twink again, the tattoo shop where he'd found Marissa three-and-a-half weeks earlier.

Lucca was doing a brisk business next door, people enjoying the restaurant's shaded patio in the unusually warm weather.

Marcos took a deep breath and pushed open the door.

"Be right with you," Rex said without looking up. The artist was working on someone's back, doing a pink polka-dot mushroom for what looked to be an extensive magical forest scene.

"Hey, Rex, it's Marcos."

Rex glanced up. "Oh, hey." He went back to work. "Marissa's in the back."

Marcos nodded. He'd figured she would come here, the last safe place she had known before he took her in. Here or with Tris, and the boy had denied any knowledge of her current whereabouts.

Marcos pushed his way through the black bead curtain that separated the back of the shop from the studio.

There was a bathroom on the left and a storeroom on the right and a closed door at the back of the hall.

He knocked, admiring the art that decorated all the walls—designs from the tattoo books he'd leafed through the last time he was here.

After a moment, the door swung open.

Marissa stared up at him, smelling like bubble gum. "You can save the pep talk. I'm happy here."

She tried to close the door, but he held it open. "Look, I just want to talk with you for a minute."

She shrugged and let him push open the door.

The room held a desk and chair, a bookshelf full of notebooks, and a mattress in one corner. A vape pipe lay on the concrete floor at the edge of the mattress. That explained the bubble gum smell. "Nice place."

She shrugged. "It's better than sleeping on the street."

"Yeah, I can see that."

She sat down on the mattress, her back against the wall. She picked up the pipe and offered it to him.

"No thanks."

She shrugged and gestured for him to join her. "So, talk."

Marcos sat down next to her, ignoring the cloyingly sweet smell. He closed his eyes, trying to remember what it had been like at Marissa's age. When he was always talked *to* and talked *about*. Never talked *with*. "Why did you run away?" he asked at last.

"I told you. My parents—"

"No, I mean, why did you take off this afternoon? What spooked you?"

She stared at him for a long moment, then looked away. "She wanted to take me away."

"Who? Carmelina?"

She nodded. "I was just feeling safe with you. Happy. I should have known it couldn't last."

She feels safe with me. That made him feel a little better. He reached over and touched her forehead with his index finger, running it lightly down her face. "You have this scar running across the middle of your life. This broken place where you used to feel loved, protected."

She shrugged again. "I guess. Everyone's broken somehow."

He nodded. "Scar tissue helps protect us. It makes us stronger where we used to be weak. It puts things back together that got cut apart." He had his own share of scars, some of them physical, most of them on his psyche. "But scars numb you too, deaden your nerves, make you forget what it felt like to be whole. It's a constant dead zone, a reminder of the hurt you went through."

She was silent, but her eyes were locked on his.

He picked up her left hand in his. "I'm scarred too. My parents threw me out when I was your age, and I spent the next twenty-five years scared to let anyone in." He'd opened up to both Marissa and Dave, and now he was scared to death to lose one or both.

"I can't get hurt like that again," she whispered.

"I know. When I took you in, I promised you'd be safe. I meant it. That hasn't changed. You can stay with me for as long as you want."

Marissa looked doubtful.

"I talked with Carmelina for an hour after you left. She wants to be your grandmother, not your mother. She just wants to know you better. She has her own scars from losing your mother."

"What happened?"

He shook his head. "I don't know much. She gave her daughter away when she was about your age, and she never saw her again."

"Just like my mother."

"Those circumstances were a bit different." He squeezed her hand. "The scarred have a special affinity for one other. We know what it feels like to be hurt, to be broken by someone we love. The three of us—you, me, Carmelina —we share a bond."

"I don't know—"

Marcos picked up his backpack off the floor and unzipped it. "I brought this guy for you." He held up Nathan, her teddy bear.

"I'm too old for teddy bears." Still, he could see a little light in her eyes as she stared at it.

He laughed. "I'm sorry to hear that. I still have mine. His name is Andy, and I hug him whenever I need a little love." He held out the stuffed animal to her.

She took Nathan hesitantly, then held him tight.

"You have your key?"

She nodded.

"You're a grown woman, or near enough. You get to make your own decisions, so I'll leave it up to you. You and Nathan always have a place with me and Dave." He leaned over and kissed her forehead. "I hope you come home."

He got up and left her there. She was almost eighteen. It was time she started to make her own decisions, but walking out of that room was one of the hardest things he had ever done.

He headed home, managing not to cry for most of the drive, and went to bed with Dave, spooning his other love and trying to put Marissa out of his mind. Eventually he managed to sleep.

In the morning, he got up early and tiptoed out of his room and down the hall.

He opened Marissa's door just a crack, and breathed a great sigh of relief when he found her and Nathan sound asleep together in her bed.

91.KARMA

Ben sat in the waiting room at U.C. Davis, staring nervously at the time on his phone. Dr. Randall had agreed to see him, though she'd already told him there was nothing she could do for him when they'd talked on the phone. He'd sent off his novel the day before. Now he had something more important to do.

She was late. It was ten-thirty a.m., and his appointment was for ten. He hoped the fact that she was running late didn't mean anything.

The hospital was busy today, humming with patients and personnel.

He hadn't told Ella he was coming here. Why get her hopes up, if it might all end up being for naught?

"Mr. Hammond?"

He looked up to see a blonde nurse in a purple smock smiling at him from the doorway. "That's me."

"Want to come with me? Dr. Randall is ready to see you." She gave him a friendly smile.

"Thanks." He picked up his backpack and followed her.

The last time he'd been to this hospital had been for his bottom surgery, and it still made him a little uncomfortable to think about it. Not because he regretted it—not at all. But it had been a long, painful recovery.

"I'm Jacqueline. Having a good day today?"

He nodded. "I guess? Hospitals make me nervous."

"You're not alone." She opened another door for him. "Here you go." She squeezed his shoulder and whispered, "Good luck."

He turned to face Dr. Randall. She was seated behind her desk, working on something on her computer. She had short silver hair and blue eyes, and he guessed she was in her mid-fifties.

"Please have a seat, Mr. Hammond. I'll be with you in just a moment."

He did as he was told, looking around the office. It was neat, with shelves of leather-bound medical journals against the back wall and color-coded patient files stacked on her desk. "Not paperless yet?"

"Not entirely." She tapped out a few more keystrokes and then turned to face him. "So what can I do for you today?"

"I'm here on behalf of a friend. Well, more than a friend." He unzipped his backpack and pulled out a photo and his checkbook. "That's Ella." He handed the photo over to her.

She took it and glanced at it, giving him a cursory smile. "She's very pretty."

"Thanks. She told me about a clinical trial for Fahr's Disease that you're running. I was hoping…"

"I'm sorry, Mr. Hammond. I have to stop you right there. The trial is full, and I doubt she would meet all the criteria for the study anyhow. I know it's hard to hear, but these trials are not for the benefit of a single patient. They're run to help us understand the disease and possible treatments for the entire Fahr's population."

"I can pay. I've got about ten thousand dollars in my savings account, and I could set up a payment plan out of my paycheck. I work at Zocalo—"

"I'm truly sorry, Mr. Hammond. That's not how it works. At least, not with any reputable research institution. We don't fill our studies with patients who can pay the most—"

"She's going to die."

"As I said, I am sorry—"

"For the first thirty years of my life, Dr. Randall, I lived in this society in the wrong body. I fought my parents, my friends, the whole fucking world to get myself to a place where I finally felt like *me*. Do you have any idea how that feels?"

She sat back and stared at him.

I went too far. He was shaking now, feeling exposed. "I'm so sorry to have wasted your time." Ben put the photo and the checkbook away and stood to go.

"Yes, I do."

"What?"

"You asked me if I knew what it felt like. I do. My daughter Lyra is trans."

"Oh." He sank back down into the chair.

"I still don't see what that has to do with the clinical trial."

He took a deep breath, and decided to forge ahead. "After I came out, I didn't think I would ever find someone to love me. To see me, scars and all, and still want to be with me." He looked away. It was hard to talk about this, especially with a stranger. "A lot of trans people go through this. I know. I'm not exceptional. But with Ella, I finally found someone who *sees* me. Who likes me for me. You don't know how rare that is. For anyone, but especially for someone like me." He put his hand over hers.

It was like an electric shock, and he could have sworn there were green sparkles in the air between them. He shook his head. *I must be more tired than I thought.*

Her expression softened. She put her hands together in front of her face, sighing. "Like I said, it's highly unlikely that she matches what we're looking for in the study. Even if we did have room. Which we don't. Someone else would have to drop out."

"I know."

Dr. Randall stared at him for a moment longer and then opened her desk and pulled out a business card. She handed it over to him. "Have her contact me and send me her medical records. I'll take a look, and if she seems like she might be a good candidate, we can have her come in and see if she fits the bill. Even then, I can't promise anything."

He nodded. "I understand."

She bit her lip. "I want to believe that Lyra can find someone to love. Like you did. Since she came out as trans… it hasn't been easy. For either of us."

"Maybe there's something to the whole karma thing."

She smiled, but there was a bit of sadness around her eyes. "I don't really believe in the karma. But I hope you're right."

"Me too." He shook her hand. "Thank you so much, Dr. Randall."

"Call me Susan."

"Thank you, Susan. I'll have her contact you."

He wanted to dance, but he restrained himself, leaving her office with some of his dignity intact. Once he got around the corner though, he did a little jig.

His phone buzzed. It was Ella.

Max is awake.

92. CAZZO

Diego scanned the crowd gathered just past the airport tram exit, hoping to see Matteo waiting for him there, as he'd promised in his text when they landed. It had been a long flight, and it was after midnight in his new adopted hometown.

They'd already gone through customs at SFO. Thankfully the customs agents hadn't questioned Gio's travel visa. They'd need to get that whole thing figured out, and soon. He only had a six-month visa. That could wait for later though. Right now, Diego was exhausted.

Gio followed him, looking far more awake and enthusiastic than Diego felt. "Everything's so new." This was Diego's son's first trip to America, and that seemed to have overcome at least some of the boy's doubts at his new living situation. At least for the moment.

"Not everything. But their old is our new." He was glad to see Gio being more responsive.

"Ciao, bello," Matteo said, emerging from the crowd to give him a hug.

They kissed, and Diego squeezed Matteo hard. "It's good to be home," he said in Italian. "This is Giovanni."

Matteo reached out to shake his hand.

Gio turned away.

"Gio! Sorry about that. He's had a long night and a long week."

Matteo sighed. "Of course. Well, should we get your luggage and then take you two home?"

"I think that would be best." Diego was keyed up by the time change but also exhausted.

They reached the long escalator that led down to baggage claim.

Gio looked up. "*Che cazzo?*"

"Language, Gio.…" At least none of the passersby knew that cazzo was the Italian equivalent of *fuck*. Diego couldn't help but laugh though. The sculpture of a big red rabbit hanging in the air over the escalators had caught the boy's attention. In fairness, it was impressive—at least fifteen meters long and three or four high. "He's called Leap, but most people just call him the big red rabbit."

Gio nodded, not taking his eyes off it. "Cool."

"You speak English?" Matteo asked as they descended to the ground floor. He was trying to connect with the boy. Diego appreciated that.

"Yes."

"Studied English since was a kid," Diego said in English. "He speaks better the language than me."

"See?" Matteo raised his eyebrow. "I told you that you *needed* to learn."

Diego kissed his cheek. "You are always right, my *bello*."

Gio snorted.

Diego was going to have to teach the boy some manners.

They waited for the luggage for fifteen minutes, but at last Diego's big white bag and Gio's even bigger orange one swung into view.

"That's quite a suitcase you have there, Gio," Matteo said, eyeing the giant piece of luggage.

"It's just my things." He squirmed uncomfortably under Matteo's stare.

"There's more coming too. I shipped the rest of it." Diego pulled his own suitcase off the carousel. "It will be here in *circa* three weeks."

"Good. We can find a place for all of it then. Come on, you two. Let's go home."

~

They got Gio settled in the guest room. He settled himself. He fell onto the bed and was asleep in seconds.

Diego put his suitcase inside the room, turned off the light, and closed the door, laughing softly. "I remember when it was so easy to go to sleep," he said in Italian, hoping Matteo wouldn't call him on speaking *la bella lingua* now that he was back home.

"Ah, to be young again." Matteo led Diego back to their own bedroom and closed the door. "Are you awake enough to talk?"

Diego nodded. "I got some sleep on the plane, and it's ten in the morning for me." He'd just gotten used to the time zone change when he'd had to turn around and come home. They sat down on the bed together.

"How's your mother and sister?"

"Valentina is good. The kids keep her busy. My mother… she's forgetting more and more."

Matteo frowned. "Do you… would you rather be back home, in Italy?"

Diego shook his head. "I'm home, *here*." He sighed. "It just means I'll have to make more frequent trips to see her."

Matteo smiled faintly.

"What?"

"You just said *this* was home. I don't think you've ever told me that before."

Diego nodded. "I guess so. Home is with you." He looked up into Matteo's eyes. "So… how are we?"

"You mean now that I know you slept with Luna while we were together?"

Diego blushed. "Yes. That."

"Why didn't you tell me?"

"I was drunk. It was when your father died. I… I don't even remember it happening."

Matteo looked away. "So you really didn't know. Or remember."

"No."

The silence stretched between them for a minute, then two.

Diego wished he could see what was going on in Matteo's head. Was he angry? Did he want Diego to leave? Did he even care?

At last, Diego couldn't stand it anymore. "Are we okay?" He tried not to sound desperate.

Matteo stared at him. "No," he said at last.

"Oh." Diego felt a little nauseous. "Okay. Sure. I can look for somewhere else to stay tomorrow. Is it okay that Gio and I stay here tonight? I can sleep on the couch. I don't think I could wake him up, in any case—"

Matteo put a finger over Diego's mouth, silencing him. "Are there any more secrets?"

Diego shook his head. "No," he whispered.

Matteo nodded. "I said we're not okay. Not yet. But I don't want you to leave."

"What then?" Diego clamped down on the little ember of hope that burned in his heart.

"We start again. No more lies. No more secrets."

The hope flared into a bright flame. Diego nodded. "I can do that."

"Can I have your ring?" Matteo asked suddenly.

"Why?" Was this a punishment?

"Please." He held out his hand.

Diego pulled it off his finger. It was the wedding ring Matteo had slipped on his finger on that amazing day, the wedding day that had been reduced to a lie by circumstance. By his own actions. He handed it over to Matteo.

Matteo took it and slipped off the bed, going down on one knee.

Oh shit.

"Diego Bellei, will you marry me again?" He held up the ring. It sparkled, throwing off little sparks that flashed in the air. "Start things fresh between us?"

It was a sign. "Yes, *che cazzo*, yes!"

"Language, mio amore—"

Diego laughed. He stood and pulled Matteo up to his feet, hugging him fiercely.

As nighttime edged into morning, they celebrated his return and their new engagement properly.

93. MAKING IT RIGHT

knocked on the door, hoping Moms was away.

"Come in."

It was Ella. Relieved, he pushed open the door.

Max was sitting up in bed. He looked pale, but there was life in his eyes again. Ella's eyes were puffy, and her cheeks were wet.

"Hi Max," Ben said, holding out a hand. "I'm Ben."

Max shook it weakly. "Nice to meet you. You're Ella's new boyfriend? She spoke highly of you."

His raised eyebrow made Ben wonder if he disapproved. "Yes. And I know all about her condition." He pulled over a chair and sat next to Ella. "Hey, you okay?" He gave her a kiss.

She nodded. "I didn't think this was ever going to happen." She managed a tiny smile. "Ish good."

Ben ignored the slur in her speech. "Where's your Moms?"

"She went to get some coffee for me." Ella kissed his cheek. "I'm so glad you're here."

"Speak of the devil." Lexi, Ella's "Moms," came into the room bearing a coffee for her daughter and a water for Max.

Ben grimaced. "Look, I know you don't like me—"

"Shhhh." Lexi shushed him with a manicured finger on his lips. "It doesn't matter whether I like you or not. Ella made up her mind, and she's made it clear to me that it doesn't matter what I think." She swept her scarf up behind her back and took a seat across the bed from the two of them. "Besides, I never said I didn't like you." She winked. "I actually think you're quite the nice young man."

Ben blushed. "Well… thanks, I guess."

"Now that Moms is back, I have something to tell you both," Max said, and he looked, if possible, even paler than before.

Lexi was on her feet in an instant, her hand on his forehead. "You feeling okay? I can call Dr. Matthews—"

"No, Moms, it's nothing like that." He squeezed her hand. "Please, have a seat."

Frowning, she sat back down, throwing Ella a stare that said, "Do you know anything about this?"

Ella shook her head.

"I did something… bad before the accident."

"How bad?" Ella's brow creased, and she squeezed Ben's hand so hard he thought her nails might draw blood.

"I was so scared for you, Sis. I heard about that clinical trial at UC Davis. I thought I could buy my way in. Maybe make an endowment or something."

"You don't have that kind of money. I know. I've been paying your bills." Ella's nails dug in a little harder.

Ouch. Ben tried gamely to ignore the pain.

"I know. I blackmailed someone."

"Holy shit, Max. What the hell were you thinking?"

"Hey, be careful! Coma patient here, remember?" Max rubbed his cheek.

"Who were you blackmailing?" She still looked angry.

He shook his head. "You don't know them. This Italian couple with a restaurant out in East Sac, whom I helped with their immigration—"

Oh shit. "Matteo and Diego?"

"Yes. How did you know?"

"They're… friends of mine. Diego just came home from Italy. His ex-wife died, and he brought home a son he didn't know he had." Sam had filled him in on the whole thing. Poor guy, dealing with all that *and* a blackmail threat from Ella's idiot brother.

Max hung his head. "I'm sorry. It was wrong. I know that now."

"You know that *now*?" Ella pulled his chin up to look in his eyes. "Do you know what damage you could have done?"

Max held her gaze for a moment, then looked away.

"You have to apologize." It was Moms who spoke this time. "You did it for the right reason. I know you love Ella. But you really screwed up this time."

Max nodded. "I know. When I'm feeling better—"

"You think it's okay to let this go on even another minute? To let that poor man wonder if you're going to wake up and bring his whole life crashing down?" She said it softly, but it was as sharp as a knife.

"No, ma'am." Max suddenly looked five years old, staring down at his crossed fingers and twiddling his thumbs.

Lexi looked at him. "Can you reach your friends?"

Ben looked at the time on his phone. "They're probably at work. But I can FaceTime them."

"Please."

He nodded. He called Diego first. There was no response. He was probably cooking for dinner. Ben tried Matteo next.

"Hi, Ben." The man flashed his beautiful Italian smile.

"Hey, Matteo. Do you and Diego have a moment?"

"Sorry. The place is a little busy."

"Damn, that's good to hear. But seriously. This will only take a minute, and it's really important."

"Okay. One moment." The view shifted.

Ben waited.

"Okay. We're ready."

Diego's hands were covered in flour. "Ciao, Ben!"

"Hey! You know the girl I've been seeing? Ella? It turns out her brother is someone you know, and he's just woken up from a coma." Without additional preamble, he turned the phone to face Max.

On the screen, Diego stiffened. "Cazzo."

Max nodded. "I deserve that." He took a deep breath. I wanted to tell you how sorry I am about what I did to you. Ella is… I had my reasons. But none of them justified blackmailing you. It's over. I'm so sorry."

Moms nodded, squeezing his hand.

Ben shivered. It felt like the room had just suddenly gone cold or that an electric shock had run through him. He turned the phone back to himself. "That's it. I just thought you should know." He expected to see scowls of disbelief or anger.

Instead, Diego was nodding, a curiously serene smile on his face. "Tell to him that I accept it."

Matteo kissed Diego and then added, "We hope he gets well soon."

The screen went black. "Well, that went well."

There was a knock at the door. One of the nurses poked her head in. "I need to check on Mr. Cucinelli's vitals."

"Come on, you two. Let's give her a little room." Moms herded them out of the room into the waiting area.

"I'm so happy for you both," Ben said, looking back at the closed door. "He's awake and seems like himself."

Ella nodded. "His old *blockheaded* self. I'm so sorry for what he did to your friends. I didn't know."

"I know."

Moms gave them a quick hug. "I'll leave you two to catch up. I want to talk to Dr. Matthews."

"Thanks, Lexi." He took Ella's hand. Can we sit down for a sec?"

"I'm tired of sitting."

"Please? It will make this easier."

"You're nosh breaking up with me, are you? 'Cause both Max and Moms will kill you." She grinned, but the creases at her temples gave her away.

"Not at all. I had something I wanted to tell you, something good about that UC Davis trial…"

94. MEMORIES AND PLANS

Marissa picked at her meal. She'd agreed to come to dinner with Carmelina under protest, and she hadn't said a word since they'd sat down with their salads. Marcos had dropped her off and was due back to pick her up in about half an hour.

Sellands was busy as usual, as people stopped by the popular H Street joint to pick up sandwiches and salads to take home.

Carmelina watched her, concerned that she'd gotten off on a bad foot with the girl. She decided she'd waited long enough. It was time.

She pulled out a bright-blue hat box from her purse and set it on the table.

"What's that, an early birthday gift?" Marissa's eyebrow arched, reminding Carmelina so much of herself that she almost laughed.

"Sort of." She looked out the lime-green-framed window at the passing traffic, wondering where to begin. "When I was younger—about your age actually, more or less—I met a boy. His name was Billy Morgan. He was the cutest guy I'd ever seen, and then I found out he *liked* me."

Marissa frowned. "Marcos said your husband's name was Arthur."

Carmelina nodded. "This was long before Arthur." Her eyes misted over at the thought of her late husband. It was still so hard to believe he was gone. She sighed. "Anyway, Billy asked me out to a school dance, and I said yes. My mother didn't want to let me go, but I begged. I was really good at begging."

Marissa smiled. Just a little.

"Billy was a total gentleman. He picked me up in his Cougar and drove me to the school dance. We spent the whole evening together on the basketball court and in the bleachers. Then in the back of his car…"

"Seriously?" Marissa was all ears now.

Carmelina laughed ruefully. "We didn't have Sex-Ed back then. I thought babies came from… well, I don't remember what I thought. So yes. Seriously. And nine months later, your mother arrived."

"What was she like?"

"You know I gave her up for adoption, right?"

Marissa nodded, and her eyes narrowed.

"I know, it's hard to understand. But at that age… at your age, I wasn't ready for a child. I don't think I would have been a very good mother." Carmelina sighed. "*Your* mother was a beautiful baby. And a lovely little girl. I spoke with the man who raised her… his name is Darryl Smith. He wants to meet you too, one of these days." She pulled a manila envelope out of the box and handed it over to Marissa. "He gave me these."

Her granddaughter opened the envelope and pulled out the photos, staring at them raptly, one after another. "She was beautiful," she whispered.

"Yes, she was. She looked a lot like you. With longer hair." She gave Marissa a few moments to go through the photos.

When she was done, Carmelina took her hand. "You can have those. I made copies."

"Thank you." There were tears at the corners of Marissa's eyes. "I've never had pictures of her before."

"You're welcome. This is for you too." She pushed the box across the table.

"What is it?"

"Open it and see."

Marissa pulled off the lid and stared at all the things inside.

"I call it my box of hopes and dreams. When I gave away your mother for adoption, I wondered every single day if I had done the right thing. To make myself feel better, I started buying her things for each birthday, things I told myself I would give her if I ever saw her again." Saying it out loud made her choke a little on the words.

Marissa pulled the objects out of the box one by one. The plastic unicorn. The baby rattle and the shoes, a golden pen, and many more.

"Do you know what happened to her?"

"Some kind of accident." Marissa held up the magnifying glass questioningly.

"In case she wanted to be a scientist."

"Ah." She put it back in the box gently.

"Andrea had been out with friends that night. She came out of a bar in

Midtown in the early hours of the morning and was hit by a passing motorist."

Marissa closed her eyes, squeezing one of the photos. "Was she drunk?"

"I don't know." She wrung her hands under the table. "Marissa, I have to tell you something else."

"What?" Marissa shut the box and set it aside.

"I know the man who killed your mother."

Marissa just stared at her. "How?" she said at last.

Carmelina sighed. "By accident. I met him about a month ago at the grocery store. He asked me out. Neither of us knew—"

"Are you still seeing him? How did you find out?"

"When I was looking for you. I found some old newspaper clippings that mentioned his name." She bit her lip. "And no. I broke it off with him two weeks ago after I learned what he had done."

She set down the crumpled photo. "Was it an accident?"

"Yes. It was late, and he'd… probably had too much to drink with his friends."

"Just like my mother."

That surprised her. She nodded.

"I should hate him." She picked up a picture of her mother again, smoothing it out between her fingers. "It's terrible, but I barely remember her. This one Christmas, her kneeling beside the tree to give me a gift. It was a pair of socks, I think."

That image broke Carmelina's heart. "I'll never see him again, I promise. It's not fair to you."

Marissa set down the photo again. "Do you like him? Is he a good man?"

"He's… besides the accident, yes. I think so. He's kind and sweet." She thought of all the times in the last week she'd wanted to call him, to tell him what had happened, what she was thinking. "And yeah. I think I do."

Marissa took her hand. Something passed between them that was deeper than words.

For a moment, Carmelina saw Andrea there. Her daughter stared at her, and then a smile crept up the edges of her mouth. Carmelina blinked, and it was Marissa again.

"You should call him. You should grab whatever chance you have to be happy."

Carmelina sat back in her seat, stunned. How old was this girl to be so mature? "Are you sure?"

Marissa nodded. "I don't want to meet him. Not yet. But one of these days. When I've had a chance to think it through."

"Okay, then." This was not what Carmelina had expected. Not at all. "The box is for you too. I want you to take it."

"Thank you. You should keep this." Marissa handed her the shoes. "I could see they meant a lot to you."

"Yes, they do." Perceptive too.

"So can I call you Grandma?"

Carmelina stiffened. *God, am I that old already?* "How about Nonna? It's more Italian."

"Thanks, Nonna." Marissa got up and flung her arms around Carmelina.

"You're welcome, *cara mia.*"

Fifteen minutes later, Marcos arrived to pick her up.

Carmelina sat there for a while after Marisa left, trying to decide what to do. At last, she decided to make a phone call.

"Hello?" Daniele sounded surprised to hear from her.

"Hi. Can I see you Friday night?"

95. WHAT HE WANTED

Diego watched Gio walk away with Marissa and Tristan for his first day of school here in *gli Stati Uniti*. Marcos's ward had agreed to show Diego's son the ropes. With the boy's good looks and Italian charm, not to mention the strict schooling he'd gotten in Italy, Diego didn't think he would have any problems.

Matteo was meeting him at the lawyer's office to discuss what happened next now that Luna had passed away.

It was a beautiful fall Sacramento morning, sunny and warm, and Diego was feeling truly hopeful for the first time in a long time. Max no longer had something to hold over his head. All of his secrets were out. The restaurant was doing well, actually bringing in a profit for a couple of weeks running, which Matteo said was a minor miracle.

And Matteo, for some crazy reason, still seemed to love him after all that had happened.

He started up the Fiat and headed downtown for their meeting, hoping he wouldn't be too late. Gio had taken forever getting ready for school. The boy had more product than Diego and Matteo combined.

Diego crossed Broadway and slipped under the Highway 50 overpass. The freeway was clogged with cars taking their occupants to work.

Grazie a dio that I don't have to do that every day. He rolled down his window and whistled a happy tune, and all the lights were green.

. . .

Across town, Matteo waited outside the lawyer's office, checking his watch. Diego was running late, as usual. He grinned. It was nice to have things back to normal.

Matteo had stayed behind, prepping the restaurant for the lunch rush. The *tavola calda* concept had proven very popular, and word was spreading. Their suppliers had been shocked as he upped his daily orders and then upped them again, and the kids from the Center had proven adept at helping with food preparation. A few of them, Ricky and Marissa in particular, had a real talent for cooking.

Matteo turned his face up to the sun, drinking in the warmth. Somehow, *un po' per un po'*, things were working themselves out. He whispered a little prayer of thanks to his mother and father.

"Sorry, am a little late." Diego kissed him, grinning broadly at his surprise. "You ready?"

"I think so." Even with their recent run of good luck, Matteo was ready for the other shoe to fall. Things were going a little *too* well, and their fortunes had never been this good. "Let's go in."

Dana was waiting for them, dressed in jeans and a black T-shirt.

"Casual Thursday?" Matteo asked.

"Something like that." She shook their hands. "Have a seat."

"You have fifteen minutes for us?" Diego asked within a sly grin.

"This morning I have as much time as you want." She smiled and sat back in her chair, putting her hands behind her head. "It's a slow week. So what can I do for you gentlemen?"

"Diego just got back from Italy."

She nodded. "How'd it go with the ex?"

"She died." Diego handed over a folder.

"Oh, I'm so sorry to hear that." She opened the folder, looking over the death certificate. "Natural causes, if my limited Italian's any good."

Matteo nodded. "She had been sick for some time."

She laid the folder on her desk. "Did you get to see her before?"

"Yes. She asked me to take her son... our son." Diego looked over at Matteo, who nodded. "He is called Gio... Giovanni."

"Wow. Did you know about him?"

Diego nodded. "I didn't know he was so young. Seventeen."

Dana nodded. "Is he still in Italy?"

Diego shook his head. "No, he's here. He has a six-month visa."

"Ah, a tourist visa. Okay, we can work on that. It may take some time, but we should be able to get him legal status as your dependent." She frowned, turning to Matteo. "So how are you doing with all this?"

Matteo shrugged. "It happened a long time ago. There were… how do you say? Migrating circumstances?"

"Mitigating."

"Yes." He took Diego's hand.

"Okay. So what do you guys want to do now? Are you separating?"

Matteo shook his head. "We want to get married. For real this time."

Diego nodded.

Dana grinned, a spontaneous, genuine expression of joy. "I was hoping you two would work it out. We'll have to file for a nullification of your earlier marriage. But with the death certificate and that, you'll be free to marry. For real."

Matteo squeezed Diego's hand. "How long?"

"How long for…?"

"How long until we can get remarried?"

"Hmmm… it might take a couple of months to get an appointment with a judge to consider the nullification."

"Ah." Matteo sighed heavily. He had hoped it could be sooner.

"Why? Is there a rush?" She smiled slyly. "Is this a shotgun wedding?"

"Shotgun?" Matteo looked confused.

"He's not pregnant, is he?" She pointed to Diego.

"Ah, no." I just want to get this behind us. We want to be married again. And we don't want to worry about immigration any longer.…"

"Gotcha." She turned to her laptop. "Let me see what I can do. I have a few family law judge friends. I'll call around."

Matteo nodded. "Thank you. That would be fantastic."

"Where are you going to get married?"

"City Hall. We just want to get it done quickly."

"Quick is good. Not every wedding can be a fairy tale, after all." She got up. "Let me make a copy of this death certificate. I'll be right back."

She left them alone for a moment.

"Did you understand all of that?" Matteo asked Diego in Italian.

Diego nodded. "Mostly. We can get married?"

"In a few months. But she is going to try to nullify our old marriage sooner, if she can."

"Thank you." Diego looked away, wiping his eyes.

"For what? Dana is doing all the work."

"For forgiving me."

For his answer, Matteo pulled Diego into a hug. "I had to. I love you."

"After everything?"

"Even after everything." He let Diego go and grabbed his ear, pulling his face close. "Don't you ever lie to me again."

"Never."

Things between them weren't perfect, but they would work it all out. Somehow.

That's what he wanted. And he almost always got his way.

The next day they got the call from Dana. They had a hearing for the following Monday.

96. TWO DATES AT FORMOLI

Marissa was much on her mind as Carmelina waited for Daniele at Formoli. She'd gotten there early, wanting to have a few moments to get settled. To think about what she was going to say to him.

Not that she'd been thinking about anything else these last few days. She'd been stunned by Marissa's response, and up until that moment, she hadn't let herself even think about the possibility of letting Daniele back into her life.

She looked down at her hands crossed in her lap. She'd had them freshly manicured and painted.

What would Arthur have thought about all of this?

"You could just ask me, you know."

She looked up to see Arthur seated across from her, looking at the menu.

He whistled. "Eleven bucks for a plate of stuffed dates. They'd better be stuffed with diamonds." He grinned at her.

She laughed. "You always were a bit of a cheapskate."

"Yeah, but look at the great house I was able to buy for you. That came from a lifetime of ordering water at restaurants and only getting my hair cut twice a year."

She chuckled. "I suppose. I thought you'd gone up to the great beyond."

"It was a bit boring up there. I thought I'd check in on my old gal."

"Old, huh?"

"But still as gorgeous as ever." He picked up her hand and kissed it.

Carmelina looked around to see if anyone else had noticed her strange conversation with her husband's ghost.

The restaurant was empty, not another person in sight.

"I thought it would be better to have this conversation with you one-on-one, my dear." He took her hand. "You know the whole story now. The one you longed to find out, all those years." He squeezed her hand.

"Yes. I never expected it to lead where it did." Andrea was lost to her, but she had a new granddaughter in return.

"What fun would life be if it was just what we expected?" His eyes twinkled.

She nodded. "I suppose so." She took a sip of her water, looking at him over his menu. "So why are you able to be here now?"

"Because you needed me. Sometimes we can pierce the veil. But only for a little while."

She considered that. "What's it like?"

"Heaven?"

He scratched his chin. "It's like pizza and gelato. Oh, and water volleyball."

"Come on."

"I don't know. It's… it's love. The people who went before us—our friends and family—there are a whole lot of them looking out for you and your friends, let me tell you. Nonna says hi."

"Dammit." Carmelina pulled a handkerchief from her purse and wiped the corners of her eyes. "You always could make me cry."

"In a good way, I hope."

"Usually." She stuck her tongue out at him.

"Glad to hear it."

"So." She sighed. "Daniele."

He sat back, arms crossed, and stared at her for a moment.

"What?"

"Just enjoying the view. Something to remember when I'm back among the pizza and gelato."

She snorted. "Well?"

A lazy smile played across his features. "Life is short. You should grab whatever chance you have to be happy."

❧

Someone was shaking her shoulder.

"What?" She looked up. It was really bright. Her eyes adjusted, focusing on the man in front of her.

Daniele.

"Are you okay?"

She nodded. "I guess I was just tired. Did I fall asleep?"

Daniele nodded. He looked a little skittish. "Yeah. You kinda did." He sat down opposite her, staring at her just like Arthur had.

The whole conversation had felt so real. "What?"

"*You* called *me?*"

Oh, yeah. That. "Andrea had a daughter."

"Oh." He looked crestfallen. "If you called me here to yell at me again…" He started to get up to leave.

She put a hand on his arm. "No, it's not that at all. Please. Sit."

He looked doubtful but allowed her to guide him back down to his seat. "What's this about, then?"

"I found her." She pulled a photo of Marissa out of her wallet and handed it to him.

"She's beautiful."

"Yes, she is."

"Did you meet her?"

She nodded. "I actually already knew her. Her name is Marissa. She's part of the cooking class I go to."

He whistled. "Small world."

Carmelina was once again reminded of Arthur. "It sure seems that way. I told her about you."

Daniele tensed up. "I—"

"Hi there. I'm Lisa. Can I bring you some drinks to get started?" Their waitress flashed them a big smile.

Always with the bad timing. "This water's fine for me."

Daniele nodded. "Me too."

"Okay. I'll be right back to take your order."

"Can you give us a few moments?" Carmelina shot her a pleading look.

"Of course. Just let me know when you're ready."

When she was gone, Daniele asked, "What did Marissa say? When you told her?"

"That she wanted me to be happy."

That took a minute to sink in. "Wait… what? Did she… are you…?"

"Sometimes things that are broken can be put back together," Carmelina said softly. She took his hands in hers across the table. "I'm saying I want to give it another go with you. If you'll still have me."

He jumped up and swung around the table to pull her into his arms, startling the other patrons. "If I'll still have you? *If I'll still have you?*" he spun her around like a ballerina, knocking her water off the table, and pulled her in for a kiss.

"So sorry," she mumbled to the waitress as she sat down.

Lisa smiled. "Don't worry about it. It's not often I get to see such a beautiful display of love."

Love? she mouthed at Daniele.

He shrugged. "I hope so. You tell me."

The rest of the evening passed like a fairy tale, and in the end, she got her prince.

97.RAGU AND REGRETS

Diego looked around at the class. It had grown to twenty-five people. Things were going so well, he was thinking about adding another course.

Their lunch business continued to grow. Matteo said they would turn a profit in October, enough of a good sign that they should be able to renegotiate their line of credit with the bank. And dinner business was picking up too.

Gio had fallen in with Marissa and her boyfriend, Tristan, at school. The boy actually seemed to be enjoying himself as he chopped carrots with the others for the *Ragu alla Romagnola* sauce they were preparing today.

"Ragu does great with any pasta," Diego told his pupils. "And of course, ragu from Emilia Romagna does the best." His mother had taught him how to make a wonderful Ragu. He just wished she could be there to see how he was passing it along.

Diego moved around the room, setting each person to doing a part of the preparation. Cooking was eighty percent prep and twenty percent applying heat.

He came around to Carmelina. "*Ciao, bella!*"

She and her companion were dutifully peeling tomatoes. "Diego, this is Daniele. Daniele, my friend, Diego the chef."

"*Piacere.*" Daniele held out his hand.

"Polite, and *bello* too." Diego grinned at Carmelina as he shook Daniele's hand.

"Matteo said you just got back from Italy?" She set another peeled tomato in her bowl.

"Yes. I brought my… *figlio.*"

"Son," Daniele supplied. "You didn't know?"

"No, I only recently found out. His mother never told me." He wished he had gotten a little more time with Luna before she had passed away.

"But haven't you and Matteo been together twenty years?" Carmelina asked, eyeing Gio. "The boy doesn't look any older than seventeen."

Diego closed his eyes. "Long story."

She rubbed his arm. "Sorry. I didn't mean to pry."

"I'll tell you one time. When things are less… *folli.*"

She nodded. "It's a date."

"I wanted to talk with you about a thing." He waved for Matteo to come over. "He is better with English."

Matteo joined them, taking a seat on one of the counter stools. "Are you ready to ask her?"

Diego nodded.

"We have a proposition for you. It was Diego's idea. You were so wonderful here when he was gone, helping us run the place. How would you like to come work with us?"

Carmelina's mouth dropped open. "Work with you… how?"

"Diego wants to train you as a chef. He thinks you could be really good at it, and with the business expanding—"

"I'd love to!" She jumped up and hugged Diego and then Matteo. "I had such a wonderful time cooking with you."

Matteo gave her the slow-down gesture with both hands. "We can't pay you a lot to start. But over time…"

"It sounds *perfect.*"

"You'd be fantastic at it." Daniele kissed her cheek. "I've had your cooking."

Matteo nodded. "So… we just heard that Marissa is your granddaughter?"

Carmelina nodded. "A little surprise of my own." She winked at Diego.

"*Ha un dono per la cucina…* She has… *come si dice?*"

"A gift."

"*Sì.* A gift for cooking. We can train her too."

"That would be amazing."

"Then maybe Diego could take a day or two off now and then."

Diego tried to imagine it, not having to be in the kitchen every day.

Carmelina grinned. "Maybe both of you could take a day off *together.*"

"That would be nice," Matteo said in his usual droll manner.

"You could help for the wedding next weekend." Diego pointed at Sam and Brad. "If you want."

"I would love to."

Just for a moment, Diego wished they could have a fancy wedding of their own. But getting married again was the most important thing. The rest was just decoration. Besides, he didn't need a fancy wedding to know how madly in love he was with Matteo, even after twenty years.

"Can you start next Saturday?" Matteo asked. "We can see how we work together on the wedding prep."

"That sounds wonderful. Do I need to bring anything?

"Just yourself and an apron."

~

Carmelina was flying. In less than a week, she'd gotten herself a granddaughter, a boyfriend, and a new job. Though she felt a bit old to be throwing around the "boyfriend" word.

Male companion?

Significant other?

Maybe just "guy."

She had a *guy*. It felt like a new lease on life, and Arthur approved.

After class, she sent Daniele on his way, promising to meet him for dinner later at Mayahuel. She had a hankering for their cream of poblano soup, but she had something more important to do first.

She'd gotten the woman's name from Marcos, and now she was just hoping she was home.

She climbed up the steps to the front porch. The home was beautiful, a mid-century mansion along the American River in Fair Oaks. It had a huge grassy front yard, green in the midst of the drought, she noted. The place had clearly been updated and was well cared for.

After a moment's hesitation, she pressed the buzzer.

She heard the sound of footsteps—heels?—inside.

The door opened. "Yes? Can I help you?"

Carmelina suddenly felt drab, underdressed, and old.

Jessica Sutton was dressed for a night out on the town even while she was at home on a Sunday afternoon. She wore a pearl necklace, a light blue top, and a matching skirt. Her heels were at least three inches high, and gold bracelets jangled on her arms.

Carmelina stuffed down her jealousy. She was here for Marissa. "Are you Jessica Sutton?"

"Yes. Are you serving me papers or something?" She frowned.

Still pretty. Damn. "No, nothing like that." She put on her best smile. "I'm Carmelina di Rosa. I'm Marissa's grandmother."

"Marissa's grandmother lives in Topeka, and if I never see her again, I'll be perfectly happy." She started to close the door.

"Wait!" She pulled out Andrea's photo. "This was my daughter, Andrea. She was Marissa's birth mother. She was killed in an accident fifteen years ago, just before you adopted Marissa."

Jessica paused. "What does that have to do with us?"

"I came here to warn you. I don't want you to lose your daughter too. Please, may I come in?"

Jessica stared at her for a long time. At last, she nodded and opened the door wider. "I don't have much time. Phillip is expecting me at the club in about half an hour."

See the ragu alla romagnola recipe at the end of the book.

98. BEHIND ENEMY LINES

"I won't take too much of your time." Carmelina stepped inside, letting her eyes adjust to the light. The house was gorgeous. A wide stairway swept up on both sides of the entryway, and beautiful travertine floors and huge paintings gave the place a museum-like quality.

As beautiful as it was, it didn't feel like the kind of place one raised a child.

"We can talk in here." Jessica ushered her into a big living room off to the right floored in wide rosewood planks with a brick fireplace that climbed two stories to the high-beamed ceiling. The furniture looked like it had never been sat upon. Carved wooden chairs with stiff backs and white leather upholstery. Two green-marble greyhound statues, one on either side of the fireplace. Glass tables with miniature crystal copies of the Eiffel Tower, the Colosseum, and other assorted world landmarks.

She'd heard of people who had two living rooms: one to watch TV and another they used only for guests. It was a little pretentious, in her opinion.

They sat across from each other. Carmelina refrained from picking up the Eiffel tower to see if it had a price tag.

Jessica crossed her hands in her lap. "So what did you want to tell me?"

"Your daughter—my granddaughter—is an amazing young woman."

"She's a brat and a thief." Jessica almost spat it out.

"Maybe so." Carmelina cast about for a way to reach her. "When I was a girl, I stole a Hershey's candy bar from the grocery store down the street from my mother's house. We all did stupid things when we were kids."

"We also paid the consequences."

"Maybe." She'd never been caught, but her father would have tanned her hide if he'd known. "Look, I know you're angry with her. And you don't agree with everything she has said and done."

Jessica nodded. "She knows what she did. I came to her school a few weeks ago. I asked her to come home—"

"But only if she renounced who she was." Marcos had filled her in on that.

Jessica shook her head. "She's just pulling this lesbian crap to get back at us. She's not a lesbian. No one's born like that."

Carmelina laughed. "I could introduce you to a bunch of my friends who might tell you differently."

"I'm really sorry, but I have to go. Ms.… Di Rosa, was it? Let me show you out." She started to get up.

"You're going to lose her."

That brought Jessica back down to her seat.

"Whether you're angry with her or not, whether you think you can change her or just want to get through to her… you're going to lose her." She held out the photo of Andrea. "I gave up my daughter for adoption, and by the time I tried to find her, it was far too late."

Jessica took it, looking from the photo to Carmelina. "It's not the same—"

"I know. But if you show up in court tomorrow and testify against your own daughter…" She shivered. She couldn't imagine doing something like that to someone she loved. "At best she gets off, and she never talks with you or sees you again. At worst… Did you know she has a real talent for cooking?"

"Cooking?" Jessica's brow furrowed.

"Yes. She has been taking a cooking class at a local Italian restaurant. They want to groom her to be a chef. She has quite a gift for it."

"A chef?"

Carmelina nodded. "She could really make something of herself. But here you are, ready to derail her dreams to send her to juvie or worse. And for what? To punish her? To be vindictive? To get back at her for daring to tell you the truth?"

"She was always so angry with me—"

Carmelina laughed again. "She's a teenager. That's who they are! And did you think about the fact that, in three more days, she'll be an adult? That you won't have any more hold on her at all?"

"I… She doesn't want anything to do with us anyhow."

"Teenagers are like that. Moody one moment, sullen the next. Look, can I give you some advice?"

"You haven't been shy about that so far."

Carmelina snorted. "Here it is. Let this go. Drop the charges and take a step back. Maybe we can find a way to get you together with her when things have cooled down."

"It's too late for that."

"Only if you let it be."

~

The next morning, the three of them waited outside the courtroom. Carmelina was nervous. What if she hadn't gotten through to Marissa's mother?

Marissa herself sat on one of the wooden benches, dressed like a respectable young woman, though she kept scratching her arm through the white blouse as though it were giving her hives.

Marcos was pacing back and forth, staring at the closed doors. "They're running late."

Carmelina nodded. "Whatever happens, we'll get through this."

Marissa looked up. "I know. Thank you guys for being here."

"It's the waiting that's the worst." Marcos sat down next to Marissa and hugged her. "You have a new family now. We'll take care of you."

"Excuse me. Are you Marissa Sutton?" A middle-aged gentleman in a sharp gray suit and wire-rimmed glasses stood before them.

Marissa nodded. "I am. Who are you?"

"I'm Chet Clifton. I'm the attorney for your parents."

"They're not my parents."

Chet shot Carmelina a confused look.

She shrugged.

"In any case, your mother—"

"Not my mother."

"—Jessica Sutton asked me to tell you that they're dropping the charges."

Marissa looked up, her eyes wide. "They what?"

"It's over?" Marcos said at the same time.

"Yes. You're free to go. The hearing has been cancelled."

"Holy shit!" Marissa jumped up and into Marcos's arms. "It's over!"

He laughed. "We're gonna go out and get something at Biba to celebrate!

"Can we go to Ragazzi instead?"

Marcos nodded. "Whatever you want."

"I have to text Tris. Can I invite him along?"

"Of course. Have him meet us there."

Marissa strolled off down the hallway, texting intently.

Carmelina smiled. She was happy that Jessica had made the right choice. Maybe there was still hope for a reconciliation between Marissa and her adoptive parents. Now Marcos and Marissa could celebrate together. She sighed.

Marcos watched Marissa for a moment, then turned to Carmelina. "You didn't have anything to do with this, did you?"

"I don't know what you're talking about." She smiled.

He grinned. "Thank you." He threw his arms around her. "Thank you so much," he whispered in her ear.

"You're welcome." She let him go. "I should head out. I have some yard work to do at home."

Marcos looked crestfallen. "I was hoping you would celebrate with us."

"Really?" It was her turn to smile. "I'd love to. I didn't want to interrupt you two—"

"You're her grandmother. You should be there."

Her smile widened to a grin. "That's so good to hear."

"I'll call Dave, and we'll make a family lunch of it."

"Got it. I'll meet you there in…" She checked her watch. "About an hour?"

"Perfect." He kissed her on both cheeks. "See you soon."

It was going to be a great day. She needed more of those.

On her way back to her car, she ran into an unexpected pair.

"Ciao, bella!" Diego gave her a hug.

"What are you two doing here?"

"We're seeing a judge about dissolving our marriage," Matteo said. "Now that Luna's no longer with us…"

"So we can marry again."

"Congratulations! Where are you getting married? At a church?" Another wedding. She loved weddings.

Matteo shook his head. "At the courthouse. Next week, if everything goes well today."

In a courthouse? "Okay. Well, good luck with that." She kissed them both.

"Grazie!"

As they walked inside, she pulled out her phone and texted Sam. There was no way her friends were getting married at the courthouse. "Sam? We need to talk."

99. YOU ONLY TURN EIGHTEEN ONCE

"We'll just stop in here for a minute. I have to talk to Matteo about something." Marcos pulled his Prius into a spot just around the corner from Ragazzi on 51st Street.

Marissa shrugged.

Seeing if I can get out of the birthday dinner thing.

"I'll be right back. Not that you're listening or anything."

"I heard." She grinned and waved him off.

~

Marissa stared out the window at the quiet street while she waited for Tris's response. A woman was walking down the street carrying a couple of those colorful Trader Joe's bags stuffed with preservative-free potato chips and fresh-squeezed orange juice.

Okay. I have something special planned.

For me?

You only turn eighteen once.

Her heart skipped a little. Tris was the first person to do that to her in years. Since Marcie.

Marcos has something planned too. He won't tell me what. Might be late.

I know. Look up.

She read that twice, and then did.

Tris tapped on her window, a big grin on his face. "Hey Birthday Girl!"

"Hey!" She pulled off her seatbelt and pushed open the door, aware how fumbly and awkward she must look as she practically threw herself into his arms.

Tris hugged her.

He smelled *so* good.

He held her out at arm's length. "Happy Birthday again!"

He'd brought her a birthday cupcake at lunch, but this was even better.

He grabbed her hand. "Come on!"

"Where are we going? Marcos is coming right back…. He'll miss me…." She trailed off as she realized he was pulling her toward Ragazzi.

He swung the restaurant door open and whispered in her ear, "Surprise!"

She stepped inside, and the whole room burst into the chorus. "Surprise!"

The place was packed. She looked around, trying to take it all in. A brightly colored "Happy Birthday, Marissa" banner stretched across the back wall over the kitchen. Diego and Matteo were there with Gio, all beaming at her.

On one side were Carmelina, Marcos, and the others from her class.

On the other side were the interns, including Ricky, looking much better than he had in the hospital.

The Outcasts were there too. Jason ran up to give her a hug. "Happy birthday!"

"Where the hell have you been?" Marissa asked, laughing.

"I got mono."

"Oh shit. Don't kiss me, then."

He laughed. "It's gone now, but I'm still tired."

She hugged him again. "I'm so glad you're here."

"I wouldn't miss it."

That old Italian song about the funnels, or something like that, started playing, and the crowd surged forward to wish her a happy birthday. Marissa spent the next half hour greeting the partygoers and figured she must have hugged a hundred people by the time it was over.

She finally got a moment to herself, sinking into a chair in the corner and staring in amazement at the crowd that had gathered. *For me.* She'd never had a birthday like this.

"Pretty cool, huh?" Tris slid into the chair next to hers.

"You helped with all this?"

He nodded. "I rounded up the kids from school. The ones you like."

She laughed. "Mostly, anyhow."

"Who?"

"Jenny has about as much personality as a goldfish. But other than that, you did okay."

"From you, that's high praise."

"Marissa?" Carmelina poked her red head through the crowd, pulling an older man in a brown corduroy jacket in her wake.

"Hey, Grandma." Marissa gave her a hug.

Carmelina winced.

"Is that okay? For me to call you that?" She was still getting used to the idea herself.

"It's wonderful. It's just… it makes me feel a little old. Nonna is better."

Marissa grinned. "Oh, right. Thank you, Grandnonna."

Carmelina grunted. "Listen, I wanted you to meet someone. This is Darryl. He's a professor over at Sac State."

"Hi, Darryl. I'm sorry, but I haven't started thinking about college yet."

"You should be." Her nonna glared at Marcos across the room. "We'll have a talk about that soon. But that's not why I brought Darryl here. He was your mother's adoptive father."

"Hello, Marissa. Nice to meet you."

Her heart raced. This man had known her mother, her *real* mother, had watched her grow up. She jumped up and hugged him. "You're my grandfather?"

He glanced at Carmelina. "I guess I am?"

"May as well be. If you wanna be a part of this crazy little family we've put together." She squeezed Marissa's hand. "I'll let you two talk. Tristan, wanna help me with the hors d'oeuvres?" Carmelina kissed Marissa on the cheek.

Marissa and Darryl sat down together.

"You look so much like her when she was your age." Darryl had a wistful grin on his face.

"Really?" She blushed. She'd always wanted to know more about her mother. "What was she like?"

"She was full of life; vivacious. Hard to get a word in edgewise with her, especially when she was angry or passionate about something."

"Tell me more." As they talked, the rest of the party faded away, and Marissa drank in the details.

~

She had no idea how much time had passed when everyone began to sing

"Happy Birthday to You." Marcos appeared out of the crowd, carrying a cake alight with candles.

It was in the shape of a chef's hat.

She laughed, putting her hand over her mouth as he set it down on the table in front of her, and then she started to cry. It was too much. She didn't deserve it.

"Hey, you okay?" Marcos whispered as the crowd went silent.

"Yeah. It's just… I can't… it's too much." She sighed. "I'm so happy. You're all so wonderful. But I wish…"

The bell on the front door rang in the silence.

Marissa looked up to see Jessica and Phillip Sutton standing at the entrance.

Their eyes met. Her parents suddenly looked small to her. Jessica's face had lost its haughty glare, and Phillip—her dad—his shoulders were sloped, his face drawn. He looked ten years older than the last time she'd seen him.

"Your parents?" Marcos whispered.

She nodded, grabbing the back of the chair to steady herself. "What do I do?"

He hugged her. "What your heart tells you."

She took a deep breath and then took a step toward them. The distance between them seemed infinite, with everyone else watching in silence. Step by step, she bridged the gap.

When at last she came to stand in front of Jessica—her mother—she had decided what she would do. "You came."

Jessica looked at Phillip then back at Marissa, her Hermes scarf clutched around her shoulder as if it were the middle of winter. "Yes. I hope it's okay. You only turn eighteen once."

The same thing Tris had said. She shook her head. "If this is going to work, things have to change between us." She had to hold her ground. Her life was non-negotiable.

Her father replied, "Things already have. Your mother and I… we talked for hours last night. You're your own woman now. An adult, and a truly beautiful human being." He smiled, just a little. "I am so proud of you, Misty."

It was his own little nickname for her, one he hadn't used in years. Marissa wiped her eyes. She turned to her mother.

Her father squeezed her mother's shoulder. "Go on."

"I'm… I'm sorry."

Those were two words Marissa had never heard pass through her mother's lips. It wasn't enough, not after everything else.

"Sorry for *what*?"

Tris came up behind her, putting his arm around her in support.

"I'm sorry for trying to make you change." She pulled a tissue out of her purse and wiped the corners of her eyes.

"I'm still bi, you know."

Her mother nodded. "This isn't easy for me. I'm not… It's not what I was brought up to believe. But I'm trying. I love you, Marissa."

That was enough. "Okay."

"Okay?" A flash of hope flickered in her mother's eyes, and the air around them seemed to sparkle for just a moment.

"Okay." She hugged her mother, and they both started to cry in earnest. "I missed you, Mommy," Marissa whispered.

"I missed you too." Her mother hugged her fiercely, and she felt her father's arms wrap around her too. When they separated, she put an arm on each of their shoulders. "I'm not coming home."

Her father nodded. "You're an adult now. We'll figure it out."

She felt the last bit of weight that had held her down lift off. She knew she could fly at that moment if she only stretched her wings.

Carmelina broke up their little reunion. "Well, come on in, then," she said, pulling Marissa's parents gently away toward the bar. "It's a party. Enough with the tears."

She turned to wink at Marissa. "I'll get them something to drink. It looks like they need it."

Marissa grinned. It was almost a perfect day.

～

The last of the partygoers slipped out, leaving just Marissa and Tris, along with Carmelina, Marcos, and her parents.

Her mother and father hugged her on their way out. "Happy birthday," her mother said, holding her for a long time. "Can we have dinner sometime this next week? We have a lot to talk about."

Marissa nodded. "I'd like that."

She hugged her father. He slipped an envelope into her hand. "Get yourself a little something special."

"Love you, Daddy."

Then they were gone.

Carmelina came next. "One last gift." She held up a pair of keys.

"What are those for?" She took them. One looked like a house key, while the other was black with a big white "H."

"The first one's a key to my place. You are welcome at any time for any reason. The second was your *nonno* Arthur's car key. His Jaguar's a bit old, but it's yours if you want it. It's parked around the corner on 51st."

"Oh my God, seriously?" *My own car.*

"Yup. I put you on my insurance. We can transfer the title later." She kissed Marissa's cheeks. "I'm so proud of you."

Marcos was next. "I'm proud of you too. And if you want to go home…" She could see how it hurt him to say it. "I'll be happy for you."

"I do want to go home."

He looked pained. "Okay."

"Is it okay if I get in a little late?"

His face lit up. "Really?"

"We've got a good thing going. Why ruin it?"

He laughed. "Yes, we do."

"Thanks for all this. It was amazing."

"Of course. See you when you get in. No later than midnight!"

"Deal." She hugged him. She wasn't sure what Marcos was to her, exactly… Not her father. Not her uncle. More than a friend. *Who needs labels?*

"You ready?" Tris asked her when they were gone.

"We should help clean up—"

"Matteo and Diego said they would take care of it."

Matteo nodded from behind the bar. "Go have fun!"

Marissa grinned. "I know what I want for my birthday."

"What? I already gave you a cupcake."

For her answer, she pulled him down by his shirt and kissed him, hard.

When she was done, he grinned. "I think I've got that covered."

It turned into the perfect night too.

100.MAYBE THE FUTURE

BEN CHECKED HIS MAKEUP ONE LAST TIME IN THE RESTAURANT MIRROR. He'd gotten off shift half an hour before and had used the time to get himself into character. He'd never done Blackula before, but figured he'd be a natural with some pointy eyebrows, a black-and-red cape, and a set of plastic vampire teeth.

He grinned, enjoying his new look in the mirror.

The door banged open, and Luis leered at him. "Handsome *sonofabitch*."

Ben grinned. "You on shift all night?"

"Yup. Until midnight. Hoping to take home a sexy cat or a sexy nurse, or maybe a sexy stewardess…"

"They're called flight attendants now, you troglodyte."

"Whatever. There's an Elvira waiting for you at the bar."

"Thanks."

"She's hot, man. If you ever break up—"

Ben threw a wad of paper towel at him.

Luis ducked out the door.

Ben pushed his cape behind him and swept out of the bathroom.

He reached the bar and then stopped awkwardly.

There were three Elviras there sipping margaritas, all with their backs to him.

He tapped one on the shoulder. "Ella?"

The man who turned to face him was definitely *not* his girlfriend.

"Sorry. But you make a really good Mistress of the Dark."

The man grinned. "Thanks."

The next Elivra turned out to be a Cher—there was a lot of overlap on *that* Venn diagram, after all—but she was very gracious about it.

The last one turned to grin at him.

He frowned. "Didn't you hear me call your name?"

She nodded. "Sorry. I couldn't resist. You're adorable when you're flushtered."

He ignored the slur. "You look a little pale," he said with mock concern.

"Ten pounds of white makeup to look thish good." She stood, and he got a look at her cleavage.

Ben ignored her slurred speech. He whistled. "Okay, I know you have a beautiful… um… body, but—"

"It's a push-up bra. You like?"

"I like." He pulled her close for a kiss. "Happy Halloween."

"Happy Halloween."

"Ready to go? I got us tickets to Scream Park."

"Oooh, I've heard that's fun."

"Luis went last night with his girlfriend."

"Really, it sounds great. But I have news first."

Ben frowned. "Are you okay? Really okay? We don't have to go if you'd rather stay in."

"What, and waste all this?" She spread her black-lace-covered arms. "No, it's good news. I had my appointment with Dr. Randall and her team on Thursday, and they called me this afternoon. They said I'm qualified for the trial!"

"Holy crap. That's amazing!" He lifted her in the air and spun her around, narrowly missing Cher. "Sorry about that!"

"Nothing damaged, honey." She turned back toward the football game.

Ella hugged Ben. "I'm not in the trial. Not yet. But it's something."

He nodded. "It's amazing!"

"It's all because of you." She took his arm and steered him toward the door. "Now let's go get our asses scared off."

~

"It's getting dark!"

Sam grinned. Ricky was peering out the front window at the sky like he was five years old. "You can go out Trick or Treating if you want."

Ricky shook his head. "No. I want to give out the candy this year. I've been out on the streets enough."

Sam and Brad shared a look. "You're probably too old anyhow." Brad carried the bowl full of Tootsie Rolls, Reese's Peanut Butter Cups, and Twix Bars to the front door. "I saved the best for us. The Peanut M&M's are in the kitchen."

"I have friends who are going out tonight."

"*They're* too old too." Brad turned Ricky around and sent him marching toward his room. "This is a rare event, you know."

"How come?"

"All Hallow's Eve on a Saturday night? This place is gonna be non-stop busy." Brad pulled out a paper bag from behind the couch. "I even got backup candy. Now get dressed. The first kids will be here soon."

"Yes, *Daaaad.*"

Sam laughed. "You kinda deserved that." He enjoyed seeing Brad's fatherly side.

"Actually, I think I liked it."

"Really." Sam put his arms around Brad's neck. "Are you thinking…?"

"I'm thinking it might be nice to have a Brad or Sam Jr. in our lives." He looked into Sam's eyes. "You said before that you wanted kids."

Sam nodded. "I always wanted to be a father." His heart was racing. "So you think you might want to?"

Brad bit his lip and nodded. "Maybe so." He looked over Sam's shoulder at Jason's door. "We can talk about it more later."

"I'd like that." Sam could picture it: the four of them as a family, big brother Ricky coming home from college on the holidays. And his mother would be in grandma heaven.

"So what did Ricky choose for his costume?"

Sam shook his head. "Some kind of superhero thing, I think? We went to that costume place in Old Sac, but he didn't want to buy a pre-made costume. He bought a wig and a jacket and a few other things."

"Which one… holy cr…ackers."

Sam turned to see Ricky step out of his room. He had on lace-up boots, fishnet stockings, go-go shorts, a Harlequin shirt, and a wide leather choker topped with a blond wig with pink-and-blue ponytails. Red lipstick, white makeup and a baseball bat completed the outfit. "Wow."

"Right? Do I look like her?"

Sam had no idea who Ricky was supposed to be. "Um… yeah. Just like her." He nudged Brad.

"Oh, yeah. You nailed it."

"Harley's one of my idols." Ricky grinned.

The doorbell rang.

"You're up, slugger," Brad said.

As Ricky ran to the door, Sam pulled out his phone.

Harley superhero baseball bat

"Ah." He held up the phone to show Brad.

"Harley Quinn," Brad read softly. "Never heard of her. Whatever happened to Superman?" He chuckled. "I hope she's a good role model."

Sam scanned the Wikipedia page and whistled. "Not so much."

"We'll see if we can find him a better one tomorrow." Brad pulled Sam over to the couch, and they tumbled down together.

"So. A kid, huh?" Sam hovered over Brad's face.

Brad nodded. "Maybe two."

"It'll ruin my lovely figure."

"I wouldn't mind." He kissed Sam tenderly. "You ready for tomorrow?"

"You kidding? I can't wait to be permanently hitched to my guy."

The doorbell rang again.

A wooden bat tapped Sam gently on the shoulder. "Your turn!"

Sam grinned. It was gonna be a busy night.

101. THE BIG DAY

Carmelina looked out onto the street, pulling the blinds open like a snooping neighbor. She'd been up at five, making sure all the details of her devious plan would come together properly.

Her hairdresser had arrived at seven, and she was very pleased with her updo…. She might even outshine the grooms. She grinned. An airport shuttle pulled up in front of the house. "They're here!"

"I don't know how you did it," Marcos said, giving her a quick peck on the cheek.

"Don't praise me yet. There are still a lot of things that can go wrong. Marissa, it's your turn with the stylist."

"Coming!"

Carmelina loved having a full house. She grinned as she went to let in her guests. This was going to be fun.

~

Across town, Sam brushed the lint off the shoulders of Brad's tux. "You almost ready, ring-bearer?" he called. It had taken them an hour to get the white makeup off Ricky's face the night before after the last of the Trick or Treaters had come by.

"Yeah," came Ricky's voice from his bedroom. "I think I lost the rings though."

"You what?" Sam rolled his eyes. That was the last thing they needed.

"Found 'em." Ricky poked his head out of the doorway holding the ring box, his shirt only half-buttoned. "They were in my shoe." He disappeared back into his room.

"Don't even ask," Brad whispered.

Sam grinned. "It's all good." He checked his phone. It was ten-oh-seven. "We have about twenty minutes before we need to go."

"Perfect. Wouldn't want to be late to our own wedding."

Sam pecked him on the cheek. "I think they'd wait for us."

"Yeah, but think of what all the gossip pages would say!" He pulled Sam in for a real kiss.

When they came up for air, Sam frowned. "Hey, we're not supposed to see each other before the ceremony, right? Isn't that a thing?"

Brad laughed. "We're gay. After not being allowed to marry for, what—well, in my lifetime?—I think we're allowed to flout convention."

"Sounds good to me." Sam pinned the red-rose boutonniere onto Brad's lapel. Then he stopped, overcome by the enormity of what they were doing.

"What?"

"I just can't believe it's here. Something I've waited my whole life for. Something I never thought would really happen."

They grinned like a couple of idiots.

"Sam, can you zip me up?" Lena called from upstairs.

"Coming, Mom!" Sam kissed Brad back and went to help her get ready.

Matteo hung the last star and climbed down from the ladder to get a look at his handiwork. This was the first wedding they'd hosted at Ragazzi, but if it went well, it wouldn't be the last. He *adored* weddings.

"*Che bello!*" Diego said from the stairwell.

"English, please!" Matteo winked at his partner.

Diego stuck out his tongue. "Very beautiful."

"Where's Gio?"

"Taking the shower." He came to stand by Matteo. "I wish it was us."

Matteo nodded. "It will be. Next week."

"I mean all this."

Matteo nodded. It was a wonderful thing to be married in the presence of all your family and friends. "We could wait and do it right."

Diego shook his head. "Fast is good. I don't want to wait."

Matteo took Diego's hand and kissed it. "Fast *is* good."

~

Ben rubbed his eyes. Something was blaring at him. He sat up in bed, looking around.

Ella lay in the bed next to him, fast asleep, her dark hair spread out across her naked back.

Ben's head pounded, trying to concentrate. That noise, what was it? *Ah. The alarm clock.* He slammed his hand on the snooze button and then collapsed back into bed.

It had been a long night. After the haunted houses and music at the Scream Park, they'd landed at the Torch Club for a little bit of blues and a whole lot of drinking. They hadn't gotten in until after two in the morning.

At least the wedding wasn't until noon.

He checked the time. It was eleven-thirty a.m. "Shit! Shit, shit, shit, shit, shit!" He nudged Ella. "Get up. Ella, wake up!"

She groaned. "I wanna sleep. Let me sleep."

"Ella, it's eleven-thirty!" He jumped out of bed and ran for the bathroom. "We overslept!"

"What?"

He flicked on the hot water. "You have to get up," he called, frantically pulling down his shorts and taking off his nightshirt. "We need to leave in ten minutes!"

"Oh crap!" She stumbled into the bathroom. "I need at least fifteen!"

"Fifteen minutes, then, tops." He hopped in the shower. "You can have it next, and then we dress like the wind!"

~

"I'll drop you two off in front of the restaurant." Lena pulled up to the loading zone. She turned to look at both of them in the back seat. She had driven her Volt all the way from Tucson to Sacramento to act as their chauffeur. "You're both so handsome." Her voice caught in her throat. "I'm a lucky mother today."

"Thanks, Mom." He leaned forward and kissed her. "You ready?" he asked Brad.

Brad stared at his fiancé.

"What?"

"I just want to remember this moment." Brad's heart was pounding. He looked out the window at the restaurant. "We still have time to head off to Vegas, you know. Quickie wedding; no pressure."

Sam laughed. "And leave all our friends and family hanging? Let's go. You'll survive."

"All right." He opened the door and took Sam's hand. "Let's do this."

They climbed out of the car together, and Sam waved at his mom as she drove off to find parking with Ricky.

He took a deep breath. "Here it goes." Brad pushed open the door to Ragazzi.

A big cheer went up from their friends and family who had already arrived.

Brad stopped on the threshold, his mouth falling open.

Ragazzi had been *transformed.*

Hundreds of silver stars hung from the ceiling, catching the light of what had to be a thousand candles. The tables had been cleared out and replaced with rows and rows of chairs. The bar was decorated with rows of twinkling lights, and there were white flowers everywhere.

"It's like getting married at Hogwarts," Sam said, a look of wonder on his face.

Brad nodded. It was so much better than he had imagined it. And so much more than they had paid for.

Matteo gave him a big hug. "What do you think?"

"We didn't ask for this."

"You don't like it?" Matteo frowned.

"Oh no, we love it!" Sam was staring at the candles.

"It's just that we didn't pay for all of this."

"Our friend Carmelina helped out."

"Ah. Where is she?"

Matteo shrugged. "She said she had a couple of last minute details to take care of."

Sam and Brad shared a grin. "I'll bet she did."

Matteo tilted his head. "What?"

"Nothing." Brad squeezed his arm. "We better say hello to everyone before the ceremony." Now that they were here, he was glad they'd decided to do this in front of everyone they loved.

"Of course. Congratulations!"

❧

Matteo glanced at his phone nervously. They were running ten minutes late, but Carmelina wasn't there yet.

The door opened, and he looked up, expecting to see her, Marcos, Dave, and Marissa come through the threshold. Instead it was Ben and Ella. "Ciao, amici!" He gave them both hugs.

"We made it?" Ben was sweating.

"Yes, we're still waiting for Carmelina and the others."

Ben laughed, sounding relieved. "I'm so glad not to be the last one here. We had a bit of a long evening last night."

"You're here now. Go ahead and take a seat. We'll get started as soon as they get here." He fidgeted his ring back and forth, looking from Brad and Sam to the door and back.

The bell rang again. This time it was his favorite redhead. "Thank God you're here," he said, kissing her cheeks.

Carmelina returned the favor. "Sorry. Had a few last-minute issues to take care of." She ushered the others inside.

He nodded. "Okay, everyone, we're ready to go. Please take your seats." He clasped his hands nervously. Everything had to be *perfect*.

When everyone was seated, Brad nodded at him.

Matteo signaled the DJ to start playing the wedding march. Well, *a* wedding march. Instead of the traditional song, Sam and Brad had opted for "Marry You." Not the Bruno Mars version, though, the Glee one. As the music started—a bubbly synth pop sound—Brad and Sam danced up the aisle. They were beautiful together.

Matteo laughed and shook his head. They didn't do weddings like this in Italy, but it was infectious and life affirming.

The audience started to clap in time with the song, and the look on Sam's and Brad's faces was radiant, pure joy as they approached the beautiful white arbor.

Matteo was happy for them. Really, he was. They deserved this.

The guys reached the arbor, and all of a sudden the music screeched to a halt.

Matteo frowned. Something was wrong. "I'm so sorry. Let me go check—"

Carmelina stood in his way, putting a hand on his chest. "Diego, come here."

His partner looked up from where he was seated. "*Io?*"

"Yes, you."

Confused, Diego stood and joined Carmelina and Matteo.

Matteo shot a look at Brad and Sam. They looked upset. *Cazzo, I've ruined their wedding.* He tried to squeeze by Carmelina again. "Please, just let me fix this—"

The bell chimed on the front door.

Matteo turned to see who it was.

~

Diego turned at the sound of the little bell that announced visitors to Ragazzi, and his mouth literally dropped open.

His three sisters stood there, grinning from ear to ear.

"No, not possible—"

Valentina had something draped over her arm. "*Ciao, cucciolo!*" She gave him a big hug.

Diego laughed. "I'm hardly a puppy anymore," he replied in Italian. "What are you doing here? How did you get here?" He stared at Cinzia and Claudia too.

"Your friend Carmelina arranged it. I brought the kids, our sisters, and someone else."

"*Tesoro!*" His mother hobbled up to him, her wizened face creased with joy.

"Mamma!" He gave her a hug, totally befuddled.

"Here. Put out your arms." Valentina lifted the thing off her arms. It was a black Armani jacket. "One for you and one for Matteo. Kids, go take your seats."

Diego obeyed as she pulled it over his shoulders. He looked over at Marco. "Did you know about this?"

Matteo shook his head. "*Boh.*"

Diego's mother pinned a red carnation to his chest, while Carmelina pinned one to Matteo's. She stood back to look at her handiwork. "You both look dashing."

"What's this about?" Matteo looked irritated.

She grinned. She waved to the DJ, and the song started up again. She grabbed Matteo and Diego's lapels and pulled them close. "You're getting married today too."

"What?" She was *pazza*. "We can't. This is for Sam and Brad." Diego turned to look at the couple.

Sam was grinning at him. So was Brad.

Diego pinched himself. Nothing changed except for a twinge in his arm. This was real.

Matteo offered his arm. "Shall we?"

Diego laughed. "*Perché no?*" He took Matteo's hand, and they danced up the aisle together as the music urged them on.

~

"I now pronounce you husband and husband," Kate, the officiant, said to Sam and Brad.

Brad had revised his opinion of her. She was more Ellen than Niles. And she was the perfect choice for their wedding day.

Kate turned to Matteo and Diego in turn. "And I pronounce you too husband and husband. You may now kiss your husbands."

Brad pulled Sam to him, tasting his sweet lips. He had waited for this for so long. Sam wrapped his arms around Brad and whispered in his ear. "I love you, Mr. Weston."

"Oh no, I'm not changing my name," Sam whispered back.

"Weston-Fuller?"

"Deal."

~

Diego held Matteo tight. They'd been through so much these last few months, much of it his fault. Matteo was still here with him though and still loved him. He sobbed quietly in Matteo's arms, smiling at his sister and his mother through his tears.

And next to his mother, there was someone else. She looked familiar.

"Matteo, *guarda!*" he whispered.

They separated, and Matteo looked where he pointed.

"Mamma!"

Matteo's mother Elena, who had passed away years before, sat next to Diego's mom.

She smiled at him and nodded, and then vanished in a shower of sparkles. Matteo's eyes were wet.

Diego squeezed Matteo's hand.

Kate raised her hands. "I present to you the newlyweds!"

Everyone cheered.

~

Carmelina was deep in conversation with Dave and Marcos when someone tapped her on the shoulder. It was Diego.

"Excuse me, boys." She got up and followed Diego outside, taking a deep breath of the fresh air. It was a cool early November afternoon. "What's up?"

"I wanted to thank you. For the wedding. For mamma and my sisters."

She smiled. "I couldn't stand to think you'd be getting married all alone at City Hall."

He nodded. "It was beautiful." He paused as if unsure what to say. "Matteo saw his mother today."

"Oh, that's lovely. On Skype?"

He shook his head. "She left us a few years ago. But she was here."

"Here?"

He nodded. "With my mamma. She came for us."

That sounded a little creepy, but she knew what he meant. "That's beautiful, Diego." She remembered her conversations with Arthur these past few weeks. Who was to say what was possible?

"Anyhow, thank you." He hugged her and then opened the door for her to go back inside.

"I'll be inside in a moment." It felt good just to have a quiet moment to herself before diving back in.

He nodded, and the door closed behind him.

She looked up at the ribbon of sky. Clouds were blowing in from the west. It would probably rain later. They could certainly use the rain.

She turned to go inside and caught sight of a woman standing all by herself on the corner about thirty feet away. She was young, maybe twenty.

The woman turned toward her. She thought it was Marissa at first, but then she realized she could see Marissa through the glass inside with her boyfriend Tristan.

She turned back to see the woman smiling at her. "Take care of my daughter."

My daughter? "Andrea!" She reached out toward the woman, but she was too slow.

In a flurry of sparkles, she was gone.

102.ALLA FINE

Sam threw an extra pair of swim trunks into his suitcase and closed it up. "You about ready?" He'd shipped off his second novel at last, and it was time to take a writing break.

They were taking their honeymoon in Tucson. They had transportation thanks to his mother, and it was a cheap trip. Plus, Brad had never been there.

"Yes, Mr. Weston-Fuller." Brad kissed him, picking up his suitcase and hauling it out of the room to take it downstairs. "I do love the sound of that."

"Me too." He popped into the bathroom for his deodorant. "Hey, I was thinking.… Can we take a trip down to the Chiricahuas while we're there?"

"Chiricow-whos?"

"They're these beautiful mountains southeast of Tucson. We could go out camping for a few nights, sleep under the stars."

"You remember I don't camp, right?" Brad called from the stairs.

"You'll learn. Just like I'll learn to love staying in nice hotels."

Brad's snort carried from downstairs.

Sam grabbed his laptop case and took one last look around the room. He had everything. He was fairly sure. "Ricky, you ready?"

"Coming."

"Mom, you ready to go?" He found her in the kitchen, drying her hands.

"Just finished putting the dishes in the dishwasher."

Sam rolled his eyes. "You didn't have to do that."

"I know, love, but somebody had to."

Sam looked around at his housemates. They were taking a road-trip honeymoon with his mother and their live-in foster child to his childhood hometown. It was such a non-traditional honeymoon, and he couldn't have been happier about it.

~

Ben put on the hot water for tea and sat down to check his email. There was the usual bucketload of spam, an email from his boss at Zocalo, and one from Red Tern Press. His hand shook as he moved the mouse to open it.

We're happy to inform you that we would like to publish your book…

Ben grinned from ear to hear. "Ella!" He got up and ran to his bedroom, flinging open the door.

"I just got good news!" they both said simultaneously.

He laughed. "You go first." He threw himself down on the bed next to her, feeling like a little kid.

"No, you go. Mine can wait."

"Okay. I just got an email. Red Tern wants to publish my book!"

"Oh my God, that's fantashtic!" She threw her arms around him. "Oh, I am so proud of you."

"Thanks. I mean, they're a small press, so there's probably not a lot of money in it—"

"It doesn't matter. It's a great start!"

He nodded. "It's a foot in the door." He took her hand. "What's your news?"

She took a deep breath. "Dr. Randall called. She said they found a space for me in the clinical trial."

"Oh my God… that's amazing!" He crossed his arms. "Why did you let me go first? I feel like such an idiot. That's much bigger news!"

She blushed. "It's just that you looked so excited to get that offer. And yours is big too."

"I am. But I'd throw it all away for just one extra day with you."

She put a hand to her mouth.

"What? Did I upset you?" He was always doing that—making stupid mistakes.

She shook her head. "No. Not at all. It's just that you said exactly what I needed to hear."

He pulled her close. Things were finally going their way.

The tea kettle blared.

Ella laughed. "Go!"

"I'll be right back. And then we're gonna really celebrate."

Carmelina shook out the tablecloth, the one decorated with lemons that she'd brought back from the Amalfi Coast on her last trip there with Arthur. This was to be their first family brunch. Marcos, Dave and Marissa were due over at ten. She hoped to make it a regular thing.

Her phone rang.

"Hello?"

"Hi Nonna. This is Marissa."

Carmelina smiled. "I figured. The 'Nonna' was a bit of a giveaway."

"Sorry I didn't call sooner—"

"You're not cancelling on me, are you?" She had been *so* looking forward to this.

"Oh, no, not at all. I just wanted to see if Tris could come along with me."

Carmelina breathed a sigh of relief. "Of course he can. When will you all be here?"

"About twenty minutes."

"Perfect. See you then."

"Everything okay?" Daniele came up behind her, slipping his arm around her waist and kissing her neck.

She nodded. "I just need to do one thing. Can you finish things here?"

He nodded. "Go. I'll take care of it."

She retreated to her bedroom. On her dresser, the little pair of shoes she had bought for Andrea, for her hopes for Andrea, waited for her.

She picked them up and sat down on her bed, holding them to her chest. "I love you, baby girl." She felt a surge of warmth spread from the shoes into her chest. *I love you too, Mamma.*

She looked at the shoes in wonder. They sparkled green in her hands for just a second and then faded to their usual pink and white.

It was time to put them away. She put them in her closet on the top shelf next to her hand-made blankets. She kissed her fingers, touched them to the shoe. Then she closed the door behind her.

Dave led Marcos toward Carmelina's front door. Marcos squeezed his hand with a smile. Dave pulled him back.

"What's up?"

Dave frowned, scratching his chin. "Do you think that'll be us some day?"

"What do you mean?"

"Like Sam and Brad. Like Diego and Matteo."

"Married?"

Dave nodded.

"I hope so. Are you asking?"

Dave laughed and shook his head. "Not yet. I just wanted to know how you felt."

Marcos grinned. "Yeah. I hope so one day."

"Good."

"Are you guys being all squishy again?" Marissa and Tris had arrived carrying a cooler. "Someone get the door?" she asked.

Marcos chuckled and rang the doorbell. "One of these days you'll be doing all that squishy stuff, and I hope someone gives you shit for it then."

"Hey, guys! Come on in!" Carmelina waved them inside. "Hopefully this will be less of a disaster than the last time I had you here for a meal."

"It can hardly be worse." Dave looked around. He'd been in Carmelina's place hundreds of times before, but there was something different this time.

"Gather around the table," she said. "Daniele has made us a fantastic Italian family breakfast."

Dave grinned. That was it. Now they were a family.

Matteo woke. Diego was fast asleep in bed next to him, but there was light coming through under the door. *Gio?* Maybe the boy was having a hard time sleeping.

Matteo got up and padded out of the bedroom. The door to Gio's room was closed. Matteo frowned. Had he left the light on when they went to bed? No. There was someone sitting at their dining room table.

He picked up the rolling pin off the counter silently and approached the person from behind. "Who are you?"

She turned around, and he let the rolling pin drop to the floor with a clatter. "*Mamma.*"

"*Ciao, Tesoro,*" she said, getting up to hug him. She was just as he remembered her, in her light blue robe and slippers, her black hair streaked with gray and held back with bobby pins. "Sit."

He stared at her.

"Sit, sit!" She gestured to the chair across from her.

He sank down in his chair, and she passed him a cup of hot tea. It was

French vanilla, the kind she always used to make for him when he was sick. He took a sip. It was just as he remembered. "How…?"

She smiled. "We all watch out for you," she said in Italian. "I know you've had a hard year, but I am very proud of you. Your father is too."

"Papá?"

She nodded. "He sends his love." She took a sip her tea and smiled. "Diego loves you, you know."

It still hurt him that Diego had lied to him. "Sometimes I don't know if—"

"He *loves* you. He will make you happy, I think."

"You think?"

She winked. "Even angels don't know *everything*."

He laughed. "I miss you, Mamma."

"I am always here with you, *Tesoro*." She finished her tea, then got up and kissed him on the forehead and gave him a hug. He could smell her Chanel No. 5, the perfume she only wore on special occasions. "Live every day like you might die tomorrow. *Ti voglio bene*."

Matteo woke up. Sunlight was streaming in through the window, creating patterns through the blinds across the bedcover. It had all seemed so real. "Diego, are you awake?"

Diego's eyes flickered open. "*Un po'.*"

"I just had the most amazing dream."

"Coffee first. Then dream." He rolled over, away from Matteo, grunting.

Matteo grinned and kissed his cheek. "Coffee coming right up." He slipped out of the bedroom and made his way to the kitchen. Gio's door was still closed. Matteo approached the table with some trepidation. It *had* been just a dream, right?

There were two mugs sitting there.

He picked one up—littered with bits of dried tea. He inhaled, savoring the lingering smell of vanilla.

He closed his eyes. "Love you, Mamma," he whispered.

Then he smiled, washed them out, and put them away.

RECIPES

Recipes courtesy of Fabrizio Montanari and his mother and grandmother.

Piadina Romagnola (Chapter 6)

Ingredients:

- 8 cups flour
- 1-1/4 cup lard (room temperature)
- 2 cups, 1-1/2 Tablespoons of milk (warm)
- 1 tablespoon salt
- 1 teaspoon honey
- 1 pinch baking soda
- 1 teaspoon baking powder

Mix all the ingredients together. Add a little bit of water to form a paste that's rather hard. Or, instead of water, you can use milk or even white wine.

Flatten a piece of the dough out with a rolling pin to form a nice, round form about the size of a tortilla, adjusting the thickness to your taste.

Sprinkle the rolling pin occasionally with flour. Otherwise the dough may stick to the wood.

Start cooking the pasta on a pancake pan on high heat, because piadina should be cooked quickly.

As the flatbread is baked, bubbles will form on the surface. Pop these with a fork. Their "footprints" will remain even after the piadina is cooked. Then turn over the piadina to cook the other side.

~

Passatelli (Chapter 16)

Ingredients:

- 1/2 cup parmigiano cheese
- 1/2 cup dried bread
- 4 eggs
- A little nutmeg and some shaved lemon peel
- 4-1/4 cups beef or chicken broth

Serves four.

You can use more cheese than bread crumbs for the best flavor.

Grate the dried bread and the cheese. Combine the bread crumbs, cheese, and nutmeg.

Then mix in the four eggs.

Knead the mixture to make a compact, hard dough.

Use a passatelli mold—if you don't have one, you can make do with a colander—and press firmly on the dough, pushing it through the holes.

Cut them to a standard length—about 2" long—with a knife at the base of the mold and set them aside until you have used all of the dough. Then cover them with a cloth.

Bring the beef or chicken broth to a boil in a pot on the stove. Uncover the passatelli and put them into the boiling broth by hand.

After eight to ten minutes, put the passatelli directly into bowls for your guests.

A sweet and delicate scent will waft from the bowl, bringing with it a great desire to enjoy this delicious and much-appreciated soup.

~

Mamma's Apple Fritters (Chapter 35)

Ingredients:

- 3 pippin apples
- 1/4 cup sugar
- 2 generous tablespoons rum
- 1 grated lemon peel
- 2/3 cup flour
- 1 cup water
- vegetable oil
- powdered sugar

Peel and core the apples and thinly slice about 3/8 of an inch thick. Mix the sugar, rum, and lemon peel in bowl. Add the apple slices. Set aside for about an hour. Mix up the batter using flour and water. Put water in a soup bowl and gradually sift flour into the water, constantly beating the flour in with a fork until all flour has been added. The batter will be thick, like sour cream.

Pour the oil into heavy skillet, 1/2-inch up the side of pan, and heat oil on high heat. Pat the apple slices dry with paper towels. Dip them in the batter, and when oil is very hot, brown them to golden brown on one side and then turn them over to other side until they are golden brown all over. Drain them on paper towels and sprinkle them with powdered sugar. Serve hot.

~

Chicken Cacciatore With Farm Potatoes (Chapter 48)
Ingredients:

- 1 chicken
- 1 tablespoon fresh lard
- 2 onions, sliced thin
- 3 or 4 ripe tomatoes (or 1 can chopped tomatoes)
- 1 glass dry white wine
- 1 sprig sage
- 1 sprig rosemary
- 1 clove garlic
- 2 lbs potatoes
- 1/2 cup olive oil
- 1 pinch salt

To cook Chicken Cacciatore, it's preferable to use lard for two reasons:

chicken today is less fatty than it once was, and lard gives it more flavor without making it too heavy.

If your chicken still has the head and legs and you don't want to use them for this recipe, you can use them to make chicken broth.

Sear the chicken in a pan on the stove to remove any down remaining on the skin. Wash it under running water and dry it, then cut it into pieces following the joints, detaching the legs and head.

Put the lard in a big pan and melt it. Lay the pieces of chicken skin-side down in the pan and combine with the sage, rosemary, mashed garlic clove, and salt to taste, and brown it over high heat in the uncovered pan.

When the chicken is well-browned, add the white wine, and when it has evaporated, add the onions and chopped tomatoes.

Mix everything carefully, add a glass of hot water, and then season to taste with pepper.

Cover the pan and continue cooking on low heat for about thirty minutes.

While the chicken is cooking, peel the potatoes, cut them into chunks or quarters, and put them to blanch in boiling water.

Let the water come back to a boil and cook for two minutes.

Drain them and allow them to finish cooking in a pan where you heated some oil with the rosemary and sage. Stir often because they may stick.

Add salt when they are cooked and serve with the chicken.

A good wine to accompany chicken is a cabernet red, spicy sweet but soft, suitable to counteract the acidity of the tomato.

~

Spiedini Di Frutta Al Cioccolato (Chapter 67)
Ingredients (serves 12):

- 8 3-1/2 oz. bars of dark chocolate
- cioccolato bianco 100 g
- 12 grapes
- 12 pieces of pineapple
- 12 strawberries
- 12 pieces of kiwi
- 12 skewers
- 1/2 cup chopped hazelnuts

Melt the white chocolate and dark chocolate separately in a double boiler.

Add a strawberry, a piece of pineapple, a kiwi, and a grape to each skewer.

Dip the skewers in dark chocolate, drain the excess, and let them dry on a sheet of parchment paper to prevent sticking.

Place the melted white chocolate in a cone of waxed paper and cut off the tip, creating a small hole. Using this, create decorative stripes across the fruit and chocolate on the skewers. Garnish with hazelnuts.

Serve when cooled. The type of fruit here is just a suggestion. Vary according to the season and your own personal tastes.

~

Potato Gnocchi (Chapter 87)
Ingredients:

- 2-1/2 pounds potatoes
- 1 cup flour
- 1 egg
- salt

Wash the potatoes under running water. Steam-cook them or boil them in salty water for 40 minutes. As soon as they are done, remove them, let them cool a little, peel them, and put them in a large bowl and mash them. Let them cool.

Add finely sifted flour, the egg, a pinch of salt, and knead the dough until you make a firm and elastic dough. Divide the dough into four parts and work them one by one.

On a cutting board covered with flour, roll the dough until you have a long rolled piece of dough about 3/4 of an inch thick.

Cut it with a knife into pieces about 3/4 of an inch long and use your thumb to press each one gently onto the flat tines of a fork to make a pattern.

Shake off the extra flour and put the gnocchi in a large pot of boiling salty water. Cook them until they float up to the top, which usually takes about two-to-four minutes.

Remove them using a slotted spoon and drain well, then put them in a saucepan with your favorite sauce, cooking both together for about two minutes. Serve hot.

To store gnocchi, place them on parchment paper or a floured cloth, separated so that they don't touch. Otherwise, they will stick together.

This recipe makes enough gnocchi for four-to-five people.

To make the best gnocchi, it's important to use the right amount of flour. Too much, and the gnocchi will be too hard; too little, and they will melt when you cook them.

To freeze gnocchi, place the tray in the freezer for half an hour and then put the gnocchi into a freezer bag. They should remain good for about six months.

~

Ragu Alla Romagnola (Chapter 97)
Ingredients:

- 1/4 cup butter
- 1/2 onion
- 1 carrot, chopped
- 1 celery stalk, chopped
- 1/4 cup pancetta, chopped
- 1-3/4 cups lean ground beef
- 3/4 cup chopped chicken liver
- 1/2 cup red wine
- Just over a pound of fresh tomatoes, peeled
- Beef or chicken broth

Serves four people. Melt the butter for about two minutes in a large sauce pan. Add the chopped onions, carrots, celery, and pancetta. Brown these for a few minutes, then add the beef and the chicken liver. Let the beef and chicken brown for a few minutes, and then add the wine. When the wine has evaporated, add the fresh peeled tomatoes. Salt and pepper to taste. Add some beef or chicken broth, spoonful by spoonful, also to taste. Let it cook on medium heat for about 45 minutes, stirring occasionally.

ACKNOWLEDGMENTS

There are a number of people who made River City possible, and I want to thank them all. First and foremost, the hubby Mark, who pushed me to start writing in the first place, and who read every chapter as I wrote it and critiqued it before it ever saw the light of day.

Next, my best friend Angel Martinez, who was my other beta reader, and who often kept me out of hot water when I wrote something stupid.

A special thanks to our dear friend Fabrizio Montanari for providing the family recipes for this book, and to his husband Marco Munda for answering my constant "Italian" questions.

I'd also like to thank Claudia Milani, my Italian translator, who rain or shine turned around chapters for me every week so the story could be posted to my blog simultaneously in English and Italian.

A big thank you to the members of the Queer Sci Fi Writer's Workshop and the QueeRomance Ink author group, who helped me workshop the blurb and to figure out how to self publish this opus.

And thanks to Freddy MacKay and Erik Schubach (and Frank) for helping me through my first self-publishing experience with minimal scarring. Frank, I owe you a box of chocolate eclairs!

As they say, it takes a village—or at least a very full clown car.

ABOUT THE AUTHOR

I live with my husband of 26 years in a leafy Sacramento, California suburb, in a little yellow house with a brick fireplace and a couple of pink flamingoes.

As a writer, I've always occupied the space between the *here and now* and the *what could be*. Indoctrinated into fantasy-sci fi by my mother at the tender age of nine, I devoured her library. But as I grew up and read the golden age classics and modern works, I began to wonder where the people like me were.

After I came out at twenty three, I decided that it was time to create stories I couldn't find at Waldenbooks. If there weren't many gay characters in my favorite genres, I would reimagine them myself, populating them with men who loved men. I would subvert them and remake them to my own ends. And if I was lucky enough, someone else would want to read them.

My friends say my brain works a little differently - I see relationships between things that others miss, and get more done in a day than most folks manage in a week. Although I was born an introvert, I learned to reach outside myself and connect with others like me.

I write stories that subvert expectations, that seek to transform traditional sci fi, fantasy, and contemporary worlds into something new and unexpected. I run both Queer Sci Fi and QueeRomance Ink with Mark, sites that bring people like us together to promote and celebrate fiction that reflects us.

I was recognized as one of the top new gay authors in the 2017 Rainbow Awards, and my debut novel "Skythane" received two awards.

My writing, whether queer romance or genre fiction (or a little bit of both) brings a queer energy to my stories, infusing them with love, beauty and power and making them soar. I imagine a world that *could be*, and in the process, maybe changes the world that is, just a little.

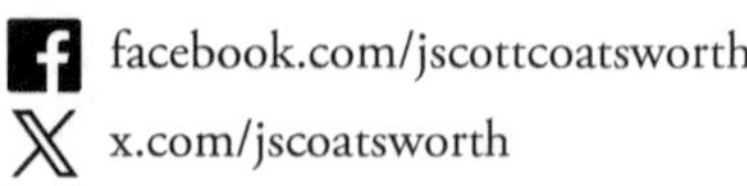

facebook.com/jscottcoatsworth

x.com/jscoatsworth

ALSO BY J. SCOTT COATSWORTH

Liminal Sky: Ariadne Cycle

The Stark Divide | The Rising Tide | The Shoreless Sea

Liminal Sky: Redemption Cycle

Dropnauts

Liminal Sky: Oberon Cycle

Skythane | Lander | Ithani

Tharassas Cycle

The Dragon Eater | The Gauntlet Runner | The Hencha Queen | The Death Bringer

Other Sci Fi/Fantasy

The Autumn Lands | Cailleadhama | Firedrake | The Great North | Homecoming | The Last Run | Wonderland

Contemporary/Magical Realism

Between the Lines | Flames | The River City Chronicles | Slow Thaw

Short Story Collections

Spells & Stardust | Tangents & Tachyons | Androids & Aliens

Audiobooks

Cailleadhama | The Autumn Lands | The River City Chronicles | Skythane